Azeron:

Beyond the Veil

By Françoise H. W. Krull

To Mary
I hope you enjoy the Adventure

(Francoise Heffernan-Walter Krull)

© 2017 Françoise Krull. All rights reserved.
Written and Illustrated by Francoise H. W. Krull
Visit the author's website at www.azeronthebook.com.

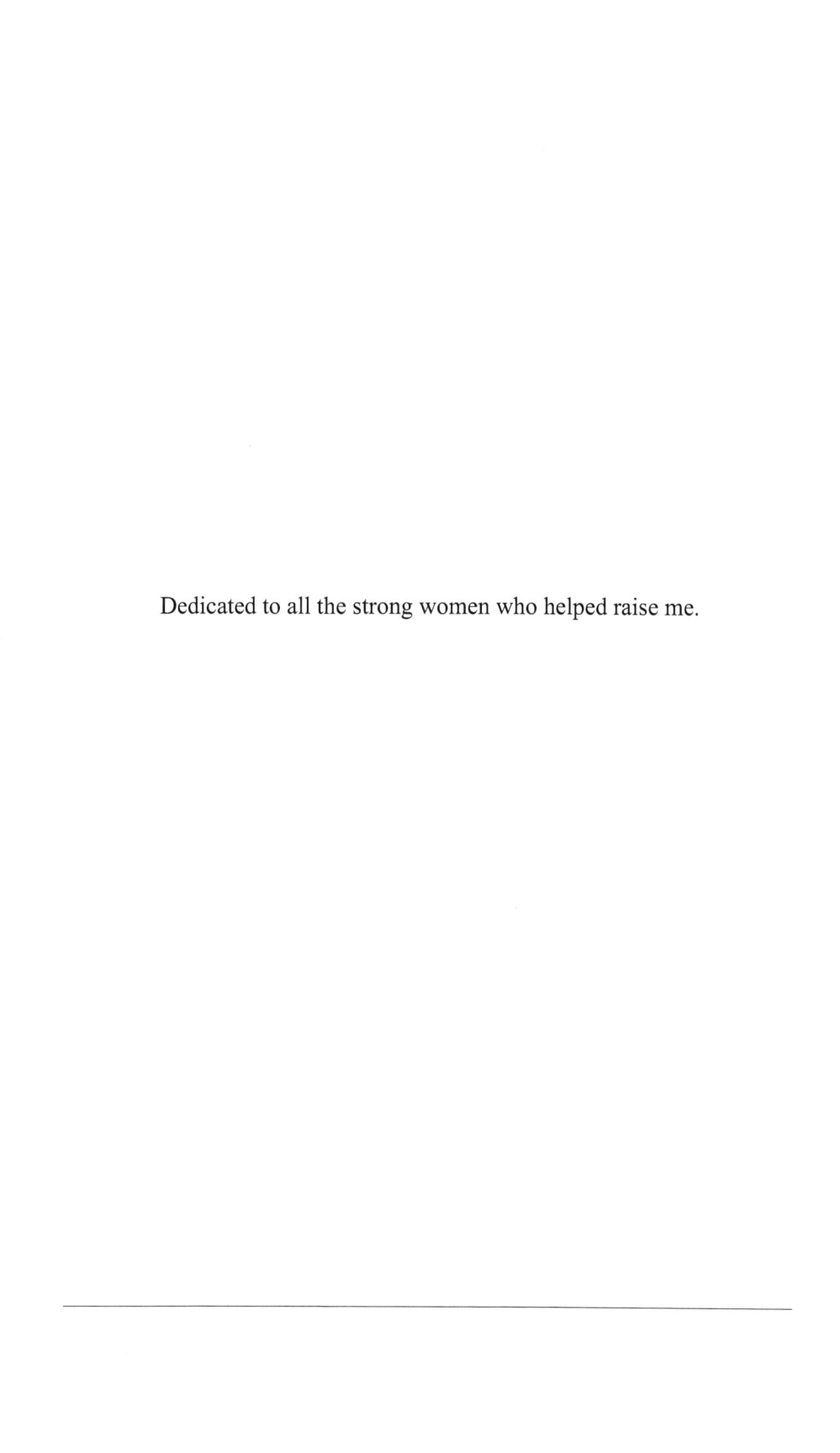

Dedicated to all the strong women who helped raise me.

Table of Contents

Day One: Part One — *1*

Day One: Part Two — *13*

Day One: Part Three — *28*

Day Two: Part One — *58*

Day Two: Part Two — *71*

Day Two: Part Three — *85*

Day Three: Part One — *107*

Day Three: Part Two — *139*

Day Three: Part Three — *174*

Day Four: Part One — *200*

Day Four: Part Two — *216*

Day Four: Part Three — *233*

Day Four: Part Four — *244*

Day Four: Part Five — *264*

Day Four: Part Six — *282*

Epilogue — *317*

Additional Sketches From the World of Azeron — *331*

Day One: Part One

"Will you kids for once just pipe down!" Anita Heyward snatched up the paper plane from her lap, screwing it into a ball and chucking it on the dash, as she looked to her rear view mirror in time to see a satchel fly across the gangway. "You know if I crash this heap of junk we could all be killed!"

A combined, "oooooh," followed by laughter and some inaudible mutters was the only response. Lucky for them all, the road was empty - it always was this close to Craven's Peak. No one else had reason to travel this far into the forest, and once she was done dropping this lot off no one else would for another three months.

She'd be happy when the year was through and she could finally say goodbye to this wretched job. Anita couldn't stand children regardless, but these delinquents were among the worst. All twenty-three on the bus had been cast out of normal state schools due to behavioural problems. Putting up with them four times a year for the past three years had already brought her premature grey hairs. Course if she'd done better herself at their age, she wouldn't have to accept hideous jobs like this one, she thought.

Terrence and Tobias, the Emerson twins, were fighting again. Morris and Harper, the two Sandras, were polluting the air with noxious gases of their cigarettes, trading one fag back and forth like two lovers; which the rumours assumed they were. Meanwhile Baxter was up to his usual tricks.

"Oh come on...." Anita hollered, "I'm not blind you know, you two put those damn cigarettes out this instant! And Robert Baxter get out of Lilly's bag."

"Oh my God!" Lilly pulled her bag off her shoulder and down onto her lap. "Get lost you thief."

"Yeah right," he laughed "Ain't like you have anything worth taking anyway... _Orphan Annie._ Everyone knows the Slaters bought you for one ninety-nine at the corner shop."

Lilly turned back to her comic book, "At least someone wanted me... Your mom's so drunk she doesn't know what you look like and what was your Dad's excuse again?"

Some of the other kids laughed, until Baxter looked around for the culprits; they all hated him but none wanted to be on his bad side.

"Bitch!" He punched her between the shoulder blades. Swivelling around she lifted her bag, clouting him over the head several times.

"Fuck you asshole!"

The others laughed more, some chanting encouragement.

"I said cut it out!" Anita yelled, half wishing she could cheer Lilly on for her spirit. Although she didn't much approve of the bright bubble-gum-pink streaks in the girl's hair, she had to admire her gumption. Baxter was by far the worst of this bad bunch; deserving every whack he got, and more.

Lilly glanced toward the front of the bus, and for the briefest second thought she was going insane: ahead of them the air appeared to be rippling, similar to heat waves on a sunny day, except this was shimmering and expanding; a huge iridescent globule, as solid as it was transparent.

"What the…"

"Fucking hell!" Hearing Baxter's exclamation, Lilly also looked up.

"Holy shi-"

The others were screaming as the bus swerved and they hurtled off road, straight into the thick of the old growth forest on their right.

Lilly heard none of it; she was too busy staring out the windscreen - her eyes drawn to that shimmering rift in the world. A second later the bus passed through it. For one long moment it felt like her entire body had been turned inside out and back again; as if that stomach dropping feeling of riding a roller coaster had extended to every fibre of her being.

The screams of the others remained muted and an incredible chill spread across her skin. Like a sudden wave of pins and needles, Lilly felt her entire body tingling. She looked frantically around, her long blonde hair swaying into her line of sight, the one dyed strip creating a halo of pink in her vision for a moment. Shaking it out of her eyes, and glancing around, she realised the others were in too much of a panic, to see the huge tree in their path and she screamed "Get down!" a split second before they smashed into it.

***

The sound of the horn brought Lilly to her senses, and seeing Anita slumped over the wheel was enough to get her out of her seat. Clambering forward she pulled the driver backward.

"Miss Heyward?" The constant bleat of the horn gave way to sobs and whimpers from the few still conscious. Seeing blood trickle down into Anita Heyward's open eyes and gaping mouth - suspended in a scream that would never be heard - Lilly grimaced before turning away.

Smoke was pouring from the bonnet, spiralling upward in a thick cloud all too reminiscent of stories from her childhood. "You guys," she moved to the door, pushing and pulling - it wouldn't budge. "Guys, we need to get out of here. Someone help me, the door's jammed. Come on you lot… we're trapped!"

Baxter was the first at her side, adding hefty kicks and profanity to the effort. The pair were soon joined by the Emerson twins, but the combined effort proved just as futile.

Lilly glanced to the bonnet again. The spiralling smoke had become a thick cloud.

"Oh God no!" The others followed her gaze and panic began to spread.

The next thing they knew the door was swaying and contorting.

"What the hell is going on?" she looked to Baxter.

"I don't know…" he shook his head, taking a step back as he added. "But I don't fucking like it." The others followed his lead as the sound of tearing metal reverberated through the bus.

Sandra Harper, who'd been sobbing in her seat near the front, started to scream hysterically. Her best friend, Sandra Morris, slapped her face - stunning her into silence, before hugging her tight.

They all watched as the door was ripped away by an unseen force; only to fly off and land on the ground below.

Lilly peeped out, expecting an explanation – there was none. The door lay engulfed in foliage below. She turned back to the others with a shrug, at which point Baxter pushed past her; almost knocking her down.

"I'm out of here," he jumped out and ran off.

"Hey wait up," yelled Terence Emerson as he and Tobias grabbed their backpacks and followed.

Wanting to do the same, Lilly turned to see a pleading look on Sandra Morris's face. Another glance to the bonnet revealed it was no longer visible under the cloud of smoke that had now begun filling the interior. Putting a hand over her mouth and nose she stepped hastily toward them.

"You two coming or what?"

"We can't," Morris shook her head. "She's frightened."

"Well, frightened or not, you can't stay here."

Lowering her voice, Morris said, "She's right, Sand we've really gotta get going, look the others have already-"

"Yeah, whatever…" Lilly grabbed Harper under the arm and pulled her up off the seat.

"Hey!" Outraged Morris rose to defend her best friend. "You can't just-"

"We don't have time for this crap OK!" Lilly yelled in her face, "This bus is a death trap! Now do you want help or not?"

"We do," nodded Morris. "We want help!"

Together they dragged Harper through the gathering smoke and off the bus, her own legs moving too little to be much help.

A few feet away Morris turned to the wreckage,
"What about the others? What about Miss Heyward? Shouldn't we help them too?"
"We can't." Lilly dragged Harper forward. "We have to get away."
Scrambling to keep up, Morris glanced backward with every step.
"But the others, we can't just-"
"It's too late for them!"
Morris stopped to stare at the bus. "But-"
"Come on!" Lilly paused, grabbing her shoulder and spinning her round. "Ain't the kind of thing you need clear in your memory OK... Just keep walking and *don't* look back!" With a look of confusion Morris did as she was told, only to cringe a few steps later when the bus exploded behind them.

***

Baxter slapped the back of Tobias's head.
"Ouch! What the fuck?"
"You told me your brother has a good sense of direction." Baxter pointed ahead to Terrence; having removed his cap Terrence had his sleeve to his brow and was resting against a tree.
"He does!" Tobias rubbed his head, anger flashing in his eyes.
"Oh yeah?"
"Yeah!"
"Then why the hell are we lost MORON!"
"Who you calling moron? Asshole!"
"You and your dim-witted twin over there that's who..."
"Yeah well, you better watch your mouth Baxter else I'll-"
"You'll what?" Baxter pushed him square in his scrawny chest; almost toppling him.
"You touch me again and you'll find out." Tobias hissed through gritted teeth.
The pair glared at each other.
"Hey! Cut it out you two." Terrence shook his head as he re-joined them. "Hate to say this guys but I think we're lost."
"Oh really!" Baxter raised an eyebrow.
"What!" breaking off his stare Tobias turned to his brother. "Oh man. What do you mean we're lost? How can we be lost, you know these woods like the back of your hand."
"I know," shrugged Terrence. "I don't get it either. Everything just looks so... different. We musta crashed a lot further out than I thought... could a sworn we should be seeing the school by now."
"Jesus Tez, it's freezing out here. You know how I hate the cold. How could you go and-"
"Hey, hey! OK calm the fuck down," Baxter pulled a pack of cigarettes from his pocket and clamped one between his lips, lighting it as he added. "Ain't his fault. He's right, we must a crashed a lot further out than we thought. I know

my legs sure as hell ain't ever felt this tired walking through these damn woods before… we've been on the move for ages."

"Yeah, well, maybe that's because we're lost!" Tobias flashed an angry look at his brother before turning back to Baxter. "Give us one would ya?" getting a raised eyebrow, he shook his head and rolled his eyes. "Oh come on. I've got a fat stash waiting for me at the Peak. I'll give you a whole pack when we get back."

Flipping the pack open again, Baxter held it out, then pulled back when Terrence went to help himself. "Na ah… these babies are like medicine for me and I don't know how long it's gonna take you to get us back. Go twos with your brother."

With that he turned his back on them, looking ahead in the direction they'd been going and ran his free hand through his scruffy dark brown curls.

"Course I wouldn't need you two sad-cases if I could just see the fucking spires. Damn this damn fog, I ain't never seen anything like it."

Tobias looked around then across to his brother, relieved to see him equally confused.

***

"Where'd you think the others got to?" Morris tugged on her jacket collar, pulling it higher up Harper's neck.

"Who cares," Lilly shrugged, throwing more twigs on the fire before prodding it with a stick. "Baxter's with them and we're better off without him around, would only hog the fire and steal our lighters anyway."

"Yeah, you're probably right," leaving Harper on the old log they'd found and joining Lilly beside the fire, Morris shrugged. "Maybe they're back at school already. Bet Mrs Askey has search parties out for us right now."

"Dunno." Lilly shook her head. "Think we musta crashed quite a ways from the Peak I ain't seen any sign of it so far."

"Me either…." Morris looked to her lap, "it's odd, last year when me and Sand got past Mr. Crick we could see the spires from most of the woods… wasn't anywhere near this cold either." She rubbed her arms. There was fear in her voice, and looking round Lilly sighed,

"Yeah well this fog is pretty thick it's not surprising we can't see-"

"Fog?" the bewilderment on Morris's face was enough to make Lilly question her own eyes. A second look showed the thick fog, which seemed to have followed them from the wrecked bus still surrounding them. She looked back to Morris who was also looking around; a baffled expression on her face.

"You really don't see it do you?"

"Errr…I see trees… lots and lots of trees."

***

"It's done!"

Vereena came running out of the hut. Thin braids of long blonde hair swished back and forth across her pale cheeks, while the mud and leaves clung to her long brown boots.

Reaching Toleth and the rest of the small group of riders, she took a moment to catch her breath before she could add, "Mai Mai says it's done! They succeeded! She's here!"

"Where?"

Her brow creased as she bit her lip, aware of the other villagers' eyes on her.

"Middle of the forest."

The other riders began to mutter among themselves for a moment till their voices were drowned out by Toleth. "Mordrel's forces?" he asked.

"Some followed, couldn't be prevented." Vereena nodded. "They're not far behind. And T'vor says we can't keep her safe long, you must go now."

He nodded, pulling on the reigns of his yimusa trundel, its head turned as he looked to the others.

"It's time, we ride!"

"Wait! Toleth." Vereena called out as the others thundered up the hill toward the forest.

She dug a hand into the deep pocket of her hooded top, pulling out an opaque silvery ball the size of a tangerine. "I'm supposed to give you this."

He nodded and took it... ignoring as best he could the stricken look on her face.

"Tell Mai Mai I was thankful and that I *will* be bringing it back."

"Of course," she bowed her head, one arm going to her chest. While those around her, watched him ride to meet his troops - they were out of sight in seconds.

Vereena rubbed her palm where the orb had left a warm tingle, and turned to return to their grandmother's hut.

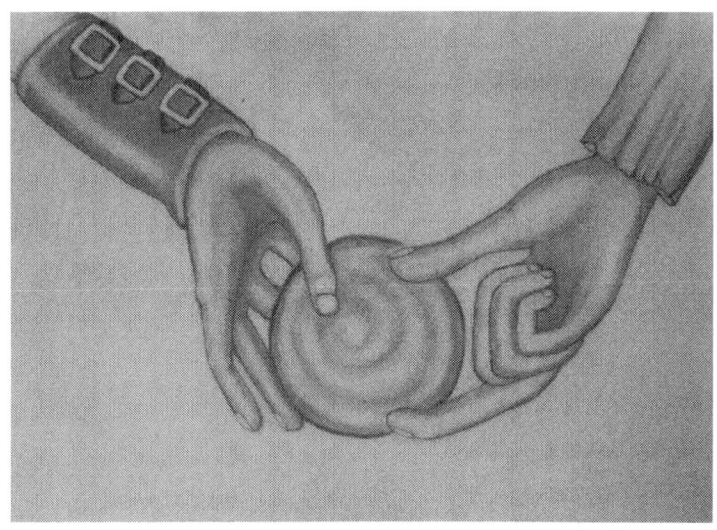

***

"Man this stinks!" Tobias complained "Which one of us put that asshole in charge anyway?"

"Not me," shrugged Terrence, snapping another large branch and chucking it on the pile behind them.

"Damn it, I'm sick of his shit. Always throwing his weight around, you know what?"

"What?"

"We should kick his ass."

"Yeah, OK." laughed Terrence.

"Hey I'm serious," Tobias watched him grab a last branch before gathering the rest together. "We could take him."

"Really getting to you isn't he?"

"You bet your ass he is, besides who's gonna stop us? Ain't no teachers here and those jerks he usually hangs with are at school already, their bus always gets in before ours."

"Can't help thinking you're forgetting something bro." Terrence took off his hoodie and tied its sleeves around the bundle.

"What's that?"

"Our kicking his ass now, don't stop him kicking ours later, even worse he'll enjoy it more that way. Wait till his crew's around him, get us one at a time, or in front of the whole school if he can…it just ain't something we need to be giving him an excuse for." He flung the bundle over his shoulder and headed back the way they'd come. "Nah, Baxter ain't the kind of guy you mess with unless you're planning on putting a bullet through his head."

"Yeah well, that can be arranged."

"Oh see, now you just chattin' shit, more specifically, the kinda shit that put us in this shit-hole in the first place."

"Why you always gotta be so fucking sensible?" Tobias followed him through the trees.

"Hell, I dunno. Maybe cos I got all the brains, you know being first and all, there just wasn't a whole lot left for you bro."

"Ah see now you're asking for a whupping."

"Right," laughed Terrence.

"You may have gotten the brains, but don't forget which one of us got the deadly physique." Tobias squared up in front of his brother, "Come on then…"

"Shhh." Freezing, Terence looked around.

"What you mean shush? You shush! Can't you hear I'm talk-"

"Bro!" Whispering he put a hand across Tobias's chest. "Seriously, didn't you hear that?"

"No," Tobias looked around also. "I heard nothing. Why? What do you think you're hearing?"

"I dunno man," Terrence frowned. "Sounded like… like a horse."

"A horse! Out here!" Tobias laughed, "Oh come on."

"I'm serious, OK, I heard a horse."

"Yeah OK bro, you heard a horse," nodding, he pushed his brother's arm away, and kept walking. "Damn man. Why's everybody gotta be tripping out, first Baxter with his invisible fog, now you with a horse!"

"Hey I'm serious all right, I heard galloping-"

"Galloping?"

"Yeah," he looked around, "lots of it! Shit Tobe, that was more than one…"

"Oh, see now, I know you tripping, ain't no goddamn horses on the Peak Tez."

"Ain't nothing in the world makes that noise but horses!"

"What damn noise? I didn't hear-"

Hearing it again, Terrence watched his brother swing around; a startled look on his face. "See!"

"Man that's fucking creepy. Why can I hear that but not see it?"

"I dunno bro." They were both looking around now. Back to back they circled one another.

"Hey, maybe it's a search party."

"On horses! OK now who's tripping?"

"Well it could be."

"Yeah sure, next you gonna be saying, Mr Crick done built a stable on Craven's Peak. Gonna teach all us delinquent city kids to ride."

Tobias came to a standstill, glaring at his brother.

"Man, why you always got to be making fun of me?"

"Why…" Terrence stopped too. "Cos you talking crazy shit and you know…"

The look on his brother's face made him swing around again.

"OK. You were right. There ain't no horses on the Peak!"

Together they stared at the bluish creature racing toward them, an armoured rider on its back.

"Terrence," Tobias hissed, as several more appeared behind the first. "What the fuck are those? And why don't they have any legs?"

"I dunno Tobes, but I don't think they're a rescue party"

"Right."

No more needed saying, in mutual, unspoken agreement the pair turned and ran.

***

Baxter stood up when he saw the twins racing toward him, and almost fell over again at the speed with which Terrence passed him, screaming, "RUUUUUUUNNN!"

"What in the…" he began yelling after them, but the steady thrumming caught his attention. Turning back he saw the creatures and their riders, bearing down and giving chase after the twins.

Well practised at evading all sorts of capture, Baxter was soon in the lead, ducking under branches, leaping over fallen logs and stumps of felled trees.

From nowhere a second group of riders; unarmoured, but on similar beasts, came from the right and one by one the boys were scooped up and each thrown across the broad shoulders of a legless equine.

***

"It's getting dark." Lilly looked around, the fog only she could see still surrounded the clearing they'd settled in. "We should get some rest, make it back the rest of the way in the morning."

"I don't think I can sleep in this cold," complained Morris, she was beside the fire rubbing at her goose-pimpled arms, thick steam escaping her mouth with every word.

"Here," Lilly took off her leather jacket and threw it over to where Harper lay on the other side of the fire, "Go lie next to her, keep each other warm."

"What about you?"

"I'm good." Lilly nodded "never really feel the cold… besides," she shrugged, "one of us should stay awake in case somebody comes."

"Right," Morris nodded. "A search party or something, well, wake me if you need a break."

"Sure." She slid closer to the fire and began breaking up more of the branches they'd gathered.

Morris spread the jacket over Harper's shoulders and crawling under it lay facing Lilly, head resting on her arm.

"They *are* looking for us by now right? I...I mean the bus exploded, that's kinda hard to miss... right?"

"Sure." Lilly nodded, staring bleakly into the fire, cracking branches into twigs.

It took her a moment to realise the sound appeared to be echoing in the distance. Ceasing all action she looked down at her still hands. The cracking continued. It was now several snaps at once, accompanied by loud thuds and getting closer.

She looked up, seeing nothing but fog. Morris propped her head on her arm and gazed off in the same direction.

"What's the matter? Oh my God!" She sat up, looking high into the trees.

"What is it?" Lilly rose to her feet, looking up also. "What do you see?"

Then she saw him too; a man darting along the limbs and branches above them. He looked down at the girls a split second before diving off the thick, moss laden branch and yelling, "Viileerium." A perfect flip left him on his feet in the clearing beside them.

Turning to Lilly he made a fist and thrust his leather clad forearm against his leather clad chest. "Lillian... We must leave now if you wish to see another sunrise"

"Err..." Lilly looked to Morris as she scrambled to her feet. "This is some kind of joke right?"

"Search me." Morris shrugged. "Ain't something I'm in on..." The man waved a hand over the fire muttering "Katat." Seeing the flames die out the girls looked from him to each other.

"We do not have time for explanations," he looked around them. "Mordrel's forces are upon us."

"Hey listen pal," Taking in the strangeness of his attire: shaggy green trousers resembling matted wool, the long brown leather vest he had over them and a thick brown belt holding a multitude of odd tools and dirty pouches; Lilly backed away. "We have no idea what you're talking about OK!" She shook her head "We don't know any Mordrel and we ain't going anywhere with a freak like you."

"I am not of clan Frik," the man frowned, the lines running deep enough to make him look thirty odd, when he'd barely looked twenty before "I am D'vey." He nodded, "and you need not know Mordrel. She knows of you, that is enough."

"Yeah, OK," signalling to Morris that he was obviously cuckoo she offered a polite smile. "Well it just so happens that I can handle myself. So whoever this Mordrel is, can-"

"Listen!" He raised a hand, silencing her. "Listen! Feel! They are almost here."

Lilly frowned, looking to Morris, and curious, they both listened. Lilly felt the hairs on her neck prickle as she heard and felt a rapid thumping.

"What in the-"

"When was the last time you handled yourself against an army girl? What you hear is at least two hundred skilled warriors with one goal in mind; To slice you in two and bring you back to Queen Mordrel in a weavel sack."

"Err... Weavel sack?" Morris shook her head. "I don't think I've-"

"Enough questions," he raised a hand. We've dallied here long enough. We must leave this place now if you wish to see-"

"Another sunrise," nodded Lilly, "we got that part already. Problem is our friend's in no fit state to-" her voice had acquired an urgency that had Morris raising an eyebrow.

"You're not seriously thinking of leaving with this loon?" she shook her head.

Ignoring her, he shrugged, "Leave her behind," glancing dismissively to Harper he added, "She makes a good decoy."

"Hang on a minute," Morris's reaction was instantaneous. "I'm not going anywhere without Harper!"

"Probably best," nodded the man. "You'd no doubt slow us-"

"Hey, hey." Lilly shook her head, assessing Morris's rising anger and raising both hands to diffuse the situation. "We're a package deal, OK! If I'm coming with you my friends are too. Besides..." she frowned "Harper's not injured, she's just... in shock or something. Our bus came off the road not far from..."

Realising he was no longer listening, Lilly's mouth hung open as she watched him pick Harper up and fling her over his shoulder before turning back to them. "We must leave... Now!"

"You do realise we're following a crazy man?" Morris whispered as she handed Lilly her jacket back, before grabbing her satchel and following them from the clearing.

"Yep," Lilly shrugged on the jacket. "a crazy man who knows my name and puts fires out with words."

"Yeah OK, so that was kinda weird... but still... crazy man... dressed like a reject from a bad Robin Hood movie, picks Harper up like she's an empty hold-all, tells us to follow him or else, and you're not the slightest bit concerned!"

"Oh, I'm concerned." Lilly paused to nod at Morris, "But something is definitely on its way here fast and I have no intentions of finding out what a weavel sack is!"

***

"Not a female among them! Toleth how could you be so careless?"

The three boys sat, huddled against a wall, on the dirt floor of the huge hut, watching the two men argue.

"They were in the mist Arteth...We had no time to look at them. Mordrel's forces were upon them... yet what of you brother? You return with nothing!"

"The mist we followed lead to an outed fire... Deebanaarie magick!"

Arteth pulled off his hood, his dark blonde hair, braided into thick plaits swinging as he shook his head. "There's no way of knowing how long they'd been gone, but the mist was down and Mordrel's troops were searching the area."

"Then they have not found her yet either."

The brothers turned as Mai Mai hobbled into the hut on her thick knotted walking handle.

"She would not listen to me, Arteth…" Vereena came in behind her. "I said I would fetch you but-"

"It is OK, Veer." Arteth approached his grandmother and the leader of their people.

"Mai Mai, you should not be-"

"What happened?" she grimaced, leaning into him as his arm went round her thin waist.

"Here," he led her to a nearby chair. "Be seated… you should not be up from-"

"You're suggesting I have a choice?" She looked up at him, her murky green eyes fixing him with an anxious glare. "It is four settings of the sun till her Kalaareem, yet Herrella's daughter remains lost to us! Do you expect me to sit silent with Mordrel's troops out there?"

"Holy shit!" Tobias muttered, pulling back against the wall as three smaller creatures entered. They were covered in thick fur, each in varying shades of brown.

The darkest looked curiously to the three boys, while the lightest, a tan coloured one, approached Mai Mai. Placing its small hand on her leg, it spoke in a low watery voice.

"She is safe… The Deebanaarie that doused the fire did so to cover their trail."

"Agreed," with a crest of thinning white hair, similar in shade to Mai Mai's, the third sprite joined them, bouncing up onto the arm of the seat, its voice more guttural than the first. "There is only one who would take the time. We can be certain of that."

"So he returns…" the expression on Mai Mai's wrinkled face was a grave one. "But we cannot be certain we can trust him with her." She shook her head.

"We must," the palest sprite put a hand over hers. "He has left us no choice."

Day One: Part Two

    Out of breath, Morris doubled up, resting her hands on her knees and panting. Even at her fastest running speed, she trailed several feet behind the others.
    "Jesus!" she breathed. "This is ridiculous!" Looking up she saw Lilly turn around and shouted, "I can't keep this up. I only took Miss Penderlay's P.E class like three times last term! What the hell are we running from any-" The look on Lilly's face had her up and turning around, just in time to see a green light, so bright it was almost white, come hurtling towards her. It slammed into her chest, sending her flying.
    White hot pain exploded across Morris's ribcage but disappeared when she landed, whacking her head off a nearby tree with a sickening crunch. Lilly screamed, about to dash for her crumpled body.
    "No!" The man grabbed her arm, dragging her forward. "There's nothing you can do for her. We must leave this place!"
    "We can't just leave her!"
    "We must!" he pulled her behind a thick tree trunk. "She is no more." More of the same bright lights hurtled past them.
    "We can't!" Lilly shouted in his face but paying no attention, he pulled a dirty red pouch from his belt.
    Ripping it open with his teeth he thrust it toward her.
    "Open your mouth!"
    "What? Why?"
    "NOW!" he pulled her closer as two more of the lights flew past their heads. Feeling her hair flutter in their wake, Lilly's mouth fell open and raising the pouch he pushed her head back and poured some of the fine – gag-worthy – powder onto her tongue.

"Hold *very* tight." His free arm went around her waist and the next thing she knew they were up in the tree. Then they were leaping into the next and the next.

With a girl under each arm – Harper still zoned out, and Lilly stunned into silence – this strange man ran through the trees, hopping from one to the other, as if part of some bizarre circus act.

Below, the troops, who had caught up to them were soon left behind.

Yet they kept moving until the man, becoming unsteady, began to slow down. Expecting something graceful like the first time he'd leapt down to her, Lilly was painfully disappointed when he tumbled down several limbs, before their fall was broken by a thick patch of prickly bushes, their combined weight squashing dozens of the bright yellow fruit growing there.

She clambered out, scanning the area before looking back at him, a shaking panting heap, sinking into the bush with every breath, and extended a hand to help him up.

He frowned, turning his palm to face the bush as he muttered,

"Ta Varee." Slowly it disappeared, leaving him and Harper on a burgeoning heap of mulch.

Lilly stared at it a moment before rubbing her eyes and shaking her head, "OK enough! What were those flying light thingies? What happened to Morris?"

"Tellemi darts." The man stood up, "From Mordrel's troops…" wiping the thick, sap-like fruits off his clothes, he added, "It was only a matter of time before they spotted us."

"Oh right." Lilly passed him by to check on Harper. "Tellemi darts." She shrugged, "Oh, but wait…" she stopped and turned to him. "I don't have a clue what a Tellemi is! Or who Mordrel is! *Or who you are!*"

Accepting her anger he sighed, "I am Kyrel."

"Good for you Kyrel, how's about you tell me what the fuck is going on?"

"You will find out soon enough." He nodded, passing her by and checking Harper over himself.

"No, no, no OK! Enough of this ta varee and running through trees, I want to know…" she barely had time to register the look on his face before the ground beneath them started rumbling. Kyrel leapt up, knocking her down and landing on top of her with a thump.

From nowhere a sapling shot up where Lilly had been standing. Ageing as it whooshed higher, it stopped at what looked somewhere between a one hundred and one hundred and fifty year old tree.

Lilly looked from the new tree to him, her eyes wide with fright, and rolling off her Kyrel got up, shaking his head.

"We're close enough to be safe on the ground from here." He turned looking at the new tree as if sizing it up then turned back to Lilly with a smirk. "Do not say that again."

"Say what," She looked to the tree. "Ta va-"

He hissed with anticipation and looking back to him she nodded. "Got it!"

"I'm sorry about your friend." He reached down helping her up. "But there's no time for explanations." He went back over to Harper, picking her up and throwing her over his shoulder again.

"Fine," shrugged Lilly but I'm telling you now, when I get one it had better not include any yellow brick roads, or ruby slippers, or a dog named Toto."

For a moment Kyrel looked deep in thought before shaking his head saying, "I'm fairly certain there are none of those things," before he walked off.

"OK," She followed him, wiping fruit and juice from her own clothes. "But we're not in Kansas anymore right?"

"Were you there to begin with?" Kyrel sounded dubious.

"Well no…" shrugged Lilly. "Was kind of a… Never mind…" she sighed. "I'm guessing a lot of my humour is lost on someone from wherever it is that we are."

"Azeron." Kyrel nodded.

"Azeron?"

"That's the name of this realm, all those lands which are under the domain of Crizoleth. All else is the Daenvekyam Outer Regions for as far as the eye can see. You were brought here by sprite magick. The mist was also their doing."

"OK," she picked her way through the trees, realising they were growing more sparse as the ground rose up, getting steeper with each step. "And where exactly are we going now?" She struggled to catch up.

"You…" Kyrel reached the top of the hill as Lilly joined him and they looked down at the small fenced off village, populated to its edges with circular mud huts: their domed roofs a patchwork of browns and greens. "…Are going home."

***

Faced with a plentiful spread of unfamiliar foods the boys looked from the table to each other, as the curtain closed behind them.

"Well, looks like they want us to eat." Baxter picked out a heavy brown roll and nibbled off a piece.

Terence watched with growing interest as he first frowned, then shrugging bit off a larger chunk and chewed.

Tobias grimaced as his brother sniffed an identical roll then bit into it.

"Ah man, don't eat that shit!"

"Not bad." Terence nodded through a mouthful.

"Yeah," Baxter grinned snatching up a wooden bowl and filling it with an assortment from the table. "Not bad at all." He dipped a finger into a smaller bowl filled with a light brown goo teeming with tiny yellow leaves, before picking it up and carrying it off to a bench by one of the room's minute windows.

"What do you mean not bad?" Tobias slapped his brother's arm away from a plate of berries. "Have you two lost your minds? Everything about today has been bad! First the bus crashes now we gotta deal with this insane fucking shit?"

"Man you need to give your bro a chill pill or something." Baxter munched away on a mouthful.

"Fuck you Baxter! Stay here and eat that funky looking shit if you want. Tez and me can find our own way outta..." he stopped; seeing Terrence filling a bowl with berries. "What the fuck! What are you doing?"

"Give me a break would ya." Terence shook his head. "We ain't had fuck all to eat all day and this stuff ain't half bad."

"You don't even know what those things are!" Tobias glared at him as he crossed the room and sat beside Baxter.

"I know it's good enough to eat." Terrence grinned and Baxter laughed.

"We've been kidnapped by a bunch of weirdos and you two think it's funny! Since when are there people living in Craven's Peak anyway?"

"Since now." Baxter looked up. "And if they wanted to hurt us they wouldn't need to feed us anything dangerous... In case you didn't notice everyone here is carrying around broad swords. They coulda slit our throats and left our bodies to rot in the forest."

"Oh great..." scowled Tobias, "...feeling much better now... Thanks!"

"Baxter's right bro." Terrence shrugged, "you should calm down. These guys don't wanna hurt us. It was that other lot headed our way we ought to be worrying about."

"Seriously!" asked Tobias. "Are you two completely fucked up? How can you not be totally fucking freaked out? Have you forgotten those horses they were riding... They had no legs! And what about those creepy fucking creatures out there? Don't you-"

"Sprites." Vereena said as she came through the curtain. Tobias turned to her and nodded as she reiterated, "We call them sprites."

She carried with her a tray with a brown clay jug and several tall wooden cups upon it as the darkest sprite came in behind her. As Tobias backed away from the creature, Vereena told him, "She'll not hurt you."

Terence had stopped eating and like his brother was eyeing the sprite curiously. "Her name's Merly." Vereena headed for the table, and hurrying round it, Terence began clearing space.

"Who are you people? These are private woods, I'm sure the school wouldn't take kindly to travellers-"

"Thank you," Vereena frowned, sliding the tray onto the table before stepping back and shaking her head at him. "We do not travel. We're Da'ariel and we've lived in these woods for more cycles than you could count."

"Err..." Tobias stepped up to continue the interrogation. "That's impossible! If you people have lived in Craven's Peak that long how come nobody's ever heard of any... Da'ariel?"

"Yeah," Terrence added. "There'd at least be rumours."

"Oh, I'm afraid you're no longer in Craven's Peak woods," Vereena looked to Tobias. "This... in your tongue at least, is Shadow-wood, sacred home-ground of the Avengturov clan and your best chance of sanctuary from Queen Mordrel's forces."

The twins stared at her, their faces blank, until looking up from his food

Baxter shook his head. "Errr... You wanna break that down for us girly?"

As she turned his way, shouts outside caught all of their attention, and getting up Baxter climbed on the bench to look out the window. People gathered in small groups, chatting among themselves excitedly while villagers bearing swords ran toward the entrance of the camp. Arteth and Toleth were among them, their swords already unsheathed.

"Something's going on." Baxter strained to make out what was being said. He turned back to Vereena with a questioning look. "Deebanaarie?"

Her eyes grew wide and she pulled a thin wavy dagger from her belt. "Stay here!"

The boys looked to each other as she ran out, meanwhile Merly bounced up onto the table, and walking between the plates on her tiny feet, grabbed a piece of meat, chomping on it eagerly.

***

"Open up these gates at once!"

"Be gone Deebanaarie Matfiac! Your kind are not welcome here."

"You'll have a lot more of my kind upon you before you know it if you don't let us in there!"

Lilly knelt beside the huge tree trunk fence, cradling Harper's head in her lap as Kyrel argued with the guards in a language she'd never heard before.

A raucous chatter was building up on the other side of the gate accompanied by the pounding of feet.

"Hear me you Da'ariel fool, Mordrel's troops are but a few strides back in the forest and if you don't let us through the barrier they shall surely find us all!"

"Kyrel?" A voice boomed over the din of the gathering crowd. "Is that you? Do you have Lilliath with you?"

"Of course!" he yelled back "But I cannot keep her safe out here for long so I suggest-"

"Open the gates!" the other voice commanded.

The noise died down and the gates were pulled back. Lilly gazed in at the crowd of curious faces. Masses of people, all bearing weapons — swords, bows and arrows, or the odd wooden pitchfork— they began dividing, and two men came through followed by more with swords.

The tallest took off his helmet, his blonde plaits falling over his cheeks.

The entrance flickered momentarily and as the man stepped forward, Lilly noticed him pocketing a small glowing orb.

"Quick Lilliath," he lifted Harper from her lap. "You must come inside at once!"

"Err..." her frown deepened as she turned to Kyrel asking, "Why did he call me that?"

"Because he knows you only by your given name," he offered a helping hand and waited for her to follow before adding, "Come on."

The crowd bared their teeth at Kyrel, raising weapons and jeering, yet when Lilly passed they became mesmerised; the fight leaving them in favour of curiosity.

"OK," Lilly took a deep breath, "Getting kind of creepy now."

***

The three boys stood up as the curtain opened again and Vereena hurried in. She was followed by a tall lithe female guard carrying Sandra Harper in her arms.

The pair took her through to a second room and moments later the guard reappeared. Baxter pushed past her, looking immediately to Harper.

"What happened to her? Was anyone else with her?" He stared at Harper's inert body on the small cot. "Another girl maybe? With scruffy dark hair and an attitude problem."

"No," Vereena pulled a small silver bottle from her belt. "None like that." she poured a few drops of thick dark liquid into Harper's mouth. "Only Kyrel and Lilliath."

"Lilliath?" Baxter looked over his shoulder as the twins entered the room. "Did you say Lilli-ath or Lilli-an?"

"What's going on?" Terence came up behind them.

"Your friend here is stunned, an effect of coming through the veil."

"Veil?" Terrence looked to Baxter who shook his head and shrugged, "She says someone called Lilli-ath was with her... could be Lilly right?"

"I guess," Terence nodded, looking at his brother as he crept up behind them.

***

"You had no right to involve yourself in this Kyrel."

"I had every right!" he sat himself on the only chair in the room, a large wooden ceremonious looking thing.

"Ny!" Mai Mai ambled toward him, her walking handle thumping off the dry red earth beneath them. "This affair is Da'ariel and we have it under control. Do not forget she is a daughter of the Da'ariel. We have planned much for these days. Your help is not needed here."

"Oh really," he put his feet up on the chunky arm. "Then you must know how close Mordrel's troops where when I reached her?"

"Get... off... my... seat, you impudent wretch!" Kyrel stared up into the old lady's eyes a moment before shrugging and moving aside. "Her friend was killed by a tellemi dart was that part of your tiresome Da'ariel planning too?"

"You are uncouth, unpredictable and far too dangerous to stay around here."

"As you wish," he grabbed Lilly's hand, "I shall take Lilliath and my leave-"

"We'll see you dead before we allow you to take her!" spat Mai Mai.

"Oh yes?" he turned back to her. "With a bowl of quiesscence and a handful of sprites? Your limited magicks couldn't even keep me from her. How do you propose to keep away an entire Deebanaarie battalion?"

"I'm not about to share our plans with you." She frowned, accepting a small wooden cup being handed to her by the white haired sprite.

"Thank you T'vor."

Kyrel moved to Lilly's side.

"You're not keeping me from her Mai M-"

"Don't you call me that!" she snapped, fixing him with a cold stare. "You're no family of mine Deebanaarie matfiack!"

Kyrel's eyes narrowed, his lips becoming little more than a feint white slit. He watched a moment as the woman sipped her drink, testing its temperature, before gulping down the lot and handing the cup back to T'vor.

"As you wish... Mairiel," he bowed his head, anger dying out as swiftly as it had flared. "But I'm here and you do need me." He gave a slight nod. "I'm the only one here with active magicks-"

"That matters not. We have the knowledge of-"

"Da'ariel knowledge will not be enough!" His head snapped up and returning her glare he switched again to that language as foreign to Lilly as her surroundings. Though he gestured her way while he spoke the only word she could make out clearly was a repeat of Deebanaarie.

Then seeming to read the confusion on her face he finally switched back. Still refusing to drop his eyes as he shrugged, "...your writings do not cover enough of the tongue to teach her all she needs. Besides, your numbers have continued to dwindle. Your chances of removing me with force are far *less* than last time."

Mairiel considered all he'd said before nodding, "So maybe your knowledge could be useful to us... But understand one thing Kyrel, you have no authority here. None! You will do only as is asked and otherwise not involve yourself in our affairs any further."

Lilly found her eyes glued to the older woman's face, with grim fascination, the deeply furrowed wrinkles appeared to be fading, plumping up and straightening out. Her hair was changing too, brightening to a shade not unlike Lilly's.

Seeing her back away, Mairiel turned her way and smiling stood up, her back had straightened and no longer needing her handle she left it against the huge seat as she walked over.

"Lilliath... We have waited too long to behold your presence again."

Lilly backed away, cowering behind Kyrel. He suppressed a smirk.

"Unless you seek to estrange the child, I suggest taking things one *small* step at a time. Her given name is as foreign to her as Azeron itself. And as the magicks in her realm are quite different to our own your pulpustuem root probably wasn't the best first step."

"You call these small steps!" Lilly stared incredulously at Mai Mai, the now handsome, middle-aged woman, standing tall beside her. "I mean OK the magick stuff... kinda cool a-and undeniably real. A-and don't think I'm not digging the whole Chosen-One thing." She shrugged, "I mean who doesn't want to be the next child of prophecy... Buffy Summers eat your heart out and all that crazy shit. But come on... You're telling me I have four days left to live, if I can't master some inherited powers so ancient that no one here has possessed them in decades."

"It has indeed been many generations." Mairiel gave a solemn nod. "But we do still possess the necessary knowledge." An attempt to call her Mai Mai earlier had resulted in a torrent of protest ending with, "That won't do at all, you child are to call me Mairiel."

Now her rejuvenated face and voice were far sterner and she stared down at Lilly. "You will defeat Mordrel," she nodded. "You must: you alone have the power."

"Hate to break it to you lady," seeing the beginnings of a frown she shrugged, adding "Mairiel, but I barely have the power to make it through school in one piece and spend the rest of my life in some dead end job, just about surviving above the breadline if I'm lucky."

"Then you are not lucky," Mai Mai shook her head, "because this is your destiny. Now open it."

Kyrel was at Lilly's other side. While Mai Mai's grandsons Arteth and Toleth stood slightly further back, watching eagerly as she stared down at the large, stone trunk. The outside of it was covered in carvings that Mai Mai had called protective writings but looked to Lilly more like random squiggles and swirly shapes.

"The Kalaareem is in four settings of the sun," added Mai Mai. "You have no choice but to be ready for the full strength of Mordrel's forces. She will stop at nothing to eliminate you now."

"But that's crazy!" Lilly shook her head. "I can barely understand what you people are talking about. How can I fight when I don't understand? I mean come on... Didn't you ever hear that knowledge is power?"

With a contemplative frown Mai Mai shook her head. "I do not believe I have."

"Fine," Lilly sighed, hands going to the lid of the trunk. "But I'm telling you now, you have the wrong girl. I-I mean not that I don't understand the mistake. Lilliath... Lillian... Fair enough there's a similarity a-and sure... My parents did die when I was younger, but it wasn't in some magnificent battle like you're making out. It was a car crash. I should know. I was there..." unconsciously running her fingers along the groove where lid and trunk met - enjoying the unexpected warmth emanating from its dark stone surface within. As she shrugged, her fingers moving faster along that groove, she added, "I mean my memory of that day may be a little sketchy. What with the being an infant and all, but I do have the shrapnel scar in the back of my head to prove it so there's no way you're telling me it didn't happen."

"Not shrapnel. Do'mass," said Mai Mai. She watched as, mesmerised by the groove on the box, Lilly felt and glimpsed a spark.

It licked at her fingertips, and startled she fell against Kyrel's hard chest. Straightening up and struggling to breathe steady, she turned back to Mai Mai. "What the hell just happened?"

"You made the connection." Mai Mai smiled.

"What the fuck is that meant to-"

"You unlocked the box," nodded the woman. "Something which would not have been possible if you were not Herrella's daughter."

"What? No!" Lilly shook her head, backing away from it. "I... I... I didn't, I was just...I-"

"Toleth!" called Mai Mai. "Cat ya vac!"

The youngest grandson stepped forward.

"Show your Do'mass."

"Oh hey... No! That's cool," Lilly backed away waving her hands. "I don't think I need to see anybody's Do'mass thanks."

With a puzzled frown and his arm over his chest, in the exact same gesture she'd seen from Kyrel earlier, Toleth nodded. "To finally know you is an honour cousin Lilliath." Then, while she muttered through clenched teeth about wanting people to stop calling her that, he dropped to one knee and flipped both head and hair forward in one fluid motion.

Seeing he had Lilly's attention Mai Mai ran a finger down Toleth's scalp. Parting his hair upward along the middle, to just above the nape of his neck: revealing a Y shaped scar with rounded ends. Lilly gasped. Her hand flew to the same spot on her head, and standing Toleth nodded once more before stepping back and re-joining his brother.

"The Do'mass is a sacred symbol," explained Mai Mai. "We Da'ariel mark our young this way when collecting their essence to seal the Eshron," she gestured to the trunk adding, "It reminds us of the true strength of Azeron: Laîoch and Tuâoch. In the Do'mass we remember them as they should be: bound by nature's laws - three mighty forces as one."

Lilly's eyes were wide with disgust.

"You carve a mark into the backs of baby's heads! That is what you're saying right? You... You bleed your kids at birth. Why would you do that?" Her nose wrinkled. "It's gross! Not to mention weird... You people are weird!" Lilly nodded. "You know that right? You know you're all real weird?"

Mairiel contemplated her quietly a moment before continuing. "There was once a time when all in Azeron were born with the Do'mass." Her voice grew sullen. "However, with the magicks parted, time was the only thing needed to bring about its demise. Unable to harness the forces of Tuâoch the Deebanaarie soon bore a different mark." The woman's gaze shifted momentarily to Kyrel and seeing Lilly look his way he sighed and begrudgingly turned around.

He pulled back his hair, showing the corrupted symbol which looked as though the right arm of the Y had fallen off, leaving only a stump. It was also flatter, thicker, and blended more naturally with the surrounding the skin.

"It's not a scar." Lilly shook her head as he turned to face her. "You... yours is a birthmark!"

"That's right," Mairiel's tone commanded her attention again, yet the woman could no longer take her eyes off Kyrel. "Some Deebanaarie," she nodded his way, "those with royal blood, are still born with the mark. It may no longer be a true Do'mass but Deebanaarie bearing it do still have limited access to the forces of the Tuâoch. As for the Da'ariel: we were forced to stop using our magicks to survive the slaughters that followed the Great War. The price we paid for doing so was a high one. No Da'ariel has been born with the mark for more than three hundred cycles. And so we long ago became incapable of accessing our once inherent magicks. That is..." picking up on the change in her tone - from seething anger to awe - Lilly turned to see Mai Mai smiling her way as she finished with, "until now!"

"No, OK!" she shook her head, backing away from the trunk. "I... I'm not listening anymore. The things you're saying are just... stupid! A...and-"

"What's stupid, Slater?" Baxter sauntered in, carrying a bowl of food, with Terrence at his side. The blonde girl: Vereena, was behind them; while Tobias, scanning his surroundings, came in after her. "If it's all this, 'you're some long lost princess with special powers' thing," Baxter shrugged. "We're way ahead of you on that one."

Lilly's jaw dropped as she glared from him to Mai Mai. Before raising an eyebrow and smirking, "Princess?"

"Yes," Mai Mai nodded. "Your mother, Herrella, was my eldest. As such she was next to lead our people. You were her only child and she died getting you beyond the veil."

Lilly blinked a couple of times before shaking her head. "So wait... You're telling me I'm next in line to lead a bunch of ragtag, mud-hut-dwelling, defenceless no-hopers?"

"Oh, ain't they told you the bit about the evil Queen yet?"

The twins sniggered at Baxter's remark.

Cocking her head to one side, Mai Mai fixed them with a stare that shut them both up. "The Avengturov family have led these Da'ariel since the days of the Do'mass council." She turned back to Lilly, "with both my daughters dead you are indeed next in line for leadership."

"Yeah well consider me abdicated, Let..." she frowned sceptically toward Arteth and Toleth. "...One of my cousins? Do it -"

"Men are not leaders." Mai Mai stated simply. "They are warriors, excellent at carrying out our orders; they do not give them."

"Phhh!" Baxter's face screwed up and everyone looked his way - Lilly doing so with a smirk. "Well come on..." he shrugged "That's just stupid!"

"Definitely," Terrence pinched some food from Baxter's bowl. "It's no wonder you're getting your asses handed to you, if that's how you think."

"Cat ya vac!" Mai Mai snarled and immediately Vereena was herding them into the far corner of the room.

"Come now, away, what's spoken here is too important for interruptions."

"Oh hey, hey watch the food!" protested Baxter.

"What about her?" Lilly watched the other girl. "She a relative too?"

"Oh yes, cousin." Vereena forgot the boys and looked back with a wide grin, "I too am-"

"Cat ya vac Veer!" Mai Mai glared at the girl. "Deng mei natuii? Cat ya vac inst!"

"Veyhi Mairiel, maenk tae." Vereena dropped her eyes, pushing the boys farther into the corner as the older woman turned back to Lilly.

"Vereena is not yet approaching her Kalaareem," stated Mai Mai. "And you cannot abdicate your destiny, Lilliath. Only you have the magicks."

"Oh yeah," huffed Lilly, "Well I got a newsflash for you I don't have any damn magicks, OK. I... I wasn't born with the mark... mine is just a scar. Like his," she pointed at Toleth. "Like I said, I get the mistake OK, a few misinterpreted similarities. No biggy... Just pop me back through one of those veil thingies and we can all get on with forgetting this ever happened."

"Yeah," Tobias spoke up, though he was still scanning every crevice of the room. "I'm with Lilly on that..." his voice trailed off when T'vor wobbled into the room and closing his mouth he backed away.

Baxter, barely noticing the creature's presence, shrugged, lending his own brand of support.

"Yeah," he looked Lilly's way. "I mean just look at her... No way scrawny-Annie is anybody's warrior princess." Seeing anger flare in her eyes he grinned, biting a chunk from his dark bread roll before adding, "She certainly ain't gonna be winning any wars for you; more like stab you in the back and run off with your valuables. I mean seriously, do you people even know what a delinquent is?"

Swallowing hard, Lilly shrugged turning back to Mai Mai.

"Look I hate to admit it, but Baxter-no-brainer over there has a point ..." the twins sniggered as Baxter scowled,

"Hey, fuck you, Slater." Ignoring him, she continued. "... None of us are the kinda kids you want around. I... mean you look like you have a good thing going here." She shook her head, shrugging. "Sure maybe not the war and oppression thing, but hey... Obedient kids! What society wouldn't envy you that? I... I mean we..." her eyes flitted over the others as she thought up more to say. "We're troublemakers, really, really bad with authority fig-"

"You, I am confident we can handle..." Mai Mai smiled. "As for your friends – If they give us any trouble we shall throw them into the Matfiack moolach and be done with it."

"Err...OK," Lilly's eyes took in the worried expressions on the boys' faces before drifting toward Kyrel as she whispered through clenched teeth.

"That would be a bad thing, right?"

"The moolach would make short work of eating the flesh from their bones, before it dissolves those also," he nodded before watching her turn back to Mai Mai, her head already shaking.

"Well see, there's also the fact that our school... The... the place we were headed to... When our bus went off the road ... Well see they'll be looking for us already and they'll be real pissed when they don't find us."

"Pissed?" Mai Mai raised an eyebrow.

"Err..." Lilly looked to the others for help.

"Angry," Terrence nodded, "They'll be real angry!"

"I see," nodded Mai Mai, her eyebrow lowering. "Does it not stand to reason, that as they will not find you they will not be able to do anything about that anger?"

Lilly frowned and all three boys sighed.

"This is your destiny, Lilliath"

"That isn't my name!" Lilly yelled at her.

"You will embrace that destiny or you will perish by Mordrel's hands."

"Oh come on," she stamped a foot. "Do we have to go back to the perishing? You have the wrong girl! I'm Lillian... Lill-ee-an OK not ath! A... a- and the mark on my head - Not a birthmark! OK... It's a scar."

"Oh that's right." added Terence, "Lilly was in a car crash when she was little that mark on her head is-"

"You have examined it closely?" Mai Mai ignored him.

"Err well... we're talking about the back of my head here... as in I don't have eyes there." Lilly said.

"Yes..." shrugged the woman, "and you were too little to remember the truth of the night Herrella escaped with you. These cars of which you speak, the accident - if it did occur - was most likely caused by the tear in the veil which brought you to that realm. I know that you are Lilliath Avengturov because I have watched you grow since the day you were sent away. As has Kyrel," she looked to him, her voice taking on a grudging tone. "He has after all had access to a bountiful supply of quiescence."

Scowling, Kyrel dropped his eyes as Lilly looked his way. Shaking her head she turned back to Mai Mai.

"Well then you were watching the wrong girl. Somewhere along the line your qui... es... whatever-the-hell-you-call-it, got me and your precious Lilliath mixed up. Stuff like this happens all the time: computer errors, underpaid civil servants. It's nothing to be ashamed of OK, no system is fool-proof."

"The Quiescence is never wrong!" Mai Mai glared at her. "And the only thing this insolence is achieving is to lower your chances of surviving to your Kalaareem!" She reached out a hand touching the lid of the slate box. "Now open your Eshron so that we might-"

"Deefak bor, Mairiel!" Kyrel's eyes burned with anger as he slapped a hand down on top of the box. An argument followed in the native tongue. Lilly and the boys watched, clueless, as Vereena became increasingly agitated beside them. While Arteth and Toleth – itching to involve themselves – were ordered back twice by Mai Mai.

At last Mairiel sighed, "Very well, Kyrel but you remember: I do not warn twice." She looked to Lilly with a nod. "We take our leave of you, Princess Lilliath," glancing Kyrel's way she added, "It is indeed a sacred rite to open the Eshron."

"The what? Oh right, the box," Lilly looked at it and shook her head, "yeah, see about that, I don't really-"

"Cat ya vac." Kyrel spat the command at Mai Mai and glaring his way she half muttered, half growled, "Deebanaarie Matfiac!" before demanding the others join her in leaving the room.

"What's going on?" Terrence asked as Vereena shunted them toward the door. "Where are we going now?"

"Back to the food with any luck." Baxter grinned, looking over his shoulder at Lilly. "Later Slater, enjoy your alone time with the freaky new boyfriend."

"Moron," she muttered.

Tobias followed him asking, "so when exactly do we go home?"

Arteth and Toleth were the last to leave and before they did Toleth threw Kyrel such a hate filled glare that Lilly felt the hairs on the back of her neck rise.

"OK," she watched the dirty brown curtain fall back over the doorway. "What's going on now?"

"Open it." Kyrel nodded to the trunk and putting particular emphasis to every word Lilly glared at him.

"The... Damn... Box ... Isn't... Mine!"

Kyrel stared at her a moment before strolling over to the table bearing the Eshron and perching beside it.

"I know you're scared, Lilly but I also know you know everything you've been told here today is true."

"I know no such thing," she continued shaking her head. "I just wish you people would hurry up and realise you have the wrong-"

"If you were not of this world your use of the sacred words would not have brought forth a new tree in the forest."

"Oh hey that... that was just-"

"If you were not Lilliath Avengturov," he glanced to the trunk, "your touch would not have unlocked the Eshron."

"This is stupid," her eyes filled with tears as she grimaced down at it, hands moving as if possessed. "I don't even understand half the things she said…" flipping open the lid saying, "I… I mean what the crap is a Kalaar…" the word froze on her lips as she looked in at the array of strange objects.

"Kalaar," Kyrel looked from her to the contents of the trunk, "Is the shuk'byaniee rotational occurrence of the day of your birth… Kalaareem is the sixty fourth rotation historically known for being the time when Azeronians gain the full strength of their powers." Taking in her blank expression he smiled cocking his head to one side, "Known to you, I believe… as the sixteenth birthday."

Staring down into the trunk, her eyes drawn to a rag wrapped around something big and square. Forcing herself to look away, she gazed curiously up at Kyrel nodding, "My sixteenth birthday. That's what this is all about? I'm not sixteen for like another mon-"

"Your true birthday." Kyrel nodded.

"Oh… right." She took in a deep and grounding breath before mumbling, "of course," then shrugging, "so this quiescence stuff… it's… you've been using it to watch me? That's… that's… it's how you and strange age-morphing woman knew to call me Lillian, right?"

"That strange age-morphing woman is your grandmother," he gave a curt nod. "She should be shown the appropriate respect."

"Oh really… Would that be like the respect you've been showing her?"

Kyrel raised an eyebrow. "You would do well not to follow my example where Mairiel is concerned."

"What! Ever!" Lilly rolled her eyes forming a W with the first three fingers of her left hand and waving it at him. Kyrel frowned.

"I have often wondered why it is that you do that. Now I think I understand. Mairiel is right," he smirked. "You are indeed insolent."

Lilly lowered her fingers with a scowl. "You know in my realm we have words for guys who like to secretly watch young girls," shaking her head she cautioned, "They're not good words!"

"Lilly…" Kyrel held her gaze.

"Yes?"

"The Eshron," he nodded to it. "Is really not so important. It is indeed your sacred right to open it without an audience, which is useful, as it rids us of Mairiel and the others for a while. But it is also your first real chance of knowing your mother." He watched her eyes flit over the cloth square again and shrugged, "Ultimately you will believe what suits you. However, the troops scouring the forest make it clear Mordrel knows you are in Azeron, and what she believes. So your two choices remain the same: You can sit here and wait for her forces to storm the gates, seize you and take you back to the castle, where she will make you wish you were dead a thousand times over before you truly are. Or you can learn to use your powers so that you might stand a chance of surviving, and perhaps defeating her." They stared at each other a moment, Lilly chewing on the inside of her top lip.

Then her eyes drifted to the dirty brown rag again and Kyrel nodded.

"Nothing can come of you taking a look unless you want it to."

Lilly gulped. She picked up the cloth bundle and hearing him sigh, "Of course…" paused to look up with narrowed eyes. "Go on…" he grinned. "Take a look."

Pulling away the cloth she contemplated the plain wooden box turning it over in search of an opening.

"Like this." Kyrel leaned forward taking her hand and running her index finger along the top of the box. It pulled away from the middle, opening up like some bizarre wooden flower in bloom. The entire top cascaded in on itself until the box's thickened edges with their multiple ridges were the only evidence of it ever having a lid.

"Cool!" Lilly's eyes grew wide as she stared in at the small hunk of yellowish metal; its shape similar to a bow-tie or hourglass. It was engraved with patterns similar to those on the Eshron and set in the middle was an oval reddish orange gem. Inside of which was a perfect Do'mass; raised from the metal beneath.

"What is this?" Lilly lifted it from the box. Examining it; the other side was identical in design.

"Your Gaashmay," he nodded.

Spotting a thin slit in either end she brought it closer to her face, her puzzled look turning to surprise as Kyrel pulled her arm back.

"Ny, ny! Nydrel!" Seeing her confusion he shook his head. "Careful!"

Lilly watched him place the Gaashmay flat on her palm, the slit ends resting either side of her hand. He folded her thumb back over it, then bent all four of her fingers upward, doing the same with them until her middle finger pressed down on the Do'mass and out of each end shot a thin blade no more than an inch in width but at least five inches long.

"Whoa," Lilly grinned, nodding. "OK… That's pretty cool."

"Yes," He smirked with recognition. "The gaashmay is.... cool! It is also deadly."

"Well now I like the sound of that too." She lifted it high above her head and hurled it toward Mai Mai's chair. The blades retracted and it bounced off, falling to the floor.

Kyrel turned to her with a bemused expression and frowning Lilly gave him an awkward little shrug.

"What! That's how Xena would have used it!"

Day One: Part Three

"How do you not have her yet?"

"My Queen we were upon the girl, and her companions, but they had help."

Mordrel's newest General gazed down at the face of her Queen, shimmering up from the surface of the puddle she'd poured.

"Help? Help! All the Da'ariel have ever known is to hide and run."

"Yes my Queen, but they're fast and they know these woods so much better than-"

"Do not make excuses, Drellaeleon."

"No my Queen," she dipped her eyes; the wrath in Mordrel's being enough to make her blood run cold despite the true distance between them. "That was not my intention," began the general, "I meant only to point out that they're using magicks and we're here with so little-"

"They're using sprites!" Mordrel's voice became excitable.

"It would seem so my Queen. We arrived at the clearing but there were mists - they're hiding her."

"They risk so much for the child?" Mordrel grinned, "They must have great faith in her powers."

A large, round, dark face appeared at the Queen's side. It was her own sprite: Neenia. A different breed to those the Da'ariel acquainted themselves with, Neenia was Gershurian. Instead of fur her squat rounded body; with its stick thin limbs, was covered with a tough hide of leathery skin. Folds of which wrinkled up around her huge blue eyes as she addressed the general with her watery gurgle of a voice.

"Look up, Drellaeleon."

As Drellaeleon looked up from where she knelt, so too did those warriors gathered around her.

Many gasped as the swarm of deadly ginat beetles hovered, dipping in and out loosely above their heads. "See how we lead the way," said Neenia, "Once they find the village the Ginaten can take down the barrier. We trust the Da'ariel will be no match for you once it's breached."

"Seize the girl and destroy the village!" demanded Mordrel, "Mairiel's clan have stood in my way for the last time... Kill everything that moves within their boundaries!"

"Yes my Queen, it shall be done." Once more General Drellaeleon bowed her head as the image faded, leaving only a muddy puddle of quiescence.

Straightening up she pulled her heavy cape back down over her shoulder, kicked dirt on the puddle, and climbing onto her armoured blue trundle, called her troops to follow as the beetles led their way through the forest.

***

Back at the huge table all three boys were now helping themselves to more food. "You heard what the girl said," Baxter piled more food onto his plate. "Those furry little critters brought us here, and they're fresh out a juice."

"Yeah well," Tobias leaned closer, lowering his voice. "Pardon my French, Baxter, but that sounds like a steaming pile of bull-"

"Sprites require a juice to function in your realm?"

All at once the boys turned to see Vereena beside them; carrying a tray atop which were two stacks of cups and two huge wooden jugs.

"Err... not exactly." Terence smiled as he stood up reaching for the tray. "Here let me help you with that."

"I'm in no need of help, Terence Emerson," she frowned.

"O-Oh no I can see that..." he shook his head, slipping his hands around the edges of the tray regardless as he told her. "You're obviously very capable... it... it's just... this is..." he raised the tray. "I-in our realm it's not good manners for a man to sit around watching others work without offering assistance."

"And your friends?" she glanced to the other boys. "They do not possess these: good manners as you do?"

"Oh hell no... these two, they're complete..." glancing their way he saw both eyeing him and looked away with a chuckle. "...obviously you don't need all three of us helping you. I... I guess I'm just... more eager."

"So it would seem," she nodded, "Still..." she pulled the tray back. "I am yet to take my taeleska and you, Terrence Emerson, are clearly not yet a man."

Baxter guffawed as Vereena made her way around the large table, placing cups and jugs in appropriate places.

"OK, but you know, there's really no need to keep on calling me that?" Terrence followed her, pausing as she did to give him a curious look.

"You said it was your name?"

"W-well yeah," he nodded "it…it is. But see it's my whole name a… and well… in our… realm," he smiled, "people don't tend to go by their whole names."

"Do they not?"

"Well no," he shook his head. "See, Emerson is my surname… err… family name," he pointed to Tobias, "We're brothers, so both Emerson; it's something we get from our father."

"Yeah," chimed in Baxter, "That, a thick skull, and some real bad habits." He snatched up a handful of berries from the table. "Why don't you tell her about those little ram-raiding trips that put you in Craven's Peak in the first place?" He sat back, "I mean you know… while you're trying to impress… why not pull out all the stops."

"Shut it!" Terrence hissed, shooting a scowl his way. When he turned back Vereena's expression had become thoughtful and she was already nodding,

"I see, yes…that does make sense."

"Man, this blows!" Tobias muttered. "I say we find our own way back."

"Somehow… I don't see these guys being down with that." Terrence glanced from his brother to the armed bunches of men dotted around the tent.

"Oh ah…" Baxter tilted his seat back and threw a few more berries in his mouth. "Something about the swords and battle axes give it away?"

"These rooms remain guarded for the protection of all within them," Vereena assured them.

"Well, there we go then," laughed Baxter. "Cos we all know we're in good hands when the people in charge are carrying weapons and doing shit for our own protection."

Vereena turned giving him a curious glance. Throwing more berries in his mouth, Baxter smiled up at her as he chewed them to mush.

"You know something…" Terence laughed, turning her away with a hand on her arm. "You should probably just go ahead and ignore this pair completely."

"Oh now that's nice!" sneered Baxter as once again the other boy separated the girl from her tray and they proceeded to make their way around the table.

"How can you be so…" Tobias turned to Baxter, "… fucking chilled about all this?"

"Aww, now c'mon… you missing The Peak that much?"

"Well now that you say it…" Tobias feigned thoughtfulness a moment before snapping at him. "Don't be a dick, man! You just said yourself these people are holding us fucking prisoner… plus, you know," he scanned the room and lowered his voice. "There's those creepy little fur-ball creatures."

"Creepy fur-ball creatures?" Baxter raised an eyebrow as he grinned. "Shit, man I get it now, you're the one that's scared of dogs. Always knew there was a way of telling you two apart for definite, well that and the fact that you're a thicko."

"You what? I'm not scared of dogs!"

***

"Are we really leaving the princess with that moolach-headed Deebanaarie?"

"You know our ways as well as he does Toleth, none of us has the right."

Around the table heads turned to Mai Mai as her grandsons followed her into the room.

"Since when is it our way to allow the likes of him into the village, that's what I'd like to know."

"You propose we get rid of him then? That I loose you and Arteth upon him and hope for the best? Do I need to remind you of what occurred last time there was an attempt to force him off our lands?" She passed the human boys and took her seat at the head of the table.

"Ny Mairiel." His head drooped as she looked up at him.

"Your parent's lives were taken the last time we tried that boy, should I allow him to snuff yours out too?" Keeping his eyes down Toleth shook his head but said nothing.

"Right now he wants the same as we do, and is our best way of ensuring it. You worry about the storm to come and leave me to worry about the Deebanaarie."

"Veyhi Mairi-"

"The Princess requires practice with her aim."

All attention turned to the door again, as Kyrel sauntered through its dirty brown curtain. Lilly, grasping the Gaashmay, followed closely behind.

"So the Eshron is opened." Mai Mai stood with a smile. "Lilliath needs to eat. Come…" she gestured to the chair nearest herself. "Sit down. Sustenance is a great aid to the concentration."

"No!" Kyrel held her back. "Practice is of far greater importance now."

Toleth's face twitched, as he watched Mai Mai calmly retake her seat.

"Then Arteth shall accompany you." She nodded to her older grandson and leaving her side he led Kyrel and Lilly out of the tent.

"Practice her aim?" Baxter looked to Tobias, and they both raised their eyebrows, before looking to Mai Mai, "Can we watch?"

"Veer," Mairiel barely glanced their way as she waved a hand at her younger granddaughter, "keep eyes on them."

"Sweet!" Baxter leapt up from the table.

"Oh, that's just great." Lilly grumbled when she noticed the others trailing behind them. Kyrel followed her gaze with a smirk.

"The eyes of your friends are but a small anxiety today Lilly. You would do well to settle on coping with the larger ones."

"No shit!" she said as they came out onto a large open dirt patch behind the tents, where huge tree-trunk posts had been planted into the ground. Lilly counted them - five. Each one scuffed and marked with huge dents.

Other spectators were appearing at doors, some peeking around curtains while others ventured out to huddle in little groups.

"Great, great, and fucking great!" hissed Lilly.

"Pay them no mind," Kyrel assured her. "Their curiosity is not what you need worry about right now." He stopped at the edge of the clearing and looked back to Arteth. "Remember this girl has never seen a Gaashmay before today. A wide berth would be best. If those present wish to give up their lives, best they do so fighting Mordrel's troops don't you think?" Though the look on Arteth's face was much like his brother's moments earlier, he turned and addressed the other Da'ariel with a short string of words in their own tongue; the crowd fell back several metres.

"Cheers," shrugged Lilly.

"Remember what I told you?" Kyrel looked from her to the Gaashmay.

"Sure," she nodded, "I'm the weapon. It's the guide…" she eyed him apprehensively. "Right?"

"Right." he nodded, before placing his hands on her shoulders and lightly shaking her. "Loosen the body," he instructed, then grasping the hand she held the Gaashmay in, he raised it above her head adding, "and most importantly… hold tight."

"Right." Lilly nodded dubiously.

"Focus." His hands went up to the sides of her head, and nodding toward the first post he told her. "Hit your target."

"Err…" A glance back to see the boys on her left watching with amusement had Kyrel's hands snapping her head back to position, "Focus!"

"Right sorry," she blinked. "I just… I don't see how I'm supposed to hit that, and hold this tight, at the same time. That's doesn't even make any-"

"Close your eyes." He waved a hand in front of her face and she did so. "Now take deep breaths." Kyrel gave her a moment to follow the instruction before saying, "when you open your eyes, you must be relaxed and concentrating only on the target."

Hearing the boys snigger behind her, Lilly mumbled, "This is ridiculous."

"Focus!" Kyrel snapped again. Seeing her jaw clench as her face tensed he added, "Deep breaths Lilly… Deep… Relaxing… Breaths. Now…" he let go of her arm and stepping back added, "Open your eyes."

Lilly did as instructed and as he lowered his voice saying, "You're the weapon Lilly."

She began echoing him. "I'm the wea-" but was soon screaming "Ho-leeeeey Shi-iiiiiiiiiiiiiiiiit!" as she hurtled upwards; body following outstretched arms: on a collision course for the first tree stump.

"Fucking Hell!" Terrence and Tobias howled in unison.

"No shit!" added Baxter. All three now thoroughly fixated on the sight of their classmate flying through the air screaming, "Make it stop, make it stop!"

"Relax…" Kyrel shouted after her. "Be guided. You *are* the weapon!"

All three boys winced, as she cracked into the stump, then they stared on with added fascination as she spun around it several times; legs flailing upward behind her, before she landed in a heap on the floor.

"Not bad." Kyrel approached her. "Though we shall have to do something about that dismount."

Getting up on extremely shaky legs, Lilly staggered slowly toward him, her voice growing shriller with each sentence.

"You didn't say anything about flying through the air! You son of a frigging bastard! That could have killed me!"

"I told you, your body is the weapon... how else did you think you would hit the tree?"

"Oh you're right," Lilly panted through repeated nodding. "It was totally obvious. I mean why wouldn't these folks be waiting for a heroine who throws herself at their enemies. It makes so much sense after..."

"Lillian! Watch out!"

With her registering the calls of the boys a split second after Kyrel had, she turned away from him, looking up just in time; to then cower at the sight of the log toppling inches from her head.

Palm outstretched, Kyrel spoke as if commanding a well trained dog.

"Ta varee." he told the post and it fell about them in splinters of damp mulch. Wiping it off her shoulders, and out of her hair, Lilly stood up throwing him an angry glance. Only then did she turn to see the boys watching her with identical grins plastered across their faces.

"Holy Fucking Hell! That was seriously heavy!" Tobias nodded as he looked to Terrence.

"You'll get no argument there bro, definitely heavy."

"Actually, Gaashmay are quite light." Vereena informed them with a curt nod. "The force comes from within,"

"Hey Lillian," Baxter called out grinning as she turned away from a growing argument with Kyrel, over whether or not she would try again. "That was fucking ace, girl!"

"Yeah..." Tobias chimed in. "Do it again!"

"Again!" Terrence echoed his brother."

Lilly's indignant glare, melted into a coy grin as she turned back to Kyrel with a raised eyebrow.

"You said something about a dismount?"

***

"Four days!" Tobias threw his arms up with his exclamation. "That's the genius plan? This bunch of village idiots teach her to fight off the militia of some bitchin' evil ho in the next four days or we're stuck here?... For keeps!"

"Stuck where?" Slowly, Sandra Harper raised herself onto her elbows.

"*Three* days," Terrence asserted, then receiving an all too familiar look of irritation from his brother he explained, "Technically Lilly has *three* days - at the most! *The 'bitchin evil ho'* needs her out of the picture by the fourth day so..."

"Where are we?" hissed Harper. "Where's everyone else?" her faint rasp of a voice remained ignored by the three boys.

"...If this Ka-laa-reem thingy is half as important as that Mai Mai woman was making out would *you* wait till the last minute to make a move?"

"What's a Ka-laa-reem?" Harper asked now as she watched Tobias suck in his thick lower lip.

The image was raw nerves; an anxiety contagious enough to surpass her overwhelming ignorance. "Guys!" She slapped the bed and forced her voice to rise in spite of the clogged sensation in her throat. "What the fuck is going on? Where's Morris?" Blank stares from each of the Emerson twins had her adding, "Is there gonna be a fight or something? Is Slater in trouble? Is that where Morris is? Did she... has she gone to get help?"

"Yeah..." Baxter glanced up from his tree stump seat. "...there's gonna be a fight. That and a whole load a something." He shook his head "And no... Morris ain't off getting help; could a done with some apparently. Though, from what we've heard, it was her trying to save your ass that-"

"Baxter!" The warning in Terrence's voice was obvious enough to tell Harper plenty.

"What?" Baxter shrugged, "She's got a right to know our entire situation, don't she?"

"What situation?" Harper fixed Terrence with a stare. "What's going on? Don't be hiding shit from me, Tez. There ain't nothing you guys can handle that I can't! Tell me the truth. Where the *fuck* is Morris?"

"Well err... she err..." Terrence looked to his brother. Tobias immediately dropped his eyes, and Terrence's mouth began to flap wordlessly until finally a response came from Baxter.

"She's dead."

"What?" Harper shook her head at him. "What are you talking about? She was right beside me on the bus. Morris was... What is this, some kind a wind up? Tez!" She turned back to him, her expression hopeful. Terrence shifted uncomfortably where he stood and nodded glumly, "Terrence!" Harper squealed at him "This isn't not funny. Tell me what's really going on!"

"You calling my brother a liar?" Tobias stepped forward but was immediately held him back by the arm of his twin.

"No." Harper's voice cracked as it rose. "I'm calling you *all* fucking liars! A bunch of no good sick, twisted, fucking assholes, if you expect me to buy that shit!"

"Hey..." crossing the room Terrence crouched at her side. "Calm down, OK. I know this is a hell of a lot to take in but I'm just telling you what we've been told."

"By who? Who the fuck told you Morris was dead? Why would somebody even say something like that?"

"Because it's true you dumb bi-"

"Give it a fucking rest, Tobe!" the accompanying sharp look was enough to close his brother's mouth as well as send him pacing. Turning back to Harper, Terrence smiled. "You're not the only one who's a little wigged out, seems we kind of stumbled into the middle of some pretty weird shit after the bus crashed and-"

"The bus crashed?"

A chuckle rose from the corner as Baxter looked up muttering, "Oh, well isn't that's just fucking wonderful... not only does she think we're four months late with the worst April Fools of all time; she also don't remember Heyward driving us off the road, like that tree we hit was a hot date with a winning lottery ticket."

"It's OK." Terrence kept his eyes on Harper but spoke up so the others could hear, "She was in shock that's all. You know… sometimes, for our own protection; the mind kinda switches off." Reaching out he placed a hand over hers. "You're fine now though… Vereena, a girl here, she gave you medicine when they brought you in. And well, I'd say your coming round means it's worked"

"Yeah well, between you and me, Harper." Baxter probed a fingernail between his front bottom teeth for food remnants. "You might wanna flick that off switch on your mind again, cos the bus exploding with everyone else inside has to be what passes as today's good news. That and the fact that school is definitely out for summer."

"What's he talking about?" Glaring through tears she shook her head at Terrence. "What could possibly be worse than Morris… than everyone being dead?"

"Well…" a quick glance to the others yielded no support, so turning back to her Terrence nodded. "Remember how I said we kinda stumbled into the middle of some pretty weird shit?"

***

Gasping for air Lilly sat hunched forward, with her back against what was left of the post. The Gaashmay lay on the ground at her right, while bearing down on her with a determined pace Kyrel came from the left.

"You must rise," he said reaching her feet. "We are not yet finished."

"Correction," she gave an exhausted nod. "You're not yet finished. Me – I'm done! You can go ahead and stick a fork in me."

"I fail to see how that would be of any help, Princess."

Sighing she looked up. "OK once again…Could you please, *please!* Stop calling me that."

"I apologise, it is difficult to remember after all the times I've seen you and thought of you as such."

"Yeah well, if you were really keeping that close an eye on me you have to know this physical shit is very far from my style."

"It's time for your style to change." Kyrel crouched beside her, hands going to his hips.

"Change! What channel were you watching exactly?" Seeing him frown she shrugged, "This *is* me changing, OK. You've just seen me give my best effort and ten times more. You must have had me fly at these damn logs a thousand times over already."

"Not at all…" shocked at the suggestion, Kyrel shook his head, "why it can't have been more than-"

"Stop it." Lilly threw up a hand, silencing him, then letting her head droop muttered, "Why must you take everything so literally?"

"Your statement was incorrect. The number of times you've used-"

"The number isn't important!"

"I disagree, Lilly. You're clearly mistaken... grossly so."

"It was a deliberate exaggeration, OK! Something you just say you know... to get your point across, that's all."

"I don't think I understand." Kyrel's puzzled expression backed up his words. "How can anything other than truth, or in fact so far from it, be expected to get your point across successfully?"

A growl escaped Lilly and rolling her eyes she raised a hand again.

"You know what? Nevermind... the real point here is that I've had enough. This flying through the air head first thing was really a kick at first but now it just fucking hurts! I'm hurting like: everywhere and I'm pretty sure that knock I took earlier left me with some sort of a concussion, OK. I really can't manage anymore... I have to rest."

"Rest cannot help you, if you do not learn, Mordrel will kill you."

"If I do not rest..." Lillian fixed him with a stare. "She won't get the chance."

A short sharp throat clearing announced Arteth's approach, and the pair looked upward as he nodded.

"Perhaps now would be a wise time for the Princess to replenish... with eating?"

A momentary gritting of Lilly's teeth was followed by her grabbing the Gaashmay and sighing as she rose unsteadily to her feet. She turned her back on Kyrel and forcing a smile nodded, "That sounds like a very good idea, Arteth. But please... I'd really much rather you call me Lilly."

"As you wish, cousin Lilly." Arteth followed her from the tree.

Rising also, Kyrel followed them inside - calling, "Do not be expecting rest after eating, Lilly. You still have much to learn before this eve is through."

***

The small crowd gathered earlier in the feasting hut were now gone. Only Mai Mai remained. She rose from her seat as the dirty brown curtain opened, and gestured to the one nearest her as Lilly approached.

Arteth and Kyrel were close behind, but Mairiel only had eyes for her newly returned granddaughter.

"You look exhausted Lilliath." she said taking hold of a nearby jug. Pouring a thick, murky green liquid from it into a brown wooden tankard, then offering a smile, she pushed the tankard toward the sceptical teen. Nodding, "Drink; it will help relax and refresh you."

"Funny," muttered Lilly wrinkling her nose as she gazed down into liquid. "Doesn't look very refreshing." Brown and yellow flecks floated on the drink's surface.

She cast a wary eye in Kyrel's direction as he took the seat on her left. He offered a slight, but reassuring nod, and bracing herself with a grimace, Lilly sipped cautiously three times before guzzling the drink down.

Mai Mai refilled her own and Lilly's cups before pushing the tall wooden jug toward Arteth who in turn offered it to Kyrel.

"I trust the training goes well?" she asked as Lilly picked out food for her plate. Kyrel opened his mouth, but the words came from Arteth.

"As well as can be expected with a lone Deebanaarie mentoring her."

A brief flash of anger passed through Kyrel's eyes, but shrugging it off he nodded Lilly's way. "Your granddaughter shows great promise, Mai Mai."

"Our people require more than promise..." Arteth hissed, before launching into a distinctly insistent sounding tirade in their native language. Kyrel responded likewise, and Lilly was forced to watch their heated argument unfold, with only their tones and barbed looks as guidance.

Mai Mai was soon involved - admonishing both men.

Watching them Lilly felt anger begin to rise; a fact clear enough on her face that a glance toward her had Kyrel switching language again as he asked, "And how many of them speak her tongue, Arteth?"

The younger man bristled, as if suddenly made aware of his cousin's presence. He looked from Lilly to Mai Mai. "Is it not enough that Toleth, Veer and I have learnt her speak, Mairiel? We can surely teach her as well as this Deeb-"

"You have no magicks, and no practiced understanding of the sacred words." Kyrel interjected. "You think stories and traditions will hold off Mordrel's forces? That ancient histories corrupted by tongue and time will stand in her way? Not even your royal line are born with the marks any more. Without Lilly your people are already lost. Nothing but an irritation creeping underneath my sister's thick skin and she will not stop until you are all obliterated."

The silence that followed doused Kyrel's anger; realisation of how much he'd just said brought a new level of awkwardness to his entire demeanour.

Lilly forced her agape jaw to close; dropping her gaze to her plate, as he sucked in a deep breath and turned back to Mai Mai adding, "Yes, Lilly has missed years of training. Youths beyond the veil are not expected to defend themselves or fulfil the types of tasks our own must on a daily basis. But there can be no denying the strength of her bloodline. She is strong, and under the circumstances, I believe she shows great determination. Allow me to proceed as agreed, Mai Mai. You know it is right. She is my charge."

"She is the ward of *all* here, Kyrel." Mai Mai's voice was firm, and he immediately offered a submissive nod.

"Of course, Mai Mai," his gaze skittered over Arteth as he added, "and know that I mean no ill respect, to you or any of the clan, but we both know none among you is as equipped as I to teach her. Allow me to continue teaching the Princess all that I can. You do already have my word: a warrior's word. I swore to you my allegiance for her sake, and for her sake I mean to keep it. "

"The word of a Deebanaarie," muttered Arteth, before switching back to their native language, his tone even more venomous than before. "Dieesh va ley mee, so eeit Herrella, lo deis draaeth-"

"Cat ya vac." Mai Mai glared his way, her tone harsh enough to make his head snap up as his eyes rose to meet hers.

"Mai Mai, Ny... Maenk tae," he switched tongues again, "I meant only that-"

"Cat ya vac!" his grandmother insisted through gritted teeth. "Inst!"

Biting her lip, Lilly watched Arteth rise. He no longer dared to meet Kyrel's gaze. His forearm already up across his chest, as he bowed first to Mairiel then Lilly, before left the room.

As the curtain fell back into place behind him Lilly turned back to see Mai Mai glaring pensively down at the table's surface. Catching her eye, Kyrel signalled with a look for her to go on eating. Then waited for her to do so before he turned to her grandmother and spoke in a tone now distinctly humbled with gratitude.

"Siiem tae, Mairiel."

The response was little more than a grunt of acknowledgment. Then she pushed her seat out and without so much as glance Lilly's way, left the table saying, "My attentions are needed elsewhere. Eat well Lilliath. I shall check on your progress later."

For a second time the curtain fell back over the doorway. Left alone with Kyrel again, Lilly realised she didn't know quite how to feel about any of what she'd just witnessed. Chiefly because so much of it had been in an unfamiliar language, but also because the parts that weren't had been illuminating enough to leave her with a bunch more unnerving questions to add to the dozens she'd already acquired through the day. Least of all being: if this Queen pursuing her was Kyrel's sister, why was he here hiding out amongst her enemies? Why was he risking his own neck to go against her? And how could he even be trusted? Lilly threw a wary smile his way, muttering, "Well you sure know how to clear a room." Then she turned back to her plate, and began picking at the unfamiliar foods piled onto it, shrugging as she added, "Don't suppose you plan on filling me in any time soon?"

A secondary glance, and his wrinkled brow told her of his obvious confusion. "The argument..." said Lilly "What was it about?"

"You." Kyrel picked up a dark brown roll, and tearing off a large chunk dipped it into a dollop of orange goo he'd added to his plate.

"No shit, Sherlock." Lilly huffed.

The expression itself was lost on Kyrel. Lilly's haughty tone was not. "What about me?" she asked. "I mean, sure, I get the part about him thinking you shouldn't be training me, something about how you won't or can't or aren't pushing me enough... To which I just have to say... whoa! What the hell? Was he even watching out there? Cos damn you are like relentless and stuff." Lilly offered a smile. Kyrel added more food to his plate. "So anyway..." she sighed, "the rest of the argument; the parts he didn't have the manners to say in *my tongue*." Again she offered a smile. Kyrel sipped his drink and tore another chunk off his roll. "OK," she muttered before pushing on. "Herrella's the woman you all think is my mother right?"

Kyrel's eyes rose to meet hers and he gradually stopped chewing. Seeing him swallow, Lilly shrugged, "It sounded a lot like Arteth mentioned her. You know... right before Mairiel made him leave."

Beyond holding her gaze Kyrel still offered no response, and nodding she added, "I'm not trying to be nosey. It's just... well it kinda sounded like..." Not wanting to add confusion to what was clearly a prickly subject, she thought a moment: to avoid the ever changing school-yard slang for what she was trying to say, "Like Arteth was... like he was insulting you?"

Kyrel's gaze shifted to his plate, Lilly pushed on regardless. "I mean obviously he doesn't like you. Actually him and that brother of his pretty much look like they'd like to rip your head off and... well... I guess I just don't get why he'd bring my mother into it. I mean why disrespect her memory by insulting you with-"

"You trust me?"

"Err... sure, I guess so. I mean you're kind of a ball-breaker, but you did save my life right... so yeah, I trust you. Why wouldn't I?"

"Because you ought not," seeing her confusion he nodded. "That is why Arteth and his brother burn with anger, Lillian. Everybody here knows better. Everyone except you. You are their best hope of finally making a difference here and they rightly fear the outcome of you placing your faith in me."

"Because you're Deebanaarie?" she frowned. "You know where I come from we call that racism, not a good word by the way."

"There is more to it than..." sighing he shook his head. "Things in our lands have been so complicated for so long; I'm uncertain how to even begin making you aware of all the truths."

"Right," she glanced around, scanning the empty room, before turning back to add, "Truths like the fact that your sister is a psychopathic megalomaniac..." getting the raised eyebrow of confusion she nodded. "Evil to the core?" and returning the nod Kyrel sighed.

"Aah... yes... I guess that is *a truth* of which, I was going to have to *fill you in?*" receiving a charitable smile for his effort he added "...eventually."

Shrugging Lilly smiled. "Well you shouldn't have worried, it's not like that bothers me."

"No? Perhaps that is because you do not yet comprehend what a threat she is."

"No. It's actually because where I come from we call that bad luck. Something my own life happens to have been filled with, so I'm hardly gonna hold it against you now am I?"

A brief smirk played over his lips and she grinned. "Besides, my shiny new Grandmother took your side, right? So she agrees you're the best man for the job. Which means even she can't think you're all bad."

The smirk faded; a scowl appearing in its place as Kyrel muttered. "Mairiel is old. Rules and tradition are the only way she knows to honour her daughter's memory... Herrella was the best of them; strong of heart and swift with her wisdom. She would have... *should* have been, one of the greatest leaders the Da'ariel has known since-"

"You *knew* her!" the accusation came with a pointed finger.

Kyrel's head snapped round, as if yanked on a cord. His eyes, meeting Lilly's were filled with such sadness, she half expected him to cry. Instead he breathed a heavy sigh and, forcing himself out of whatever reverie had caught him so off guard, he pushed away her plate.

"Enough eating."

"Are you insane? This is the first thing I've had all day."

"Good!" he slapped her hand as she reached for the plate. "Too much eating will hinder our progress."

"What? But Mairiel said-"

"Mairiel is not training you. I am." Receiving a vexed look he pushed her cup toward her.

Refilling it as he added, "Here, Gaawa is by far the better nourishment." Seeing her scowl into the cup he shrugged, "Or leave it if you wish. Either way you must hurry, if I don't get you into the room of sacred writings soon, further arguments are certain to arise."

"So that's what that was all about?" Lilly sighed as she raised the cup to her lips. "Getting me into the local library? Well score one for Arteth," she gulped down a mouthful, "maybe he isn't so bad after all. You know I really thought he was saying you should be pushing me more - physically."

"He was... your efforts with the bindings shall prove far more tiring than all you've achieved so far with the Gaashmay."

"Oh... then I take it back. That new cousin of mine is clearly an asshole."

***

Kyrel hadn't lied about the effort. Less than two hours into this second leg of training and Lilly was exhausted. This however was less a physical weariness, and more of a mental one. The room they now occupied, was easily among the largest in the village. In addition to its size difference, the walls were thick, well built and housed actual doors. It also boasted a separate adjoining passageway: a narrow, sparsely lit corridor with the odd torch of dim green flame. From what little Lilly could make out there were at least two other closed rooms. To be certain of anything was difficult when Kyrel kept ushering her about with such haste. A whole bunch more of anything could have been down that corridor and she wouldn't have known.

Once inside what was obviously the Room of Writings Kyrel had referred to earlier, Lilly was immediately taken aback enough to forget the minor irritation of being hurried from one location to another. As she'd suspected this was obviously a sort of library. Barring the reddish, hard dirt floor, and the apparent standard of sparse roughshod furniture, little else seemed on par with what she'd seen of the rest of the village. Unlike the roughly packed down inner walls of the other huts, these had dedicated panels, narrow and individually smoothed out with slots carved into them for the room's half a dozen lit torches. Every other available inch of wall space was lined with small, uniformly carved out square nooks; sandwiched between two single rows of considerably larger rectangular ones. Aside from those latter sections skirting the ground; which clearly served as storage for a wide range of objects - all unfamiliar to Lilly - while all the other sections including the larger ones above were each crammed with tightly bound rolls of leather - it was a set-up which lent the room a distinctly cramped atmosphere despite its larger size.

Kyrel began dishing out orders the moment they crossed the threshold, instructing Lilly to move aside the few furnishings: a chest, a table, two benches and two short but chunky wooden stands. He threw himself into the task of inspecting the various nooks: rifling quickly through their contents. He dashed about the room in a manner which, could almost be described as wild, if not for his obvious familiarity with whatever system of catalogue prevailed in this dimly lit library.

    When he was done Lilly learned she'd been creating adequate space on the floor for them to each sit cross-legged and face one another. Either side of them Kyrel placed a small flat stone; upon each, sat a small mound of crystals. He then struck some of these crystals together, creating bright whitish green sparks, before placing them carefully back atop their respective mounds. Now each sat emanating a soft green glow akin to that which the rooms torches already provided. Between them he had also placed two small pots of earth, and several of the leather rolls. Lilly referred to them initially as scrolls but he quickly corrected her with the word: veldii, which he immediately translated to 'bindings,' a word which made considerably more sense as she then watched him untie them, unfurling, from within each, a length of lightly waxed fabric. No two pieces measured the same, but all were inscribed with markings similar to those etched on Lilly's Eshron.

    At first Kyrel pored over these *bindings* in silence, some bringing a scowl to his lips, while others had him smiling in a way that illuminated his entire face. Intrigued at first Lilly enquired repeatedly - what was he looking for, and what it was he had found. Eventually however, after being shot down with wave after dismissive wave, she lost interest.

    Reclining a little she relaxed as best she could. Her gaze falling vacantly on the pot of earth before her, silently admonishing herself for not being quicker to try more of those unusual foods offered earlier. Her stomach was growling and the more insistent it became, the more she felt it was calling her out as a coward for not daring to eat her fill.

    A rustle and a murmur had her looking up to see a gleam of satisfaction in Kyrel's eyes, as he more fully unrolled one of the lengthier bindings, out in front of him on the floor; pushing all others aside and looking to Lilly with a triumphant smirk.

    Thus commenced her first hour of studying the Laîoch: words from an ancient language. As a matter of course, Kyrel explained how despite these words being considered sacred among the Da'ariel - being those which their ancestors had once used to direct their magicks - they no longer held much practical use as *Laîoch* was also the name of the forces in question, and their people could no longer draw any magicks from it. Ultimately Laîoch had become a dead language in more ways than one.

    "Do as I do," Kyrel instructed between his continuous insistence that she straighten up and concentrate on the pot of earth nearest her.

    With arms outstretched, they held their hands over their respective pots, while he led her through a series of hand gestures. He called these forms and the exercise had Lilly grumbling about the pointlessness of being expected to learn sign language when she was meant to take down some evil Queen. No more capable of understanding her quips than he was of being amused by them, Kyrel told her again to concentrate and moved onto the next hand-form.

Lilly exhibited a level of patience her adoptive parents would have marvelled at. The swishing wrist actions he had her reproducing had her arm aching up to the shoulder. Yet she persevered until the ache began to spread down the length of her shoulder blade, and sweat dripped from her brow. Her hunger had long become a constant yearning and, despite the relatively small portion of her body in use, the pain was becoming too much to bear.

Finally her arm gave way- dropping to her side like a felled branch and suddenly overwhelmed with her own failure Lilly scrambled to her feet and let her anger give way too.

"OK, that's it." She shook her head, "I've had enough."

"We are not finished." Kyrel didn't look up. Instead he took the opportunity to study more of the binding he'd been instructing her from.

"Finished what?" Lilly's voice began to rise. "Our sign language lesson? Sorry mate, but unless your sister's deaf, and the aim is for me to nicely talk her down, I really don't see how any of this crap is helping."

"Lilliath, sit down."

"No! And it's Lilli-an OK, not *Princess*; or *child*, but Lillian!"

The growing anger in her voice finally drew his attention away from the document, and the weight of his sudden stare seemed to damp at least a little of Lilly's rage. Adjusting her tone she shrugged, "That or just plain Lilly."

"*Lilly...*" Kyrel's tone remained even, "enough of this insolence; sit down." His choice of words however, was more than enough to bring her straight back up to the boil.

"I'm fucking starving, OK!" She yelled down at him. "There's nothing insolent about that, you're meant to be teaching me magicks remember?" Her voice rose higher with the beginning of every sentence. "Sacred words, my foot! So far all I've learnt is how to play a symphony with tummy rumbles. That and how much I really hate sitting here with my legs crossed like some gormless kid still stuck in primary school; waggling my fingers over some dumb pot of mud; like something amazing, or even vaguely interesting is going to happen - when the truth has to be that *you* are fucking with me. Maybe," she began shaking her head now, "... just to see how long you can string me alon-"

"Kiiat vash." Kyrel spoke over her; his voice distant but firm.

Lilly had been too busy ranting to pay much attention to the hand-forms he'd been practising over his pot before speaking. She'd had little time to register his actions at all before the dirt floor opened beneath her feet. Startled and terrified, she screamed as the growing hole swallowed her down to the shoulders. Then it immediately began filling back up. A few seconds later and she found herself in the awkward position of being buried up to the neck in the hard dirt floor. A vantage point from which, she was struggling to not hyperventilate while glaring Kyrel's way.

"Effective," he nodded; brow bouncing up as he told her, "I was uncertain that would do anything at all."

"What the fuck?" hissed Lilly, unable to bat away the pink strands of hair now jabbing at her eye, "are you mental or something?" she asked, trying to blow the lock away.

"I'm sensing this 'fuck' word you use so often has little in the way of genuine meaning." As her jaw dropped he added, "Also that it is, perhaps not very nice."

"You're damn right it isn't, Asshole! Get me the fuck out of here!"

"So you may abandon your training... so early on?"

"Early on! Training is all you've had me do since you got me here! What the fuck is early on about that?"

"There you go again with that word," Kyrel's eyes narrowed. "Do you believe it will fend off my sister?"

"What?" She began shaking her head, but stopped as he asked.

"You find great strength in it, do you not? This word, the 'fuck', it carries upon it a great power from deep within you. Is there enough to keep Mordrel's armies from seeking you out? From dragging you to her for a slow painful execution?" As Lilly dropped her eyes and bit her lip, he sighed, "Then it is as I thought. You remain defenceless unless you learn." Nodding down at her now he added, "I am offering you words with real power: the power to defeat my sister."

"Alright," forcing herself to calm down, Lilly slowly met his gaze. "So I need to learn. Fine! But haven't we done enough for now?"

"You, yourself were just saying you've learnt nothing of any value."

"OK, look, I'm willing to admit I might have been mistaken-"

"Aah, you were exaggerating again..." he gave a knowing nod. "...to make your point?"

"No." Lilly's lip trembled. "I mean sure," she returned the nod, "You're right. That's exactly what I was doing. I mean seriously, why would I ditch? Like you said, I need to learn, and well, who else is going to teach me this stuff?"

"I would hope you've realised by now that no other can? Da'ariel lost their magicks over three hundred cycles ago and of the few Deebanaarie that still practice, none but me would dare defy my sister."

"Right, so you're sticking your neck out for me," she nodded. Kyrel frowned, and Lilly sighed, "Taking a risk." When recognition sparked in his eyes, she added, "I get that. Totally." Then she was shaking her head. "Look I'm sorry OK. I was being a bitch, I know. I'm just... really tired, and hungry and aching like everywhere. But seriously, I get it, none of that will mean shit when they come for me: I get it!"

"Now that is a point well made," nodded Kyrel.

"OK," Lilly was shrugging again. "So you let me up out of here and I'll be good. I'll stop the complaining and I totally won't try to leave."

"I think not."

"But I won't, I swear. Just let me up, get me out of here..." it was her turn to read his expression; shaking her head she sighed. "You're not letting me up, are you?"

"You want up," Kyrel shrugged. "Make it happen."

"You can't be serious!" Lilly attempted to wriggle - nothing. Tilting her head in a futile attempt to glance down she asked. "Do you have any idea what a tight fit this is? I may as well be a... a... a: fence pole, for all the room I have to move in here. I can't climb out of this! I... I'm not even sure I can move. No joke, OK? How am I supposed to-"

"These fence poles... do they possess any of the power inherent to you?"

A mirthless chuckle escaped Lilly. "Well no, but it's not as if we've proved I have any power, you could still be wrong about me you know. I mean sure it looked like I got that box open."

"The Eshron."

"Right," she nodded, tears stinging her eyes. "And maybe I got that Gaashmay thingy activated."

"If you were not Lilliath Avengturov of the Da'ariel neither event would have been a possibility."

"So OK, then, maybe that's true. Maybe I am this long lost princess you all keep talking about. I accepted the possibility didn't I? I've been a real good sport about this training thing. I've spent all day doing everything you've told me to. Doesn't mean I actually have any power! None of the others do right? Not even Mairiel and she's like the queen of her people. So I have some stupid birthmark on the back of my head. What if you're all wrong? What if it means nothing? What if I'm just another powerless Da'ariel who can't do anything to defeat this evil sister of yours Kyrel? Then how am I meant to get out of this hole?"

"If that is true then it does not matter," he shrugged, "if you truly cannot raise yourself from out of there, then I am wasting both of our time and, I may as well take my leave before Mordrel has the chance to exact her vengeance on me." Fixing her with a stare that said he was contemplating such action he added. "If it is true... I should do you the kindness of sinking you deeper, for you are already as good as dead."

"Kyrel please... I honestly can't do this."

For many seconds they stared at each other until he muttered, "Very well then," and shook his head. Lily watched him rise slowly to his feet. He stretched out a hand, letting his palm face the hole as he repeated the gesture he'd used to create it adding, "Deeper it is then..."

"No!" Lilly writhed in fear. "Don't OK. For fuck's sake please... please don't." Seeing him frown she nodded. "I'll try. I swear to God I'll give it everything I've fucking got just please... j-just tell me how?"

"Have I not already given you instruction, Lilly?"

"Well sure, you said do as you do but..." seeing his eyes drift to his hand she followed his gaze. His two forefingers and his thumb were all tucked snug against his palm. This left only the two lower fingers outstretched. It was one of the many gestures he'd taught her earlier, and she realised now the exact one he'd used to sink her. Forcing her voice to stay calm she nodded. "OK I get it, a-and I can do that," Pressing against the wall of her makeshift dirt cell she wriggled the hand he'd had her practicing with until it formed the same shape as his. "There's words too though right? What do I say?"

"Were you paying so little attention?" scowled Kyrel.

"It's not that," Lilly shook her head. "I did hear what you said before. At least I think I did, but that put me down here right? If I repeat it how do I not just drop further?"

"Only you have the power to go in the direction you choose."

"You're sure about that?"

"Make a choice, or I make the only one you leave for me."

Dubious Lilly nodded. "OK, OK, here goes." Maintaining the hand-form, as steadily as she could under a couple of feet of shifting dirt, she pointed those two lower fingers as much toward her own feet as was possible and somewhat cautiously mumbled, "Kiiat vash"

"Speak up," instructed Kyrel. "You are giving an order. The voice must be clear; strong. It is not enough to know what you want: you must demand it."

Still dubious she lowered her head. Her hands held firm, although the strain of keeping them in such an unnatural position, with so little space to do so, was making them shaky. Lilly closed her eyes, took a couple of deep breaths and raising her voice to a more commanding tone said again, "Kiiat Vash."

The moment those words were done rolling off her tongue a second time, she became aware of movement beneath her feet. Lilly opened her eyes and instinct took over, spreading her arms for balance, she rose slowly up and out of the cold damp earth; her face now the picture of shock, as gradually her head levelled up with Kyrel's.

He grinned with obvious pride, and attempting to offer a smile in return she unwittingly relaxed her hand, and felt herself drop to the now almost even ground, in a quivering lump with her forehead pressed to the dirt as she muttered.

"Holy shit... I did it!"

"Yes you did...." Kyrel sat back down across from her adding. "...and on the second try too. I must say I am impressed. I was certain it would take you several more attempts to free yourself."

Lilly raised her head to glare at him again, and barely capable of getting the words out, told him.

"You're such a fucking asshole."

"And you," he afforded a brief smirk. "Are very powerful"

"Fuck you!"

Ignoring the comment Kyrel pushed the nearest pot of earth up next to her.

"Not that it shall be much of a challenge now, but after such an achievement, I'd say you deserve a little something."

"What?" Lilly threw him a vile look. "You call that a reward? What the hell am I meant to do with-"

"You were hungry, were you not?"

"Not enough to chow down on a pot full of dirt."

"You do not yet understand the power of your bloodline."

"So I filled in your stupid hole." She straightened up to the cross-legged position. "What's that supposed to mean? How's it meant to make me any less frigging hungry?"

Kyrel stared at her a moment longer then sighed.

"As a Deebanaarie I had only the power to sink you in the hole; to remove, or to lessen, that is what's in my blood: the power to take. But these writings are Da'ariel and the Da'ariel; they are bringers. In you flows the magicks to make of the very ground you stand upon; anything it will naturally sustain."

Looking from him to the pot she muttered, "Anything? Like today in the forest… that tree that grew..." as her eyes went back to him he issued a confirming nod, and Lilly began shaking her head. "You're saying I can grow anything I want in this pot? Right here, right now. Apples, Oranges, Pears, whatever I feel like eating-"

"Well, I'm not sure about the fruit of your…" seeing the doubt growing in her eyes he raised his hand; all fingers on it splayed, and demonstrating waved it over the pot nearest himself telling her, "Just try. Run your hand over it as though feeling for the surface of a stream - or a river! Think of food growing. Of picking it; tasting it…"

"You're serious?" asked Lilly, having recovered enough to sit up and glare at him now, she began to wonder if she was being deliberately made a fool of, and wished she had the strength to pick up the damn pot and hurl it at him.

"Yes." nodded Kyrel, "Give in to your hunger, let the desire flow."

Realising he was absolutely serious, she relented with a sigh, asking, "And say what?"

"One moment," he picked the Da'ariel document up again, studying it a moment before turning back to her and nodding "Na-ich vaneesh." Picking up on her trepidation he nodded "It's OK, this won't be like the tree. These are not Tuâoch, but Laîoch words: the tongue you were born to speak - try."

Taking a deep breath Lilly braced herself and did as he suggested. Then they sat watching the earth in the untouched dirt in the pot.

A few seconds later Kyrel was offering her a smile of encouragement, "It's OK, you did not fill in the hole on your first attempt - try again."

Several more attempts followed, with Kyrel checking and rechecking her hand movement along with the old Da'ariel binding and consistently offering further advice that failed to help.

"Perhaps you are not as hungry as you believed," he shrugged as her latest effort also brought forth nothing.

"Maybe you've read the words wrong." Lilly threw him a cutting look.

"Ny." he shook his head. "These writings may have been lost to the Deebanaarie since the Great War but our ancestors shared a common tongue, and we never turned our backs on our inherent magicks."

"Then why are the words even different?" She asked with genuine confusion. Letting her arm drop to her side, she leaned back asking, "Why do you have to go scouring through these ancient unused writings. Why can't you just teach me the words you already know?"

"You are Da'ariel."

"So? Wasn't it a Da'ariel word you used to stick me in the ground?"

"Well yes, I suspected the word was transferable, a rare few are. Also I've had many cycles to hone my-.."

"And in the forest today… that was a Deebanaarie word right? Or was it transferable too?"

"No," he murmured, "it was true Tuâoch; and a base word at that... But you were upset; your essence was displaced. It could have-"

"Just let me try. What word would a Deebanaarie use? Tell me, let me try."

"I will not."

"Why not? Don't you want me to learn? What was that word earlier? I'll try that one."

Sitting forward she muttered a string of rhyming yet incomprehensible sounds to herself in an effort to jog her own memory. However, earlier now seemed like a lifetime ago, and a lifetime was plenty of time to forget a foreign word she hadn't known before. Nothing sounded quite right. Turning back to Kyrel she sighed, "You're supposed to be imparting wisdom remember? If you just remind me I can probably-"

"Concentrating on the Tuâoch would be wasting time. Your demand is futile. Herrella was Da'ariel. Her essence was Laîoch, and essence flows from the mother. Even if you-"

The curtain behind Lilly swished open and Vereena's head poked inside.

"The other out-worlder..." she began, "has woken and-"

"Cat ya vac!" yelled Kyrel, "Nydrel inst!"

With a flinch Lilly almost toppled over, while the younger girl disappeared without another word.

"Aah ha!" nodded Lilly, she waved her hand over the pot of earth as Kyrel had instructed so many times and mindful of the tone in her voice said, "Ta Varee."

Kyrel shot her a look of annoyance but sighed with relief when nothing happened. Lilly looked more disappointed than anything.

"I told you," he began, "You are Da'ariel, you cannot just..."

Seeing her face light up with a smile, he followed her gaze to the pot where a tiny sprig of green had poked up through the earth. Growing in width and height while uncurling, it began sprouting leaves.

"Cool!" Lilly grinned; drooling the word out slow like a thick string of saliva. "I did it!"

"Veyhi," Kyrel nodded in astonished agreement. "That is truly..."

The pot began to shake, and already at a height of just over a foot, the plant continued climbing, picking up speed as it grew. A single loud crack, gave way to a chorus of the same, as thick off-white roots poked their way out of the sides of the pot and plunged themselves deep into the hard red earth - tipping over Kyrel's demonstration pot and the two flat stones; their glowing crystal mounds dying out as they dispersed across the floor in a splendid yet short-lived light show.

"Whoa...." muttered Lilly as the stem of the plant grew thicker and it continued it ascent, sprouting separate limbs which in turn became even thicker boughs, while it unleashed yet more branches.

Kyrel tore his gaze from Lilly's creation, and turned instead to her.

"How hungry did say you were?"

"Err..." following his lead: she clambered to her feet, both backing up and stepping aside as what had been a fresh sprig moments earlier, was now a trunk so thick it obscured her view. She peered around it with a guilty smirk shrugging, "Very, *very* hungry, why?"

Though clearly still maturing, the tree had slowed in growth now and Kyrel hopped carefully around its ever spreading root system. Their further growth created enough noise to have him shouting his next question. "And just which of your native fruits were you concentrating on?"

Reaching Lilly's side he grabbed her arm; pulling her toward the door, as it too began to disappear behind the drooping foliage. The tree's thick branches; upon which an array of flowers were beginning to bloom, seemed unwilling to stop their outward spread.

"Err… I'm not sure," said Lilly as he dragged her under a low hanging branch, while younger ones continued growing more swiftly toward them. "Maybe all of them," she told him, "do you think that matters?"

Kyrel pulled her through the door too swiftly for either of them to avoid a lone root now snaking its way along a portion of the adjoining passageway; poking up through the previously flattened dirt floor.

The pair thudded to the ground as the walls between them and the Da'ariel room of sacred writings began to crumble.

First back up on to his feet, Kyrel grabbed Lilly again; under both arms this time. He lifted her half up on to her feet, all the while, dragging her backwards for several more steps, until she was fully upright again, and together they made their way carefully toward the outer entrance.

They were almost out when Arteth and a handful of armed Da'ariel burst in - swords bared. Mai Mai followed close behind; flanked by her other two grandchildren. Vereena carrying Merly in her arms, while T'vor, the white haired sprite, wobbled along at Mairiel's heels.

All froze in step at the sight of the thick gnarled branches poking out through the walls.

"Ny dilur!" Mai Mai muttered, "Ny mech!" She shook her head as her mouth fell open.

The tree's growth had slowed significantly now and with petals raining to the ground, everyone watched as the buds from each blossom grew larger before their eyes. With no enemy in sight Arteth sheathed his sword; the others followed suit.

"Mairiel…" Kyrel turned to her, then seeing her eyes begin to narrow he addressed her correctly, "Mai Mai." He launched into what Lilly could only assume to be an explanation in their native language. His tone was unmistakably apologetic, his expression and gesticulations too. It was also clear; from Mai Mai's scowl, and the way her eyes kept flitting between him and the huge tree: that his explanation was insufficient appeasement.

Nonetheless Mai Mai sighed, her eyes straying to Lilly as she said, "It would seem your training goes better than expected."

"Yeah…" Lilly twiddled her thumbs and shook her head, "I'm really sorry about the room." She looked more like a child now than she had all day. "I know it was important to-"

"Are these…" Mai Mai pointed to the tree where fat apples, oranges, and pears were now visible. She raised an eyebrow, "They are fruit from beyond the veil, yes? You ate them in the other realm?"

"Err..." Lilly glanced upward, taking a first real look at her creation and began to nod, "sure, these are... well where I'm from they're all very common."

"And they all commonly grow together on one tree like this?" asked Mairiel.

"Err..." Lilly gave the tree a second look, spying plums and peaches in among the foliage now. "Actually," she shrugged, "I'm really not too sure how that happened."

Mai Mai gave a knowing nod before casting her gaze over Kyrel again.

"Perhaps the Princess should continue her training outdoors from now on."

"Veyhi Mai Mai." He returned the nod with an added dash of embarrassment. Mairiel turned to Vereena, issuing some command in their language which had her scurrying away; then she turned and shooed the others from the room as well.

Watching them leave Lilly whispered to Kyrel,

"I got you in trouble again didn't I?"

"We should go," he whispered back.

"I get to eat first though right?"

"One moment." He told her. Then he ran over to where several branches protruded from the demolished wall. Leaping up to grab the lowest hanging one, he swung up on to it, and quickly disappeared from sight. For a short while Lilly could hear the rustling of leaves as he made his way up through the tree. Then a minute or two later he reappeared through what was left of the doorway, with a grin on his face, like a child returning from an unexpected opportunity to scrump, and he soon revealed to her a decent sampling of the fruits all stowed in the front of his top.

***

For Lilly it felt as though darkness fell very slowly that first evening in Azeron. Although she would later agree with Terrence, that her perception at the time was mostly coloured by her own anticipation, and an outright assumption of being able to call it a day when the sun went down. It had however soon become evident that Kyrel had other ideas. The sky darkened: first turning a soft pale shade of pink before dimming through the purples; while he showed no sign of letting up. All above them stars began to shine, and behind them the village huts began emanating that same soft green glow: as the occupants struck their crystal torches and flat-stone lamps to life.

When Kyrel noticed the sun was down he whirled around using a hand-form previously unseen by Lilly - this was the first time she witnessed him use both hands to draw on his magicks.

"Kratack!" he told the air around them. One by one several tiki style torches - apparently also filled with the flammable crystal substance - lit up illuminating a perfect circle around the edges of the clearing - bathing them both in that same soft green.

Throughout the afternoon many in the village had stopped by; quietly keeping their distance as they stayed a while to watch her train. Very few remained by the time Kyrel set those torches blazing. Still there was no mistaking the fearful awe evident in those Da'ariel who did witness it. Seeing this, Lilly realised that as much as these people loathed the very sight of Kyrel, their responses to his actions also seemed to reveal a certain level of respect. Eventually the last of these onlookers drifted away, and seeing the obvious yearning as she watched them depart, Kyrel slipped in a remark about everyone else in the village having duties to attend, before aiming the correct hand-form at the ground between them and sending a growing fissure straight for her. With a startled expression Lilly moved to use her own powers but overwhelmed with uncertainty, leaped out of the way instead. By the time she came rolling to a stop Kyrel was already shaking his head at her with obvious disappointment. While her class mates, the only spectators left, were thankfully too impressed with his skills to pay much attention to the state of Lilly as she slowly picked herself up off the ground. Shortly after this even they became disinterested enough to slip away into the night. Yet still Kyrel kept her out in the training field until long after the sky's purple hues had grown a dark inky blue. In fact he showed no inclination toward letting her rest, let alone call it quits and it was only when her new cousin, Vereena appeared at the clearing's edge and insisted upon on it - another assumption on Lilly's part as they conversed entirely in the native language.

Despite her self proclaimed exhaustion, when she finally realised she was being given an out, she was so overjoyed that she couldn't get indoors fast enough.

However she was barely through getting her fill of the various foods on offer before she'd had enough of being quizzed by the locals. While few actually spoke her language well enough to hold a conversation with her, and the table she was served at seated only a dozen; the hut they dined in had clearly reached capacity several villagers ago, and with Kyrel, Vereena and occasionally Arteth providing translations, it seemed everyone there had come to learn more about the human world and their princess' human companions. None of whom were currently present, although Lilly felt certain she'd spotted Baxter hovering amidst the crowd when she'd been led through earlier.

Aside from Kyrel, and Mairiel's two grandsons, everyone else seated around the table was female, something Lilly only noticed halfway through her second tankard of gaawa, when nodding her way through yet another barrage of questions she realised how much more willing to speak up these women seemed in comparison to the three men; who so far as she could tell, never spoke unless first spoken to and immediately quietened without question any time the women, prone to talking over them, deigned to cut them off. They would even interrupt the answers to their own questions - then exhibit frustration at their own continued lack of understanding.

As clan matriarch Mairiel made for a somewhat sombre contrast; quietly observing the interactions between her long lost granddaughter and the rest of her subjects. She had declined most of the foods and barely touched that which she'd accepted from the servants. Content instead to sit back in her huge chair at the head of the table; allowing Vereena almost full control of the conversation. She herself, was of course not above interrupting; but she actually seemed to do so indiscriminately, and often with little more than a raised hand effectively steering the discussion's course without much need for words of her own.

All privileged enough to be seated at the table, had been formally introduced to Lilly as one relative or another and often with accompanying grand titles from General, and High General, to Lady. Vereena reeled off their names with all the expertise of daily familiarity, apparently completely unaware of how long, complicated and foreign it all was to Lilly's ears; hitting her tired brain as little more than well mannered gibberish. One by one, the noble-women had bowed respectfully; before all taking their seats at Mai Mai's behest, only to shoot expectant glances Lilly's way as they allowed servants to load up their plates. Unsurprisingly, two large bowls filled with fruits harvested from the tree Lilly had unexpectedly grown in the room of writings, were among the first foods to disappear; and for a short while at least it seemed all the questions might be dietary.

Unfortunately for Lilly - who had been just about getting into the swing of such easy questions - foods of the human world turned out to be one of those topics Mairiel vetoed before it truly found its legs. Far sooner than she would have liked, the conversation returned to more pressing matters: how her training was progressing, speculations on the impact of her arrival in their realm, and her opinions on leadership, were all but a constant in their concerns. Along with the recurring themes of the social attitudes, and mating habits of humans.

Suffice it to say, Lilly was pushed from her comfort zones repeatedly in a very short space of time. More so as none present seemed aware of her growing embarrassment. She felt interrogated and overwhelmed and after what couldn't have been more than three quarters of an hour, she was making her excuses and retreating from the room.

***

Lilly's departure from the dining hut had been sudden enough for her to neglect considering where she might retreat to. Realising, only as she hurried through the poorly lit village, that she knew very little about her surroundings. Worse yet, she had no idea at all where her classmates were and was in fact certain of only two things: the location of the village entrance; and its training ground, each being at opposite ends of the compound from one another. She had no inclination to leave, having seen more than enough outside of the village to feel far safer inside its well-guarded, badly fenced perimeter. She also had her doubts about whether those guards would actually allow her to leave if she tried. Hence she found herself doubling back, she took a slightly alternate route; giving the area where the dinning hut resided a deliberately wide birth, and made her way back to the training field. A small forest now stood where there had previously been only the remainders of tree stumps - a product of her training. Lilly lay at its centre, with her hands under her head, staring up at the sky, noticing again how different it was from what she'd grown up looking at. More a faint purple now, than the deep blue of earlier; the stars flickered mostly with a pinkish hue. Cloudless as it was there was no North Star or moon lighting up the night, yet up ahead was a tightly packed swirling cluster of stars - so dense she had at first mistaken them for a cloud. The combined light from them was both abundant enough to ensure visibility on the ground, and eye-catching enough to keep her from noticing the footfalls heading her way.

"Lilly?"

With a slight turn of her head she saw Sandra Harper standing a couple of feet away. She had one hand stuffed in her pocket, the other: grasping an orange, hung at her side. Shuffling from one foot to the other she looked more uncertain than Lilly had felt all day.

"Hey…" Lilly sat up, groaning she added. "…You're awake. I didn't know."

"Yeah," said Harper, "Have been a while." She shuffled closer, nodding to the ground beside Lilly. "You mind if I…"

"God no, go for it."

"You were busy," Harper said as she crossed her legs in front of her and tossed the orange from one hand to the other. A quick scan of their surroundings had her adding, "Learning new and interesting ways of kicking ass and now making your own little forest apparently." She turned back to Lilly with a shrug.

"Aah," Lilly offered a smirk, "I take it the guys have been filling you in."

"Oh yes, I've had the lowdown, other world, long lost heiress, magical powers and you and your little flying gizmo thingy. Gotta say I don't think I've ever heard Baxter sound so impressed as when he was trying to explain that bit. Course," Harper shrugged, "that was nothing compared with Tobias's reaction to that tree in there. I only wish you could have seen his face when that Vereena girl said we should pick all we can before they have it removed." She glanced around again at the other trees. "Are all of these really your doing?"

"These… yeah…" Lilly sighed "Pretty fucking crazy, huh?"

"Yup," nodded Harper, "Definitely crazy, course that does seem to be the order of the day."

"Yet you seem to be taking it all miraculously well." Lilly said as she watched the orange going back and forth.

"Well actually, I came out here to talk some sense into you. Snap you out of believing all the shit these people have brainwashed you into thinking, so we could all make moves and get the hell outta here."

"Oh yeah?"

"Well yeah, course then I went and made the mistake of looking up - so now I guess we're both brainwashed."

"That is one hell of a night sky," smirked Lilly. "Kinda wish it had been night when we arrived; could have saved myself a load of argument just by looking up. Less doubt might have been nice too."

"I dunno… from what I hear we're talking the mother-load of lunacy out here and that's long before the fruit tree to end all fruit trees came into it. I'm thinking doubt was in the deal no matter the time a day."

"Ha!" Lilly chuckled "Yeah, you're probably right. You know I'm not sure what's more frightening, the fact that I willed that tree into existence or the fact that Kyrel says he's never heard of anyone doing anything like it before."

"Kyrel?" Harper's orange stopped in her left hand. "He's the one they call a Deebanaarie, right?"

"Right"

"So what's the deal with him?"

"Oh, he's all right. You know in a… pushy, strict, humourless sort of way. It's not as if he's fun to be around but well..." she pointed to Harper's orange, "As you've seen, he's been teaching me some pretty neat stuff."

Putting the orange down the other girl turned to face her.

"You trust him then?" Lilly raised an eyebrow and Harper added, "I mean aren't his people like the enemy or something? The army of crazies?" she gestured with a nod to the village behind them while adding, "the ones these other… crazies brought you here to take down?"

"Actually his sister is the biggest baddest crazy of them all."

"Oh?"

"Yes, but… He's not like her. He's not like any of them."

"How can you be so sure? For all we know, he could be working for her; teaching you a little here and there as he gains your trust. I mean seriously Lilly, you've barely known him a day!"

"A day in which he saved yours and my life… He's a good guy, Harper."

"So good he let his own people murder the best friend I've ever had?"

For a second Lilly's mouth hung open, then she was snapping it shut and shaking her head.

"It wasn't like that. There was nothing either of us could do."

"And you're sure about that?"

Lilly's mind returned to earlier that day: when she, Morris and Kyrel had all been running through the forest - he with Harper over his shoulder. Then the sudden onslaught of bright greenish lights; starting with the one that had slammed into Morris.

At the time Lilly had burned with the anger one gets from helplessness. She'd wanted to go to Morris, to get her up and bring her with them. Now she knew better, the other girl's skull had cracked against that tree's trunk, leaving her dead as she'd crumpled to the ground. Lilly knew this because in retrospect the incident took on a clarity she'd been blinded to during the moment. Despite her limited perception then, allowing herself to think back now meant hearing that crack, clear as a klaxon whenever she let her mind's-eye bring up the image.

She also knew Kyrel had taken many risks this day. Carrying her and Harper up into the treetops out of the way of those lights had to be high up the list. Yet it was far from the height of his efforts. Confident as he seemed of his own powers, bringing her here to the relative safety of the Da'ariel village, where he knew she'd be safe - while those around them reacted like a lynch mob craving death at the sight of him - couldn't have been easy.

The hatred felt here among the Da'ariel for anything Deebanaarie was made plain in their reluctant tolerance of Kyrel's presence. Yet tolerate him they did, on the orders of their Mai Mai and under the watchful eye of her grandchildren, who'd been only slightly more hospitable. The entire village was trusting Kyrel to help them defeat his own sister.

With a nod Lilly turned back to her classmate, a girl she'd hardly noticed during their previous school year.

"How much do you know about me, Harper?" The other girl's mouth began to open but Lilly was already adding, "I mean beside the fact that I lost my real parents real young, and have a bit of a thing for breaking rules."

"I know you must have broken some pretty big ones to end up at The Peak."

"Sure, I was pretty much uncontrollable in the three normal schools I passed through before being sent away; drove the Adoptives to the ends of their wits and back again. What with my constantly running away from home only to be picked up by the cops from a whole host of the wrong places at the wrong times. We're talking again and again, and well… you get the picture." Seeing Harper grin, her eyes flashing recognition, Lilly shrugged. "But that doesn't really tell you anything about me does it? We're all so alike at The Peak. So alike that we break all the same rules and complain about the same things: the teachers, the room checks, the same shitty platefuls of food. Doesn't mean I know you, so why should I trust you anymore than I do Kyrel?"

"He's a stranger, Lilly, as in *complete*. At least we go to the same school."

"So most of the year round we're forced to breathe the same air day in day out because we've been thrown into the same shit-hole; because we've made the same mistakes. Doesn't mean we know each other. Certainly ain't a good reason to trust each other."

"What are you saying?" It was Tobias, and both girls turned to see the three boys watching them.

The pair had been so deep in conversation they hadn't noticed the approach of the three boys. Each carried a small sack of fruit, with another piece in hand. Before Lilly could answer Tobias was adding. "You trust these people here more than you trust us? They brought you here so they could use you to fight some dumb war and you think they've got your back?"

"Chill out, Tobe." Terrence spoke up between mouthfuls of pear, "That wasn't what she meant. Obviously she trusts us, why wouldn't she?"

"I dunno," shrugged Baxter "did kind of sound like Orphan Annie's building quite the rapport with that Kyrel fella."

"You do know the Annie crack is way past old?" Lilly glared at him. "Something you might have noticed by the fact that everyone gets it and nobody laughs."

"Oh hey, no need to get touchy." Baxter's hands flew up. "Ain't saying I blame you – Mysterious older man, super-powers, did the heroic swooping in and saving your life thing, plus…" he let his hands drop. "There is the rugged, long haired rebel look he has going for him, how can you resist?"

"Easier than you by the sound of it," her eyes narrowed. "Do let me know when you need me to put in a good word."

"Blam!" Tobias offered Lilly a hand, and reaching up on automatic she high-fived it. "There ya go," he grinned, "That's the serious burn you're laying on him girl, you keep that up."

"You think that's funny asshole?"

"Motherfucker, I think you been all up in all of our faces, all damn day and it is high time someone put you in your place."

"My place?" Baxter's eyebrows bounced up, as he took a step toward Tobias. "You got yourself some ideas on where that might be exactly?"

"Hell yeah I got me some ideas-"

"Tobe!" Terrence side-stepped between them, but pushing him aside Tobias hissed, "Stay outta this bro." Then he was also stepping forward.

"I ain't scared-a you, fool. Case in point we didn't make it to Craven's Peak and you do not have your crew backing you up."

"OK seriously…" Harper glared up at them. "Could we take the dick measuring somewhere else? It's getting a little hard to breathe out here with all the testosterone in the air!"

"Come on Tobes, don't do this."

Pushing Terrence away on his second attempt to intercept, Baxter kept his eyes locked on Tobias. "You heard your brother," he said through gritted teeth, "this is between me and him…"

"…so come on, fraidy-dogs, let's do this…"

"You are so gonna lay off." Tobias nodded.

"Yeah…" sneered Baxter. "Am I? You really think so? Come on then Fraidy, fraidy, fraay-dee puppies, make me lay off already. Put me in my place."

"You know you two are-"

Before Lilly could finish Tobias sucker-punched Baxter's stomach with a swing that would have winded most, instead it brought a smile to Baxter's face as Harper hissed, "shit,"

Terrence muttered, "Ah fuck,"

Asking, "That your best shot… Fraidy?" Baxter unleashed a head-butt severe enough to knock Tobias off his feet.

"OK, that's enough!" Lilly jumped to her feet, arms splayed as she stood between Baxter and the stunned, sprawled out Emerson twin.

"I don't think so Princess," Baxter pushed her aside and glared pointedly down at Tobias. "I don't take orders from royalty. And I sure as hell don't need no damn crew. Case-in-point motherfucker! Now how's about you get back up, so I can give you the ass-kicking you've been itching for all day!"

As Tobias's head began to clear, the stunned look on his face became one of rising anger as Harper edged toward him saying, "Just stay where you are Tobes, he isn't worth it."

Shaking his head Terrence said. "Don't you dare get up."

Tobias ignored them both. He had eyes only for Baxter and in them burned rage. Scrambling to his feet, he hissed, "You… are so… going down."

The pair ran at each other; no one noticed Lilly aiming a hand at the ground as she issued the command.

"Ta Varee." The thunderous roar of her newest creation drowned out the combined growls of the boys even after they turned to screams.

Lilly, Terrence, and Harper watched as the tree whooshed upward carrying the pair with it, until they were so high they were barely visible. With their lives depending on it, they dangled precariously from opposite sides of the tree's upper limbs.

"Whoa," muttered Harper as the tree's ascent came to an abrupt stop. "That's just…" Lost for words she stared up at what was easily Lilly's tallest creation so far and shook her head.

"OK," nodded Terrence. "You made your point Slater, you can let them down now"

"Can I Tez?" She turned to him. "Can I let them down? Have I really made my point? You're the one who thinks I should trust you all right? Well you know what I think, I think I couldn't have a stronger point right now!"

"It's OK Lilly, you can calm down. We get it." Harper's hand went to Lilly's shoulder, but pulling away she turned on her.

"Oh I can? Well thank you for permission, I'll just start calming down right now then. I mean for a moment there I was getting kinda worried. Thinking none of you did get it." She glared momentarily at Terrence. "That maybe I hadn't made my point! What with your not being able to make it off the bus," She glanced Harper's way "and Morris not being able to make it through the forest."

"Oh hey man, not cool," hissed Terrence. "That's not the kind of shit you say."

Lilly ignored him; her gaze going instead to the upper depths of the new tree. Neither boy was visible for foliage now but both could be heard yelling at each other, between their shouts to be let down.

"Then we have dumb and dumber up there," Lilly nodded to the tree top. "Well they just can't make it through a five minute stretch without wanting to tear each other's throats out. Hell… on a good day, most of us can just about stand the sight of each other," she snarled at Terrence. "So why don't you go ahead and let me know when you figure out a reason why there should be any such thing as trust between any of us." A quick turn on her heels and she stalked off. Left in the clearing with Terrence calling after her that she couldn't just leave the other two boys up the tree, as she disappeared through the mini forest.

Day Two: Part One

Again and again the bus crashed its way through the forest, and Morris tried ever faster to outrun the bright light that sent her hurtling to her death. These images combined with others long past: of acrid smoke thick enough to be lost in, and a fire that stung the eyes watching it.

The only sound that rose over the roaring of the flames was the screams of the dying, which although within the dream, proved shrill enough to wake Lilly.

She sat upright with a start, gasping for breath as her hand went to her forehead. Only when she drew it away soaked did she realise she was dripping with sweat. Slowly her eyes adjusted to the dim light of the morning's early hours and wrinkling her nose as she realised she was under a patchwork of stinky animal skins, she climbed off the narrow cot with a grimace, grabbed her leather jacket; draped over the end of it, and crept from the room.

Outside she found her door flanked by two guards who immediately stepped in line to follow her.

"I don't need an escort." Lilly grumbled sleepily at them. When this did nothing to keep them back she realised they didn't understand. Shaking her head as she paused to look at them she forced her mind into gear and raising a hand said "Ny." The men frowned, holding position, and with further thought Lilly forced her voice to take on a more persuasive tone. "Cat ya vac!" both men's arms went across their chests, their fists clenched in the now familiar bow, as they backed up. Lilly nodded and continued on alone.

A few Da'ariel weaved their way through the village and a variety of sounds lingered in the air: a clanging here, a pop and hiss there, the occasional stamping or snorting of animals and the recurring slosh of water as it was carried and poured.

Leaning against a log-pile Lilly gazed up at the strange pink sky - it's colour fading to the more familiar light blue. A light rustle at her back had her glancing over her shoulder.

The two guards she'd dismissed watched from the nearest doorway as Vereena hovered cautiously near.

"I should have known they'd fetch one of you." grumbled Lilly.

The other girl nodded, stepping forward but keeping a respectful distance.

"Orders are that you're kept within our sights at all times Princess."

"Course they are." Lilly's gaze returned to the sky. "You know if you must watch my every move," she sighed "You may as well come closer." Sensing trepidation she added, "Really… it's OK. Screw up as much as I have and you kinda get used to being watched."

"Our concern is only for your well-being." said Vereena as she stepped up to Lilly's side, "The men say you make noises as you sleep, sounds of distress, of pain."

"Just dreaming."

"Dreaming?"

"Yeah you know," Lilly threw her a sideways glance. "Funky pictures, or memories the mind conjures up while you sleep." Vereena's face showed no sign of recognition so Lilly shrugged. "All perfectly normal where I'm from. Nothing for you or Mai Mai's men to worry about,"

"Oh these are not Mai Mai's men," the girl corrected. "She was already at rest when Kyrel left the order and I'm afraid all other guards were assigned already. These are men from my own troop."

"Your *own* troop?"

The surprise in Lilly's voice triggered a note of apology in Vereena's.

"Yes cousin, I'm lacking in the authority to order other men from their posts at this time, but you have my word these two are of the clan's best. Each highly regarded as warriors, and their courage is not easily matched even among the best of both my brother's troo-"

"It's OK," smirked Lilly. "I wasn't doubting you, I mean them," her eyes drifted to where the guards hung back, awaiting instruction. "I'm sure they are both very capable. I just… well I-I guess I was impressed, you know with the 'you having warriors to call your own.'"

"Aah," Vereena nodded. "I forget how different your life has been. Is there no such thing as a noble beyond the veil? None to lead your clan?"

"Well yeah," said Lilly, "sure there is, I mean we don't really have clans, but we have got plenty of titles: Lords and Ladies, Dukes, Barons, hell where I'm from we even have a royal family of our own - oddly enough they're also led by a Queen."

"Oh? We saw nothing of this in the quiesscence. Do they not also each have their own personal guard?"

"Err… well…" Lilly frowned, her thoughts going to Beefeaters and the statuesque Queen's Guard outside Buckingham Palace – neither looked anything like Vereena's guardsmen. "Yeah," she nodded. "I guess they do, but it's all very different to here. I mean it's not as if our royals spend much time among the regular folk. Everything about them has to be better,"

"Then we are not so different," Nodded the girl. "It's because we are the best that the Avengturovs lead our people. Our males almost always return successful from their marats, and as well as being among our clan's most accomplished warriors and scholars, Avengturov women have always been our clan's most fertile. Of course we are direct descendants of Leyavanya so it is only to be expected that those of our bloodline excel from the earliest years of our training."

"So what, you're telling me being a warrior here is something that's in the blood?"

"Ny," shrugged Vereena. "You're in the inner regions of Azeron now cousin - to be warriors is merely how we live. Being the best; that is in the blood, in our essence."

"That's ridiculous!" Lilly's eyes rolled as she shook her head.

"Perhaps," shrugged Vereena "However, we also train far harder and longer than the other houses, the people know this - they both expect and appreciate our dedication."

"Yeah well, see I was talking more, their *lifestyles*. Nobility beyond the veil is more about privilege. They have better homes, cars, clothing; whole squadrons of servants catering to their every whim."

"Well we do also have servants," Vereena spoke in a doubtful tone as she added, "although I am unsure what a whim or indeed this catering is, so I cannot truly compare."

The more Lilly explained, the more confused this new cousin of hers looked, then she told her. "Our royalty sure as hell wouldn't be happy living in huts made of mud like you lot are. Or eating most of anything you all call food." and Vereena's face lit up with a smile.

"Veyhi!" she nodded. "This I can understand. Those fruits you grew were unlike anything I've ever tasted; such flavours. Why if I were pampered as the royalty of your world, I'd have my servants bring me one of each of those fruits for every meal."

"I dunno," snorted Lilly. "A diet like that'd probably make it difficult to get off the loo... plus, I reckon it'd get real old, real fast. Anyway, royalty of my world dine on far more than a piece of fruit per meal."

"Really? What else do they eat?"

"Oh I don't know," sighed Lilly, "Foie gras, caviar, that sort of thing. Generally if it's rich, expensive, or considered a delicacy, then royalty and other nobles are probably eating it"

"Delicacy? As in easily damaged?"

"No..." Lilly chuckled. "Delicacy as in... the normal everyday folk like what I was beyond the veil are generally very happy if we can't afford it."

"Ah... then this Foie gras and Caviar they are... a responsibility, something to be endured?"

"Well they are in my opinion." shrugged Lilly.

"Do they study?"

"Huh?"

"Your nobles and royals… Is there much to learn for their duties? Do they train?"

"Err… well they're often sent away to big important schools, so yeah I guess they must do."

"Was Craven's Peak not a big important school you were regularly sent away to?"

"Well yes, but of a totally different variety… pretty much the opposite in fact."

"Oh," Vereena looked thoughtful. "Me and my brothers have always trained and studied a lot. Every generation of our family does. Since the days of the Do'mass council. Learning from the sacred writings ensures the wisdom of our ancestors remains among us."

"And just how helpful has that been?"

"It is our history."

"Well yes OK, history can be good. I get that. In fact beyond the veil we have a saying about it, 'those who don't learn from it – are doomed to repeat it' or something like that… Point is all the Da'ariel seem to do is repeat it. I mean seriously no offence or anything, but generation after generation of you all hiding out in these woods, and committing to memory what are no longer anything more than a bunch of useless old words, really does seem like a big fat waste of time to me. Not one of you has the power to use any of what you've learnt."

"But you do."

"Well yes, OK, but I'm one girl and before I was born, no one here had any way of knowing I would be…" frowning she asked, "Or did they? Mai Mai did mention my destiny. There wasn't like some prophecy or something was there? You're people weren't like sitting around for hundreds of years, waiting for me to born."

"I don't believe so cousin." Vereena looked confused again. "How could they? No one knows what's to come so far in advance. Do these prophecy things happen often beyond the veil?"

"Only in stories." Lilly shrugged, "It's kind of a recurring theme." Seeing the confusion increase she muttered "Never mind I'm being silly."

"Then like us, the most you can do is be brave enough to shape your own futures?"

"Yes," nodded Lilly, "but see that's what I'm getting at. Hiding out here while you mull over times past doesn't seem very brave to me. What future have the Da'ariel shaped by doing that?"

"Hiding you beyond the veil kept you from Mordrel's grasp, while hiding ourselves has allowed us to survive long enough to bring you back."

"Yeah alright, fair point, but-"

"We also have clans spread in secret locations throughout these lands who grow in number while the Deebanaarie, whose numbers were so much greater than our own after the last Great War, have started to dwindle."

"Then isn't it time to try something different?"

"We shall, once you're safely past, your Kalaareem"
"Yes but what if I'd never been born?"

"But you were."

"But I'm a fluke! I might just as easily have never happened. Even without magicks, your people can fight. Instead of all the hiding, and studying, wouldn't it have been way better to pick up your weapons and take the fight to your enemies? When your history is that you got your ass kicked, how is it a good idea to sit around repeating it?"

"Mai Mai is right about you." Vereena smiled.

"She is?"

"Oh yes," she nodded. "You have much heart. I never truly knew your mother, but it is said she was a great woman and would have been one of our best leaders. Mai Mai insists you've inherited almost all of her strengths. When you were sent away, she added the studying of the tongue of those beyond the veil to our family studies. A task often easier for myself than my brothers, I'm afraid. To them it was quite the burden – even in the First House we do not usually ask that our males study so intensely. Azeronian men really are more suited to the physical, you understand," Seeing Lilly's eyebrow begin to rise Vereena sighed, "Whereas I was selected for Qin Am Ness as an infant," she shrugged, "Studying you was always a great deal of my daily routine."

"Well I guess that explains a lot," it was Vereena's turn to raise an eyebrow, and catching it Lilly told her, "Not counting Kyrel, you've now said more to me than any of the others."

"Aah," Vereena smiled. "It's not that they haven't tried. Even Mairiel has found it difficult to understand a lot of the language you speak. It seems so often to fluctuate and increase. Still she's insisted we try harder. Always telling us how important it was to be ready for your return. She's even had our messengers spread word of you to the other villages in order that all Da'ariel learn of your existence."

"No pressure then," muttered Lilly, before shaking her head. "OK seriously, it's not bad enough I have everyone here looking to me as their saviour, now you're telling me there's a whole bunch of other Da'ariel outside this village all waiting on me too?"

"Mairiel has never failed her people. Her faith in you is all the rest of the clans need know."

"Right, that's it, I have to ask… Why does she have two names?"

Vereena's face became a blank so Lilly sighed, "Is she Mairiel or Mai Mai?"

"Oh," the younger girl laughed. "Mairiel is her given name. Mai Mai is… more a title… like the nobility of your realm?"

"OK," said Lilly, biting down on her lip a moment before nodding, "So then that's why she… she was insisting Kyrel address her only by title. But then, does that mean he once addressed her otherwise?"

"Aah…" Vereena nodded back at her, "Kyrel's relationship with our clan has indeed been a strange one. Like those in charge at your Craven's Peak, you call them Sir or Miss… I often wondered why it was that they all had the same name."

"Yes!" chuckled Lilly "that is exactly... well... kind of what I mean."

"These titles, the Sir and the Miss-"

"And the Mrs," added Lilly.

"Yes those... are they, is there... do you mean to show adoration and respect when you say them?"

"Well err... respect sure... adoration... not so much... for respect and adoration we'd be talking more a title for family, like you know to our mothers... kids beyond the veil don't call their parents by name. We say mom and dad."

"Right, that is it. Mom and dad are titles much more like Mai Mai."

"But I hear loads of the people here calling her that? In fact I think everyone I've heard address her directly has called her that."

"She is the mother of the clan, that is what Mai Mai means, it says all here look up to her in both respect *and* with adoration."

"Guess that makes sense, except by that logic I don't know how she's cool with letting Kyrel address her at all. Perhaps it's time for another..." seeing Vereena bite down on her lip, Lilly asked "What? Am I missing something?"

"Err..." the other girl shook her head. "Missing something? No cousin," she glanced around them. More Da'ariel were milling about the village now but none, including the two guards still hovering in the doorway, could hear or understand a word the two girls said. "There is nothing to miss," Vereena shook her head, "I simply-"

"You're simply a really bad liar who's trying to hide the fact you know something."

"What? I am not lying. I was not even born when Kyrel came here before, and was but an infant when he left."

"Well now I know it's something to do with Kyrel being in the village before."

"I didn't say that Princess, I wouldn't have, I... I just... Some things are not for me to-"

"Oh come on. I already knew he'd been here before and I also know he knew Herrella, I'm just trying to understand the how's and why's. Your brother Arteth called to him by name before he let us through the gates and Mai Mai obviously has a history with him. If the Deebanaarie are so bad why is Kyrel even here? Why did he risk so much to save me, and why is he training me to be the best weapon you have?"

Looking like she might say something, Vereena shook her head then clamped her mouth shut. A response which frustrated Lilly into saying, "OK seriously how is it he even has a history with this clan if..." long before she noticed the younger girl's gaze had drifted to over her own left shoulder.

When she did, her mouth also closed and turning around, she saw Arteth watching them from the corner of the nearest hut.

"I shall take my leave of you cousin," Vereena said, clapping her arm to her chest before scurrying indoors with her guards following behind her.

"Princess..." Arteth nodded Lilly's way. "Mai Mai requests an audience with you."

***

With her Eshron removed, Lilly was able to lean back against the table it had been on the day before, as she stared again into the face of an aged Mai Mai. Kyrel stood at her side also, and with the sprite T'vor carrying a wooden cup toward the now older woman seated on the large wooden chair, the feeling of deja vu was uncanny, yet tainted by the fact that they were the only ones in the room.

Arteth had seemed eager to stay, but upon arrival had been swiftly dispatched, by his grandmother.

As before, Mai Mai thanked T'vor while taking her drink, then tested its temperature with a sip, leaving Kyrel and Lilly to wait patiently as she drank the lot.

This gave them enough time to exchange glances, his eyes carrying a warning she was at a loss to decipher.

"I'm told your training goes well child."

"Err… yes." Lilly's eyes snapped back to Mai Mai as the cup was handed back to the old white sprite. "I…" her gaze flitted to Kyrel but he looked away, "…I think so. Sure left my mark on your training ground yesterday," she grinned.

"You will not defeat Mordrel with trees!" snapped Mai Mai. Lilly's grin disappeared. With her face beginning the changes brought on by her pulpustuem root, the older woman turned her cutting tone on Kyrel. "Have you not yet explained to the Princess the basis of her power?"

"She does still have much to learn, but focus remains an issue and I felt it best not to overwhelm her so close to her arrival."

"Or perhaps my grandsons are correct and you simply do not wish her to know her full strength, hmmm?"

"That is not true." Kyrel's eyes widened, his face showing genuine surprise. "You cannot truly think it so."

"Can't I?" Mai Mai's eyes narrowed, her voice shedding its age with each word she said. "Was it not fear of Da'ariel power that provoked your ancestors?"

"I am not my ancestors, Mairiel. Anyway, you're the one who continues to insist…"

"Deefak bor!" Mariel snapped, then softened her tone. "Enough. Today we shall see some real progress, correct?"

"As you wish, Mai Mai." Kyrel stared impassively at Mairiel.

"Wait!"

Both turned enquiring eyes on Lilly, and biting her lip she raised a finger, shaking her head as she consciously adjusted her tone. "Can I just… you're saying I can do more?" Mai Mai's eyebrow went up on her now younger face as Lilly added "I mean I thought we did pretty well yesterday. I for one busted my ass off and so did your man Kyrel here. I'm just saying maybe you could try cutting him a little slack. You know, it's not as if he isn't trying."

"Lilly, that's enough." Kyrel looked to her with fresh warning. Lilly glanced to him then heedlessly away.

"I don't think it is. I mean, seriously?" She turned back to Mai Mai. "The way you and your grandsons have been breathing down his neck *like* every step of the way, I'm surprised he's even bothered sticking around."

"Lilly, this is not necessary."

Stepping forward, she ignored him.

"You guys need his help. I *need* his help! Have you forgotten that he's the only one here with any real power? Without him I couldn't grow a blade of grass never mind those trees out there-"

"Enough!" Mai Mai whacked her walking handle off the arm of her seat, startling Lilly into silence. "You use a lot of words, granddaughter. A shame none of them will be any help when Mordrel seeks you out. With only three days left until Kalaareem we cannot sit idly by waiting for her to make her move. She knows where you are, and no doubt has her forces, scouring the forest in search of our village." Biting her lip, Lilly took a step back, returning to Kyrel's side, as Mai Mai nodded his way. "As things stand the Princess is still vulnerable. We cannot hope to have her ready to fight in time, I do know this, as you know all here are ready to lay down their lives defending her."

"Yes Mai Mai." Kyrel bowed his head.

"You realise also that such action may not be enough?"

"Yes Mai Mai."

"Then you *will* do all you can to see she can protect herself by this eve's night fall."

"Yes Mai Mai," he nodded. "As you will it, I shall do."

"Mordrel's time is soon passed Kyrel. Do not forget you are sworn to make it so. Much still rests with you."

"I know Mai Mai, I do not forget."

"Good, then you will not fail Azeron now, by failing her."

Seeing his jaw clench as he nodded one last time, Lilly dropped her eyes, aware that yet again their conversation had surpassed her meagre level of understanding. Straightforward as the words seemed, details were being left out and all she was certain of was the serious note she heard in both their voices and how it was reason enough to not ask for answers now.

***

"I just don't understand," Lilly whispered from the corner of her mouth as she and Kyrel made their way out to the training area. "You have all the know-how, all the power – that should mean something." She glanced over her shoulder to where Arteth followed a few feet behind. "You're worth at least ten of the men in this village. Yet they all talk to you as if you're nothing. How many years have they spent in hiding here with the likes of your sister kicking their butts? Now along you come, an honest to God decent chance of turning the tables. You have no reason to, but you're willing to help. Do they thank you or make any attempt to show even the slightest gratitude? No, of course not."

"Lilly please…" he also spoke in a whisper. "I told you already these things are not your concern." Throwing her a cutting look he shook his head. "You should not have spoken to your grandmother that way."

"She's no grandmother of mine." Kyrel paused, a pained look on his face.

Relenting Lilly shook her head, "Yeah OK, fine, given the circumstances and all, you've shown me so far, she most likely is my grandmother… I just meant…." sighing she shrugged, "it just makes me so angry to see her treat you that way. The way she talks to you, it pisses me off. You're the one who got to me in time. If you hadn't gone out of your way to get me here the Da'ariel would already have missed their chance. How is it no one sees that? You should be ruling this roost Kyrel! You should be calling all the shots. Instead they push you around like some lackey and speak to you as if you're the one charging your sister's army towards this place."

After a quick sideways glance to where Arteth had also paused, keeping a distance respectful of their privacy, Kyrel closed his eyes, taking in a deep breath before he offered Lilly a smile.

"Please know that I am grateful of your concern for me. Indeed I am honoured that you think so highly of me. However it must all end here. There is much you cannot understand; things I do not have the time to explain."

"Like why you were here in this village during the time of my mother?" Lilly's hands went to her hips.

"Lillian!" Kyrel's voice rose with a mix of scorn and exasperation that caused her to lower her eyes. His tone softened, and he added, "Do know that Mai Mai is right to consider *you* the single most important being in this village right now. I cannot afford to put my pride above your needs, and it is only right that she not let me."

"Oh please, we both know she's all talk, when you refused to leave yesterday she dropped the subject real fast. What can she possibly do to you today that-"

"She can wait till I sleep then send you away from here."

"What?" Lilly chuckled but the lack of humour from Kyrel soon had her shaking her head. "Why would she do that? You're like, the best protection I have."

"Well that is not something we all agree on," Kyrel lowered his voice to a whisper again. "You already see that standing to fight is not the way of *these* Da'ariel. If I had not brought you here the plan would have been to move you from one village to the next in the hope of keeping you alive long enough to see your Kalaareem."

"But… that doesn't sound like such a bad plan."

"It is if I am to stay with you," hissed Kyrel, his gaze flitting to Arteth, who watched broodingly from afar. "This is the only Da'ariel village I know the location of, and Mai Mai is no more about to let that change than I am to let you travel without me at your side."

"So your training me is a compromise?"

"Compromise?"

"She can't get rid of you and she can't guarantee you won't find me again if she does send me away. You, on the other hand, can't be sure you would find me. So as much as you can't stand each other, the only option left is for you to trust that you really do want the same thing and work together to achieve it."

"Then yes," nodded Kyrel. "This is compromise."

"OK." Lilly gulped and continued walking, "so let's see if I have this straight," she glanced briefly in Arteth's direction. "The change of plan isn't exactly to everyone's liking, and if Mai Mai doesn't see the results she wants we're gonna be forgetting there ever was a compromise."

"Correct."

"So... Either I learn some real shit-hot stuff today or the next time you get some shut-eye it's gonna be back to plan A, with me on my way to some other Da'ariel village before either of us knows it."

"Not to worry," Kyrel's hand went to her shoulder as he kept step beside her. "You *will* learn some truly 'shit hot' stuff today," seeing her grin he nodded, "just remember to pay attention and do as-"

"You do," added Lilly. "I remember."

As they reached the training area she saw most of the newly formed trees were gone. All that remained in their place was a bunch of fresh training stumps and several large mounds of mulch.

Her eyes went to what was by far the largest mound and realising it was the tree she'd sent Tobias and Baxter skyward in, she groaned.

"Awww... dammit, that was like my best one."

"Indeed it was," Kyrel followed her gaze. "Imagine my surprise when clearing yesterday's efforts I found those two boys among the mess."

"Aah... right..." Lilly's eyes grew wide as she popped out her lips and scratched behind her right ear. "I probably should have told you about that."

"No need, the other two from your realm were quite informative."

With a meek laugh she shrugged, "It's OK, you can skip the lecture. I saw that dumbass Spiderman movie in the cinema twice, don't ask me why... anyway that whole 'with great power comes great responsibility' speech... well OK... actually I think it's a load of over-righteous crap and if you ask me Tobey Maguire like totally did the right thing letting the thief run off with the bag." Seeing Kyrel's arms criss-cross over his chest she nodded, "Still... I get it. Thou shalt not abuse thy powers. It's the path to the dark side and that way lies no good yada yada yada..." his eyebrow went up and letting loose a tremendous sigh she muttered. "OK fine, I went overboard. Go ahead, lecture away."

Staring her way with a thoughtful look Kyrel finally said, "You did well to take such decisive action. Setting your friends apart so swiftly was preferable to the alternative... Also... that tree itself was quite the display of your power. I was most impressed."

It was Lilly's turn to stare at him, it took her a long moment to decide if he was serious, then she grinned, "You really meant that?"

"Why would I say it otherwise?" Kyrel looked puzzled.

"Because... I don't know... I guess I don't usually get... the praise, when I lose my temper."

"I know," he smirked, "I've seen many of the incidents, reactions included."

"Right," she nodded, watching him make his way to the nearest stump. "Of course you have..."

"I also saw you attend that movie. The Spiderman, what I caught of it was… most interesting."

"You saw me watching that?"

"I believe so." He called back to her, "very large, brightly coloured warrior swinging from structure to structure. I believe I also know why you went twice."

As she raised an eyebrow now he added, "I've seen the many large pictures you place on the walls of your room. That warrior was on many…"

"OK," Lilly glared at him. "How's about you never mention that again… like never ever."

"Sure." Kyrel, now a good distance ahead of her, stretched his arms wide. "Raise the earth around me so I am concealed from sight and you shall have my word."

"Great," muttered Lilly, "yesterday I'm fighting for the right to eat, and today it's the right to not be humiliated."

***

In a rage Mordrel howled, and threw her steaming goblet across the great hall. Her newest general hadn't checked in with her since the day before and patience wasn't her strong point. Fortunately for Drellaeleon, and everyone else in her court, this anger was witnessed only by Neenia - as she rarely left her Queen's side.

"Why have they not found her yet?" she growled. "We know Mairiel's village is in the forest. For the first time in so long they risk using magicks and still they evade my troops. Your ginaten are not doing their work Neenia."

"My Ginaten always do their work." The sprite hopped down on to the lower floor and made its way to the trail of brown goop left by Mordrel's goblet.

"Then why have they not led my forces to the girl yet? Why is she not here before me so I can dres verfelt those unsanctioned powers from her?"

"We know the magicks that brought the girl to our realm must have been potent."

"Potent and ill timed." Mordrel paced the floor beyond her quiesscence bowl, and muttered mostly to herself. "My troops were so close. If only the Da'ariel hadn't interfered I would have had the girl's essence by now."

"Mairiel's people have grown evermore wily in the forest. She must have known the girl would become more detectable as her essence grew in strength." Neenia stuck her long pink tongue out and lapped at the thick brown trail. "She probably used the last of her quiesscence over these last few days merely watching for you to make your move."

"Yes, but who could have guessed she'd move so quickly; transporting the girl from one land to the next without leaving us so much as a chance to blink?"

"It truly was an impressive feat. Her people can't have many sprites left. Even working together, they may well have exhausted themselves. The creation of the mists could have been the last of their power."

"You're suggesting there was nothing left for the Ginaten to follow?"

"Tekurian sprites do require much time to recover."

"Time is not something I can allow them to have more of; the girl's Kalaareem grows ever closer!" Mordrel's pacing slowed, and she turned to watch Neenia lick her way along the spotty goop trail, then deep in thought, she brought her hand up to her chin, tapping with one finger as she muttered, "Still if that is true: Mairiel's clan are at this moment more vulnerable than we have ever known them to be."

"Presuming general Drellaeleon can find them." Neenia chimed in before lapping up what was left on the floor with one big swish of that long tongue and adding. "Perhaps you were too hasty getting rid of S'gleeros." She picked up the cup and slurped out the few drops left in it.

With gritted teeth Mordrel glared at her sprite. "An example needed to be made, do not tempt me to make another. Even you can become expendable."

"Now now, Mai Mai," said Neenia. "What a way to speak to your oldest friend? And just when I may have come up with a possible solution to your tracking problem."

"Better be a solution that actually works this time…"

"Even you cannot ever assume success Mordrel, still if the chance of failure means you are not interested-"

"Just tell me!" she hissed loudly. All teeth, the sprite grinned, raising its tiny hand, discarded goblet and all.

"How likely is it that Mairiel would leave her people completely at your mercy?"

"Not very," sighed Mordrel. "I'm sure she's equipped her Second Hand with some of their puny Da'ariel weapons…" her voice petered out as she cast a more knowing gaze at her oldest friend. "You speak of magickal defences."

"Veyhi, have we not always assumed it was Mairiel's sprites that kept her village cloaked? Now if their magicks are truly used up and still your warriors cannot locate them…"

As Neenia paused, Mordrel sucked in her lower lip and deep in thought, stood a moment, watching her own foot as it tapped in time with the finger at her chin.

Finally she looked up.

"Mairiel must have some other way to continue cloaking the village."

"Some other way?" asked Neenia suggestively.

"But there is only one other way, and that is not possible."

"Isn't it?"

"All the other orbs were destroyed Neenia." Mordrel stated with a dismissive wave in the sprite's direction. "Leyavanya herself was said to have hurled them into the seas of Ceshori in the first days of the Great War."

"Yet your family has had two in its possession since before your grandmother's time."

"Yes but… You're genuinely suggesting others survived? That's madness… Why would Mairiel… why would any of the Da'ariel have remained hidden so long? Access to such potent magicks might at least have allowed them to even the odds."

"Now you assume too much," Neenia threw the empty goblet to Mordrel. She caught it without blinking. "What if they've only had the orbs a short time?" asked the sprite. "What if—like you—they have but two… or perhaps only one. Leyavanya's magicks were potent yes, but that war tore her people asunder and as you well know, the orbs are little more than relics to those low in essence. Separated they are even less formidable, and you yourself have two. The ability to keep up the cloak on the Da'ariel village, may well be all the power Mairiel is ever going to draw, from however few of the orbs she has in her possession."

"You are right," Mordrel's bright yellow eyes fixed the dark leathery sprite with a gleeful stare. "My family lost many seeking out our two orbs and they themselves were almost devoid of Leyavanya's essence. The chances of many others surviving *and* being recovered is…" grinning she chuckled. "…Laughable. Mairiel would surely have rallied her people and mounted some kind of an offensive by now if she had any real power. Yet one more orb, probably… at a stretch two and she would be able to at least keep her village's precious cloak up."

"With your permission…" Neenia ambled back toward the Queen, "I can sample the essence from one of your orbs and give my Ginaten a far better idea of what they're hunting for."

"Oh you have my permission." Mordrel stalked off in the direction of her large throne. "I shall get you one this instant. As for Mairiel, well… maybe she's worth more to me alive after all." Behind the throne a door known only to a very few slid open and Mordrel disappeared from sight.

Day Two: Part Two

Lilly managed to successfully raise the ground around Kyrel, trapping him inside several perfect circles, one after the other. But as she'd begin to take a breather, he was already using his own power, as he'd free himself with the creation of a door. He soon had her struggling to keep him inside the one circle as pitting his power against hers, he created door after door and she in turn closed them. Finally he brought down the entire ring before telling her she was doing well.

Then he blasted her into a hole so deep it took several tries for her to raise enough earth to get back out again. Kyrel shook his head, "Too slow, you can do better," and again he blasted her down below ground.

Hissing obscenities and clawing at the ground around her, Lilly made it to the surface with only three tries, and seeing him stretch out a hand to sink her a third time, made an effort to roll away muttering, "Don't you dare!" Not fast enough, she found herself plummeting again. This time, it was face first, and before the earth stopped moving, she howled "Kiiat vash".

She reappeared with such force that she coughed up dust and clods of dirt both clung to and fell from her hair. Anger burned in her eyes; Kyrel grinned.

"Much better, now to improve your focus."

For this next part of the lesson he had her mould the dirt into various constructions around the training field. Several times she towered above him on columns of raised dirt, or called from the ground a perfect set of steps to run up.

Impressed but not satisfied, he used his own powers and often the same words to bring the entire lot down around them before instructing her to combine both the earth rising and tree growing to create more elaborate structures.

An attempt to prove she had plenty of focus saw Lilly recreating what she thought a perfect replica of her favourite building back home: the local shopping centre.

"Ny mech!" Arteth gasped, his eyes growing to drink in every detail – tiny people and a car park full of cars included.

If it hadn't been for the miniature proportions of the stores, Lilly felt sure he would have wandered around each one with that same gormless look on his face.

Yet dismissing the entire thing with a wave of his hand and the words, "Ta varee," Kyrel let it crumble around them, leaving a mixture of mud and mulch at their feet. Trudging over the mess he nodded. "Good enough, but you will not dazzle Mordrel into submission, stop wasting your energies on nonsense."

Under her breath she mimicked his words as she followed him across the mound. Then as he spun to look at her with a raised eyebrow, she offered an overly wide smile, and asked, "So I have that down. What's next?"

The answer was another of the hand gestures she'd practised the previous day – almost a fist but facing outward and with more palm on show.

"Kimst", said Kyrel, his arms outstretched. Following the instruction without question Lilly copied everything down to his stance and with her now well practised, firm voice found herself flying backward - bowled over by an airflow of her own creation.

"You have got to be kidding me!" she clambered to her feet, "that was... was that... I can create air too?"

"Of course," Kyrel shrugged. "Does your realm not sustain the exact same force?"

"Well yeah, I guess... I mean sure we have air but-"

"You do not yet appreciate the gifts bestowed upon you."

"No. No that's not true, I totally get it," nodded Lilly. "Well OK. I kind of get it. I can... create stuff, like out of nothing, like apparently... air," she grinned. "Very cool by the way! And you... well... you can take it all away again, also... kinda cool." Her expression grew puzzled and she shook her head. "Can you? Take air... away again?"

"It is said that before the great war-."

"Aww come on!" muttered Lilly, "Not another history lesson." Narrowing his eyes Kyrel continued. "Lilly!" Kyrel's eyebrows went up and sighing she rolled her eyes muttering in a less than enthused voice. "OK... Carry on."

"Yes," said Kyrel. "I can diminish the air too. When I found you in the forest you had a fire. I-"

"So that's how you did it!" Lilly's head tipped back and she grinned. "Man this is like so freaking cool. Why didn't you tell me I can do so much?" Then she was replicating the stance again, her arm outstretched as she said, "Katat."

This time it was Kyrel who was bowled over. The far stronger gust took him by surprise and he rolled over backward several times.

"Holy shit!" Lilly gasped as a snigger escaped Arteth and he turned to hide a smirk. Coming to a stop Kyrel crawled to his feet with a grimace. "I am so sorry..." she shook her head as he threw her a vexed look. Then offering a meek smile said, "Plus side – I have a bitchin memory." And when his only response was to raise an eyebrow as she added, "That was the word you used for the same force right? To out the fire?" Seeing him sigh again, this time as he began wiping traces of the red dust and mud from his lower garments, she shrugged. "At least we know I can do it."

"Yes..." Kyrel relented, "At least we know you are capable... if not *ill* focused."

"Ill focused!" the words left her mouth with a snort. "I just knocked you clear off your feet pal. I have focus up the waazoo, OK. I kick ass. Suck it up."

"Do not think too highly of yourself yet Lilly. Mordrel will not tumble so-"

"Yeah yeah, blah blah blah... I'm holding my own against you pretty well. How much tougher can she really be?"

"What Kyrel means cousin," Toleth stepped out of the shadows and strode past his brother toward her and Kyrel. "Is that he is but a man," Arteth stepped forward also.

"Toleth ny! Diest nydrel. Elt Mai Mai dien."

"For that matter..." the younger brother ignored what was clearly an order from his older sibling, his gaze shifted from Lilly to Kyrel "... he is one who's shirked his place as a fighter among his clan. Do you not think if his powers were any match for his sister's he would have returned to his family home and faced her long ago? Instead he hides, and he runs, and he further disgraces himself through his deals with us - Da'ariel." He spat.

Kyrel threw Mai Mai's youngest grandson a dark look.

"I make deals for the good of all Azeron, Toleth. To rid us of the dark days both our peoples endure."

"Dark days your people brought down upon us," nodded Toleth.

"That is so," said Kyrel "of course I, like you was many cycles away from existing at the time and cannot be held responsible for the mistakes of either of our ancestors."

"Of course," Toleth's eyes narrowed, "Still many wonder: were it not for you losing grace with your sister, being thrown from Crizoleth like the last coteli in a moolach bog, would you ever have noticed the darkness?"

"Toleth! Cat ya vac inst!" ordered Arteth, and turning his back on Kyrel and Lilly, Toleth hissed, "Chorosh K'bar, ti hishliv't Matfiack!" and strode off past his brother, the two of them barely exchanging glances.

Kyrel's lips curled back in a snarl as he took a step to follow. Lilly shot out a hand, the words "Kiiat vash," leaving her mouth before her brain had time to register the motion. From where she stood to far beyond Kyrel, a two-foot thick wall sprung from the earth - separating him from the brothers in seconds.

As Lilly hurried to his side Kyrel's hand went up to give him passage through the wall. Grabbing the arm she yanked it away before he could speak the necessary words.

"Don't, OK."

Immediately his jaw tightened with visible knots just below his temples and he turned to glare at her. "I'm sorry," she shook her head, "But whatever that was he said just now... it doesn't matter. You're supposed to be teaching me remember? Mai Mai wants me ready to protect myself by tonight." Again he went to raise his arm but Lilly kept her grip on it. "I'll quit giving you attitude, OK. I'll focus. Just forget him and teach me. I need to learn Kyrel. Teach me more." Slowly his fist unclenched and he was nodding,

"You are right," he waved the now relaxed hand at the wall muttering "Ta varee."

As it dropped, revealing only Arteth with a look of concern on his face, Kyrel said. "You do still have much to learn." And turning his back on the older brother he added, "Come... let us practice your skills with air."

True to her word Lilly held her tongue. Keeping at bay the sarcasm, which came so naturally to her, yet was generally pointless among current company.

As per instruction, she practised combining her power over air with all Kyrel had taught her so far.

Before long she could propel herself into a freshly sprouting tree only to come running down a steep set of steps she'd called from the ground up to meet her.

As she reached the bottom Kyrel nodded, his voice full of pride. "A sight to behold!"

"Really?" Lilly grinned, gasping for breath. "That was good?"

"Oh yes," he nodded. "You are truly making progress. Do you not feel it?"

"Actually," still gasping she doubled over and let her hands rest on her thighs. "I think what I'm feeling... is my heart about to explode."

"Come," Kyrel tucked a hand under her arm, pulling her upright. "Let us get some gaawa in you. You have earned a rest."

"Oh please no," mumbled Lilly as he guided her away, "not more of that funky brown stuff. Can't I just have some food? Maybe some of that fruit I grew?"

"Gaawa is better," said Kyrel as Arteth took hold of her other arm.

***

On reaching the dining hut the two men got her seated, then leaving Kyrel to attend her needs, Arteth disappeared through the curtain opposite the one they'd entered.

As he'd done through much of the day Kyrel went back to lecturing her on the history and principles of her powers. "Even at peace the Deebanaarie and Da'ariel were always opposites," he explained. "Before the wars it is believed our ancestors lived and worked together. With the natural push and pull that governs our powers there was little they couldn't achieve, and all Azeron thrived."

"Mmm hmm..." mumbled Lilly, working on her second cup of Gaawa. She was only half listening to him, then Vereena wandered in through the same curtain Arteth had disappeared through. She carried a huge bowl of the assorted fruit grown the day before, and sitting back, Lilly's eyes lit up.

The other girl conferred briefly with Kyrel in their language before apparently obtaining his permission to set the bowl down close to Lilly. "For you cousin," she nodded, and looking up to offer thanks Lilly was distracted by the sight of four faces peering in at her from the edges of the dingy curtain. It was the others from Craven's Peak and all at once they ducked back from view; one of them apparently injuring another in the process as a whispered but sharp, "Ouch!" rent the air.

Vereena frowned then spoke in a lowered voice. "Your friends have been discussing you for much of the day. I believe they seek an audience with you."

"Well they obviously know where I am," Lilly didn't bother whispering. "Why don't they just come on in?" The other girl's eyes drifted to Kyrel.

"Well there were orders that..." she bit her lip and following her gaze Lilly saw Kyrel nod.

"It is all right Lady Vereena. I am certain you did not mean to give the wrong impression by telling them where your brother had bid you bring these fruit. Their presence shall not be held against you." As a grateful smile spread on her face he turned his attention to Lilly and raising his voice added, "They may enter only if Lilly wishes it so."

"Sure..." she rolled her eyes. "Whatever... I don't care, let them in."

Harper was first into the room and after her the boys pushed through the curtain in one impatient clump.

With the replenishing properties of the Gaawa juice slowly taking effect on her body Lilly leant forward, picking fruit from the bowl and only when she'd picked out a fat plum did she notice the silence which now filled the room. About to bite into the fruit she looked up, realised all eyes were on her, and setting it down turned to Harper - currently the nearest of the four - with a sigh.

"OK you know what. If you guys are looking for a warm fuzzy heartfelt apology... well frankly I'm not feeling all that sorry and I'm-"

"We're not." Harper's arms went up and looking past her to the others Lilly shrugged, "OK... so like what? You're here to watch me eat?"

"Actually," Terence spoke up, "We were kinda hoping you'd accept *our* apology."

"Yeah," added Tobias after his brother pushed him forward, "we err... we didn't mean to be inconsiderate and shit. We're all just really freaked out here man. We wanna go home you know and-" a slap up the back of his head, had him yelling "Hey!" as he turned to shoot an enraged glance at Baxter who shoved past him adding, "What eloquent here is trying to say is: much as we enjoy giving you a hard time, we do know that you have a lot on your plate right now, and none of us really meant to add to it." Lilly's hardened expression began to soften, and shrugging Baxter added, "Actually seeing as you're apparently our only chance of getting out of this crazy place in one piece, we figure we better quit behaving like a bunch of useless morons and give you a hand."

"Yeah," Harper nodded, twiddling her thumbs as she spoke. "We want to help. Just you know... tell us what to do."

Lilly stared at them a moment longer, stunned into silence by such a hefty olive branch, then a smirk broke out on her face and she shrugged. "Well as uncomfortably touching as that all was... I really don't see how you guys can help. I mean you know, besides the obvious like making this village impenetrable or turning every man, woman and child in it, into a fighting force worth attempting to pit against an army-"

"Err..." Baxter stepped forward, his hand raised slightly. "I reckon I can give that a decent shot."

A sceptical eyebrow went up on Lilly's face and he shoved his hands deep into the pockets of his jeans "Not the whole turning women and children into a decent fighting force thing, but I reckon I can maybe make this place less vulnerable."

Lilly's sceptical look seemed contagious as one by one the rest of the group turned to look at him. "What?" He eyed them all. "I'm not saying I'm the expert or anything just that I've seen enough of this place to know I can make some improvements... anyone from our world could... haven't you guys ever watched action movies?" The scepticism seemed only to increase, so he added. "Historical fiction? Braveheart? Robin Hood? Look if we can get a few spare hands there's got to be plenty we can do to slow down that army headed this way."

"That's right," support finally came from Terrence, "these people are practically living in the Dark Ages. Even without decent weapons there's gotta be a shit load we can come up with."

"Totally," Tobias agreed "Tez knows heaps about that kinda shit too."

"It's a fair point Slater," added Harper. "You do have three teenage boys here. Violence and defeating evil overlords is pretty much their staple TV diet back home."

"Look..." Lilly shook her head. "It's not that I don't appreciate the offer, but come on... This isn't TV, and we're definitely not back home!"

"So you'd rather we just don't try?" asked Harper. When the three boys each threw her similar dubious looks she shrugged. "What! Girls don't watch action movies? Get real already. Anyways, in case you all forgot, women are like the leaders here, you *guys* are probably gonna be needing my help if you expect any real cooperation."

"Yet another fair point," shrugged Terence as he and the others all turned back to Lilly. "So what's it gonna be Slater? We can't make you any promises-"

"*Or* an army," added Harper.

"Right," agreed Terence. "Can't make one of those for you either, but we can at least try to make some use of ourselves."

"Plus... we're all really bored," added Baxter with a shrug.

"You lot are serious?" She sat back, her eyes going from them to Kyrel. He was busy examining an orange but paused to look up as she said, "They're serious!"

Then she was turning back to watch them nod in unison, with Baxter adding, "As a heart attack Slater."

"Qin Am Ness...." said Kyrel, again Lilly turned to him. He however was looking to Vereena. "What say you; can volunteers be rallied at Lilly's request?"

"Of course." she nodded, with the first grin Lilly had seen on her, "All are honoured to do anything our Princess requires."

"Then I see no reason not to let them try," he turned back to Lilly with a nod.

"Reason!" she glared at him. "They shouldn't even be here!"

"This time yesterday you thought the same of yourself," he shrugged.

"So you've been kinda convincing since then, what with the trees and air and mud manipulation. But this lot are innocent bystanders Kyrel. They don't have any powers, how's that for a reason?"

"Nor does anyone else in this village," he shook his head.

"Innocent bystanders," Tobias sniggered, "That's one I've never been called before."

High-fiving him Baxter added, "Damn straight!"

For a moment Lilly stared at them, the change in their attitudes since the night before had her more perplexed than angry, but given a second to mull it over she still snapped. "Oh shut up guys! You know exactly what I mean. None of you are meant to be here. Those sprite thingies didn't mean to bring a whole bus load of Craven's Peak delinquents through that damn veil, OK? It was a mistake!"

"Actually..." Vereena spoke with obvious hesitation, "The entire bus was brought through intentionally, Princess." Receiving a questioning look she shrugged, "With Mordrel's forces already through the veil time was not in our favour and keeping a lock on your essence was proving more difficult than anticipated." Seeing Lilly raise an eyebrow as the others also turned to look at her Vereena shook her head. "No harm was meant, but a decision did have to be made; it was better for Merly and the others to bring the entire moving construction through to our side."

"A decision had to be made?" Harper glared at the young blonde girl.

"Harper," Terence stepped in front of her, but pushing him aside she added,

"Fifteen of our classmates are dead!"

"I know," nodded Vereena, "And I am very sorry, but the sprites did only what had to be done… I am confident they made the correct-"

"You're confident! My best friend was killed because your unreliable furball pets brought us through that stupid portal thingy."

"Sandra!" As Lilly rose, so too did her voice. "Stop it!" She fixed Harper with a warning glare. "You have no right to speak to Vereena that way. She has been nothing but good to us since the moment we got here." Forcing her tone to soften she added, "I know you may not get that cos you were out of commission a while there, which as it happens was not your fault, but it wasn't hers either, and actually if it wasn't for her you probably wouldn't be back in the loop at all so you *will* ease off… right now!"

Harper glared at the Da'ariel girl a moment before shrugging, "Sorry." She bit her lip a second then added. "I… I didn't mean to…" she nodded to Vereena shrugging as she repeated. "Sorry."

"That is all right." Vereena offered a smile. "I too am sorry. It is regretful that you lost your friend."

"Sure," Harper stepped back, her eyes going back to Lilly as she shook her head.

"You have to let us do this, if I have to keep sitting around this place watching everyone else here doing-"

"OK, OK…" Nodded Lilly, her hands going up, "I get it alright. If only for the sake of keeping the peace, you guys go ahead and see what you can do to improve things here."

"I will speak with Mai Mai about raising volunteers…" offered Vereena, "Our warriors keep a guard at the walls but there are still many able villagers she can call on."

"Thank you." Lilly sat back down. "That would be very helpful."

"Oh it is my pleasure Princess."

"Great," muttered Lilly as the other four pulled out seats. "We're back to the princess bullshit again."

"Wait!" Kyrel called as Vereena turned for the door, pausing she faced him with a bow of her head and reproducing the gesture he said, "May I suggest you have your cousin Arteth placed in charge of overseeing this matter. It is after all most important that Lilly's companions can fully communicate their wishes and I am sure Toleth already has his hands full as Mai Mai's second."

Again she looked hesitant, her gaze flitting from him to Lilly then back again as she asked.

"Is it not my cousin Arteth who already has the task of overseeing your training of the Princess?"

"It is yes." Kyrel smiled.

"Then I do not understand. Has he in some way offended her?"

"Rest assured he has been nothing but polite where the Princess is concerned,"

"Then I am sorry Kyrel but I do not believe it wise to-"

"So then you choose to forsake your role as Qin Am Ness?"

For a second her mouth fell open then she was shaking her head.

"Ny," her gaze grazed Lilly, "I... I would never make any such choice it is just..." she swallowed hard. "You do see I am still young."

"I see that you are no younger than your own Mai must have been when she too was called"

"Niamma was exceptional." Vereena's tone was matter of fact.

Lilly looked up from the plum she'd just bitten and tilting her head to put Vereena back in her sights asked, "OK what's going on now?"

Neither of them registered her.

"But you are schooled, correct?" Kyrel asked the younger girl "You've received the training? Undergone the rituals?"

"Veyhi." Vereena nodded, eyes drifting to Lilly she checked her language. "I mean yes...Yes I am trained."

"Then it is settled," Kyrel smiled. "Consider yourself called."

"OK wait, hang on just a minute," Lilly turned to him. "Called? For what? What have you just settled?" a glance Vereena's way showed her frozen, only her throat moved with repeated gulps. "Kyrel!" Lilly clicked her fingers at him. "You gonna tell me what the fuck is going on or what?"

"Your cousin Vereena will be accompanying us for training from now on," he nodded, "That should give you ample time to discuss the matter with her. Still you should probably *dismiss* her first, so she can go speak with Mairiel on your behalf." Turning around, Lilly took in Vereena's fearful gaze before the other girl dropped her eyes.

An unidentifiable weight plonked itself on Lilly's shoulders and sighing, she waved to the girl. "It's OK, you can go."

"Whoa!" muttered Baxter. "I do believe Lilly just acquired herself a slave."

"What!" her eyes roved between him and Kyrel as she snapped, "Don't be stupid! Why would I need a slave? I'm more than capable of-"

"No." Terrence shook his head, "Not a slave. You're royalty... the heir. You were brought here to lead these people. Everyone here is willing to bow down and tend your needs. Vereena just made that clear. But she's... She's royalty too..." He then turned to Kyrel "She's... the advisor... Right? That's what Qin Am Ness means? You referred to it as a role. It's a title. She's Lilly's rightful second in command?"

Clearly surprised, possibly impressed, the Deebanaarie stared at him a moment before nodding.

"How is it you know this? You cannot be familiar with our tongue, yet you know our ways."

"I... I don't know how..." Terrence shook his head, "body language I suppose?"

"Baxter went with body language and he got slave," pointed out Harper.

"Yeah, but Tez is smart," added Tobias, to the obvious humour of the others. Baxter seemed not to notice the slight, while Kyrel nodded,

"It would seem so."

Lilly shook her head saying.

"A bit more than smart I reckon. Even trying to follow the conversation I pretty much got zip. Well, except the same as Baxter: Vereena seemed terrified to me too. So how'd you come to the conclusion of advisor?"

"Well, there was tone of voice too... maybe I just picked up on-"

"Bullshit!" sneered Baxter, "your grey matter has been doing over time since we got here." He nodded Lilly's way, "everything he sees he's gotta ask questions about, it's getting kind of irritating actually."

"So I'm interested," shrugged Terrence. "We've stumbled on a whole new civilisation here, this entire world and everything in it, the people, the places, the animals and any other life-form... everything here is previously unheard of... how are you not interested?"

"Oh I am..." Baxter leaned back, throwing what looked like a grape into his mouth, "Interested in getting back to civilization - and cigarettes."

"So you observe," suggested Kyrel, barely noticing the intrusion, his eyes skirted Lilly as he nodded, "It is a good way to learn."

"What else have you figured out?" asked Lilly in an indignant tone.

"Not that much..." Terrence said with a chuckle and an eye roll. "I mean it's not as if I actually *know* anything. I just..." as her eyes narrowed he added, "Well OK, I think I might have the dynasty here pretty much worked out"

"What, that cheesy eighties soap... that comes on cable?" Harper's face screwed up, "how exactly is that relevant?"

"He's talking about line of succession you moron." Baxter threw an amused look her way. "You know... how monarchies work. Like Charles being next in line for the throne and all that jazz."

"Oh," she nodded as Terrence added, "Exactly... Except not! Seeing as our monarchy, like others in Europe is what's known as male-preference primogeniture." Between rising eyebrows and blank stares Kyrel looked the most confused, while Baxter turned out to be the least.

"That does just mean guys rule, right?" he asked.

Shrugging Terrence said, "Well sure but it's cognatic..." this produced further blank stares all around and waving a hand he added, "you know what, never mind... the point is females can rule too... you know, provided there's no male heirs before them."

"And that's how we have a Queen?" suggested Lilly.

"Right!" nodded Terrence. "But then there's other types of succession. Like Agnatic Primogeniture, A.K.A Patrilineal Primogeniture, which basically means females are excluded completely, and the line of succession goes from eldest male to eldest male."

"Which is how the Da'ariel do things?" said Tobias.

"Also the Deebanaarie," added Kyrel "except that here in Azeron it is us males who are excluded from leadership."

"Yeah," snorted Tobias. "No wonder your world's fucked."

"Actually," said Terrence "it might be uncommon in our realm but it's not like it's unheard of. It's what we'd call a Matrilineal Primo-,"

"OK that's it," sighed Baxter, "if this is gonna be some fancy way of saying girls rule I may have to get up and hit you." The others chuckled as he narrowed his eyes at Terrence.

"Sorry," a sly smirk appeared as Terrence shrugged, "I'll try and stick to English." He turned to Lilly. "OK so you're the only daughter of the eldest, which makes you the rightful heir. Course, all that really tells us is that these Da'ariel brought you back for more than just your abilities."

"I dunno," Harper shook her head. "They've been getting their asses handed to them for hundreds of years and Lilly's their first real chance of stopping that, what better reason could they have?"

"He didn't say they had a *better* reason," Baxter sat back with a smirk. "Just another one." The others all looked to him as he added "That Mairiel woman is on her way out, you must have seen how she looks in the mornings, like she's ninety or so years old…"

"One hundred and twenty seven I believe," Kyrel interjected, then seeing the jaws around him drop simultaneously he muttered, "Which is of course unheard of in your realm, but as you've seen, a Mai Mai has ways of preserving and extending their youth." The others all glanced around each other, and shrugging Terrence added, "This eldest to eldest, daughters only system leaves the Da'ariel with no successor but Lilly; they need her to take over."

"Yes." Kyrel nodded.

"No!" Lilly shook her head at him. "That's not even an option. The deal is I survive to this Kalaareem thingy, become what's known as 'way out of your sister's league' and those sprite creatures send us all home: me included!"

"That is a matter you will have to discuss with Mairiel," said Kyrel, with a solemn shake of his head, "There are very few sprites left in our realm. Their abilities are not something many have access to." He sighed and shrugging, returned his attention to Terrence. "And what of Vereena, how did you reach your conclusion on her?"

"Err…Well in our realm, many ancient civilisations learnt things can get real messy when a line of succession ends abruptly. So we have what's commonly known as regents. They're not true heirs so they have to move over as soon as one becomes apparent, but they can rule if one is absent and while a monarch is still in place they're generally a person close to the throne. Someone the reigning monarch can trust above all others, like a blood relative or an advisor, or…" he shrugged, "as in Vereena's case they're often both."

"Regent," nodded Kyrel. "This is what you call a Qin Am Ness beyond the veil?"

"Yeah I… I guess so." Terrence nodded, "Though for what it's worth, if I am right, then as long as Lilly's breathing, the title of advisor seems way more accurate to me."

"How the hell do you know all this?" Harper shook her head, "I definitely don't remember any lessons on-"

"He watches The History Channel whenever we're home," explained Tobias.

"Ha!" Terrence threw his brother a look of contempt. "What? Why would I be watching-?"

"How the hell should I know? If you ask me, the stuff on there's boring as shit," his brother scowled, Tobias shrugged. "What? It's not like anyone cares," then added, "Seriously he loves all that crap. There are times we don't see him for days."

"Shut up!" Terrence kicked him beneath the table, causing a yelp and receiving an evil look in return.

Lilly's eyes narrowed as the others turned to look at him, and shrugging he laughed, "OK so maybe I have watched The History Channel in the past, but only a little OK and only because-"

"Stop being a schmuck Tez." Harper rolled her eyes. "Your brother's right OK, none of us give a shit."

"I do," Baxter sat back with a smirk. "I think it's priceless. Gonna have a blast telling everyone back at The Peak what a dorkus you are when we finally get-"

"Give it a rest Baxter!" Lilly snapped his way before turning back to Terrence. "You know he's just winding you up. Having an actual clue what's going on here isn't exactly something the rest of us are going to hold against you."

"Princess..."

Following Kyrel's lead everyone except Baxter rose from their seats, as pushing aside the curtain Mai Mai stalked purposely into the room. She had Vereena and Arteth close behind her, and waved for the others to sit back down as she addressed Lilly. "I am told you've taken it upon yourself to issue orders now?"

"Err..."

"Stand your ground," whispered Terrence as he sat slowly back down.

"Well," Lilly offered an awkward smile. "Yes," she nodded. "Yes I have, that is my right as this clan's Princess isn't it?"

Mai Mai's eyebrows bounced up her forehead and crossing her arms she glanced suspiciously in Kyrel's direction.

"There's no need to look at him," Lilly sidestepped into the way. "We do have Princesses beyond the veil too, I do have some idea how things are meant to work."

"Oh?" The older woman turned back to her granddaughter with a look somewhere between surprise and scorn.

"Yes," nodded Lilly, "and as it happens, I've had enough of being pushed around. I know you're like in charge here and stuff but if you really expect me to take on this... this role of leadership, this being your Princess and stuff, then... well... frankly, I damn well intend to have a say."

***

"Can you believe the way Lilly spoke to her?" Harper giggled, clapping her hands together as she whispered. "Man I thought the old witch was gonna have herself an aneurysm or something."

As they were following close behind Toleth and a small contingent of villagers, Baxter also kept his voice low. "What I can't believe is that she didn't chicken out, she so wanted to, you could see it in her face."

"Nah," said Harper, "Lilly's a lot tougher than she lets on, I remember seeing her lay into Kirsby last year; I swear to God he was like redder than a fire engine and this close to blowing his top."

When she illustrated with finger and thumb Baxter hissed, "Fuck off, nobody gives Mr Kirsby lip. Well, except me that one time his fat bitch of a wife caught me selling ciggy's round the back of the technology block. Still, I didn't get him anywhere near blowing up. That man's got more patience than a dance instructor in a room of one legged ballerinas. Bastard chucked me in iso for five whole days without a frigging word, then it was *'alright Robert how are we doing today'* fucking prick... if they let us take stationary in there I'd a stabbed him in the eye with a pencil."

Giggling more Harper said, "Yeah see I think that's why they don't let us take shit like that in there... And anyway, he chucked Lilly into iso too, but I swear the way he dragged her away, man I thought I was about witness a Homer style strangulation right there."

"Serious?"

"Serious!"

"I don't think I believe you." Baxter shook his head. "What set it off?"

"Kirsby's fat bitch of a wife of course."

This time he giggled with her, grinning, "Of course."

"Fuck the Kirsbys, man." Tobias grumbled, from behind. "The only thing I can't believe right now is that Slater kept Tez with her." Baxter turned to him with a raised eyebrow.

"You what – We've crossed over into some fucked up other-wordly dimension, where horses have no legs, magic is commonplace, and as well as being expected to sleep on a bunch of straw, we're now off to fortify a magically hidden village in the middle of a forest; against an army sent by an evil warlord bitch – and Slater keeping your brother at her side as her resident brainiac is the *only* thing you can't believe?"

"Hey our helping out was his idea in the first place." added Tobias.

"He is helping out," said Harper, "Besides, if you ask me he got the bum deal; observe and decipher, then relay the info. Sounds like any old lesson at The Peak to me."

"Yeah," nodded Baxter, "Got that straight... way too much concentrating... Plus, and I urge you both to take a moment on this one... because we are not just fortifying..." as Toleth paused up ahead Baxter nodded to the larger crowd that had gathered to meet them and grinning added, "...we're in charge!"

It took a moment but looking to the group of men Tobias grinned also, and sighing Harper shook her head saying, "Man this is gonna be fun."

***

"This is why we use different words to direct our powers."

"Aah yes... but see when I use the Deebanaarie words I get some pretty bitching-"

"If we wish to achieve the *desired* results..." Kyrel's voice was stern through his tightly gritted teeth. "...we learn to use the *correct* words."

"I happen to like the results I get when I..."

Lilly's voice tapered off; worth more than a thousand words, the look on Kyrel's face stilled her tongue. With a smirk she turned away to where Vereena and Terrence sat watching from the edge of the training field. Kyrel shook his head and tried again.

"As you have seen, where *Kiiat Vash* raises the ground for you, allowing shaping and building, my use of the same words, does not remove all you've created,"

"And *Ta Varee* does!"

"Yes." Agreed Kyrel. "Because for me, for all Deebanaarie, it projects the correct force."

"But it does for me too."

"Ny."

"Don't you Ny me! You saw it yourself. The Da'ariel words don't always work for me and when they do the results aren't nearly as-"

"This is why you must focus," he sighed "the Laîoch and Tuâoch are so different in their nature. So far from one another that one can no more replace the other than it can control it."

"Well maybe you just have it all wrong."

"Wrong!"

"Yes, wrong!"

"If you even knew how long I have studied these magicks-"

"It wouldn't matter because they've still been around way longer than you have."

"Err guys..." with the pair shouting at each other now, they failed to notice Terrence attempting to interject.

"Just because you know more than me doesn't make you automatically right."

"Lilly," tried Vereena. "Kyrel... please." Neither of them noticed her.

"Ny dylur!" Kyrel's hands went upward, "All those times I wondered how it was, those humans who took you in found it so difficult to speak calmly with-"

"Oh no no no... don't you dare even go there."

Terrence and Vereena both frowned as they glanced to each other. "You don't get to start in on the Adoptives OK," added Lilly, "just because you played creepy old voyeur watching me all these years doesn't mean you can even begin to understand what I've-"

"What I understand is that Mairiel is right to call you an insolent child," hissed Kyrel. "How am I to teach you anything when you refuse to follow even the most basic principles of-"

"OK, OK..." Terrence jumped between them, arms outstretched and voice rising to a shout. "...Time out you two! Enough! No more! And please... for the love of all that is holy: no gesturing with the hands or saying words I can't understand, because you pair are seriously scaring the shit out of me."

They immediately stopped glaring at each other to glare at him instead; Kyrel with an eyebrow bouncing upward in illustration of how little of the statement he'd understood.

"OK," Terrence's voice came out as a slight laugh as he looked from one to the other. "We have quiet, that's... good. Now here's what's gonna happen: Lilly..." he pointed at her. "You're gonna go that way..." he nodded beyond her, then ushering Vereena with a wave added, "Vereena will go with you and neither of you is going to come back until you have seriously chilled out..." as the other girl nodded her agreement, her hand going to Lilly's shoulder, she gently guided her away. Terrence muttered, "or you know, at least until you're over the comment about your parents," before he turned to Kyrel adding, "Never a good idea by the way."

Kyrel sighed, making it clear this was a statement he did understand.

"Come on," Tez put a hand cautiously to his shoulder. "Let's see if we can't teach you a thing or two about the women from my realm."

"Lilly is not yet a woman." Kyrel shook his head and so did Terrence.

"Mmm hmm... and just like that we have a place to start."

Day Two: Part Three

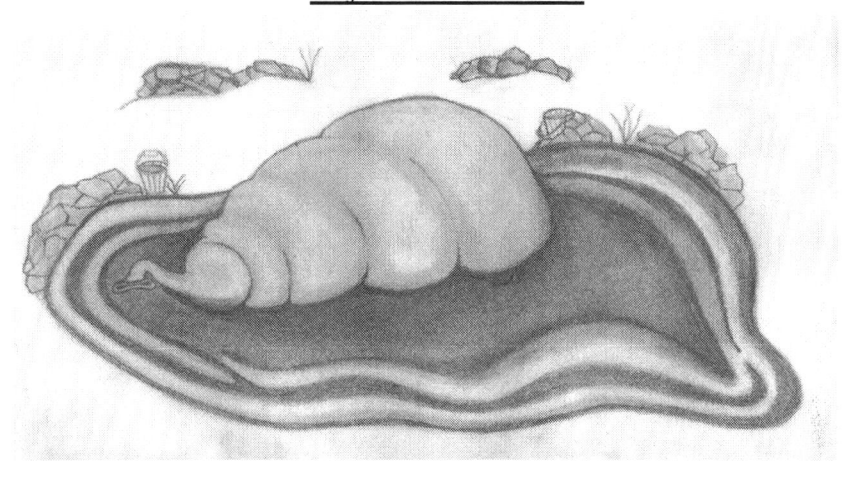

"OK, that's just disgusting." Harper held her nose as she and Tobias stared down into the trough of thick translucent green liquid.

"Shit man. What is that?" added Tobias, as using the stick he was carrying Baxter waved for the four men holding the trough to set it down. They did so very slowly.

Speaking in a pinched nasal voice Baxter covered his nose also. "You remember that stuff the old woman threatened to chuck us into yesterday?"

"Yeah sure," Tobias made gagging sounds between his words. "The moolah-ma-jig."

"Moolach," corrected Baxter "The matfiac moolach in fact."

"Yeah, whatever." Taking a step back Tobias nodded, "I remember. That part about it eating the flesh from our bones was…" more gagging was followed by: "kinda difficult to forget," as he took another step back. "Still doesn't exactly tell me *what* it is."

"Well apparently a Matfiac is a large slug like creature." Baxter grimaced. "And I don't mean large like the African variety OK… I mean… large like a frigging elephant. And this stuff… the Moolach… well near as I can tell…" with a deep measured breath he forced himself on "…is its slime."

"Slug slime?" Harper frowned. "That's our super-duper secret weapon… stinky slug slime"

"Super-duper stinky *extremely corrosive* slug slime," corrected Baxter. "Besides I'm pretty sure a great deal of it is also… the creature's faeces."

As they threw each other fresh looks of disgust, he prodded his stick deep into the foul substance and shrugged. "Turns out wood is impervious, but that part about it eating flesh…" he poked around a moment then carefully pulled the stick back out. On its end dangled the skeletal remains of some small creature which, covered in the goop, hissed and popped as it dripped a thick but steady stream of Moolach back into the trough.

"Eww gross." mumbled Tobias, while Harper, stepping closer for a better look frowned,

"Tell me you didn't-".

"Not me," shrugged Baxter before nodding in the direction of Toleth and his troop. "They felt I needed a *demonstration* and this little guy," he raised the stick higher. "Well, he was in the wrong place at the time…" the remains fell into the trough and the three classmates jumped back to avoid being splashed. "Kind of sad really…" Baxter shrugged, "looked like he would a made a great pet."

***

"Why can she not just do as she is told?" Kyrel sounded more puzzled than angry, as pacing back and forth he made his complaints to Terrence. "I thought she at least knew my main reason for being here is to help her. To see my sister does not succeed in her efforts."

"I think she does know that." Terrence shrugged from his spot on the ground. "I don't think I've ever seen her get on so well with anyone the way she's trying to with you. If you must know she's kind of a loner in school. Never stops to give anyone else the time of day"

Kyrel paused to frown at him.

"But why should she be expected to do so? Does your great sky flame not indicate this as ours does?"

"Our great sky…" watching Kyrel glance to the sun Terrence nodded, "Oh! Yes… yes of course it does. I just meant… no you know what never mind… the point is I really don't think Lilly's trying to be disagreeable. I mean she wants to be heard and she wants to know everything that's really going on here but bottom line, I do think she trusts you. If you could maybe just give her a bit more explanation on that whole using the right words thing I'm sure she'll be more willing to do things the way you tell her."

"The people of your realm truly do have peculiar ways of making their points." Kyrel shook his head with an irritable expression.

"You think so?"

"Saying something you do *not* mean," He frowned at Terrence "as a means of stating something completely unrelated to it that you *do* mean."

"Yeah," the twin chuckled. "I… I guess we kind of do."

"You really think knowing more will make Lilly compliant?"

"Err… compliant, maybe not totally, but sure… I mean… if it's relevant why shouldn't she know?"

"So many things are occurring both inside and outside of this village that could be deemed relevant." Kyrel sighed.

"Then I guess she needs to know many things," suggested Terrence "Just another thing peculiar to the people of my realm; we have a real issue with knowing where we stand."

"I do not prevent her from looking to her feet." Kyrel frowned and grinning Terrence nodded "You know if I didn't know you're clueless I might think you were trying to be deep."

"Deep…" Kyrel's frown increased.

***

Across the field, beyond a raised embankment, the girls sat side by side with Lilly tearing up handfuls of grass while ranting to the younger girl.

"I mean seriously, what is his deal? I thought he wanted me to win this thing. If this sister of his is as uber scary as everyone's making out, shouldn't I be allowed to pull out all the stops? It's not as if I'm making shit up. You all saw how much more power I'm getting from those Laîoch words-"

"Tuâoch." Vereena corrected.

"Yeah whatever… the ones he uses. They're doing more for me so why should I be stuck using that other set?"

"Because your bloodline is Da'ariel," suggested Vereena. A scolding look from Lilly had her adding, "I believe Kyrel is concerned about your abilities to control the Tuâoch. The Laîoch is your birthright. It is the force you were born to use. You may feel very much in control now, but the ability to wield the forces… it is much like that of the Gaashmay, it is a power drawn from within and if Mordrel's troops are upon you… well you may find yourself less capable with that which is not truly natural to you."

"Like any of this is natural to me." Lilly's hands went up. "Anyways, last I checked I'm the one whose life is in peril here. I think I have a right to choose a few risks of my own."

"I can see why you would think that," Vereena spoke carefully. "But Kyrel has a far greater understanding of the risks than you or I can possess. He has studied many of the sacred writings of his own people and mastered more elements than most males ever do."

"Yet you're all convinced he would lose against his sister?"

"He is still *only* a man Lilly. You have been told how these powers work. You know it is the women who bear more strength in the magicks."

"Sure, I know." She sounded glum and Vereena's tone perked up in response.

"Still… even among my people Kyrel's skill is revered. Why, it is said he could stand well against those that practised before the last Great War."

"So he's good. So what? I'm good too. In two days I've got a pretty decent handle on my Gaashmay and I've learnt to control three different forces. Doesn't that count? Isn't that something to be revered?"

"Oh yes," nodded Vereena. "It is of course. All here are impressed with your progress. Only today I heard my cousin Arteth speaking of you with much pride."

"You did?" Lilly turned to stare at the other girl. "What did he say?"

"Yes. Yes I did. He was speaking with Mai Mai, when I went to give her your message earlier. I… I confess I heard a good deal before I could get their attention."

"And?"

"And Arteth speaks highly of your abilities. He says the swiftness with which you're learning each force, is encouraging. That you will soon be unsurpassed even by those of your-" pausing there Vereena looked to her feet, before adding "even by Kyrel."

Sighing Lilly said, "Sure, I get it: Good as he is only *I* can take down Mordrel. I'm not *chosen;* I'm screwed. New world, new powers, new problems; same old shit: I'm on my own."

"No." Vereena turned to face her cousin. "Your being alone before could not be helped, but now you are home and with your true family. Your mother sent you away only to protect you, and we as your clan will stop at nothing to do the same. You must believe this Lilly; if you trust nothing else here you must trust what you mean to us, to your people."

"What I mean?"

"Yes. Your existence brought a hope back to the Da'ariel that had been lost for generations. The first Da'ariel in over three hundred cycles to be born with the mark. The *full* mark! Even before you learnt of your powers you were a sign that all is not lost. That the old ways *can* return. You are the living hope of the Da'ariel, Lilly. That is the real reason Mordrel seeks to end you."

"It is also why she is too late." Both girls turned to see Kyrel staring down at them. Terrence stood a short ways back, hands stuffed in his pockets and a smug smirk on his face.

"The lessons of time have been harsh on all of Azeron," added Kyrel, "and now that your people know of you, now that they know there is hope; there isn't a one among them who would stand by and watch the likes of my sister take that away from them again."

With a nod Lilly rose slowly to her feet. "And what about you? You're not Da'ariel. How can you want so much to help me take down your own sister? How can you-"

"All... of Azeron... has suffered... Lilly." His tone had softened from earlier, but as their eyes met, there was a hardness in his that had her gulping. "What these Da'ariel know of my people, is not all there is to know. I am not the only Deebanaarie opposed to my sister's continued rule," he assured her. "I am just the only one able to seek a solution."

"And that's me? That's where I fit in... I'm your solution?"

"You are so much more than that."

Again pride filled his eyes. Lilly turned to Vereena with a raised eyebrow.

"Both people suffer? The Deebanaarie-"

"Are a dying race." Kyrel added as the younger girl nodded.

"It is true," Vereena's eyes met his a moment. "The Deebanaarie control most of Azeron's lands and they raid our villages continuously, but it could be said they do so only because their own resources are so much less than-"

"Most of my people are starving." Kyrel shook his head. "In Crizoleth it is easy to ignore how barren the lands have become. Supplies arrive daily and trade goes on. There is little reason to ever leave the comfort of my ancestral home. Yet beyond the walls of the city... outside is but wasteland and those Deebanaarie unfortunate enough to dwell there; Lilly they need you every bit as much as the Da'ariel do."

A small gasp escaped Vereena. Muttering she covered her mouth with her hand. Seeing this Kyrel hissed something in their language at her.

"OK no!" Lilly raised a hand. "No more of that shit. I want to know everything... what was that all about."

Vereena threw her a hesitant look and Kyrel added.

"Either you do your duty Qin Am Ness or I will," and looking distinctly cornered Vereena nodded.

"Forgive me cousin. It is just that I do not believe Mai Mai wants us discussing such-"

"She's deliberately keeping things from me?"

For a second Vereena's mouth flapped wordlessly until she said, "It is not that she-"

"Your grandmother does not believe you knowing the plight of her enemy, would be advantageous to you in any upcoming battle."

"Her enemy?" Lilly turned to Kyrel. "I thought they were *my* enemy? I thought the Deebanaarie and the Da'ariel were all en-"

"Lilly." His tone stilled her tongue and a heat rose in his eyes "... Am I not Deebanaarie? Have I not been here from the beginning to ensure your safety? I tell you in my lands... every day... many perish because they need this change every bit as much as those you see around you. Our lowborns know it though. Their offspring are always the first to go, and the rations assigned to their classes were pitiful to begin with. They *are* Deebanaarie. They are *not* evil. They need so much of what the Da'ariel have, yet archaic beliefs that persevere across all of Azeron steer them to desperation."

"Seems there's many things your grandmother chooses not to share with you," said Terrence. "Sorry," he shrugged, as Lilly's gaze landed on him. "I just... I figured you might want to know; there's a lot more going on here than meets the eye..."

Closing her eyes she took in a deep breath before opening them again and shaking her head with a sigh,

"I really can't do this."

Watching her walk off Vereena also sighed,

"That was not necessary Kyrel, you should not have forced me to-"

"She should know everything and it is *your* place to tell her."

"Everything?" Vereena turned to him. "Including the truth about you?"

***

By the time Kyrel caught up to Lilly she was at the village walls using her new-found powers to raise huge pillars of earth.

"Vrelgest Dylur!" Kyrel covered his nose as he approached. "Moolach?"

"So I'm told," she said as another pillar went upward. "Where's Tez and Vereena?"

"I gave them leave to visit the room of sacred writings." Kyrel's voice came out distorted beneath the hand he was using to pinch his nose. "The boy: Terrence – he believes with translation he may find information of use to you."

"Good old Tez," muttered Lilly, "always thinking way too much."

Watching as she sent another trough of the stinky Moolach just above the village's fenced boundary on a tilted pillar of earth, Kyrel gestured to it. "Why are you-"

"The others say this stuff is wicked corrosive," she explained. "They think it'll make a solid defence against your sister's troops."

"The intention is to pour this down onto them?" his tone was dubious.

"Yes. Why?" she turned to face him. "Do you see a problem with that plan?"

"Ny... No..." Kyrel shook his head, eyes glued to the currently rising pillar. "No problem. Done correctly it shall devastate them. It is a very good plan."

"Yeah, that's what I figured."

"Who... if I may ask-"

"Baxter," she sighed. "He's had Arteth's men moving this stuff since they left us earlier."

"An impressive plan, I should like to hear any other ideas he has."

"Yeah well they're all off finding weapons. After hearing how we were ambushed in the forest earlier Tobias thinks we should probably all be armed too, he has the others convinced the Da'ariel must have more of an arsenal hidden somewhere."

"I fear they will be disappointed," muttered Kyrel. "The Da'ariel are not known for their wealth of arms." Catching a sideways glance from her he added, "Still, your friends show initiative. Certainly more than I expected, we should have put them to work sooner."

"Or maybe we shouldn't have put them to work at all."

"Oh no, I would say you made the right choice in letting them-"

"Maybe none of us should be helping out here... maybe we should just refuse to get involved on account of this whole damn place being screwed up and there being nothing any of us can possibly do to fix such a broken world."

A moment's silence followed before Kyrel said, "You are still upset."

"You think?"

For a moment he looked to his feet, while Lilly moved along to the next trough.

"I am sorry," he moved to her side, "about earlier and anything I said that offended you." His tone was solemn. "I have always been... prone to impatience and it is difficult for me... to choose my words carefully when using your tongue."

A chuckle escaped Lilly and seeing confusion as she glanced his way she shrugged, "Language," before commanding more earth upward with another "Kiiat Vash," then she sighed, "Tongue just kinda sounds... weird, especially in sentences like that one." Getting no sign of comprehension from him she added, "Beyond the veil we would more often say language, not tongue."

"Oh! Of course," he nodded, "My mistake. I apologise for that also."

"Are your people expecting me to save them too Kyrel?" she moved on to the next trough and following her he shook his head.

"That is something they could use, but no... Most Deebanaarie would never speak against my sister. Daring to hope of being saved from her is..." giving it further thought he swallowed hard adding, "Most still believe we are too great a people for things to ever need to change in Azeron now."

"So they suffer in silence, believing things are as good as they get?"

"I suppose that is what they do yes."

"Beyond the veil we'd call that content. It's not generally a bad thing."

"Then I suppose I should be more happy for my people."

Lilly threw him a cutting look and Kyrel sighed, "I did not tell you in order to distress you further. Your friend Terrence, he… he thought you would want to know the *whole* truth."

"Of course I do." she hissed. "I just don't know what I'm meant to do with it is all. The Da'ariel believe in me, they want change. The Deebanaarie," shrugging more she shook her head, "from what you say they might need me but…"

"I suppose what you should do, is exactly what you have been doing."

"And how does that help them? Those poor starving children you mentioned, how does that help any of-"

"They are *my* people Lilly. You help me, by helping *yours,* and I shall do what *I* can for *mine.*"

"Then that's why you're here? Why you're helping me and these Da'ariel? You want to overthrow your sister for the good of your people?"

Kyrel shrugged, clearly considering for a moment how to answer, before he asked, "Is it not as good a reason as any other?"

"Yeah, sure… I guess it is." Lilly sighed.

She shot another pillar of earth upward with the next trough and asked.

"There's still a lot left for me to learn though isn't there?"

"Yes." nodded Kyrel "A great deal. However I am not-"

"And these powers…" she turned to him. "The forces we control. How many more are there?"

"There are said to be more than ten separate forces." He sighed. "Still… even if there were time, I regret that I cannot teach you any others."

"What? Why not? Because you're scared I'll lose control when things get a little hairy and I'm faced with actual battle?"

"No," shrugged Kyrel. "I… I cannot teach you more because the only other forces I myself have mastered are outside your abilities."

"Oh come on!" she snorted, "Vereena was just telling me how kick ass everyone's saying my skills are. Apparently Arteth can't stop talking me up. You, I had pegged as my main supporter. Are you telling me now that you're doubting me?"

"There is no doubting of you Lilly. The power in you *is* immense! It is just that the forces are much like the ton- the language… some are good for all; others are… blood specific."

"You're saying I can't learn everything you know because I'm not Deebanaarie?"

"I'm saying you are meant for other things… *because* you are Da'ariel."

"And by other things…" Lilly's head snapped round and she fixed him with a calculative stare. "You mean other powers…right? The forces… there are some I can learn that you can't… That Mordrel can't! That's what you mean isn't it?" When his only answer was to sigh she said, "So there's still lots I can learn."

Following her to the next trough Kyrel watched it rise as he added, "You have truly done well and yes your control is much improved, but we really should work on honing your use of the Gaashmay and these three forces you've learnt already."

"Sorry Kyrel but three out of ten, not gonna cut it."

With returning confusion he began to shake his head, "I do not think I-"

"It's not enough!" her voice rose slightly, only to lower as she gazed upward adding, "Even the clouds here are wicked crazy. What is that anyway... some kind of storm?"

Also looking up, Kyrel's eyes widened and he stumbled backward muttering, "Nydrel dylur!" and grabbing her arm he almost pulled her over.

"What is it?" asked Lilly. "Is something wrong?"

"Everything!" His grip increased as he yanked her away from the wall. "Everything is now wrong."

"Hey!" Lilly's protests were a reflex only. Sensing from him some new unknown danger she began running with him. "What about the plan? I only have a few more of those pillars to raise."

"The plan is ended. We are out of time. Faster! We must get you away from here." Raising three fingers to his lips he let loose a shrill whistle, which carried across the village only to be taken up by others as he yelled "Ginaten! Ginaten! Cat ya vac Ginaten!" The call was also taken up by others and he and Lilly were soon pushing their way through a throng of Da'ariel, all armed and racing the other way towards the gates.

**

"I really don't like the sound of this." Tobias trailed behind his two classmates, with him a selection of weapons larger than he could make use of, while Toleth lead them through the growing crowd.

"You must all move faster." He paused, holding open a curtain on the hut he'd reached and waved for them to keep moving through the increasing crowd of Da'ariel. "Inside, inside..." he beckoned, "All of you be faster!"

"OK," Baxter mumbled in Harper's ear. "I think this place just went to DEFCON One."

"Funny..." she told him, "looks more like blind panic to me."

"That's because they don't have a Defcon One." Tobias cut in. "Only armies led by guys come up with cool shit like that. That's how screwed we are right now!"

"Yeah, gotta say," Baxter looked skyward where a dense cloud of darkest black had settled above the village. "Things do not seem to be looking up." At first it had been a blip, now as the three watched, it blanketed enough of the sky above to have turned the bright sunny day into an impenetrable night.

"Definitely *not* good!" nodded Baxter.

"Oh shut up." Harper pushed both boys aside with a sneer. "Let's at least find out what's going on before we join in on the blind panic."

They followed her to where a group, including Lilly and Kyrel, had gathered around Mairiel's large wooden chair.

With most discussion spoken in Azeron's native language; all three were instantly submerged in an incoherent babble of white noise.

Elbowing her way through to Kyrel's side, Harper spoke around him to Lilly.

"Do you know what's going on?"

"Not really."

Mairiel barked orders and men and women scurried away as swiftly as others were entering the hut.

"Well, I could be wrong," Baxter poked his head in between theirs. "But that whole battle to the death thing... I reckon it just started."

"Then we should be out there." Harper's gaze skirted the door, "Finishing those-"

"None of you will go outside." Kyrel gave them a cursory glance. "Without protection from the Ginaten you will *not* return." Turning back to the crowd he addressed Mairiel in Azeronian and the babble quietened to a lull.

"Ginaten?" Harper whispered over to Lilly; who pointed to the door then back with a shrug.

Hearing, "Qin Am Ness" in Mairiel's response to Kyrel, Lilly scanned the room, muttering to herself, before she too became engrossed in the conversation she couldn't understand.

A few seconds later, the curtain they'd entered through was pulled down by a male villager who fell inside and rolled to the ground. Screaming, he writhed, one hand clutching the back of his neck.

Most in the room had unsheathed some sort of blade and a handful of them sprang forward ready to defend. A command from Kyrel had them backing up cautiously while he leapt forward instead. He pinned the man belly down, with a knee either side to keep his arms from flailing. Scanning the faces around them Lilly saw fear and awe in the eyes of everyone but Mai Mai. The man's shrill screams turned to a blood freezing roar when Kyrel pressed two fingers to the back of the neck and speaking through tightly clenched teeth said, "Ta esta, ta'at, ta dres verfelt inst: Ta varee."

Both Kyrel and the Da'ariel beneath began emanating a mild yellow glow. Then, as if pushed by an unseen force Kyrel's head tipped back, the same glow showing through his closed eyelids and shooting momentarily from his nostrils and mouth, before the latter fell open in a silent scream.

"Shit!" hissed Tobias.

"Yeah," Baxter nodded as they all watched the glow fade to a single light at the nape of the man's neck. "I can definitely second that."

Tearing the blob of light from the man, Kyrel tossed it to the ground where its glow diminished, leaving a shiny black beetle the size of a child's fist.

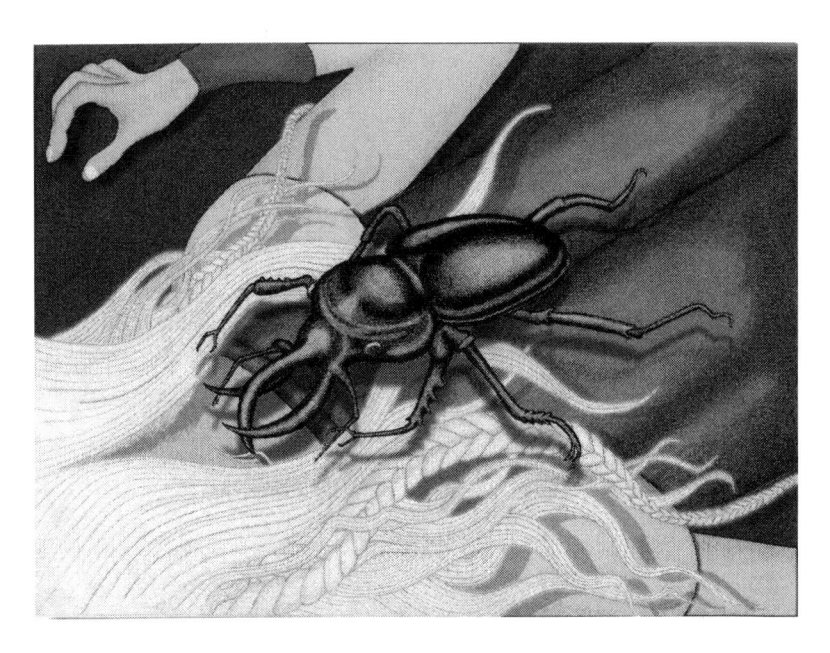

It skittered about, jerking in circles. The two hooked pincers protruding viciously from its head snapped open and shut several times. Then a woman leapt out of the crowd, pummelling the creature with the end of her staff until there was nothing but pieces of shell and dark purple goo all splattered together on the floor.

Kyrel slowly rose to his feet, head and shoulders slumped forward, as he almost toppled back before achieving steady enough footing to stand straight.

"OK, I don't even want to know what that was." muttered Tobias.

Outside the hut the shouts of angry surprise were fast becoming screams of fear, and turning to Mai Mai once more Kyrel said, "Will you continue this? Or are we getting her out of here?"

A solemn nod from the older woman saw her stepping aside as she gestured to the door at the rear of the hut.

"There is more cover this way, Arteth will see you reach the paths."

"Come!" Kyrel grabbed Lilly's hand and pulled her with him.

"OK," Baxter took up pace behind them, "I reckon that's our cue."

"What about Tez?" Tobias trailed behind.

"Hey if you wanna go look for him, be my guest," replied Baxter "But it's not as if *you* stand a chance if he ain't had the sense to get *his* head down... he's the smart one after all."

With a scowl Tobias kept moving, following the others from that room to a next, then out into the open, for a brief but revealing moment.

Dozens more Da'ariel were dropping to the ground in agony, hands pressed to the napes of their necks.

"Pssst! Come on!" Tobias yanked Harper's cuff as she froze watching a woman whose body had stopped writhing and was now contorting and bending at unnatural angles. Harper wrenched her eyes away - following the others into the relative safety of indoors. Through one more door and they had reached the central dining area. Two of Arteth's troop set about moving the huge table and its chairs, off its dirty threadbare rug.

"Ny Mech!" Kyrel muttered at the sight of the huge trapdoor. Arteth threw him a cursory glance; registering his surprise but saying nothing of it and proceeded down the narrow steps that had been revealed.

Clinging to the walls in the darkness the group converged a few steps down as Arteth pulled a torch from the wall and dipping it into a bowl of fluorescent green liquid, bashed it on the wall three times before striking it like a giant match.

All four classmates stared at the bright green flame which sprung to life atop it.

Dust fell from above as Arteth's men could be heard putting the rug, the table, and the chairs back into place.

"Whoa!" Tobias clung to the walls a second time and following his gaze the others did the same.

The area they'd stopped on was a platform linking the enclosed steps they just descended, to what appeared to be a million others all spiralling downward with a vast chasm at their centre.

"Where are we going?" Tobias grumbled from the back.

"Away from here." shrugged Harper.

"Yeah but what about Tez? Shouldn't we go back to-"

"Look, he isn't dumb enough to be out in the thick of that," Baxter whispered, a dash more compassion in his voice now. "And he isn't dumb enough to be looking for you either. You gotta trust that he's OK, like he'll be doing about you right now and figure the rest out later."

"There is no need for concern." Arteth called back to them. "The other you should join us soon."

"What the fuck's that supposed to mean?" mumbled Tobias as they turned a corner in through a door that led them upward in a second enclosed space. "How the fuck is he meant to find us down here?"

"He is with the Lady Vereena…" Kyrel's voice came out strained, "and she is now a called Qin Am Ness: she *will* return to Lilly's side."

"But what about-"

"It means shut your frigging cake hole," hissed Baxter. "No one here has any wish to go back up through those doors and we all know that means you included, so give it a fucking rest." He glanced around as they came out of another door and back onto a spiral staircase. "In case you haven't noticed, this place is a goddamn maze and I for one am trying to pay attention."

"You OK?" Lilly whispered up to Kyrel. In the darkness no one but her had noticed how the hand he'd grabbed her with had become the one he now clung to her with.

"I will be fine." He forced a nod "I am just… I am-"

"Looking like you're about to pass out is what you are." Though she was still all whispers, her tone was all concern. "Not that I can see much of anything, but I can feel you OK, you're like... drained or something." When he didn't respond she added, "Well, you *are,* right?"

"Yes," he hissed with effort, "but I will be fine."

"It's because of what you did to that man isn't it? Some kind of magicks right? Can I do-"

"You will not try!" Kyrel's tone became sharp, enough to bring on a wheeze that became a cough.

"Kyrel?" Arteth called back.

"Keep moving," instructed Kyrel, "All is... OK." turning back to Lilly he added. "*Never,* you understand?"

"Sure," she sighed, "I get it, never try that, like I could anyway I barely caught a word of it."

They made their way up and down stairs, in and out of alcoves, with the dim green light Arteth carried guiding their way.

The stairs eventually gave way to tunnels, the rankness of damp earth enveloping them as doorways—leading to further dark—dotted the walls around them.

"This place is immense!" muttered Harper.

"And thousands of years old," said Baxter.

"You reckon?"

"Hey," he nodded her way, "this is one hell of an excavation. I reckon the Da'ariel are still working on it."

"These tunnels are not Da'ariel." Kyrel's voice seemed a bit stronger now. "They are not Deebanaarie either. My people mostly consider this place a myth. So assuming my eyes are not tricking me, we are now deep within the lands. Tualavan; Ancients built this place. The magicks they must have possessed..." he gazed around, voice croaky as if choking up for a cry. "This explains so many things."

"You didn't think this place was a myth did you?"

"Well I spent two cycles in Mairiel's village and never knew of that entrance." He scowled toward Arteth, adding, "but yes I did believe some may still exist and possibly nearby. Your mother she..."

"What?" Lilly looked up the second he hesitated. "What about her?"

"The eve on which she left with you," interjected Arteth "Kyrel killed many of our clan in his attempts to recover information as to where she'd gone."

Kyrel turned away as Lilly's gaze intensified. "He suspected an entrance to these tunnels existed," added Arteth, "and may have stopped to search had Herrella not been spotted heading away from our village."

A muscle tensed in Kyrel's jaw but he said nothing and a few minutes later Baxter was pointing ahead of them.

"Hey fraidy-dogs, check it out."

Seeing the two blobs under a second green torch with a handful of men behind them, Tobias muttered, "Thank fuck!" and pushing his way through the others, ran ahead yelling. "Tez! Shit man where have you been?"

"There was this entrance... by that room of writings." Terrence explained as he handed a heavy sack over to Baxter. "We came down all these steps, then we were here... in these tunnels. How amazing is this place?"

"Yeah we're all pretty psyched," sneered Baxter, "did you see those creatures up there? And what the fuck is all this?" he waved the sack at Terrence. "We're making a getaway here. What the fuck are you doing?"

"They're Veldii." Terrence shrugged. "I mean bindings... I mean err... scrolls, I meant scrolls! A lot of them talk about powers like Lilly's, the others are... well I think they could all be important. I've carried them a long way though. You don't mind right?"

Baxter lifted the sack over his shoulder with a grumble and continued after Lilly, Kyrel, Arteth and the men of Vereena's troop. The others hung back discussing their not-so mass exodus from the Da'ariel village.

A few minutes later Vereena was trotting along the edge of the slightly increased group and sidling up to her cousin Arteth. "Are Mai Mai and Toleth to meet us at the Pass?"

"Toleth will surely be there. Mai Mai diesh ny."

"Ny! What do you mean?" Shock made Vereena's voice rise and her cousin lowered his in an effort to convey she should do the same.

"She could not leave, Veer... Deelurg eêst a Leyavanya..."

Kyrel perked up to listen as Vereena glanced over her shoulder, and Lilly noticed the obvious distress on the girl's face. Turning to Kyrel she asked in a whisper what the pair were talking about, and raising an eyebrow he nodded toward them.

"Ask her."

"Who, Vereena?" a snigger escaped Lilly as she watched the younger girl gesturing along to whispered words. "She doesn't really look much like she wants to tell me."

"Qin Am Ness..." Kyrel barked, "Lilly wishes to know what you speak of!"

Everyone paused as Vereena and Arteth turned to face them.

"Arteth is returning to the village," she said, checking everyone's faces with a quick scan. "He and the others will meet us by first light."

"Meet where?" asked Kyrel. "At Duruth Schtaal? Surely that's not possible... Just how much of this cave system do you Da'ariel have mapped?"

"Enough to hide from you Deebanaarie when the need arises," cut in Arteth. Ignoring the curtness in his voice, Kyrel shrugged,

"And why is it your people are not hiding down here right now? Those Ginaten are here by my sister's will; her sprite Neenia is at work. Surely Mairiel would not rather lose her people. Lilly is here. What else up there is worth fighting for?"

"Our home is up there." Vereena's words came out as a sharp hiss.

"Ginaten do not care for Da'ariel homes, Qin Am Ness." Kyrel spat back in an equally ferocious tone. "Ginaten care for magicks and Mairiel claims no access."

"You dare to expect the *truth*, Kyrel?" Arteth shook his head. "What have you ever done to deserve truth from my people?" A second's hard staring had Kyrel turning away with a heavy sigh.

Arteth nodded and pulling a large bag off his shoulder he turned back to

Vereena, "Remember, first light or you keep going. Don't stop until you're inside Zanreal."

"I know." She took the bag from him. "I remember, OK. Just try to hurry," her pained expression belying her true discomfort with the plan despite her calm demeanour..

Kyrel pulled his hand from Lilly's, placing it to her shoulder instead. "Do you still trust me princess?"

"You kind of told me not to." She bit her lip sensing from his tone how disappointed she was about to be.

"Well trust that I will return to you."

"Return? Where are you…" she glanced to where Arteth now headed back toward them. "You can't! You have to stay with-"

Kyrel's arm hit the wall as he stopped Arteth in his tracks. "I am returning with you."

"But the Princess…" a quick look to Lilly had him changing tack, "I'm no fool to your magicks Kyrel I know how low you must be right now. What use can you possibly be to-"

"Those Ginaten are on the scent of the last Tuâlavan. You have an orb of Leyavanya up there!" Arteth's jaw dropped and Kyrel nodded, "If I could figure it out, you must know Mordrel has too. If she gets hold of that, Lilly's Kalaareem will be meaningless and if I am *not* up there she *is* going to get hold of it." He turned back to Lilly, "If I do not go you will never be safe." She nodded and he turned back to Arteth. "Well… Lead the way!"

***

Watching the protective sphere around the Da'ariel village first appear, then dissolve beneath the swarm of Ginat beetles felt like a triumph in itself to Drellaeleon. Despite relentless searches and the losses of many troops the Deebanaarie had never succeeded in finding this place.

The Da'ariel were good with secrets and the location of Mairiel's clan was among their best kept. Now three days as Mordrel's General and she had already uncovered it. Her Queen would be pleased, even if her sprite had played a significant role in this discovery.

Signalling for her men to wait she watched as what was left of the swarm began to depart. These creatures were more voracious than dependable; charging in too early could be as disastrous for her forces as it had been for the village.

***

"Mai Mai will not be pleased at your returning with me." Arteth scrambled through the hole Kyrel had created and out into the foliage just behind the village.

"Mairiel should have told me the truth." Kyrel crawled out after him. "If I had known I never would have kept Lilly here."

"She told you it was never our plan; you are the one who did not want to listen. Insisting you could protect my cousin, yet now you abandon her for the chance of a bigger prize."

"Is that truly what you see… me seeking out the orb for myself?" Kyrel clung to the nearest tree, steadying himself as Arteth turned to him with a scowl.

"What am I supposed to see Kyrel? Should I be fooled by you again? Make-believe that you've changed?"

"You should see the truth. That I did what I had to at the time."

"You did what came easiest because you could not decide where you stood."

"That is *not* true."

"No you're right. I am sorry. You betrayed my people as readily as you betrayed your own. So obviously where you stood was always at your *own* side."

The obvious hurt in Kyrel's eyes compelled Arteth to drive the knife deeper.

"Oh yes, the Great Kyrel D'vey; so consumed by his hunger for the magicks, that all around him cease to matter."

"You all mattered to me Arteth. Surely you haven't forgotten so much of those days; I know you were young but…"

Grabbing Arteth's arm he pulled him down among the foliage and pointed.

Turning slightly the younger man spotted the handful of Deebanaarie warriors heading toward them on foot and his hand went to the hilt of his sword. Instantly Kyrel's hand was over his and turning back to see him shake his head with warning in his eyes Arteth scowled whispering.

"Even without you I can take them!"

"Are you so eager for the fight? They're scouting for signs of life this side of the hill. If they don't report back many more will come. If they do report back, telling of nothing here we keep a clear escape route for Mairiel and the others."

Arteth's eyes narrowed and he turned to watch the troop a moment longer then seeing they were indeed passing by drew his hand away from his sword, muttering, "So be it. Just know that I have forgotten nothing!"

"Except how you once trusted me-"

"Oh no, that I remember clearest of all." The words came out strained. "Both mine and Lilly's mothers are dead because of the trust we *all* placed in you."

"And you think I don't regret what happened?" Kyrel kept his voice low. "The way things ended was…" He shook his head, "I would give anything to bring them back…" seeing the troop disappear from sight he shook his head. "We do not have time for this. Your grandmother has made certain you will never trust me again and for that I cannot blame her." He stood cautiously. "On the other hand… if her desire to keep things from me has endangered Lilly unnecessarily the blame will lie only with her. Come…" he peeked out around a tree. "Let us go while we still can."

***

Inside the village, Mairiel and what was left of her own and Arteth's troops were gathered in what passed for their clan's armoury. They'd set fires in both its doorways to keep out the Ginats and were now waiting out this first wave of the attack; with hopes of being able to make a run for it once their own people were done ripping each other apart at the behest of the giant beetles.

It was a decent plan in theory but keeping the fires effective and controlled was a delicate task and every time balance was a little off something unexpected would go up in flames or a Ginat would dive bomb into the room; compelling many in the group to lash out fiercely at the same time.

Mai Mai would have demanded more self-control but these creatures brought a chill even to her spine. Her three sprites gathered around her all cowering at the sounds from outside. With their taste for anything rich in thar the Ginats were no friend to these sprites, who could not control them as Mordrel's gershurian sprite Neenia could.

As the noise outside began to die down, their hopes were raised, then dashed by the sound of a horn signalling Mordrel's forces to move in.

"We must make a break for it now Mai Mai." One of the women in the troop spoke as she backed up closer to their Queen. Like everyone else in the room she would give her life before letting anything happen to Mairiel.

"No." said Mai Mai. "If we leave now what's left of the swarm will converge on us. That call was many leagues out, we have time to-"

Beneath them the floor began to rumble and the troops parted as a small fissure was followed by a crack which weaved its way halfway across the hut floor before crumbling in to reveal a hole.

"Dig!" Arteth's voice called up through the hole. "All of you. Dig!"

In seconds the first to reach the hole were down on all fours tearing up earth like a pack of dogs. The others kept guard on the doors, one man close enough to peer out reported being able to see Mordrel's troops tearing down the hill that surrounded the village. A second later he ducked his head back and swatted a Ginat from the air as it breached the flaming barrier. With singed wings it couldn't rise from the ground and another man splattered it with the hilt of his sword but its presence still brought enough fear to have the doorway fires stoked and the group at the floor digging all the faster.

After a few painfully long minutes the hole was big enough for Arteth to poke his head up and call for Mai Mai to depart the room first.

The three sprites followed her and as she crawled a few feet and sat against the wall – standing room was not provided – she stared speculatively at the crumpled heap that was Kyrel as her companions joined them one by one in the narrow tunnel.

Visibly exhausted, Kyrel's eyes fell to the large pouch she had tied at her waist and nodding he mumbled,

"Just how many do you have?"

Mai Mai's nose went in the air. "Do you not have a ward to take care of Kyrel?"

"Take care of her is exactly what I am trying to do," his words came out as a sneer. "How could you have even one of those here this entire time and not tell me?"

"I will not discuss Da'ariel matters with you."

"Your Da'ariel matters put everyone, including the Princess in danger."

Arteth scrambled over to them.

"We do not have time for this."

"Had you not brought him with you we wouldn't require it." Mai Mai turned her indignant tone on her grandson; un-rattled he replied,

"I would not have been able to get you out if I had not," before turning to Kyrel and asking "Can you do it?"

"Do what?" Asked Mai Mai, "The Deebanaarie is exhausted! I will be surprised if he can crawl back out of here."

"I believe so." Kyrel ignored her invective as his eyes drifted to her pouch again.

"Give me one." She looked from him to Arteth and seeing the pleading in her grandson's eyes she began to shake her head.

"You can't seriously expect-"

"If you saw the legions descending on our village Mairiel you would know we do not want them on our trail. Yes, Kyrel is exhausted, but with its aid he can cover our tracks."

Grudgingly she untied the pouch enough to stick a hand inside and pull out one of the luminescent balls.

Drained as Kyrel was his eyes lit up and seeing this Mai Mai handed the orb to Arteth, "Stay with him. I will lead the others out."

"Yes Mai Mai. There are few Ginaten where we entered but you will have to double back to find the ancient seal. Close it after you. Kyrel has enough drelga for the two of us to make it to Duruth Schtaal."

"See you *do* make it." She crawled away calling back. "Cat ya vac inst!"

Kyrel and Arteth pressed themselves to the walls as the others clambered on past them.

Once there was enough room for them to crawl back toward the hole Arteth helped Kyrel along asking,

"You are sure you can do this?" as he steadied him.

"Just get me close enough; the orb will do the rest."

As they knelt at the hole Arteth placed it into his outstretched hand.

Taken aback by the cold emanating from it Kyrel hissed before muttering, "Let this work," and mustering what strength he could, called out, "Viileerium."

The din above was tremendous as he drew his—now glowing—hand back and the entire hut above them caved in on itself. Debris fell into, then blocked up the hole and for a second Arteth stared at the Deebanaarie as the glow in his hand spread up his arm then faded out across his body.

Kyrel gasped, falling back against the wall, though stunned he appeared stronger and shaking his head as if to clear it grinned, "Well I think that worked."

"You look…" Awe filled Arteth's voice. "You are feeling better?"

"Very much so." Kyrel grinned, clutching the orb as he stared at it in amazement. "The power in this is…" then seeing the way Arteth looked dubiously at it he knew they shared similar thoughts: With him back at full strength there was no way the younger Da'ariel could hope to take it from him. "Here…" Kyrel's smile waned "…you should probably-"

"Yes," Arteth dropped the orb into a pouch of his own. "We should go."

***

"My God we've been walking ages." Harper grumbled. "Is there even an end to these tunnels?"

"There are many endings and many beginnings to Tuâlavan. We shall not reach the exit we seek for quite some time yet."

"Then I'm officially calling a time out." Baxter set the sack he was carrying down and pulled his crumpled pack of cigarettes from his pocket, looking in disgust at the broken remains of his last one. He shoved the pack back in his pocket and sat beside the sack, glancing to Terrence as he asked, "don't suppose there's any food in here? Or a drink maybe?"

"Soz." Shrugged the other boy. "It's not like there was any of that in the room. When Kyrel got rid of that tree of Lilly's he really got rid of it."

"What?" Lilly also shrugged as they both turned to her.

"You could grow something." suggested Harper.

"That is…" Terrence looked to Vereena, "if it's cool for us to take a break?"

Looking from her troop to the expectant faces of the others, Vereena's gaze landed on Lilly. "I suppose a short break… if my cousin grows tired?"

"Oh I grow tired." Lilly nodded and Vereena added,

"… is probably wise."

"Great!" said Tobias as Lilly sagged down the wall opposite Baxter.

Vereena joined the five classmates, digging the base of her torch into the ground, at their centre. Terrence plopped down next to her, while the men from her troop took up standing positions either side of the small group.

"So?" Baxter nodded Lilly's way. "Food?"

"If you think I'm growing anything in here you're crazy." She shook her head at the disappointed faces. "What?" she asked them all, "It's not like I grew that tree on purpose. If I fuck up in here I could bring this whole place down around us. Sorry but unless one of us has something stashed, we're all gonna have to wait."

"Ooh!" they all turned to Vereena as grinning she pulled a satchel from her back. "I have some Drelga bark we can share."

"Bark!" Baxter's face scrunched up with disgust and looking to him the others stared a moment then one after the other burst into fits of giggles.

Over the past two days they'd each seen him shove all manner of strange things down his throat, now to hear him complain when their predicament left little choice, at least seemed amusing enough to lift their spirits.

Vereena, the only one not laughing, pulled the thin gnarled chunks from her bag and tearing the largest one in half she began handing out those and similar sized pieces until everyone had one to gaze curiously down at.

"It is good, with much energy," she reassured them, "Just do not swallow."

"You're saying we can't even eat it?" asked Harper.

"Well you could," she frowned "but doing so usually involves bringing it back up again - an unpleasant experience."

"Yeah," Lilly grinned, "We're not too fond of puking beyond the veil either."

"We chew," she stuffed a chunk of Drelga bark into her cheek, illustrating her words. Dubious as they all were the others followed suit and were soon chewing along with her.

***

"Foolish Da'ariel," muttered Tai'at, Drellaeleon's second in command, as he made his way inside the previously concealed village. "They truly believed they could keep this place hidden forever."

The inert bodies littering the ground posed no threat other than the prospect of tripping anyone failing to constantly check their footing. "And all this over one girl-child! When will they learn their place?"

"None but the Da'ariel has seen this village in hundreds of cycles." Drellaeleon came in after him. "Seems much like forever to me." Looking up she studied the raised pillar of earth before asking, "And what are these?"

"We're not certain," Tai'at followed her gaze "Perhaps they had plans of fortifying with a new wall."

"Perhaps they should have planned sooner," nodded Drellaeleon, a wide smile spreading across her face. "Less magick for the Ginats to seek would have served them well."

The men around her laughed, and whipping around to face them she scowled. "Do you not all have your orders? The girl and the Da'ariel Queen are to be brought to me alive. Kill any who try to stop you."

Disbanding into small search parties the other Deebanaarie scurried off, ransacking what was left of the village. Turning to Tai'at Drellaeleon added, "I expect to be notified of any larger concentrations of the Ginats, understand? Our Queen has her sights set on more than that girl and if she is not satisfied I will not only blame you, but offer up your essence to prove my desire to solve the problem."

With a gulp Tai'at nodded,

"Of course, I will see that the troops tear this place apart until we have all we seek."

"You do that." Drellaeleon glanced up at the pillar again before snorting and wandering off to further inspect her surroundings.

***

"These tunnels are really something else!" Harper gazed around the walls. "I don't know what kind of rock this is," she stopped to stroke a section, "but did anyone else notice the way it sparkles? It's so pretty."

"Pretty?" Baxter called from ahead of her. "More like endless, I swear this place goes on forever."

"Yeah," agreed Terrence, "It's like some mythical Labyrinth; I keep expecting the Minotaur to jump out at us."

"I don't think the Minotaur's labyrinth was anywhere near this pretty." muttered Harper, her gaze still on the walls.

"There she goes again with the pretty," Baxter rolled his eyes, "Girls!"

"That's it." Tobias dropped the weapons he'd been carrying to the floor, causing a clatter that startled the others and had Lilly and Vereena turning his way with near identical frowns. "Screw this shit," he swayed as he spoke. "Who needs weapons anyway? I mean…" he kicked a small crossbow contraption across the floor. "I don't even know how to use one of these! Do any of you know how to use one of these?" He looked to the others and seeing the puzzled faces singled out Vereena's men, with their sheathed swords and similar contraptions strapped to their backs, as he chuckled. "Except you guys of course." Expressionless, they watched him wave his hand adding, "Obviously you all know how to use this shit. But then you already have weapons right so why the fuck am I carrying these all this way?"

"You know I bet the Minotaur's Labyrinth was pretty magnificent," Terrence told a clueless Vereena, as he watched Harper; who had gone from simply stroking the walls to practically hugging them as she went on muttering "So beautiful! It's all just so… so… pretty."

"Had nothing on this place I'm sure," Terrence was nodding, "but we are talking about the ancient Greeks right... and those guys could really build. I mean talk about your timeless architecture."

"Seriously," Tobias was asking again. "Won't somebody tell me why I was carrying all this. " Glaring at the weapons with frustration he ran a hand over his hair. "Was there a reason? I... I'm almost certain there was a reason."

"OK then..." Lilly's raised eyebrows dropped as she turned a puzzled look on Vereena asking, "Is it just me, or is everybody acting a little... crazy?"

"You know architecture is a real amazing art-form." Terrence leaned so close to Vereena that he almost fell on her. Offering him a smile she pushed him gently upright and turning to Lilly shook her head, saying,

"It is *not* just you."

"Hey what gives? Am I on my own now?" Baxter called from far enough ahead to be a strain on the eyes. "Are we not leaving anymore? You know what, fine, that's how I like it anyway fuck you lot! I'll get out of here by myself."

The warriors looked to Vereena and nodding for them to go after him she looked to Lilly.

"I fear something is very wrong with your friends, cousin Lilly."

"You don't say."

***

Toleth and his troops made their way through the forest. As escort to more than half the villagers - all those not of the warrior classes who'd managed to evade the Ginats and reach the meeting place - and with most on foot, it was less of a hasty retreat than it was a concerted effort to keep everyone together at a steady pace.

The troop guarded front, rear and sides of the pedestrian caravan. Each three-fighter contingent keeping look out for any sign of the enemy, they rode atop their yimusa trundels ready for action. Every sound in the forest was suspect and every person present was twitchy. Nonetheless they proceeded without incident and with Toleth at the head of the group, pondering the survival of their clan now that their village had been discovered after being hidden so long.

There was no going back for his people now. They had been a vexation on Mordrel's family since long before the last Great War. The blood of the original Da'ariel royalty survived as long as the village had remained hidden, meaning Deebanaarie rule had always been at risk.

Now, as reigning head of the D'vey family, Mordrel finally had the chance to wipe them out. There was no doubting her troops would make good on the opportunity. They would spare none in their search for Lilly.

One of Toleth's lieutenants rode up from the left flank.

"Riders have been spotted this side of our line; permission to take a troop and slow their progress?"

"I cannot yet allow you, the people are our main concern and we are too thin on the ground to protect them," Toleth scanned their group. "Tighten them up. We shall put more distance between us and our pursuers before any engagement is attempted."

"Of course my Liege." The man bowed back, drawing away and proceeded to relay the orders quietly among their others warriors. Minutes later a hand signal was issued and the entire group picked up its pace.

A few leagues later the same man rode to the front.

"They still follow my Liege, what will you have us do?"

"Take one troop, set traps, then return to us. Engage only if necessary, understand?"

"Yes my Liege."

Off he rode, signalling three others to join him, a troop's worth as specified.

They disappeared into the trees as Toleth urged all remaining with him to move faster.

***

"What do you mean nothing is here?"

General Drellaeleon's rage showed mostly in her cheeks, which glowed bright pink as words huffed out of her.

"There are many dead though my Liege," shrugged Tai'at. "The Ginaten have-"

"An orb, the girl and Mairiel!" shrieked Drellaeleon. "If it is not about an orb, the girl, or the Da'ariel Queen then I do not want to hear it."

"One building does look promising." Tai'at offered. "The Ginaten definitely converged most heavily upon it. It has… caved in."

"Caved in?"

"Completely my Liege, it appears to have been set on fire… from the inside…"

"To keep out the Ginaten," muttered Drellaeleon.

"That is how it seems. Inside is mostly crushed from the force but underneath the dead Ginaten and rubble we have discovered only one body so far. The area is still being searched. If an orb is present I will of course notify you immediately."

"You had better hope an orb *is* present." hissed the General. "Giving word to the Queen that we remain empty handed will mean more than my essence, understand? Take me to the location, *I* will see it is searched properly"

The Deebanaarie warriors spent all night searching the Da'ariel village. An effort which turned up nothing until Drellaeleon, reluctant to report to Mordrel, ordered a second search during which they discovered two survivors and evidence of a tunnelling underneath the imploded hut.

Day Three: Part One

Most pockets of Da'ariel had run out of drelga when Arteth had been a boy. As such it had been that long since he'd used it in powdered form to aid him in journeying through the trees, a skill most Deebanaarie did not possess. Kyrel, now stronger from the essence his body had absorbed from the orb, was clearly the better for it and took extra care to stay close to Arteth.

There could be no conversation with the concentration the journey took and the pair made swift progress over the tree-tops.

Night travel this way was notoriously treacherous, but with Kyrel's supply of drelga used up they kept going to make the most of what they'd consumed.

As day broke over the forest they could see Duruth Schtaal, which Vereena had translated as "Bridge Pass" in the distance. Another hour maybe two, of being flanked by leaves as air rushed by, and they could rest.

Having been no farther than half a league ahead the entire night Kyrel broke away, his speed increasing. Squinting from the sun Arteth watched as the distance became a full league and a half, and kept growing until the Deebanaarie was barely visible.

As he muttered words of irritation to himself, Arteth's eyes drifted off passed Duruth Schtaal. Now he spied a dark blue line, in the valley beyond the forest but moving steadily toward it – Compelled by dread he too sped up.

This contingent of Mordrel's troops numbered at least three times what she'd sent upon the village and were sure to reach the rendezvous before he or Kyrel could.

If Vereena's group had made it there as they should have hours earlier, they were likely preparing to move on already, but unaware of the troops heading straight for them may well linger in hopes of being re-joined. The valley would keep Mordrel's troops hidden until they came up over the Pass and Vereena and her companions would find themselves set upon the moment that happened.

Kyrel was long gone from sight, leaping from tree to tree as fast as he could without losing his footing; Arteth was still many leagues from the tree line.

Once in a while he thought he saw the Deebanaarie up ahead but knew in truth that he was clueless.

A half a league from the tree-line, an unknown yet familiar bird-like coo caught his attention and swinging his head to look, Arteth toppled down through several branches. Certain he was about to hit his head on the next thick limb he flailed, grabbing at everything but catching nothing. Suddenly his arm was caught just above the wrist and he dangled on the end of Kyrel's grasp.

"Swing up." The Deebanaarie's strained voice came through gritted teeth as he lay belly down over a thick bough.

Arteth did as instructed, and together they ascended higher.

"Apologies, I could not let you risk running into Mordrel's troops." explained Kyrel. "They are at the pass."

"Already? I saw them in the valley but how-"

"There are many." Trepidation was as evident in the Deebanaarie's eyes as in his voice and nodding Arteth asked,

"What of my cousins; the Princesses?"

"No sign."

"They could be well on their way to Zanreal."

"True, but we cannot risk attempting to pass or the possibility of leaving them to face such an ambush alone."

"Then we must get closer. As near the entrance to the seal as we can."

"No. I must do this."

"You are not the only-"

"You are not fast enough to make it on what little drelga remains in you." Kyrel fixed Arteth with an impatient glare. "And should the need arise… I am not strong enough to take on so many without…"

"So now I should just give you back the orb and tell you exactly where the entrance is so you can go on without me?"

"Arteth, it is-."

"I am certain Mai Mai would not want -"

"Your grandmother is not here!" hissed Kyrel. "But she too may be about to walk out into that ambush and with no magicks but her sprites. Are you so much more certain of their abilities than you are of mine?"

Arteth's eyes rolled upward as he loosened the orb's pouch at his waist muttering,

"Mai forgive me for trusting the Deebanaarie who brought your death."

Kyrel's face showed slight irritation but he held his tongue; allowing Arteth to instruct him on the location of the ancient seal, as he took the orb and slipped it into a pouch of his own before responding with:

"Leave the trees only when you have to and do not be too long over ground. Your help may yet be needed."

With that he leapt from the tree they were on, to higher up the next one and repeated the action until he was yet again running along the leaves at the top of the forest.

***

The troops at the edge of the woods were steadily dividing. Half were heading across the old stone bridge in the same direction of Zanreal while the others continued on a forward path into the forest, toward the village of Mairiel's clan.

Cross legged, Kyrel sat watching from the top of one of the tallest trees near the edge of the forest. The purposeful way in which they rode past the rock's concealed entrance, to the ancient remains of Tualavan, before passing directly beneath him, told him they remained oblivious to the location of both.

However, getting near enough to the entrance would prove tricky, and without doing so he could not know if Lilly and the others had already come through. A plan formed quickly in Kyrel's mind.

Climbing slowly down the tree he rested a few limbs from the bottom and watched the men passing by beneath him.

Keeping their uniform stride through the forest was no longer possible. Instead those on trundles weaved in and out of the trees while those on foot ran along the forest floor, hopping over felled logs and pausing intermittently to glug from their animal skins.

Picking out a young male warrior doing just that, Kyrel descended further and clutching the lowest bough with his legs, he swung down catching the man's throat between his arms. He twisted until the neck snapped, then dragged the lifeless body with him up into the tree, stopping only when he reached halfway, where he propped the corpse alongside himself and began removing the dark blue armour.

***

"This is it!" Vereena's eyes widened as she studied the wall being illuminated by the torch of one of her men. "We near the exit," she told Lilly as she and the others drew closer.

"Err…" wiping his bleary red eyes Terrence asked what the others were thinking. "How can you tell?"

To them this section of wall looked no different from any other. Vereena saw more. She pointed upward to three deep gashes a foot down from the tunnel ceiling. They were far paler than the rest of the wall and the warrior at Vereena's side raised his torch, so the green light shone on them. They sparkled and the grating of rock on rock rent the air as the wall began to move.

"OK," nodded Tobias "That's kinda cool."

"See," Harper cried, "I told you all I saw crystals in the walls!"

"Yeah, you also told us your middle name and your bra size," muttered

Baxter as he passed her by.

"What?" Harper glowered after him, as she followed him and the others through to a much narrower corridor.

"Yeah," Baxter chuckled as they made their way up an ascending walkway. "That bark stuff may be better than caffeine but man did it make you guys loopy."

"Us," asked Terence. "What about you Mr Keen-sense-of-direction?"

"Yeah," agreed Harper. "If you hadn't got lost we would have been out of here ages ago."

"Oh come on…Who wouldn't get lost in this crazy place?"

"Err… Anyone not stupid enough to wander off when they have no idea where they're going…" Lilly suggested from in front of them.

The others chuckled and blushing in the darkness Baxter shrugged.

"Yeah OK, fine so that stuff made us all kinda loopy."

"Except for Lilly." said Terrence.

"What about me?" she called back.

"You err… you didn't lose it like the rest of us."

"Yeah," chimed in Tobias "you had the bark too, how come you stayed so cool?"

"Maybe it wasn't the bark," she suggested.

"Oh, it was definitely the bark." said Baxter, to the unanimous agreement of the others.

"Then I don't know," she told them. "Maybe it's because I had some before."

"Oh right!" snorted Baxter. "Like you were hitting this shit and didn't tell anyone?"

"It wasn't the same stuff."

"But you just said-" began Harper.

"It was a powder." said Lilly. "Same stuff just not as bark. Kyrel gave it to me, got to admit though, Baxter's right, it is definitely better than caffeine."

Leaving the walkway they came out onto yet another spiral staircase, which resembled so much the one they'd entered down the previous day that doubts were voiced as to whether or not they'd gone full circle.

"There are many such staircases throughout these tunnels." Vereena assured them. "We have taken longer than expected but we are not lost." She turned to Lilly, "Our ancestors lived many generations down here."

"Underground?" asked Harper. "Why would anyone choose to live underground?"

"So the land above stays unharmed," said Terrence. "It's believed the ancestors of the Da'ariel people had a profound love of the world around them. Seeing the damage they were doing on its surface they used their powers to burrow underground. Here they created a network of cities without marring the beauty above."

"Funny looking cities." shrugged Tobias.

"We haven't seen any," Terrence nodded. "The tunnels are more like… well… roads"

Baxter turned to give him a sideways glance in the torchlight.

"OK, not only does most of what you just said make next to no sense, but you should probably know: you're enjoying those scroll thingies way too much."

"Yeah," Terrence smirked. "Well, to be honest, a lot of that does seem to be speculation on the part of modern day Azeronians. Still... the scrolls really are kinda fascinating."

"Yeah sure, just know they'd better be some kinda helpful as well, or I'm gonna kick your ass for roping me into carrying them too. In fact, why don't you quit reading up on the long gone ancestors of the Da'ariel and concentrate on finding Lilly the most kick ass powers she can have?"

"You know it's not that easy when my translator has to go off on a wild goose chase after you."

"Shh!" Lilly hissed their way as Vereena and her men slowed to a halt. Catching up to them, she stared up into the darkness. They could all hear the rumbling, like a constant thunder. "What is it?" asked Lilly.

"Maybe it's your cousin Toleth," Harper looked to the Da'ariel girl. "You said he would meet us here with his troops."

"My cousin does not have that many troops."

"The whole Da'ariel village didn't have that many troops," agreed Terence.

"I will go see," Vereena whispered. She tapped one of her own troop on the shoulder telling him, "Cat ya vac Malat," as Lilly grabbed her arm asking,

"Shouldn't I come with? You know, in case you need back up?"

"I do not intend to need back up cousin. I am Da'ariel, we're good at hiding remember? No one shall see me."

"Even so," Lilly pushed past her and went on ahead, "As I'm the only one here with active magicks I'd rather if we're *not* being seen together."

As the others watched them disappear up the spiral stairs Lilly hurried alongside her Da'ariel cousin, who was so much swifter than herself. "You think it's Mordrel's army don't you? You think it's her troops?"

"I think it a likely possibility."

"Sounds like a lot." Lilly panted as their hastening steps became a run. She hadn't taken the amount of steps into consideration when she'd insisted on going along.

"Perhaps you should talk less," Vereena suggested with a smile. "It helps when moving swiftly and we cannot be sure these tunnels have not been compromised."

"Right," nodded Lilly, "shutting up now."

A moment's rest was needed once they reached the top as gasping for breath; she informed her cousin of a need to sit, then promptly fell down.

The thunderous rumble, which had continued incessantly above them, was now so loud they were forced to speak with raised voices.

"Are you sure you are ready?"

"Sure," Lilly nodded to her cousin as the guard Malat helped her to her feet. "I'll be fine, just do me a favour?"

"Anything in my power cousin."

"When this is all through...." Lilly wheezed between renewed panting, "remind me to teach you people about the benefits of elevators."

"The benefits of elevators," nodded Vereena "It will be an honour to remind you-"

"Yeah OK how's about we lay off the honour stuff and you tell me what our plan of action is here."

"Very well; the entrance above us comes out behind a large bridge known as Duruth Schtaal."

"Duruth what now?" Lilly asked.

Vereena patiently translated... "I believe you would call it 'Bridge Pass,'"

"The rendezvous point." A blank look from Vereena had Lilly adding, "Where we're to meet Kyrel and the others right?

"Right," nodded Vereena. "Of course they probably think us far ahead on our way to Zanreal by now." For the first time, Lilly had noticed, the other girl appeared almost glum as she added, "And if Kyrel's right Mordrel has sent a far larger second wave of troops toward my village. This requires them to also pass by the bridge." She pointed to the rough dirt ceiling and following with her eyes Lilly said,

"So worst case scenario: we're now on our own with an evil army camped out above us."

"It would seem so."

"OK, again I ask... plan of action?"

"As little *action* as possible." Vereena pulled a torch from the wall and struck it as Arteth had done the previous day. The green light flared and spat but settled as they made their way up the last steps and out into a deep square like hole.

The rumble seemed more distant now, muted and no longer all around.

A crude wooden ladder had been affixed to the wall directly opposite them and making her way over to it Vereena put her torch into a holder on the wall before waving for the others to follow as the flame fizzled out.

"Mordrel wants something else now doesn't she?" Lilly asked as she took second place on the ladder. "That's why she's sent more troops... She's figured out your people have something else hidden. Whatever Kyrel went back to get, it's something she wants almost as much as she wants me."

"Possibly more." agreed Vereena "But now is not the time to discuss such matters."

"Right," Lilly muttered to herself. "Shutting up again."

Vereena helped her up onto the short ledge and they waited for Malat. He then led the way through a large crevice in the otherwise sheer rock face, with the two girls moving hip to hip behind him.

A few feet around a couple of bends and they could see light. They could also hear voices and the constant marching. With everything spoken in the native language Lilly could barely make out actual words as they crept closer to the opening. Dense foliage surrounded the exit, a curtain of thin tendrils above and mid-height shrubs across the ground.

Vereena pressed her face tentatively up to the leafy curtain and grimacing unsheathed her small wavy dagger.

"Whoa hey!" Lilly eyeballed it. "I thought there was no intention of being seen?"

"I cannot see anything."

"You're not thinking of going out there?" her amazement was surprising to the Da'ariel girl.

"I must see if we can pass." nodded Vereena.

"But…"

"You will be fine here with Malat." She nodded to the willowy guard behind them. "He will not leave your side."

"Oh sure, like you're not leaving me now and like Kyrel didn't leave last night? There's no way I'm falling for that again." She slipped through the shrubs before Vereena could stop her.

"Ny dylur!" whispered the younger girl as she and Lilly crouched low, pressing themselves to the outer face of the cave. "You are not safe here cousin, you must go back inside."

"Oh right and I guess you're just peachy," Lilly hissed as she looked out across the vast scrubland that faced them.

The cave's entrance was cut into the back of a large boulder. It was one of many which spread out in clumps and were the only cover for as far as could be seen.

"I do not understand… Peachy?"

"Look I'm not going back inside without you, so do you want to see what we're up against or not?"

Malat had joined them now too and with no further protest they made their way slowly around the set of boulders.

As her cousin stopped dead, hissing "Ny mech!" Lilly caught sight of the armoured men passing by within metres of her. "Holy shit!" she pulled her head back around the corner and Vereena did the same. "Shh! Quiet." she whispered. "They must not see us."

"Right," nodded Lilly "That would be bad. What are we going to do?"

"We cannot hope to pass by them." Vereena shook her head and turning to Malat spoke a moment in her own language before turning back to Lilly.

"They do not seem to be stopping here. We will wait until they are passed."

"Yeah OK." Lilly turned for the cave.

"Wait!" hissed Vereena. "Two… no three! Three approach."

"But they can't see us right?" Lilly swung around a little too fast and tumbled into the wall.

"No," Vereena threw her a pained look "They cannot see us but please… you *must* be quiet."

"Right." Lilly whispered. "Sorry."

Taking another peek she watched the men walk purposefully by and sighed when their footfalls faded. About to turn back they heard returning steps; now significantly closer.

Lilly froze with her companions, for what seemed like forever until Vereena whispered.

"It is OK, they did not see us... come, let's go back..."

The sound of small rocks falling down the other side of the boulder made her eyes widen.

"Oh God!" Lilly's voice dropped lower as she pressed herself to the rock again. "Someone's behind us"

"Quiet." mouthed Vereena.

A scrambling about could be heard above them now, and she waved for the other two to back up toward the cave's entrance.

Malat took the lead and as such was the first to encounter the two Deebanaarie soldier's leaning against the opposite side of the entrance.

One of the men held an animal skin up to his mouth and it was obvious they were slacking off. A fact which changed the second they caught sight of this tall Da'ariel male and his two young female companions.

The few feet between them served as a running board for Malat as he sprang into action, leaping at the nearest man, while the one with the water skin let it drop to his waist and unsheathed a broad sword as he dived for the girls. Pushing Lilly to one side, Vereena stepped the other way and the man wound up hugging boulder.

As he stumbled backward Vereena's arm snapped out and she thrust her dagger into the back of his neck. The man collapsed to his knees between the girls. His eyes watered and blood spurted from his mouth. He was dead before he hit the ground. The younger girl knelt and jiggled her blade in an effort to retrieve it.

On the back of the other guard, Malat had lost hold of his weapon and forced to improvise, was bashing the man's face repeatedly into the hard ground. Vereena hurried over to help, plunging her dagger into yet another neck.

"Fuck!" Lilly muttered as the man stopped flailing and less than a foot from the entrance she backed into the boulder.

As if from nowhere a third man appeared from around the corner where the first two had been leaning. His eyes gleamed as he set his sights on Lilly. His lips pulled back for a growl as he made to lunge.

"Shit! Shit! Shit!"

She turned to run inside but the man pounced, dropping her with a thud that reverberated through her back, ribs and skull. She thrashed about in his grasp, narrowly avoiding his raised short sword several times over through the sheer will of her terror as the warrior - a young man not much older than herself - spluttered a string of incomprehensible words into her face.

With his saliva coating her in a fine spray Lilly found herself incapable of screaming because the fall had knocked the wind from her.

Vereena and Malat turned to see her as a fourth uniformed man dropped from the top of the boulder. He landed beside the struggling pair and drove a short sword deep enough into the young man's back that a couple of inches of the blade's tip protruded from his sternum. Blood spattered Lilly's upper body and face then slowed to a steady trickle.

When they realised what had happened Vereena and Malat were already mid lunge. Kyrel had to move quickly to avoid injury and they both pin-wheeled to the floor.

The entire situation was now too much for Lilly to take in; horrified she stared at the dead man on top of her, eyes drawn to his seeping wound.

Kneeling beside her Kyrel gestured for her to stay quiet as he yanked the body aside and retrieved his blade with ease.

"Are you OK?" he wiped her face clean with his sleeve. "Are you injured? Can you move?" the urgency in his voice drew her distant gaze to him, and she breathed out a barely audible,

"Sure. I... I think I can..." she raised herself on one elbow before muttering "Kyrel..." and passing out.

***

Darkness surrounded them as Lilly opened her eyes. A familiar green glow emanated from behind her. This also seemed to be in front of her, as it was the actual direction of their motion.

"She wakes!" Vereena's squeal echoed around them as her upside down face appeared in front of Lilly.

"Oh good I'm being carried," she mumbled, "least that explains why the world's gone topsy-turvy."

"You became unconscious." Vereena told her cousin, as Kyrel stopped to place her carefully on the ground.

"Yeah," nodded Lilly. "I guess that would also explain it."

"How do you feel?" asked Kyrel.

"Oh you know, insane mostly. Just tell me it's all over OK. That I've been out cold for days and it's time to go home now?"

"I'm afraid you were not out nearly long enough for that." Kyrel offered a tentative smile.

"You came back." Lilly's lip trembled as she gazed up at him.

"Of course." He nodded, "It is my duty to protect you. I cannot do so if I am not at your side."

Sighing, Lilly pushed herself up off the wall.

"I guess we should probably get back to the others."

"There is no hurry," he rose with her, "we're safe here; if you need rest you can-"

"It's OK." she steadied herself on the wall. "I'm good."

Malat had already gone on ahead and they met up with him and the others near the top of the stairs.

It was here that Kyrel insisted they sit listening to the rumbles above, in hopes of the sound signalling an absence of troops by dying out soon.

Two hours later the noise let up, and making their way up the rickety ladder and out of the tunnels, the group were joined by Arteth; who'd been waiting nearby unable to get close enough to enter the caves before Mordrel's troops had completely passed.

In the stark light of day Harper saw the dried splodges of blood that covered Lilly's neck and upper body. She stared a little too long but saying nothing forced a smile and moved along.

In the time they'd waited Lilly had done little but hug her own knees and stare into space. Whatever had happened when she'd left the tunnels earlier clearly wasn't something she wanted to discuss.

Once out they divided into smaller groups, Malat and the other guards were deployed to lookout positions, while their mistress, Arteth, and Kyrel, stood a few feet from the boulder conversing in their own language as the classmates huddled together near the entrance. Lilly stood alone to the left of them where she continued her vigil of staring at nothing.

Despite an awareness of the others whispering about her she couldn't focus enough to listen. Her mind was too busy going over recent events with a growing certainty that she was going to die in this strange place called Azeron.

A world where girls younger than she did battle and took life without hesitation, here the fact of her existence made her a walking target and many had already died in the crossfire. How else could this bizarre situation end? She had seen with her own eyes more than a thousand men marching past these boulders; each with hopes of bringing her back to their Queen as a prize. Now freshly stained with another's blood and dismally aware that fresh clothes or a warm shower were not on the itinerary, Lilly felt despair digging in its heels. She was the farthest she'd ever been from the home she'd despised so long and all she wanted now was to be back there.

"Lilly," slowly the world around her drifted into focus. "Lilly," nodding she gazed up into Kyrel's eyes. "It has been decided we shall wait for Mairiel to join us." He told her, "She entered the tunnels shortly after leaving us and could have new orders once she knows a good many of Mordrel's troop also went over the bridge towards Zanreal."

"Is that what *you* think we should do?"

Kyrel smiled, touched by her need for such clarity.

"It seems every one of us could use the rest." He nodded.

"We just rested," Lilly's voice came out faint, little more than a murmur as she added. "It was noisy."

"I know," he stroked some strands of hair from her face. "I was thinking this time you could sleep. From what I'm told of your night in the tunnels you need to."

"I don't know." She stared at the ground, "things have been so crazy, like a dream that won't stop. How am I supposed to sleep when I'm already dreaming?"

"I know not this dreaming but lying down..." he patted the ground between them. "... and closing the eyes usually brings sleep readily to me."

"Sure," Lilly lay down and curled up into a foetal lump. Kyrel watched her eyes close and moved to get up.

"Don't leave me," her hand clutched the hem of his ragged shirt and there was a pleading in her eyes that couldn't be ignored.

"Of course not," he smiled. "I will remain."

***

The first stars were twinkling overhead when Lilly woke. One of the strange whirl-like clusters they formed reminded her: this wasn't the sky she knew. Sitting up slowly she turned to see Kyrel dozing beside her.

His head flopped forward with his chin on his chest. In his hands he clutched one of the ancient Da'ariel bindings.

Some of the others had fallen asleep too. Harper and the twins lay curled up around a smouldering fire and a few feet from them Vereena and Arteth were stretched out side by side. She was fast asleep surrounded by a small clutch of similar bindings, while Arteth lay propped up against a rock sharpening his longsword, and pausing he glanced up as Lilly got groggily to her feet.

The guards also slept, each with their hands on the hilts of their weapons as if expecting to rise for a fight.

Unable to see Baxter, Lilly assumed he couldn't be far, and checked vigilantly around the other side of the large boulder before dropping her pants and squatting to pee.

Halfway through she heard his voice.

"Well that's not very princess-like." Looking up she saw him sitting atop the huge boulder grinning down at her.

"Oh shut up!" hissed Lilly as she stretched out an arm, steadying herself on the rough rock and finishing up considerably faster than she'd planned to. Straightening up she fixed him with a squint asking, "How'd you get up there anyway?"

Baxter pointed to the cluster of smaller boulders, which clung to the side of the one concealing the cave.

"Took a climb." he shrugged "Though I don't think that's considered very princess-like either."

"You'd be surprised what royalty get up to around here," she said as she made her way up.

"Yeah," Baxter stared out at the landscape.

The bridge to Zanreal took up most of it. Made from the same rock as those around them, it loomed large in the faint light. "That explain why you came back all zoned out from your adventures today?"

"What do you...." she followed his eyes to her blood spattered top and closed her mouth.

"You saw something kinda shocking up here, huh?"

"I'm fifteen Baxter!"

"Yeah I know your age Slater. We take most of the same classes remember? I'm fifteen too."

"Yeah well you're not fifteen with a price on your head. You didn't just find out you have a bunch of strange powers and a whole world expecting you to use them to take down the wicked witch of the East"

"Err... that'll be the West."

"What?" Lilly threw him a puzzled frown.

"In The Wizard of Oz," he nodded.

"No." she shook her head. "I meant the bad one, not the good one"

"Good cos Glinda's North."

"What?" her frown deepened and he rolled his eyes.

"The wicked witch of the East was the one squished under the house at the beginning. She was the sister of the wicked witch of the West who then spends the rest of the movie trying to get revenge."

Lilly's mouth fell open and her face said her already low opinion of him was declining.

"What?" Baxter shrugged. "I have an older step-sister who loved that shit growing up OK. Consider my knowledge my scars."

"Yeah OK," a smirk formed on Lilly's lips only to fade as she became solemn again. "There's like this huge army out looking for me Baxter..."

"Yeah I know," he shrugged "We all got the memo."

"Yeah but you didn't see, there were like thousands of them up here. Maybe thousands on thousands, I don't know..." as if still seeing them she stared out across the expanse. "Point is they're all out to see me dead. As if that isn't bad enough a bunch of strangers have appointed me their next Queen and are actually expecting me to free them... No, wait! Their entire world! From some tyrannical regime that's existed here for decades. I mean come on... do the Da'ariel not know the meaning of 'too much responsibility'..."

A short sharp hiss escaped Baxter as he leaned back.

"If we're talking about the same Da'ariel, then no, I doubt they do." Seeing her frown he added, "The only responsibility these people have had for hundreds of years is ensuring the survival of their race. Doesn't matter how rough things get. They've kept going no matter the odds. Every one of them is willing to do whatever it takes to make that happen and I for one don't really have a problem with that."

"Yeah, well, I do. I wasn't raised here. What works for them isn't what works for me. They're expecting too much. I'm used to a hot meal every day and curling up in a warm bed at the end of the night. Clearly I'm not equipped to deal with this."

"Oh? See now I thought the point *was* you're the most equipped person here."

"If I was Da'ariel maybe"

"Err hate to break it to you Slater but clearly you are. I mean look at you." Tilting his head back he examined her profile. "You even look like one of them."

"Shut up, no I don't."

"Sure you do, I always thought your hair was the most amazing shade of blonde. Minus that 'I'm so different' streak of pink you went and stuck in it of course."

"You what!?" Lilly snorted. "You thought my hair was an amazing shade? Now I know you're talking crap."

"Nah really," he shrugged. "Until I clapped eyes on you I figured a blonde that translucent could only come from a bottle. In fact I was never a hundred percent on yours not being bleached till we wound up here and I got to see everyone walking around with that same hair."

"Yeah, well." Lilly examined a few strands between her fingers. "It's just hair. Doesn't mean anything."

"Yeah, alright," he nodded. "So we're just not mentioning that odd yellow tint your eyes seem to have from time to time?"

"Odd yellow..." Lilly began with a shake of her head, "What are you talking about?" her nose wrinkled with confusion.

"Seriously?" Baxter cast an incredulous glare her way but getting that same blank stare, soon shrugged. "Alright, fine, what about all that magic shit you can do? That's just coincidence is it?"

"Well no... of course not." said Lilly, immediately flustered "That's... well it's..."

"Awesome?"

"I was thinking more: overwhelming." She shrugged. "Like I'm cramming for the most important exam of my life. Quite literally, seeing as my life apparently depends on it! Only it's also the most completely unfair exam of my life because I have like no previous experience of the subject, and I'm not even the one who left everything to the last minute this time."

"Yeah, that does kind a blow... Still... we are talking magical powers here." He grinned. "A burden I would so take from you if I could."

"You're a chronic thief Baxter, you'd pinch your granny's knickers if you thought you'd get away with it."

"Oi oi, no need to get personal. It ain't like you were shoved into Craven's Peak for being Miss Squeaky Clean now is it?"

"Sorry," she sighed staring into space. "It's just... I wish the powers were the burden."

"Yeah I know it's all that pesky expectation that's the problem. But then with great power comes-"

"Oh please don't you start talking about Spiderman too. Already had enough of that particular conversation with Kyrel." Baxter's eyebrow bounced up again and rolling her eyes she sighed, "He saw me watching the movie..."

"Come again?"

"Through that Quiescence stuff," she nodded. "Seems he had access to a lot more of it than the Da'ariel. That's why he speaks our language so much better than Mai Mai and the others – well maybe not Vereena, learning about me was a duty for her. But Kyrel saw a lot more of me growing up."

"Right," nodded Baxter, "Makes sense, being Deebanaarie probably makes a lot of things easier in this world."

"Maybe, but I'm getting a serious vibe that he's been shunned by his own people for quite some time. God, this is all so weird."

"What?"

"You know... us sitting here, talking about being in a whole other world to the only one we knew existed three days ago."

"Aah," sighed Baxter before frowning, "But which is the weird part exactly... the whole other world thing, or us sitting and talking?"

Again Lilly smirked.

"Yeah, I guess you have a point there."

Baxter also smirked then his expression grew thoughtful.

"Look, I don't want you to bite my head off OK and I certainly don't want to go for another tree-top joyride, but have you bothered asking Kyrel why he has such an interest in you?"

"It's something to do with him knowing my mother..." Lilly shook her head. "He and Mai Mai obviously have more history than this whole race war thing."

"So that's a no then? You haven't asked him?"

"I've wanted to."

"Then why-"

"Kinda seems like a touchy subject with him," shrugged Lilly. "With all of them actually. The only one who's come close to discussing any of that stuff with me is Vereena and she pretty much shut up when that cousin of hers showed up." She nodded Arteth's way before turning back to Baxter and lowering her voice. "I think maybe they trusted Kyrel once. That even though he's Deebanaarie he was accepted by the entire clan and that... that for some reason... somehow: he betrayed them."

"Then you think he's trying to make amends? That that's why he's looking out for you?"

"I don't know... sure, maybe."

"Must have been one hell of a betrayal if that's the case."

"Why do you say that?"

"Oh come on, how many times has he saved your life already? Once wipes most slates clean back home. And it's not as if he just happened by and took the opportunity either. This fella's watched over you since you were a baby just so he could jump out of a tree and risk his life for yours? That's the definition of dedication right there."

"Yeah," Lilly looked to her toes. "Guess you kinda have a point there too."

"Believe it or not I have loads of good points," he told her. "Unfortunately for you none of them are answers."

"Well Kyrel's pretty tight lipped about it all so I-"

"Then ask somebody else." He nodded to Vereena, "Isn't it like some sacred duty of hers to keep you informed?"

"Something like that, but… well I think that's more a Royal font of knowledge thing. Like you know keeping me informed of kingdom affairs or something… At least I figure that's what would be her duty if the Da'ariel actually had a kingdom."

"Right." nodded Baxter "They do however have a shit load of history."

"So what… you think I should be asking Vereena more about their history?"

"Hell no," he looked disgusted by the idea. "We already have Tez for that crap; good appointment by the way."

"Thank you." she gave a prim nod.

"Yeah, he's so loving his new role as royal scholar slash historian," said Baxter. "A little too much I reckon. In fact if he doesn't quit trying to fill my head with the 'nuggets of info' him and that cousin of yours keep pulling from those dumb scrolls I may have to bash his skull in."

Laughing out loud Lilly saw Arteth lift his head to glance their way then went on sharpening his longsword. She lowered her voice, muttering, "Sorry, maybe I should have let him know he didn't need to bring them with him in the event of an escape."

"Oh but these ones could be very important." The familiar mocking tone in Baxter's voice had been absent long enough for Lilly to notice its return, then it was gone again as he said. "Correct me if I'm wrong, but your mother's royal blood made her duties your duties right? So doesn't that also mean her Royal business is now your royal business? As in… you know… the business of Kyrel? You say you think he knew her-"

"Oh I *know* he knew her," nodded Lilly, "There's been like no hiding that. Not that I have any real clue what's being said, but it seems the standard for shutting him up is saying her name in what I'm fairly certain is a tone of seething hatred mixed with a hefty dose of accusation."

"A hefty dose of accusation…" echoed Baxter ."Sounds to me like a pretty good place to start."

"You're suggesting I ask Vereena about my mother?"

"Err… Duh! Yes. Answering your questions is her job."

"Well sure but come on Baxter, she's like a year or two younger than us! How much can she really know about the hows and whys of events before I was born?"

"More than you do." He shrugged. "Besides you did say she started telling you something before, why don't you just give her another opportunity... see where it leads?"

"I dunno, maybe cos I get the feeling I'm putting her on the spot or something."

"Kyrel's the one that put her on the spot. He pointed out her role in all this and so far he's the only one I've seen taking advantage of that role."

"Taking advantage?"

"What? Like you haven't noticed how he gets you to question her?"

"Sure, but I don't think it's like-"

"Don't you get it? She can *say* no to him, he has like no right to ask anything of her. Apparently you do... you, she *can't* say no to."

Biting her lip Lilly nodded,

"OK... so that I did kinda notice."

"Course you did, she's like your beck and call girl."

"Maybe I don't want a beck and call girl."

"Oh so you just prefer to whinge."

"Whinge! I haven't been whin-"

"Yeah OK," Baxter snorted, "boo hoo the expectation. Whaaaa..." He rubbed his eyes dramatically. "...the responsibility. What a world! What a world... and all on my puny shoulders."

"Fuck you!"

"Oh come on," he chuckled, "You get to gripe but I don't? You've been declared a Princess, Slater. What more could a girl ask for? You're next in line to rule these people. Sure the kingdom is kinda crummy, I will give you that. But so fucking what? You still get to be their leader. Besides it might not always be. The Da'ariel don't just expect from you, they believe in you. They look at you and they see all this magnificent power. How often do any of us get to say that?" he watched her gulp, staring at him with doubt. "I know your story Slater, little discontent rich kid." Looking to her toes again she bit her lip as he added, "Shit the Peak is actually a better place for me, but if I had half of what you had..."

"You know I've heard all this crap before." She scowled "The rest of you all think-"

"No you haven't," he dismissed her with the slightest of head shakes. "See I always figured that kids like you chose this life. That you never fit in anywhere because you didn't want to. Only you're different and I think maybe I get that now. I look at this place and I think maybe... I understand you now. Nothing back home can ever compare to here." He gazed up at the sky "Just look at that..." hugging her knees Lilly also looked up. "I can't for the life of me figure out what's going on with the stars but it is bloody gorgeous." Hearing her chuckle he turned with a smile. "Do I need to mention the magical powers again? Or do you get now how nothing back home is ever going to compare with this place?"

"OK sure, it is kinda pretty to look at, but I grew up in the same world as you Baxter. I'm not from-"

"You came from here Slater!" Her gaze remained on the sky as he said,

"No matter what you say, you know this is where you were born. That means you really are like the rest of us. You've never belonged, and that had to be something you felt. I mean seriously... magic is a way of life here. We're not talking rabbits out a hats or card tricks either, but real honest to flipping God *magic*. You can't tell me that deep down you didn't feel, you know... even a little of the power you have in your blood. How could you ever have been content with anything in our world? In this world you're powerful."

"I'm not powerful enough to get us home."

"OK one: I'm sure we already established that you *are* home! And two, last I heard, that isn't actually one of your powers. Besides, why the hell would you even want to?"

"You saying you don't want to go back?" it was her turn to throw an incredulous look his way.

"Am I saying... Nah," Baxter shook his head, "course not but hey the Da'ariel have promised to send us ain't they?" He shrugged. "And come tomorrow those sprite thingies should be jacked up enough to do it."

"So the theory goes." muttered Lilly.

"OK so things look a little different now, we're not back in their village anymore and the furballs aren't around, but we'll find a way back to that shit-hole of a school – it's just our dumb luck. And hey... bright side: tomorrow is also that calorie thingy."

"Kalaareem." corrected Lilly.

"Whatever..." Baxter shrugged "point is: all you have to do is stay alive a few more hours."

"See that might be comforting if I hadn't seen the size of the army out looking for me."

"Yeah but in case you didn't notice, you've also got some pretty bitching back up here. I might not have seen what happened out here today, but I know you came back in one piece."

"Define one piece."

"Oh give it a rest Slater, what do you think this is? Share time... sorry but I don't do hugs."

"You're such a jerk sometimes." Lilly hissed with a roll of her eyes.

"So what?" Baxter shrugged. "If you don't like it why you even here talking to me about this shit?"

"Because you're the only one awake?" she threw him a quizzical look.

"Because I don't sugar coat anything, that's why. Right now, that's exactly what you need. Ain't like you're the only one stuck here you know... you're just the only one lucky enough to have an advantage. I wasn't joking when I said I'd gladly take your powers. Nevermind that flying blade thingy; also fucking awesome by the way! Course the rest of us don't have any of that. You think Mordrel's army are gonna stop at you if they catch up with us? I get that something went down up here today and I get that you're freaked. But I also get that family or not your new pals over there took care of you. Yes you were right under the noses of Mordrel's *thousands* but you're also still around to tell the tale."

"I very nearly wasn't."

"But you are! She's got this mighty army that can't find you to crush you; you've got people who give a shit. Oh, and by the way, if she's so hard, why hasn't she just taken you out herself already?"

"Odd how I'd rather not think about that." nodded Lilly.

"Because she can't that's why; she *ain't* that hard."

"Yeah OK. You do realise she grew up using her powers?"

"And you do realise she's a Queen? Not in the pitiful Da'ariel sense either, she rules the land right?"

"Yeah... so not helping!"

"Just how much of her own dirty work do you really think she does?"

"What you're saying... maybe she's rusty so no need to worry?"

"Well, Vereena says you're very powerful."

"Please... I have a couple day's training, some abilities I don't understand, and a weapon I can barely use... I'd hardly call that powerful."

"Well Tez seems to think there's something to it. He's had her translating shit for him since back in the village. Turns out there's a bunch more of these powers you can learn."

"Not from Kyrel there isn't."

"Why do you say that?"

"Because he does. He knows more, I'm sure of it. But he won't teach me anything else."

"Has he said why?"

"Kind of," she shrugged. "I think he's mostly angry because I won't stick to one type."

"You mean that whole Lâioch, Tuâoch thingy?"

"Yeah... get this, when I use his: the Tuâoch, not only does it work for me but I also get like way more power! But he doesn't want me doing that."

"Should that even be possible?" Baxter's expression became thoughtful.

"Well no... but apparently some of the words can be a bit transfery. You know, like the one which brought that tree up in the Da'ariel library... I was going more for something in the potted plant variety."

"Right," He raised an eyebrow, and Lilly muttered.

"So yeah Kyrel says it's too unpredictable and I can kinda see where he's coming from-"

"But it's still fucking wicked!"

"Thank you!" Lilly's hands went up. "See I just don't get why he won't let me keep working on it. Instead of busting my ass over *focusing* on the piddly crap I can just about do with the Da'ariel words. Shouldn't I be playing to my strengths? And anyway, it ain't as if he doesn't use the Da'ariel words when he wants to."

"He has had a lot longer to learn than you. Maybe he thinks that makes him good enough."

"Can we stick to you agreeing with me please? I like that way better."

Baxter chuckled, then hearing her sigh, told her, "You're gonna be fine Slater. Come tomorrow this Mordrel won't have anything on you. She's running out of time and she knows it. Besides your faithful servant over there told Tez, the royal Deebanaarie have grown less and less capable with their powers since the wars too? Seems whatever stripped the Da'ariel of their mojo is still busy. That mark on your head is rarer than you think."

"Oh I know, Kyrel only has a half mark"

"Yeah but did you know it's meant him working twice as hard to be as good as he is?"

"I thought that was cos he's male."

"Well yeah OK. So apparently that's a factor too, but no I mean all the Deebanaarie do. Well the few of them who still have magic anyway. Your man Kyrel there is considered a master for being half as good as he could have been before their wars. Tez says the effect is universally diminishing but he thinks your full mark might mean full powers."

"Full powers?"

"You really should go speak to him yourself," nodded Baxter "You're the one that told him to find out all this shit." Hearing a yell behind them he turned around adding, "Oi oi what's this then?" Lilly swivelled around too.

A child of around ten had sprung from the forest and was running full pelt toward them. After him came two women, then a man, then dozens more people left the cover of the trees, many were injured, some helped along by others.

Dotted about were several groups of three on the equine creatures known as trundels – at a lower speed it was clear they actually did have legs. None wore the dark blue armour of Mordrel's forces.

"Must be Toleth," Lilly rose to her feet atop the boulder. "He and his troops were escorting survivors from the village."

On the ground the others began to wake, as Lilly stepped down the boulders. Arteth and Vereena's two men were already bounding over to meet the group.

"Doesn't this mean your granny should be here already?" Baxter followed her down.

"I don't know," Lilly said as she reached the ground and he clambered down after her. "Yeah I guess so," she turned to see Kyrel joining them.

"Hey." Baxter gave him a nod as they stood either side of Lilly.

"Toleth?" Kyrel looked to Lilly.

"Err… Yeah…" she told him. "I think so."

"What of Mairiel?"

"Not here yet." She shrugged then seeing concern in his eyes asked, "That's not so good is it?"

"Perhaps not." He sighed before asking, "What of you Lilly? Are you feeling well now?"

"Oh I'm fine," she folded her arms across her chest. "Sleeping helped I suppose." Nodding to Baxter she smiled. "Then there was talking, and now I'm feeling much better"

"I am glad." Kyrel gave Baxter a cursory glance before stalking off toward the approaching Da'ariel.

Watching her bite her lip as they watched Kyrel catch up to Arteth,

Baxter shoved his hands in his pockets.

"So you gonna start asking some questions or what?"

"You really think I should don't you?"

"Doesn't matter what I think. Matters how much you give a shit." Shrugging he disappeared around the side of the boulder leaving her to mull it over.

***

Having discovered another of her own troop injured among Toleth's forces, Vereena was off conferring with Kyrel and her cousins. So unable to quiz her, Lilly set her sights on Terrence.

"Hey," she plonked herself next to him at the re-stoked fire.

"Oh, hey." He looked up from the binding he was studying.

"Do you have any idea what any of it says?"

"Well I can tell you it's titled Lee... a... vash Lass... a... oo and that it's something to do with water," scratching his head he turned back to the document muttering, "Or is it fire?"

"You can tell all that just from looking at it?"

"What?" Terrence turned back to her, "Oh... No...Veer told me."

"Veer?" Lilly's eyebrow bounced up and grinning Terrence nodded.

"Yeah, she err... well see your other cousins call her that. She err, she said it was cool if I do too."

Looking slightly embarrassed he rolled the binding back up and placed it with others beside him.

"So err... How's it going, Princess?"

"Please don't." Lilly scowled, and grinning he said, "Sorry, it's just all so cool, like something off the telly you know?"

"Sure... except no, wait; TV's fun! Light entertainment if you will... So no, I guess I actually don't know."

"Right..." he nodded, "things have been pretty intense for you."

"That's a word. One *you* might use... but hey enough about me. Baxter says you've found out a bunch of stuff?"

"Oh sure, Veer's like a wealth of knowledge all on her own. Did you know in addition to learning all about you she had to go through some ancient ritual as a baby that basically forced the memories of every Qin Am Ness before her into her head?"

"Honestly?" Lilly's eyebrow went up and her nose wrinkled, "That sounds like one hell of a headache."

"I know, right," Terrence glanced around at the young Da'ariel girl in obvious wonder adding, "She's really quite amazing!"

"Yeah, OK..." sighed Lilly, "Has she told you anything about my mother?"

"Who Herrella, err... no." He turned back with a frown, and shook his head, "Not really." Then he was grinning again, "but she's translated loads of stuff for me. I know you probably have a lot more powers. You know..." he averted his eyes, "if Kyrel will teach them to you."

"Do you know why he won't?" asked Lilly.

"Err... I know some of the powers he has are... well, I guess they're considered taboo."

"Taboo? As in... forbidden?"

"Well not anymore; with no one to govern them but yeah... See that council they had before the war, they outlawed the use of certain magics. In fact I think it might have something to do with how the war actually started."

"Well I'm not interested in a war that ended hundreds of years ago. I need to know how to escape an evil Queen now."

"Yeah I know, but actually I think some of it might be relevant."

"How?"

"Well the last person in Azeron to have that full mark on their head like you do..."

"The Do'mass," muttered Lilly.

"Right." he nodded, "Well she was also the last surviving member of that council. And get this: The other members all died on the same night."

"What? How?"

"Well..." he pulled a notepad from his pocket. "We haven't actually found anything saying so but I'm thinking poison."

"Poison... you're sure?"

"Well no. Like I said nothing's written down, but Veer did say something about the water at their last meeting being bad. So yeah, I err... I think it's a possibility."

"And what about this surviving council member?"

"Well I guess she didn't drink any water that day," he shrugged.

"Yes, but what makes her relevant now?"

"Oh right... well I might have this a little screwy but apparently this Leyavanya gathered the essence of her co-councillors and fled Tualavan."

"The tunnels."

"Actually no, Tualavan is one of many cities within the ancient tunnel system. It was pretty important I guess, like a capitol or something. The council convened there and stuff like that."

"Right," nodded Lilly "And what about this gathering of the essence thing?"

"Oh well, I'm not too sure how literal that part of the story is meant to be..." he frowned flipping through his pad to another page. "Somehow it made her the strongest being in Azeron..." looking up he added, "like ever!" Lilly raised an eyebrow, and Terrence shrugged, "Anyway, after abandoning the city she's said to have taken to the forests, settling her people in small protected pockets before vanishing herself."

"Her people? You're saying she was Da'ariel?"

"Not only that, it seems your family here: the Avengturovs, they're directly descended from her."

"OK," Lilly frowned. "So you're saying my powers come from her somehow?"

"I'm saying I think," He shrugged. "Turns out translating ancient Da'ariel to modern English isn't all that easy. Vereena's unfamiliar with some of the words and others she simply doesn't know a translation for."

"Right, but what about the Deebanaarie?"

"Err Slater..." he lowered his voice, "I really don't think he likes being called that."

"I meant in general, dufuss," her eyes rolled. "Or you know at least his family as a whole – those of Royal blood. Do we have any idea who *they're* descended from?"

"Oh right. Course, well I'd have to guess another council member, but no," he shook his head. "Fascinating as they are these scrolls, or bindings as they call them, only seem to cover Da'ariel history, so nothing solid, sorry. Maybe you could ask..." his eyes drifted over her shoulder. Lilly's followed his gaze. Kyrel approached on her left.

"Doesn't look much in the mood for twenty questions," she muttered before turning back to thank Terrence and asking him to keep digging.

A quick swivel on the spot had her facing Kyrel as he reached them; a stricken look on his face.

"Something's wrong?" Lilly asked as Vereena ran to join them.

"Gather your things," said Kyrel "We're leaving."

"What is it? What's happened?"

"Kyrel!" Vereena caught up to him, a pleading in her voice as she let loose a torrent of words in their language. Seeing Lilly and Terrence rise to their feet she switched to include them. "Your rights do not go this far. You cannot just take her, you know this. Mai Mai was very specific on not giving you full charge for-"

"She was also very specific on us keeping your cousin as far from Mordrel's troops as possible," he growled at the young girl. "There is no way Mairiel would allow such foolish action and neither will I."

"Err... guys?" Lilly tried to get their attention, as the other classmates began joining them and Vereena's cousins made their way over. Despite the courteous switch of language the pair remained too engrossed in argument to notice those around them. Even when Lilly resorted to waving as she said, "Hello? Guys?" and the others began questioning what was going on.

"We can discuss it more," Vereena tried. "Find another way."

"What discussion is there when your Moolach headed cousin is so determined to disagree with me that he would risk everything?"

"Kyrel..." it was Arteth joining in from a few feet away. "The Lady Vereena is right, let us talk more."

"Have we not wasted enough time here?" Kyrel whirled to face him. "Mordrel is not yet exhausted of troops. If she sends more they too will pass this way."

"We all know this," Arteth assured him. "But you cannot just take Lilly with the matter unresolved."

"OK, seriously!" Lilly spread her arms between them as she stepped forward. "Somebody needs to tell me what's going on."

They all turned to her and a second later Kyrel was on the floor with Toleth on top of him. Harper shrieked, jumping aside as they rolled passed her, heading straight for the fire. Chasing after them Vereena and Arteth called,

"Cat ya vac!"

"Cat ya vac!"

The pair stopped rolling less than a foot from the bright green flames and after some scrambling around wound up with Toleth straddling Kyrel and yelling in his face.

"No!" Screamed Lilly, as the glint of a dagger being pulled from its sheath caught her eye.

Kyrel could do nothing but squirm, his arms clamped to his sides. Vereena ran at her cousin but growling, he flung her aside with a quick sweep of his arm. She tumbled over, reminding Lilly of a rag-doll. A thought which disappeared the second she turned back to see Toleth now grasping his blade in both hands, and raising it high above his head, ready to plunge.

"Kimst!" shouted Lilly aiming the appropriate hand gesture at Toleth.

He went flying several feet through the air, before smacking into the nearest boulder large enough to stop him.

The air filled with gasps as all around her the Da'ariel stared in awe. The village had been so busy the whole time she'd been there, that few had actually seen her learning her powers.

Kyrel also looked to her with surprise but only for a moment before he sprang up and made a dash for Toleth.

Determined to reach his brother first, Arteth ran ahead. Hearing Kyrel shouting, "Nydrel! Cat ya vac! Dieesh Ginat! Inst cat ya vac!" and coming to an abrupt halt mere feet from his younger brother he stared warily down at the crumpled heap.

Kyrel joined him and together they slowly circled Toleth.

"Toleth?" Arteth looked uncertain as he called out to his brother. "Toleth di eena valen mer? Di eena Toleth? Cat ya vac."

Others drew closer to the three men, many readying their weapons as, like Lilly, they began to realise what was happening.

Toleth began to move, gradually at first, his hands, then his arms. Arteth tried speaking with him again and in response to his own name he leapt up. Tearing his broadsword from his waist, he swung it side to side in a deadly arc as he ran full force at his brother.

"Kyrel!" Arteth's eyes grew wide as he backed away, ducking and weaving, to avoid the blade's edge.

Cat ya vac!" Kyrel yelled and launched himself onto Toleth's back. Bringing the younger man down with a thump, and pushing his face into the ground. Arteth ran up and kicked the sword from beside his brother's hand as Kyrel put two fingers to the back of the neck and spoke the same string of words Lilly had heard him use back in the village.

A hush fell over the other Da'ariel as they watched the glowing lights that emanated from both men's bodies before converging in the beetle on Toleth's neck. It was far smaller than the one they'd seen at the village but Kyrel seemed every bit as wary. He threw it aside then toppled to the floor as Arteth ran to the creature and stamped his heel down so hard that it popped under his boot.

"See how they react," Terrence whispered to Lilly as his eyes roamed the crowd of Da'ariel now gathered around the scene. She followed his gaze and recognised the wary expressions, somewhere between disgust and awe, which she'd seen when Kyrel had done the same thing back at the village.

Baxter caught her eye with a nod toward where Vereena was slowly getting to her feet. Lilly hurried over to the Da'ariel girl - helping her up.

"Are you OK?"

"I am." Vereena checked her daggers - establishing they all remained correct and present, while asking, "Toleth, he is-"

"He's OK." Lilly brushed dirt from her cousin's long brown coat. "It was one of those ginat things, a young one I think. Kyrel took care of it, Toleth's fine."

"Yes..." she nodded, still catching her breath.

"Look I need you to tell me what's going on?"

"Veyhi..." Vereena nodded as she drew her gaze from where Arteth was now helping his brother to his feet; it was a shaky ordeal and they held each other all the way to the fire.

"Of course," Vereena glanced back to see Kyrel, still lying on the floor. "Now they will both require time to recover, maybe I can."

"Where is Mai Mai?" asked Lilly. "Soldiers from your's and Arteth's troops came out of that forest. People I know you both left with her."

"Yes," Vereena gulped. "They *were* with her... they say she did not make it into the tunnels,"

"But Kyrel said-"

"He and Arteth did get them out of the village," she nodded. "But there were too many Ginaten near the entrance when they reached it." Her voice became grave as she glanced out across the newcomers. "They could not get in but they could not wait to be discovered." She shook her head.

"Of course not."

Lilly nodded and her cousin went on to explain how a trek through the forest would have seemed the best option. How Mai Mai and the others had put great distance between them and the village when they were spotted by a scout troop heading straight for them.

The facts were relayed as Vereena had heard them. A short chase had ensued, and insisting her guards focus on helping each other Mai Mai had wound up among those taken. The others would have fought for their Queen but the remainder of the Ginat swarm was seen heading straight for them and without Kyrel's abilities none stood a chance of fending them off.

Of the few who'd escaped with their lives most had caught up to Toleth's group soon after and together they managed to avoid anymore of Mordrel's forces. Two of Mairiel's sprite are however among those still missing.

"You're saying Mordrel has my grandmother?" Lilly asked.

"We cannot be sure." Vereena shook her head. "But it is her the Ginaten seek now."

"Those bugs are after her! Why would-"

"Because she still carries something my sister wants," looking far better than Lilly expected, Kyrel came around the boulder the girls were leaning against. Seeing Vereena avert her eyes he added. "The time for discussion is long past. A decision needs to be made. Will you join us or follow your cousin Toleth to where I will not be able to save him a second time?"

"That's what you were arguing over?" Lilly turned to Kyrel with a look of disgust that caught him off guard. "You want to leave Mairiel to the mercy of your sister?"

"Given the circumstances," he nodded. "It is the correct thing to do."

"How the hell is that the correct thing to do?"

Lilly's rising voice brought her classmates over to investigate. Terrence sidled up to her, while the others remained a few feet away.

"She would not want us to return for her." said Kyrel. "Nothing could be more foolish."

"You can't possibly be so cold."

Frowning he put one hand to the other, checking his temperature as he asked, "My feelings on this have nothing to do with how hot or cold I am."

"For Godsake!" Lilly muttered, her eyes doing a quick roll before she said, "We're talking about the woman who raised these guys. She's the closest thing they have to a mother. You can't just expect them to abandon her".

"I cannot make your cousins do anything Lilly, but they know as I do that Mairiel would not expect us to put her life before yours. You *must* come with me."

"And let them go on their own? Without any magics!"

"We two are the only ones here who can provide that; and I will not again leave you to go ahead without me. This morning was... I believe you say? Too close a call?"

"Yeah, I know," she lowered her gaze. "I froze when I should have-"

"It was not your fault, Cousin." Vereena spoke up. "I should have paid better attention."

"No harm done." Lilly shrugged.

"This time!" Remonstration filled Kyrel's voice. "You were both foolish to leave the tunnels at such a time. Had I not arrived when I did-"

"Yeah OK, you can back off now." Baxter stepped forward, his hands leaving his pockets. Kyrel barely afforded him a glance before shaking his head at Lilly. "You going back for Mairiel is not an option, and she would agree. Getting you out of my sister's reach is our task right now. Not heading toward her."

"She's the closest thing I have to getting decent answers about my real parents Kyrel. I don't think I'm ready to give up on that just yet."

For a moment he appeared visibly taken aback by this, but quickly overcoming it he shook his head.

"What could be so important to know, that you should risk your life?"

"Oh smell the beans already. My life's been in danger since before I got here. Your sister seems to have sent her troops out in every direction looking for me."

"Yes and far more of them await us if we go after Mairiel, than in any other direction. So few of us escaped the village already," he told her. "If Mordrel gets her hands on you every death will have been for nothing."

"We can't just leave her, Kyrel!" Lilly shook her head.

"We have no hope of saving her!"

"We do if we get to her before they reach the road into Crizoleth." Arteth came around the same boulder Kyrel had moments earlier. Toleth stepped, sheepishly, out after him. He and Kyrel glared at each other a moment until Arteth sneered, "We do not have time for this! You saved my brother's life Kyrel. He thanks you."

"With the dres verfelt!" spat Toleth.

Kyrel's jaw tensed visibly but Arteth pushed his brother forward, his tone more commanding as he again said.

"He *thanks* you!"

"Siiem tae," mumbled Toleth. "I am in your debt Deebanaarie." There was more glaring from each of them until Kyrel turned pointedly away from him and back to Arteth.

"You would do well to remove this one from my sight." They stared at each other a moment before relenting Arteth sighed,

"Cat ya vac," and stepping back Toleth passed him hissing.

"I ready my forces now brother."

Arteth watched him stalk out of hearing range then turned back to Kyrel. "You know he would never have drawn his weapon on you if not for the Ginat."

"He was under no such influence when he spoke as he did."

"I know." agreed Arteth, "and he was wrong but understand he was young. He does not remember as well as he believes."

"If he speaks her name in my presence again," Kyrel hissed through his scowl. "I shall dres verfelt his tongue from his head."

"Well that sounds nasty." Tobias muttered, as Arteth nodded.

"Then you have my word he shall not," he turned to Vereena. "I am still Mairiel's First-Hand, I *must* leave with Toleth. But Kyrel is right; we cannot risk Lilly being so near Mordrel's troops."

"It is already dark and they have almost a day's ride on you," said Kyrel "Even on your fastest trundels Mairiel will be at Crizoleth long before you can reach her."

"I know," agreed Arteth. "That is why we will be leaving those trundels near the edge of the forest." Kyrel shook his head with obvious confusion.

"How is it you believe you can—"

"We know of another tunnel entrance on that side of the forest."

"Ny!" Vereena spoke up. "You cannot! Kyrel," she turned to him for reason, "he cannot! It is forbidden!"

"It is necessary." Arteth turned to her. "Mai Mai still has one of the orbs. We must do all we can to prevent it from reaching Mordrel. They are *that* important."

"Yes but those tunnels you speak of go deep under Crizoleth." She dropped her eyes as Kyrel grabbed Arteth's arm.

"Is this true?"

"Veyhi," nodded the younger man. He swallowed hard before adding,

"There is no need for concern, your people remain unaware of them."

"Nydrel Arteth," Kyrel shook his head, "you are speaking of going up into Crizoleth itself."

"Mordrel's lands?" Lilly muttered just loud enough for the others to hear.

"Yes," Kyrel's whole face told his opinion on the matter but this didn't stop him from voicing it.

"It is the swifter route and Mordrel's troops shall not be expecting it."

"This is too risky. You would need to go above ground to stand any chance of finding Mairiel. How will you even know where you are going?"

"You will tell us. T'vor made it out with the others and he is certain he sensed Quiesscence not more than a league back in the forest. I have already sent a troop to gather what they can. We shall divide it between us."

"Don't trouble yourself," Kyrel assured him, "I can locate my own. Those that attacked earlier," he began to add, "You can-"

"Take their armour?" asked Arteth his eyebrow rising. "We've already stripped them of all we'll need and the men joining us shall be as captives."

Kyrel's eyebrow went up also, and a faint smile played its way along Arteth's lips. "Be trusting. I swear to you I know what I am doing."

"You are not the one who concerns me," Kyrel's eyes flittered across to where Toleth waited atop his trundel watching them with an impatient scowl.

"You *had* better know what you are doing." Vereena stepped forward. "Don't make me have to come looking for you." Arteth tore a pouch from his waist and held it toward Kyrel.

"I know enough that I cannot risk taking this with me. There are obviously still Ginaten in the forest and we definitely can't let Mordrel get both of these." Vereena sucked in her lips as she watched Kyrel accept the pouch.

"Hey wait a minute." Lilly grabbed his arm as he went to attach it to his own belt. "This is what you went back for?" Kyrel raised an eyebrow at her. "I want to see," she shrugged.

Tense glances were exchanged between him and her cousins. "Go on!" she insisted, "show me what was so important."

Kyrel sighed, tipping out the opal white orb, which glowed through his fingertips.

Exclamations of awe echoed around the classmates, as Lilly's face drifted closer to Kyrel's hand. The beauty of the soft lights and swirly glowing clouds inside it seemed to have her mesmerised.

Knowing better Kyrel said,

"You too feel its power."

"What?" she lifted her eyes slowly to meet his, then blinked several times. "What is that thing?"

"Err…" Terrence tapped her shoulder, "You don't think maybe it's…" he gulped, "the gathered essence of a council member?"

Kyrel's eyes flickered over them both as he returned the orb to its pouch.

"I see you have learnt much." Nodding he added, "Just one of these makes my sister a far stronger enemy."

"Then shouldn't we be helping to keep them from her?" asked Lilly "If

Mai Mai has one too Mordrel is going to get it."

"Yes," agreed Kyrel, "and if it reaches her before we reach it, you *will* be powerless against her."

"I think I have to side with him on this one Slater." Terrence shook his head. "We're talking about the ancient magical life force of someone from an entirely lost civilisation. There's no way to know how powerful these things are. Letting Mordrel get her hands on one of them is bad enough, we can't waltz in there with a second for the taking."

"Course not," she shrugged "we'll come up with a plan, there must be some way to-"

"Err I'm kinda hoping it ain't just me." said Tobias "but I really thought letting those who know what they're doing go after the other glow ball thingy… while the rest of us put as much distance between you and the woman who wants you dead was a pretty good plan."

"I totally second that." Harper nodded.

"We did try the planning thing already," Baxter shrugged, "It rained bugs and we barely got out with our lives."

"Your friends are right," said Vereena, "you cannot risk going back. If there is a chance of getting Mai Mai or the other orb back before all is lost then Arteth and Toleth will do so." Her lip trembled as she turned to Arteth. "I also cannot risk leaving the Princess. I am called. I must-"

"We know," Arteth smiled and held her chin up between his finger and thumb. "You are already proving to be a very worthy Qin Am Ness cousin. Do not despair over doing what you know is right." As she offered a weak smile, Kyrel turned to the others.

"We should be getting on our way. If you have things to gather-"

"Oooh, right," Terrence hurried away calling back, "won't be a minute."

"Great!" muttered Baxter "We're 'perky' otherworldly refugees now." His gaze drifted to Lilly but only for the second it took him to realise Kyrel was watching him. "Oh don't mind me," he shrugged, shoving his hands in his pockets. "I'm good with just the clothes on my back."

"Veer," Arteth said as his sister turned to leave, "Deeis vulath del Shenti." His eyes strayed to Kyrel who looked away as if embarrassed. "We will re-join you as soon as we can. Until then we must use what quiesscence we get as little as we can."

"I understand," she nodded. "Be concerned only for Toleth and yourself cousin, we shall be fine."

"I will see to it." Kyrel's head bowed slightly, his arm going up across his chest. Doing the same, Arteth's gaze shifted to Lilly, he switched languages again: speaking so fast she could barely make out the separate words. With no such impediment, Kyrel seemed vaguely embarrassed again, as also speaking their language his eyes went to Lilly too. Twice he mentioned Mairiel before resting a hand on Vereena's shoulder and finishing with, "The night only offers its cover so long Qin Am Ness."

"Of course," she turned to Lilly "We should-"

"Are you sure this is what you want to…" Lilly's defiant tone simmered to sympathetic and consoling when she looked into the other girl's eyes. "Right…" she nodded "Guess we're on the move again."

***

Forcefully separated from her entourage by a sizeable contingent of Deebanaarie warriors, Mairiel walked alone amidst her captors. Having already concluded the huge double doors ahead must lead to Mordrel's throne room, she was bleakly aware of her form's growing frailty. Her body's stores of pulpustuem were diminishing swiftly. It felt as though she were ageing with every step they took, through the wide, sparsely lit corridor.

Yet even ageing as she was, Mairiel took every step with visible pride, though deep down in her stomach there was no escaping the weight of dread. She would soon return to her true age: the one at which her granddaughter Lilly had first encountered her.

Nonetheless she would not let those caught with her see so much as an ounce of fear in her. If for no other reason than to be their strength, she kept her head held high, determined to face what were most likely her final moments with the same dignity and courage with which she had faced every trial of her life before now. Under the watchful eye of twice as many Deebanaarie warriors than their Queen, the other Da'ariel captives shuffled along wearily about ten steps behind her.

Shackled as she was, Mairiel stumbled; not for the first time, and losing patience one of the older female guards lashed out with an elbow: popping Mairiel on the left side of her face just below the eye socket.

This almost toppled her, and as a surprised moan escaped her the rest of the captives began to stir in angry protest. There was a smattering of worthy warriors within the tightly packed cluster of Da'ariel prisoners, most being somewhat worse for wear; having been injured during capture. Still, they already seethed to fight back and avenge a multitude of fallen comrades and clan siblings. Watching their Queen being disrespected by her lessers could well turn out to be more than they could tolerate.

"Ny vac dimst" Mairiel took a second to address her people, deliberately catching the eye of Lasaya - the most senior among them. It was all the time needed to signal with the slightest shake of her head and a definitive glare in her eyes: there was to be no further resistance. Most of the rag tag mob caught alongside Mairiel were actually low-borns. They did not come from prime fighting stock. Regardless of this and their injuries, she knew all would fight to the death should she order it.

Instead, she steeled her resolve and prepared herself for the end. It was not that she harboured doubts about the abilities of her people, she was in fact confident they could take a fair few of these Deebanaarie matfiack with them before they inevitably perished. She also understood their desire to fight back. Even aging as swiftly as she was, the warrior's blood coursing through her own veins boiled. She too itched for retaliation; to avenge all her own had lost, over so many generations - at the hands of these insatiable oppressors, however she also knew it was a move they could ill afford.

As a Mai Mai; born and raised to lead a people for whom survival had always been a numbers game, her own desires had never been relevant. Among the clans of the Da'ariel, no one person's wants could ever be put above the needs of the many.

Furthermore, Mairiel knew Mordrel's desires included far greater prizes than a Mai Mai already in her last days, and a dozen or so already weakened lowborn villagers.

Lilly's essence was one such prize, and she could at least be thankful that her granddaughter remained far from this place. She remained hopeful that Lilly was still safe among those sworn to protect her. However if Kyrel was correct, and Mordrel did now suspect the presence of Leyavanya's orbs, she would absolutely be seeking those out too.

While the Da'ariel referred to this ancient, supposedly common ancestor as: The Lady, The Mai of Mai's, and Mother to all Azeronians; The Deebanaarie, generally knew her as The Last Tualavan and had developed an altogether different viewpoint.

In general they doubted the virtues of her intentions in the creation of the orbs, and saw her primarily as a paradise destroying aggressor, while some among them no longer believed Leyavanya had ever existed at all.

They were also said to have done away with their own line of Qin Am Ness; killing off most of her acolytes, the Douleks, along with her. The few who were spared were eventually elevated to positions of slightly lesser power in her place. Such events had been so tumultuous to the realm that they were noted in many Da'ariel historical bindings.

Due to the nature of Azeronian politics, those actions had ultimately allowed Deebanaarie Queens to ditch some of the most restrictive traditions of their people, and maintain a more absolute rule; reigning unchecked and unhindered by what most Deebanaarie had since come to see as tiresome councils.

All of this, including all of the great wars, was now ancient history. Few among the realm's living population ever had access to - let alone would be capable of reading - the ancient records. Hence, for most, the details had become an amalgamation of possible facts and grand speculation, and were now as subjective as the average Azeronian imagination.

The orbs themselves had been swept up into the mythos long enough ago that few ever gave them much consideration outside of expecting them as a staple in their oldest and grandest tales.

There was however one thing both races were known to agree on. If these ancient orbs did exist, they could contain, and be used to wield, some of the mightiest forces ever known in their realm.

For Mairiel there were no doubts. House Avengturov was believed to be directly descended from the Leyavanya bloodline and as well as ruling the Da'ariel clans, their noble house had also secretly kept possession of one of those orbs for several generations.

Through many cycles of sheer determination; they had succeeded in both holding onto it, and discovering a second.

Now because Mairiel had been - by her very nature - too cautious to hand both orbs over to her grandson, as long as he remained in the company of Kyrel. There was an all too real risk she was about to lose this long sought after treasure of her clan - to a woman who was arguably the biggest threat her people had known since the Great Wars had ended.

Fortunately, Merly: the youngest of Mairiel's sprites, had initially been captured right along with them. The Deebanaarie had already hunted the creatures to near extinction for their particularly potent essence and the ambushers had gleefully seized upon the opportunity to present this rarity to their Queen, not something Mairiel was willing to see happen. It wasn't until they were already within the great city of Crizoleth that the guards let their guard down. All the same, Mairiel had seized upon the opportunity. She hoped to rectify her earlier mistake by managing to discreetly hand the orb over to Merly, just moments before ensuring her escape. These Deebanaarie warriors had never seen a Tekurian sprite before today, let alone actually dealt with one.

As expected they had been duly surprised by the agility of the chubby looking, furry little creature. Given the change in the moods of their captors since that embarrassing moment, Mairiel felt fairly certain they would be far less eager to inform Mordrel they had captured her a tekurian sprite if that then meant explaining how it had outwitted and outmanoeuvred them.

Now the young sprite was out there alone; presumably lost and terrified, a thought which made Mairiel's heart ache. She consoled herself with the knowledge that Merly was a clever little thing, who knew better than to remove the orb from its carefully crafted pouch -- created solely for the purpose of concealing its potent essence. Merly also had a decent knowledge of the ancient Tualavan tunnel systems - unbeknownst to the Deebanaarie, some actually ran directly beneath their vast city. The sprite would not seek an opening during the day, she would hunker down until the quietest hours of the evening, then make her move to find one of those tunnels. If there was any way of making it out of Crizoleth alive she would find it.

The only way Mairiel could help Merly further was by stalling. It was for this reason the old Da'ariel Queen now strived to keep her own people at bay. The grandiose double doors looming ever nearer up ahead, made it clear their doom was imminent. They were so deep down in the belly of the beast that any escape attempt would be futile. Worse still, these guards would not dare to kill them, although Mairiel doubted they had any such qualms about beating them to within an inch of their lives. If that happened Mordrel would surely seize upon those most wounded, and dres verfelt any information out of them that she could before they perished.

If she did so, she could easily learn of Merly's escape long before the Sprite had time to find a decent spot to hide in. This would completely ruin Mairiel's plan of keeping her counterpart occupied and unfocused enough to hopefully miss the age old treasure, which was currently as good as under her nose. Fortunately none but she and Lasaya knew that Merly had the orb, but a hunt for the sprite could reveal it all the same.

Wiping away the blood now trickling down her cheek, Mairiel watched as the same Deebanaarie who'd just struck her puffed out her broad chest upon reaching those double doors and nodded for the sentry to let them through.

The posted guards wasted no time obeying; throwing both doors open to a hall so large, on first glimpse, it seemed bigger than the entire Da'ariel village. Far from packed, it currently held at least a couple of hundred Deebanaarie nobles and some servants. The hum of activity which remained heavy in the air, made it obvious a hush had befallen this crowd the moment those doors had opened.

Heads were in fact still turning, as flanked by guards Mairiel found herself shoved over the threshold.

"Cat ya vac!" growled that same guard, urging her on through the curious bunches of distinctly separate crowds dotted around. All of them parted in a deliberate gulf, which lead from the doors to a three tiered dias so large it could have held all of Mairiel's throne room atop it. Here sat the lone, huge, stone throne of Mordrel.

It was a considerable distance from the doors, particularly for Mairiel whose vision was beginning to be impaired by her drastic aging. Still, the hall was lit far better than the corridor, which had preceded it.

The dias alone was bathed in the bright greenish light of a couple dozen tellemi torches. They threw long ominous shadows over the nearest Deebanaarie, down on the main floor, all the while illuminating their Queen, somewhat overbearingly from behind. The few torches planted on the walls either side of the platform were hooded, so they gave off just enough light to cast a powerful haze around Mordrel and Neenia, her sprite, who sat perched cross legged up on the top right side of the huge stone throne.

There sat Mordrel, crowned with a gleaming crop of braids piled high, with the sort of meticulous precision that required more than one terrified servant. Her royal sceptre lay resting above her lap, across the huge stone arms of the lone throne. Vaguely reminiscent of Mairiel's walking handle - which hadn't made it out of the village - it also ended with a bulbous gavel at the base. That however, was where the similarities ended. Mordrel's was noticeably shorter and the wooden shaft was several shades darker; with a reddish hue that told Mairiel it had been cut from an ataki tree. The gavel end was darker still; crystalline and black. Its polished surface sent a myriad of streaks shimmering across the vast ceiling of the great hall, as Mordrel tapped it back and forth over her throne's thick stone arms. Her eyes had immediately affixed on the older Queen, with a triumphant smirk seemingly carved into the lower half of her narrow face.

Day Three: Part Two

Unwavering were the stares of all other Deebanaarie in the great hall. Their curious gazes clung to Mairiel as she ambled past those who stood first along her wide, empty path. Each pair of eyes added their load to the weight of dread in her stomach.

She couldn't have been more than a third of the way along when Mordrel's eyes narrowed. She stopped tapping her sceptre, allowing its momentum to peter out, while sitting back and raising a hand.

It was a movement so sudden and graceful, Mairiel barely had time enough to register the use of a hand-form. In that same instant she lurched forward with enough force to immediately lose her shackled footing. Her own people groaned; some of them crying out, as though they sympathetically felt her pain.

Having hit the ground face first, Mairiel left a thin and haphazard smear of blood in her wake. Flailing and skidding, she tried her utmost to assuage the unseen force now manoeuvring her to the podium. Ultimately the best she could muster was to tuck herself up into a protective ball moments before careening into the first step with a loud thump.

The crowd exploded into laughter and jeers. Mairiel couldn't have been gladder for it. Winded and bruised, with the taste of blood in her mouth; she much preferred this revelry at her own humiliation, than those utterly demoralised cries of her own people.

As if somehow aware of this, Mordrel ensured it was the briefest of respites. Pounding the gavel end of her sceptre on the floor alongside her throne, "Show some respect!" she commanded, as the revelry ceased.

"Do you not see…" she eyed her subjects on both sides of the room respectively, her tone serious enough to cause more than a modicum of confusion among them as she elaborated. "We are honoured by the presence of an Avengturov!"

Although only slightly elevated, Mordrel's voice carried easily over the now enraptured audience as she added, "And not just any... Nydrel!" She shook her head, her tone growing more acrid with every word. "We have before us, the very one the Da'ariel of *my* lands choose to *call* their Queen!"

More jeers were unleashed by the crowd - no laughter this time. No Deebanaarie present was at all amused by the notion of Da'ariel who didn't know their place.

Then a fresh stirring flittered through them, a whispered wave of verbal curiosity, which Mordrel immediately quashed with a single bash from the gavel end of her sceptre. Looking down to where Mairiel had finally recovered enough wits to begin un-crumpling on the ground below. The younger Monarch shook her head again, her expression one of abject pity as she huffed, "From a house that claims lineage all the way back to the Last Tualavan…" she raised the royal sceptre above her head, waving it over her shoulder as she sighed, "I expected so much more."

The sceptre's rounded wooden top bobbed side to side in front of Neenia's big, blue eyes - for all of a second, before the dark leathery sprite reached out, grasping it in one slender hand. Relieving her mistress without question, she tucked the sceptre up protectively; folding it in with her skinny little crossed arms, all the while remaining silent and perfectly balanced up on that one corner of the throne. Her diminutive size helped create the odd illusion that each end of the sceptre now protruded from her sides, a preposterous sight to behold, yet familiar enough among present company to go largely unnoticed.

The opposite could be said of the only other movement made by the sprite: those huge eyes of hers. Known to have unnerved the most seasoned of warriors, the large glistening orbs seemed to follow Mordrel's every move.

The Deebanaarie Queen rose up from the huge stone seat. Signalling toward the back of the hall, she beckoned with one narrow finger, then she began descending the podium. Her long dark cloak cascaded to the ground, pouring out from beneath her heavy metal pauldrons like a sleek dark blue waterfall. Shaking her head, Mordrel scowled down on her counterpart; while speaking up for everyone's benefit.

"All those times, I was told of a fearless and cunning warrior," she said, slowly crossing the large stone slab that was her second step down off the podium. Her eyes remained steadfast on Mairiel. Spluttering and wheezing the older monarch was barely up on all fours yet.

Mairiel was drawing the conclusion there was no point attempting to hide her agony. That extended tumble up the walkway had taken quite the toll on her already weakened form. Her entire body now felt alight with pain, the likes of which she had certainly felt before. The life of one raised to the role of a Mai Mai was nothing if not arduous. Still, it had been many a cycle since she'd felt anything near this level of hurting. She had also aged at least another five years between the doors and the podium, regardless of the unwanted assistance.

The blood she had tasted earlier now welled up in her mouth, along with an excess of saliva. Gagging and retching, she spat a fair mix of both onto the hall's polished stone floor.

Mordrel seemed not to notice. Enamoured with her own voice she sauntered across the next large stone step, booming. "All across *my* lands the Da'ariel insist on proclaiming their allegiance to some wise and magnificent Queen," down she stepped again, "They espouse their undying fealty to House Avengturov, and the so called true bloodline of The Lady. Yet all I see before me is a tired old thing who does not see when she has lost." Stepping down onto the final level above the floor, Mordrel paused to stand directly over Mairiel, asking "Where is she?"

The older Da'ariel queen looked up, gazing solemnly at the younger Deebanaarie queen. Mordrel barely allowed time for a response, before she fell to a crouch - her finely crafted armour bending easily at the knees. She gazed right back into the rheumy eyes of the older Queen. Taking a moment to study the face of her conquered enemy, from wrinkled chin to wrinkled forehead, before repeating her previous statement. "Tired... old... thing," her words came with a quick head nod, as if in agreement with herself, then smiling the widest of smiles she added, "But this will not do at all. The truth of you is that of a relic... How many of your own people have ever even seen you without your boiled root keeping you upright?"

"I cling to life only because your people made it necessary," hissed Mairiel.

"You have discovered your tongue!" Mordrel's entire brow rose; her delight as feigned as her surprise was genuine when she added "Treacherous, slanderous tongue," then asked, "My people!? Nydrel Mairiel! Surely you mean the chorosh k'bar that was my brother? All Crizoleth knows the near extermination of your pathetic line to be his last deed of any true greatness. Would you snatch this mere hint of redemption from the otherwise contemptible memory of his existence? He was after all: *exiled* from my lands…" Lowering her voice to a more private volume she tacked on, "long before he dishonoured himself mixing with your ilk."

Intrigued whispers stirred instantly, with many around the great hall speculating on the conversation they could no longer hear. Somehow, they were oblivious to the fact they were effectively ensuring a further zone of privacy inside which their queen was now telling the older one, "The Da'ariel shall not have another Mai Mai to look to, no fresh hope shall be ignited for them. They will never know the face of your granddaughter. All who aid her will be hunted down, and extinguished alongside her, and her essence shall be forfeit to me - long before any can carry tales of her re-emergence in the realm." Mordrel's amber eyes narrowed on Mairiel, "This defiance of the Da'ariel has gone on long enough. It is time for them to admit defeat and *that* begins with you."

"Killing me will gain you no ground." The older woman laughed, but only for a moment before she was wracked with coughing. The crowd grew quieter; more attentive, as if expecting her frailer older body to give out at any moment - and desperate to not miss a second of it.

Glad of the opportunity to disappoint them along with their Queen,

Mairiel wheezed in a couple of sharp breaths, before carefully adding, "Those tales already roam free among my people. *All* stand ready to swear their fealty to Lilliath and the kalaareem must be upon her by now. Soon we Da'ariel shall at last have a Mai Mai whose powers can truly rival your own."

Mordrel responded with laughter of her own - a truly amused cackle, as she straightened up from her crouch.

"The only thing truly fierce about you, old woman, is your optimism. Your wretched little village is destroyed, along with all of your sacred bindings and any chance your people ever had of teaching that runt how to use any powers her weak Da'ariel thar could possibly manifest. How long has it been since your puny race could tap into the essence? Three hundred cycles? Four? Yet somehow you convince yourself this girl's powers could rival my own!" Mordrel let loose another round of laughter. Although less of a cackle and more of a dry disdainful guffaw, there was no decrease in the level of amusement when she added, "What's more, old woman, she and those who fled your village with her *have* been spotted and measures have already been taken to ensure they're delivered right into my hands."

Mordrel glanced up at her sprite.

"The T'karas have arisen," said Neenia. With a blink, her gaze finally shifted off of her mistress and over to Mairiel, whose wrinkled swollen face was now flushing with fresh dread.

"Oh, that's right." Mordrel feigned surprise, her hand going to her chest for effect. "You probably didn't know Gershurian sprites can call forth a whole multitude of beasts to do their bidding. So much more useful than concealment magicks I always thought - not that we Deebanaarie have ever really known reason to hide."

Mordrel nodded over to Mairel's right, issuing yet another quick signal with her hand.

The General Drellaeleon - the same woman who had captured their village, stepped forward. At the same time Mairiel realised she could hear the clanging of chains and shuffling footfalls behind her. Turning for a look, she barely had time to register the rest of the prisoners, before they were drawn to a halt by the contingent of guards still upon them, and she realised she was being released of her shackles.

Drellaeleon's face held its stony expression as she removed Mairiel's wrist restraints; then blithely held out the same key so she could free her own ankles.

Taking the opportunity to wipe her bloodied face off along the length of her sleeve, Mairiel eyed the key suspiciously.

"Take it, instructed Mordrel.

"To what end?" she asked defiantly. "I am defeated already. Broken, weaponless and as you say - old. I am already nearing my end. What should I gain from playing along for your amusement?"

Again Mordrel signalled beyond Mairiel and the other Da'ariel, to one of the guards keeping them at bay. A moment later a scrawny teenage female was dragged from the group. Grasped firmly by the back of the neck she was pushed forward a couple of steps until she could be held in place halfway between the others and their queen. Mairiel glanced up at the girl: one of her personal servants who'd been too slow in evacuating the village. Revealing nothing of such recognition she turned back to see Mordrel was now running a finger slowly up the length of her own belly.

It was another signal, one common enough that all who witnessed it, including the servant girl, knew what to expect next.

"Mai Mai please-" was all she managed to whimper before the guard holding her plunged a dagger deep into her abdomen. Mairiel looked back in time to see it being wrenched upward as the now gurgling teenager put her hands to the wound. Slowly it gaped open, spilling blood then innards, all over the shackles on her wrists as she tried in vain to hold herself together.

Unhanding her, the guard stepped back and the prisoners at her back began to wail and moan as they watched her, slipping and sliding helplessly in her own blood. Eventually she lost her footing, and heels over head, landed slap bang on top of the steaming pile of her own guts.

The Deebanaarie of the audience sniggered their appreciation, while the rest of the Da'ariel prisoners were beginning to lose it. The other low-borns in the group were all terrified; assuming they were next for this agonising, honourless death, while the warriors among them, whether still capable or not, were all vying to fight back regardless of their own shackles.

"Calm yourselves!" Mairiel spoke up firmly to her own people and distraught as they were, all obeyed.

Barely able to contain herself any better, she threw a venomous stare at Mordrel.

The younger Queen merely looked down at the twitching body with a shrug.

"Such a waste. I probably should have mentioned that without your cooperation the rest of the prisoners are worthless to me." She turned back to Mairiel and correctly reading the doubt in her eyes added, "I had thought to spare at least a few. That is after all, the best way to ensure word of your demise reaches other Da'ariel. Not the warriors of course, they shall serve me as shraeka, but trade with the outer regions is good and a great many of their provinces have need for slaves." A salacious note crept into her voice, "I dare say they can find use for even the scrawniest males among this rabble of yours. All these lower born females however… well they're another matter entirely…" Slowly and very deliberately she let her eyes rove over the prisoners - the last thing anyone needs is more of your clan out there breeding. Now..." Mordrel asked as she again looked down on Mairiel, "is this truly how you would prefer I get my amusement?"

Mairiel glanced from her people - with so many low-borns among them - to Mordrel; and then onto the young servant girl's body. The twitches were decreasing now, her slow death being imminent but not yet completed. Snatching the key from General Drellaeleon's hand Mairiel began to unshackle her own ankles.

Drellaeleon unsheathed her own long sword, laying it on the floor alongside Mairiel; before straightening up, bowing Mordrel's way and fading back into the crowd.

The older queen gave the blade a cursory glance, as she slipped the key into her second foot shackle.

Out from the opposite side of the crowd to where the General had disappeared, two young Deebanaarie males - in servant's attire - stepped forth. One of them carried a small clay cup, the other an oblong shield so wide he was largely obscured until he put it down. It was then, as the battered metal shield was placed on the other side of her to the General's blade, that Mairiel realised Mordrel's intentions. The shield bearer's companion stood patiently holding the cup out to her.

"Siiem tae," she told them both and accepted the cup.

One of the youths actually afforded her a smile before they moved onto their next task: dragging away the now inert corpse of the servant girl.

With a wave from Mordrel the rest of the prisoners were also dragged away, some of them in tears, others yelling encouragement and declaring their unwavering loyalty.

Mordrel was removing her cloak as a young Lieutenant brought her two gleaming short swords. Glancing Mairiel's way, as she draped the heavy blue cloak over his outstretched arms, she correctly read the older Monarch again.

"Not that I would know, but I am assured you have there some of the finest pulpustuem in the realm. Considerably more potent than anything your people can brew up I am sure. Though the palace healers are certain you already have the withers. Something you've no doubt been keeping from your people." Relieving the Lieutenant of both swords, she checked each one over in turn adding, "I'm told any more than what you have there could well make your heart explode. Still, they've assured me it is more than enough to get you on your feet."

Apparently satisfied with both swords she dismissed the Lieutenant and sighed, "It's no wonder you brought the girl back now. Did you even know we had located her and were set to do the same?"

Snubbing the question, Mairiel lifted the cup to her mouth instead. Mordrel smiled, watching the older woman glug, she came down off the last step of the dias adding, "let us see the wise and cunning warrior now." Almost immediately a hot flush flooded its way through Mairiel's body, forcing a groan from her as it coursed through her tired old veins and spilled out across her muscles. Seizing up involuntarily, she became rigid. Both hands clenched up. The one grasping the cup tightened until a loud pop sent a mist of grey dust spraying over her hand and up into her face.

Around the hall the crowd hissed with delight. A bustle of activity now as some fought back others to be nearer the front. The rest of the prisoners were all but forgotten as their eagerness saw them flooding the back end of the walkway. All wanted to see their mighty Queen take down the other in what they perceived to now be an honourable and fair fight.

By the time the wave of what had felt like searing heat was done assailing Mariel's form, it had also fixed, fused and replenished her from head to toe. Slowly she unclenched her fist from around the broken cup. More dust and several huge chunks of clay tumbled to the ground. Mordrel proceeded to circle her, swords drawn as she taunted "The Da'riel may live refusing to bow the knee to me, but it is your name on their lips that sends them to their deaths."

Mairiel took up the unfamiliar sword and shield, with the steady, well-practiced hand of a truly skilled warrior. Getting to her feet she glared at Mordrel from her now considerably younger face. "There she is," Mordrel laughed, as both women now circled the other, "proud descendant of The Lady…" she nodded. "Finally we meet. Now let us see how much ground can truly be gained from your death."

**

Instead of crossing the bridge, Lilly, Kyrel and the others all crept alongside it. The remaining villagers travelling with them formed a far smaller caravan than had been possible when they were still lead by Toleth and his troops.

Together they picked their way across the muddy terrain of what had once been a vast river. The silt bed beneath their feet clung in thick clumps up to the calves of most and threatened to pull off even the tightly fastened long boots of the natives.

Slick silver creatures poked their heads up from the dark brown surface, occasionally jumping out only to dive back in and disappear from sight. That was if they weren't caught by Kyrel or one the Da'ariel first.

Their determination to do so prompted Harper to ask Tobias, who walked at her side if he thought "those things" were going to be dinner?

"Dinner," Baxter grunted as he came up between them. "We should be so fucking lucky. I was beginning to think we landed in a world of vegetarians."

"And what would be so wrong with that?" asked Harper, hand going instantly to her hip. He gave her a curious glance then nodded "Right… forgot that'd be right up your ally." Smirking he passed them by and made his way over to Lilly.

"So?"

"So what?" she spread her arms wider as they navigated through a particularly squishy patch.

"Found out anything interesting yet?"

"Did you see me get the chance yet?" she afforded him the briefest sideways glance.

"What you so afraid of Slater?"

"You know what I'm afraid of Baxter. We're on the run from her, remember? Scary lady. Powerful magicks."

"Yeah alright, you know what I'm on about."

"Sure, but in case you didn't notice: between the arguments, that fucking horrible Ginat bug thingy and the news that Mordrel's troops made away with the woman I'm meant to believe is my granny, I've been a little preoccupied. OK."

"Yeah OK, so things did get a little hairy back there. I mean seriously, how much trouble are those bug things? But hey, you saved Kyrel's life."

"You reckon?"

"Oh man definitely." he nodded as she turned to look at him. "He was toast without you. That Toleth was so going in for the kill."

"Yeah, I guess," mumbled Lilly as she glanced across at him, giving a hesitant smile. "That just kind of happened. I mean," she shook her head. "I saw the blade and I had that... you know... that helpless bystander feeling. I just wanted it to stop you know..."

"So you stopped it," shrugged Baxter. "Was pretty cool too."

"You think?"

"Totally... but you know... out of curiosity... which err... which set of words was that from?"

"Set of... oh right." she nodded giving it a moment's thought before saying. "I... I think I used the Da'ariel one. The Laîoch"

"Well it didn't look weak to me at all."

"No," grinned Lilly, "Guess it wasn't."

"Pretty focused too I reckon. You didn't send Kyrel flying as well or anything. Maybe he's onto something; when he says you should stick to it."

"Maybe. I'm just glad I didn't freeze up again like this morning."

"Forget this morning," he waved a hand. "...it ended this afternoon."

"And now is the night." Vereena tilted her head back to speak with them. "Your friend Robert Baxter is right Lilly. You saved Kyrel from our cousin's blade. It was an impressive display of your powers. I am sure Kyrel was pleased. You should be also."

"Not too sure your cousin Toleth agrees," said Baxter. "His one solid opportunity to stick it to Kyrel and not even get blamed and Lilly goes and stops him."

"Had Lilly not, they both would have been dead now. We Da'ariel have no way to remove a ginat without killing the person they're attached to."

"Oh!" A great deal of Baxter's smugness slipped away.

"We could not have let him live." Vereena explained "As you have seen, those who fall to ginaten lose all ability of reason. They become like the dangerous animals of the Nihidi pits; attacking all in sight until they are stopped and there is only one way of doing so without magicks."

"About that," leaving Baxter's side Lilly came up alongside Vereena. "how come when he does that everybody looks at him like he's some kind of alien?"

"I do not understand this word... alien?" Vereena shook her head.

"Sorry..." Lilly sighed "I mean why does everyone look so... errm... well..."

"Disgusted?" Baxter chimed in from behind.

"Exactly..." agreed Lilly, "He's doing what he can to help. What your people apparently can't. So why does everyone react as if he's just grown horns?"

"Oh that is nothing like when a male's horn grows."

Behind the two girls an immediate yet choked off guffaw escaped Baxter, as taking a second to gauge Vereena's seriousness with a look, Lilly pointed at her saying,

"OK... now *that*... we totally *need* to have a conversation about later. Right now though, I want to know about Kyrel and those bugs."

"The Ginaten." Suggested Vereena.

"Yeah them... Ginaten, ginats whatever you wanna call them"

"They are Ginaten when they are more than one," explained Vereena.

"Aah..."

"Plural and singular." Terrence said as he came farther up the line.

"Yeah I got it, thanks," said Lilly as he passed them on his way to Kyrel. "So anyway..." she turned back to Vereena, "What gives... why do the Da'ariel all look as though they'd really rather Kyrel hadn't helped at all?"

"Many fear Kyrel delves into that which none should."

"You mean the forbidden magicks don't you?"

Seeing an eyebrow on the rise Lilly nodded after Terrence. "Tez was telling me about it earlier?"

"Aah..." Nodded Vereena "For a male he is... most capable of the task you have set; learning eagerly of the way we live."

"Oh it's been noted." Lilly offered a brief smile. "Tell me more about these forbidden magicks."

"Of course cousin - What is it you would like to know?"

"Well... why such useful magic would be forbidden for a start. Why do your people fear them? Also... how did Kyrel learn them? I mean sure I'd be lost without him around to show me all the... you know..." she gestured with her hands adding, "The hand thingies, but he has had quite a bit of trouble figuring out those bindings of yours."

"Kyrel is very accomplished in the magicks. He has a rare strength in it for a male and has learnt four out of the six forces his sister knows, as well as another one beside."

"Cool... I guess"

"Many do not think it so cool," said Vereena. "When he uses magicks such as the dres verfelt he taps into the wild magicks."

"The dres verfelt? That's what the ginat zapping power is called?"

"The dres verfelt can be used on far more than Ginaten." Vereena threw a shifty glance in Kyrel's direction, "but these wild magicks require much energy; a hunger can develop."

"A hunger?" Lilly gulped. "For what? And what's so wild about these magicks anyway? All this power and forces stuff seems pretty wild to me. Why exactly were they outlawed?"

"It is the person who becomes wild cousin. All that has life in Azeron has thar: essence flowing within. Even we Da'ariel who can no longer manipulate the forces, remain connected through the essence."

"Connected?"

"In time you will understand. For now all you need know is sustaining the wild magicks requires more essence than even our ancestors had in their blood. Magicks such as the dres verfelt also require much focus. It is possible to lose control. The amount of essence needed to maintain the one doing the channelling increases a great deal each time it's used."

"The amount of... no OK, you've lost me." Vereena's blank expression had Lilly adding, "I don't get it. What exactly is this essence stuff? I mean I kind a figured it was blood but now you're saying it's *in* the blood? And what about this needing more of it thing… is that why Kyrel seems so…" she shook her head and shrugged, "so wasted after he's done that verfelt thingy? Why it drains him so much?"

"He shows exceptional control by allowing himself to become this way. He could easily take from all around him when working such magicks. As I said, all that has life in Azeron-"

"Has the essence within," added Lilly.

"Yes,' Vereena nodded. "To tap the wild magicks is to put at risk anything nearby which lives. This is why they were as you said 'outlawed.'"

"OK… I guess I can see how that could be a thing to fear."

"Yes. His sister is said to have given in to her hunger a very long time ago. Before the days of their mother, the Deebanaarie had mostly given up on capturing our people. Their ancestors had taken all they needed from us. It was no longer worthwhile to raid our villages. In the time of our mothers such things were close to unheard of, did you know our parents once played in the forests surrounding the clan's village? Deebanaarie soldiers passed through so little it was considered safe.

Our days are very different cousin, Mordrel has seen to this. When her hunger became so much that it ceased to meet an end and she could no longer exercise the will to keep from endangering her own lands; causing an outcry among her own people, she found herself a solution: Us. Who would miss the Da'ariel? We've had no power here since the last war ended and little in the way of presence. When she rounds us up who's to care?"

"OK wait, you're saying she rounds up the Da'ariel to… to what exactly?"

"To drain us of what little essence remains in us."

"She can do that?"

"It has long been considered the purpose of the dres verfelt." said Vereena. "To take life from another. We believe that is why it was first forbidden. Our writings tell us using such magicks against each other was once severely punished. Of course like many things this changed during the Great Wars. The forces became weapons and lacking the destructive capabilities of the Tuâoch we Da'ariel suffered the most damage. Though it is difficult to achieve and control the dres verfelt was regularly used against our people. It is why we came so close to being no more and it is what Mordrel will do to you if she gets the chance. You were born still tapped into the active Laîoch; if she succeeds she will gain considerably"

"How considerably?"

"It is doubtful that even she knows. There has not been another Da'ariel with active magicks for more than three hundred cycles. None alive have ever seen such a thing."

"Right," nodded Lilly. "Course they haven't. So err…" her gaze wondered to their limited view of Kyrel's back, a few feet ahead of them. Terrence had brought him one of the bindings and looking over it he was attempting to explain its contents. "He has this wild magicks thing under control though right?" asked Lilly. "I mean we all saw him, he didn't look as though he was about to go all... soul suckery on any of us that maybe have a little Da'ariel blood."

"You do not have a *little* Da'ariel blood," Vereena smiled. "You are one of us. Eventually you will feel it."

"Yeah well no offence but I'm not exactly planning on sticking around to feel anything. So do we need to worry about Kyrel or not? He's used that dres verfelt thing like twice now? He still seems in control right?"

"I'm afraid there is no way of knowing. It is an ancient Deebanaarie force. Other than being one of the forbidden magicks and its ability to bring death, there is little in our writings about it."

"Right," Lilly scratched her head. "What about that orb thingy? What was with this last member of the Do'mass council? She's the one Kyrel called the last Tualavan isn't she?"

"Yes. These days our people have many names for her. In her day she was simply Leyavanya. It's said she was formidable from the day she took her seat and I'm told many Deebanaarie say what happened to the rest of the council was her doing, while others consider her to be a myth."

"But what does the glowing ball do?"

"It is a vessel; it contains much power."

"Right," nodded Lilly "The power of the council members?"

"Only one," corrected Vereena, "it is said Leyavanya collected the essence of each into separate orbs."

"How?" Lilly looked as baffled as she sounded but Vereena merely shook her head.

"I could not tell you cousin. Such abilities are long lost to we Da'ariel."

"Course they are." Lilly's eyes rolled as she sighed.

"We have found much written on how to use the orbs though." Vereena informed her "A set of words which allow the power in them to be channelled for different uses."

"Always with the words?"

"The writings teach that the words protect our world from-"

"I know, I know, they're kind of like a safety right... stopping the magicks from going off at the wrong times."

"Yes." There was surprise on Vereena's face, prompting Lilly to explain.

"Kyrel might have mentioned it."

"Of course," smiled the younger girl. "And this is a good way to see it. The amount of power held within the orbs would have made this 'safety' a most important need."

"High priority," shrugged Lilly "So what can they do? The orbs... what can they be used for?"

"I'm sorry cousin but I am nowhere near as studied in such magicks as Kyrel. Perhaps these are questions you should be asking him."

"Sure, he doesn't even want to teach me more forces. As if he's going to want me knowing much about this 'vessel' of great power he's carrying around now."

Vereena threw her a sideways glance.

"I do believe his decision to be the correct one cousin. He seeks only to protect you. That is his place he is-"

"Yeah why is that exactly? How come he even gets to make decisions?"

"Because you are his ward."

"Yes." nodded Lilly. "I get that and I see that it means a lot. The rest of you, even Mai Mai, always seem to give in when he's arguing that position but why? What makes it his place?"

"Cousin if you are unhappy with Kyrel I think it best you speak with him."

"I'm not unhappy with him OK. I just want to know how he has that... I don't know... right, I guess. Is it because he saved me? That first day I was here... is it because he knew Herrella? Did she... did my mother give him some kind of power of attorney over me or something?"

"I do not know this attorney power cousin. Maybe if you tell me what it's used for?"

"Nevermind..." Lilly sighed, before shrugging. "He's a Deebanaarie right? The sworn enemy of your... I mean *our* people, and a Prince too. So how is it he's even involved? Better yet... what does it have to do with me? Cos I'm telling you now if it's something creepy, like one of those 'royal treaty by marriage' things... I am so not in."

"Marriage? What is this word?" Vereena frowned, "It is alike to the *married* word yes? I have heard both said many times by those beyond the veil; mostly by the adults."

"Err... well that'll be because kids don't really do it. It's like you know... a ceremony for adults who want to... err... You know what, why don't you ask Tez about that. I bet he'd love to explain it to you"

"Thank you cousin, this is a good suggestion, I shall do so."

"No problem," Lilly's gaze shifted to Kyrel. "So... can you at least tell me how Kyrel came to know our clan? He obviously has a history with Mai Mai and your people. How did that happen? Why doesn't he take his sister's side?"

"Kyrel told you how his people lack resources, how outside of Crizoleth they starve and thirst."

"Sure." nodded Lilly. "I remember, he said they raid your villages mostly from necessity."

"Well he does speak the truth: only... well it is a necessity they created. The Deebanaarie did not do as well for themselves as they first believed when they subdued our people. The loss of Da'ariel magicks was a sign that the Laîoch and Tuâoch had become unbalanced; a balance our world has relied on since its beginning."

"The balance symbolised by the Do'mass."

"Yes," agreed Vereena "The essence of our lands and both forces combined."

"But wait... I can already work three forces. No hang on..." Lilly shook her head. "You meant the Laîoch and Tuâoch?"

"Yes cousin. These are the forces which bind the other powers, allowing you, and our ancestors before you, to harness Azeron's essence for yourself."

"OK," nodded Lilly "go on…"

"Have you not seen for yourself how both magicks oppose each other?"

"Err…"

"While your Da'ariel blood allows you to bring forth trees, and shape the very land beneath us, Kyrel's blood allows him to remove things in his path, to take away the very air we breathe."

"Yes, you're right!" comprehension flooded Lilly's face. "His power: the Tuâoch it…" her face became a doubtful frown. "His power is… Destruction?"

"Yes," Vereena beamed a smile at her cousin, "Now you see. This is the true difference between our peoples." her smile faded, swept away in a mixture of disgust and sympathy as she added, "As they draw ever closer to the forests our lands disappear, suffering the same effects they've already had on so much of this realm. Imagine it: five hundred cycles of destruction. Course I have not myself been within any Deebanaarie stronghold. In truth I barely left the village before you arrived," glancing Lilly's way she smirked, "Every day for me was studies and training. It is nicer to be with you, I think. Still…" she sighed, "I have heard it told that the air itself is thin in Deebanaarie controlled lands. How any place they settle as a people withers under their feet."

"But I thought most of them had no magicks either? How are they-"

"Like us they still have essence within. These ancient bonds to our ancestor's magicks have been good for us. The Laîoch, keeps our lands growing. Yet for the Deebanaarie… well the Tuâoch alone… it is." Vereena sucked in her bottom lip a moment before shrugging. "I am unsure but I think you would say curse?"

"Right." nodded Lilly. "A curse, I get it. Where the Da'ariel settled things grew but the Deebanaarie… they get only decay, destruction. That is what you're saying right?"

"It is." Nodded Vereena "This is why they did stop hunting our people before. Kyrel's grandmother believed that without us Azeron itself would die. Our peoples remained apart but much is said to have changed during her time and her daughter kept to her ways. Mordrel is different. Her hunger does not let her see the damage she does to this world."

"More likely she just doesn't care." shrugged Lilly.

"Yes," Vereena's tone grew more solemn, "That also is possible."

"Well yeah," agreed Lilly "We have people like that beyond the veil."

"You do cousin?" Vereena's frown told of her surprise. "There are those such as Mordrel in your world too? They would seek more and more power until your lands are desolate and all that was once around them is no more?"

"Well err…" Lilly shrugged. "We might not get quite as dramatic about it but sure… we have heaps of people who are, well almost exactly like that."

"I saw nothing of this when watching through the quiesscence," the younger girl shivered. "The human world must be a frightening place."

"Oh it's not really that bad."

"Many who are almost exactly like Mordrel!" Vereena's eyes grew wide. "I cannot think of much that could be worse than-"

"Err no, OK see that wasn't what I..." rolling her eyes Lilly sighed, "you know what... why don't you take that one to Tez too. Try... I dunno... McDonalds. Or no even better ask him about Nestlé, anyone claiming to have a social conscious usually has some problem with them."

"Do either this Nestlé or the McDonalds have powers? Can they access the magicks of your world as you do here?"

"Well yeah sure, in fact they both command two of our worlds' most powerful, most dangerous forces." seeing Vereena's entire brow bounce upward Lilly gave a brief nod, "The Money and The Lawyers... formidable when separate but put them together, and I'm told they're devastating."

"Aah yes. The money..." Vereena was beaming again. "I have heard many beyond the veil speak of this power. The people there seem to think highly of it."

"Yeah you could say that..." Lilly forced a smile. "So... about Kyrel... you're telling me he's basically a mommy's boy?"

"Mommy's boy?" Vereena frowned, "Kyrel is a man."

"OK yes. I just meant... is he here because he believes what his mother and her mother did?"

"Oh but this is a certainty. He was of course raised to lead the D'vey armies as is tradition for the eldest son, but some say he spent more time at his mother's side than is appropriate for a prince."

"Appropriate? What's that meant to mean? Why should being a prince have anything to-"

"Remember... our ways are not like those you have come to know. Things are different here. Our men are our strongest fighters, they are known and remembered among the people by their abilities in combat."

"Aah, see now that's not all that different. Men can be like that beyond the veil too."

"But human places of learning, they are filled with males," Vereena frowned, "Instead of improving their skills for battle they're allowed to fill their heads with histories and actually expected to decide on their own futures."

"Well sure, what's so wrong with that?"

"Forgive me cousin, I meant not to criticise, it is only... to understand Kyrel's position among his people you must first understand that while males of royal blood do study here, it is mostly in combat. So as men they might live and die with honour, protecting their people as has always been Azeron's way. To most here the very idea that any male would prefer to indulge in learnings is... unacceptable."

"Well where I'm from we have this thing called equal opportunities; anyone regardless of their gender or which people they belong to may live and fight to change our world for the better."

"Equal opportunities," Vereena nodded. "I know these words from the human world, I am not sure I truly understand them."

"Yeah well most of us don't either, but it's definitely one of our better ideas."

"Then you are *for* it? This equalness of the people?"

"Err the word's equality, and sure I'm for it, but then most women are in the human world."

"I admit I find this somewhat... odd, still it is perhaps a shame we are not there, things could have been very different if Kyrel were allowed his mother's throne."

"So what..." asked Lilly, "people look down on him because he bothered to learn more than the average Prince?"

"Here people follow the queen. For the Da'ariel Mai Mai is a mother to all. Sharing wisdom and keeping us from chaos. The Deebanaarie, I believe, are similar. Mordrel is their rightful leader and she, I'm told, never enjoyed Kyrel spending so much time around their mother. As the rightful heir it was indeed her right to receive all the knowledge of previous Deebanaarie mai mai's. Kyrel has no such claim but was said to be a very good study and with Anniiada's interest in the ancient writings there was much to learn."

"So she was like what... a scholar?"

"This word I do not know."

"Err..." Lilly's lips scrunched to one side. "I mean she was the smart type... you know learned, a bookworm, liked reading up on things,"

"Aah veyhi," Vereena nodded, "It is said that she was. She's also said to have considered Mordrel to be... hmm... lazy?"

"Right," said Lilly.

"The strength in Kyrel's magicks can never be so, but his own knowledge of the forces is said to be far greater than his sister's."

"So Mordrel's jealous of him?"

"Perhaps this is so cousin, all I know for sure is two days after their mother's death Mordrel ordered him to take his place leading the Deebanaarie armies and he did do so, but the arrangement did not last."

"Why not?"

"I am not sure, but Kyrel was soon banished from his sister's domain, it is how he came to be with our clan."

"But you have no idea why?"

"Forgive me cousin but we are speaking of events which were long ended before I was born."

"OK but what about things now? Obviously Mai Mai doesn't think much of him. So why trust him with me?"

"He is the best able to teach you the active magicks."

"Yes I know but I see so much... disgust... in her eyes whenever she looks at him." Vereena bit her lip, looking ahead to where Kyrel was catching another of the slick mud dwelling creatures.

"Princess..."

"Aah ah!" Lilly waggled a finger.

"Sorry," the Da'ariel girl gave a slight nod "Cousin. I do not know all details of Mai Mai and Kyrel's agreement." her gaze flashed to him again. "What I do know is some things are for others to tell you."

"You're saying you *won't* tell me?"

"I'm saying I really think any questions you have about Kyrel should be brought to Kyrel."

"But you're supposed to tell me everything I want to know. That's your duty right? As the Qin Am Ness."

"I believe you misunderstand cousin. My duties are to tell you the things you *need* to know and offer what advice I can. I have told you of Mordrel and advised you to speak with Kyrel. I do not know of anything else which you need know of him from me right now. Only things you believe you want to know and as I know very little I'd rather not muddy things with misinformation."

"Right." Lilly sighed, plopping her foot down with a splash. "Cos things aren't already muddy."

"Voar!" Kyrel turned, addressing the entire group. "Voar inst! Voar inst!" he shouted as he made his way through the others toward Lilly.

"Come," said Vereena, "we must take cover."

Pulled under one of the bridge's immense stone arches by her cousin, as the other Da'ariel did the same, Lilly turned to see Kyrel beside her with a finger to his lips and asked, "What is it?"

"Shraeka." he muttered and seeing fear in her cousin's eyes she asked. "And that is?"

"Shhh." Kyrel and Vereena instructed in unison.

"Remain here," he added before slipping out into the shadows.

"OK what or who is a shraeka?"

"You might call them the moaning," explained Vereena. "They are victims of Mordrel, those she has not drained fully. They walk only where she sends them. Like extra fingers capable of drawing essence from others as she herself does. Only it does not rest in them. They are no more capable of keeping it than they are of keeping anything in their own heads." She tapped her temple. "They no longer function for their own benefit, all they encounter is passed on to Mordrel."

"Great," muttered Terrence. "She's sent her walking zombie-cam to watch over us."

"Oh they do not watch," Vereena told him. "The sight goes swiftly under the dres ver felt."

"Then why are we even hiding?" asked Lilly.

"Their eyes no longer being intact has little to do with the functioning of the ears."

"Right," nodded Lilly, "course it doesn't."

"Shouldn't Kyrel stay too?" whispered Lilly. "Why isn't he hiding?"

"Perhaps he seeks to lead them away." Vereena looked dubious, "Though I do not know a way he could. I do know he does all he does for your protection."

"Funny, I'd feel way more protected if he stayed at my side"

"I doubt he will go far. Quiet now."

"Sure," muttered Lilly, "make like the Da'ariel and hide."

The following silence seemed endless to Lilly. Having seen Tobias and Harper being swept into the neighbouring arch, she wondered how they were faring with no one to impart information of all that was happening.

Above, the bridge began to rumble; a constant yet far off sound, which progressed to a slow beat as many feet passed overhead. The boys criss-crossed their arms over their heads as dust fell from minute cracks.

Compared to the legions which had passed earlier this was a notably smaller contingent and the beat was soon rumbles again until minutes later it had faded to nothing.

The entire group eyed each other cautiously, none daring to speak, until raising an eyebrow at Vereena, Lilly received a nod in return and poking her head out the archway muttered.

"Where is Kyrel?"

"I am here," he came in the other side dragging an inert body on the end of a short rope. Everyone present turned to watch him.

"Oh man!" muttered Terrence as he stared down at the eyeless, emaciated, face.

The lips were a bluish white but the rest of the skin had a greyish hue.

"What have you done?" Vereena's eyes grew wide as she hurried over to him. "This is too dangerous. He remains connected to the other shraeka. To your sister! You risk every-"

"I risk nothing." Kyrel stood to face her. "He is no longer in any state to supply information to Mordrel and he had no awareness of my presence when he was."

Vereena bit her lip, staring down at the prone form in its scant and filthy clothing, her voice came out solemn.

"This man is Da'ariel."

Kyrel glanced down then stepped to one side, obscuring the views of her and the others.

"This man is a means of gaining knowledge, a thing we could do with far more of don't you agree?"

"Yes but-"

"Then go tend to the others," Kyrel put a hand on the young girl's arm. "See all are ready to continue on our way. I shall not be long."

"I don't understand," Baxter said as an order of cat ya vac had the Da'ariel following Vereena from their shelter. "What's he gonna do, torture the poor sod?"

"I don't think so," muttered Terrence. Neither they nor Lilly made any attempts to leave; Kyrel seemed not to notice. "Magicks made him this way." Terrence nodded toward the figure as Kyrel turned it over. "More specifically: Mordrel's magicks."

"You think it keeps him linked to her somehow?" suggested Baxter, he and Lilly both turned to Terrence and shrugging he said, "Sure, from what Veer said these guys are basically walking transmitters right? What they learn is passed on to Mordrel. So what if that's a connection that can be made to go both ways?"

"What's going both ways now?" Harper asked as she and Tobias joined them. Both noticed Kyrel beside the body at the same time and shaking his head Tobias asked.

"Whoa? What did we miss?"

Terrence and Baxter turned to explain, and leaving them to it Lilly made her way to Kyrel, crouching at his side she asked.

"Are they right? Is he still connected to your sister? Is that how you're going to get information out of him?"

"Yes," he pulled down the top of the man's hooded shirt and parted his dirty hair. Just above the nape of the grubby neck Lilly spied the Do'mass scar so similar to her own and was jabbed with an unexpected pang of loss. She pushed it aside, watching Kyrel's fingers form a claw as he put his hand to the symbol; grabbing the man's neck as Lilly had once been taught to grab kittens. "You're going to use that dres verfelt thingy on him aren't you?"

Kyrel's hand snapped back and he turned to look at her, studying her a moment before he said "You should be readying to leave. Take your friends and join Lady Vereena. I shall meet you out there."

"Hey hang on... I get that we have to do what we have to do OK. I was just ask-"

"This is not a thing you have to do Lilly. It is a thing *I* have to do. Now do as I say, so we may again get moving."

Anger flashed in her eyes and she opened her mouth to speak. Kyrel didn't give her the chance.

"Leave!" he insisted in a voice, which assured no arguing, and sighing as she slunk away Lilly muttered,

"Whatever."

"OK what was that all about?" Harper asked as she and the others followed Lilly out from under the bridge.

"There are magicks Kyrel doesn't want her learning." said Terrence. "They're too dangerous or something."

"That's stupid," said Tobias. "Shouldn't he be teaching her everything he knows, especially the dangerous stuff?"

"Not if it's mostly dangerous to her." Harper turned from him to

Terrence. "Is it?"

"I dunno," he shook his head. "But I bet you he's about to use some of that magic right now."

"Hence the kick out," nodded Harper. "He doesn't want her watching him. Never know what she might pick up."

Lilly had already joined Vereena and they were deep in discussion by the time the others joined them. Turning to address them Vereena explained that there should only be a couple more hours walking before they hit the cover of the forests on the bridge's other side.

"Then we get to rest right?" Tobias interrupted, "I'm not sure I can get that far but if it means settling somewhere safer I'm all for it."

"Yes," Vereena told him, "We shall rest and it shall be safer. The wounded will need tending to before this night is out and we could all do with eating."

"Yeah," agreed Lilly "I can't believe Baxter's gone so long without complaining... hey," she looked around "Where is he anyway?"

Curious glances passed between the group and shrugging Terrence said. "He was with us when we came out from..." Lilly's gaze followed his to the darkness of the arch they'd just left and rolling her eyes she sighed.

"For crying out loud!" Stalking off in that direction, her stride slowed as she neared, then peered inside. Almost immediately she spotted Baxter, he had pressed himself against the wall and was watching Kyrel. Lilly made her way quietly over to him, whispering from behind her hand, "What are you doing? He said we had to leave."

"Don't pretend like you ain't curious." Baxter whispered back. "Anyways does he look like he's paying attention to us right now?" Lilly looked to where Kyrel grasped tight at the man's neck. His closed eyes were moving as if he dreamed and his deep rhythmic breathing told of complete engagement.

While they watched his hand and arm shake from the strain; Kyrel watched image after image flashing before his mind's eye.

He saw himself as he'd been when last in Crizoleth and the faces of Lilly and Mairiel swam by too. These were followed by Leyavanya's orbs. First there were two, side by side on matching pedestals. Then another appeared beside them; then another and another - in all nine glowed around him and as he realised what a beautiful sight their light created, his sister's army stomped it all out.

Legions upon legions of soldiers marched across Azeron. Everywhere they went devastation followed. Fires brought down homes as deadly swarms of Ginaten converged on an ever increasing amount of villages. Dead Deebanaarie soon accompanied dead Da'ariel in decorating the lands with their blood.

Lilly and Baxter watched with growing horror as unknown to Kyrel the Da'ariel shraeka began convulsing silently beneath his hand, and he himself began gasping and gulping as though the air were being sucked from his lungs. Through his strained gulps came the repeated moans of "Mai Mai," and "Nydrel, Ny mech."

Before Baxter could stop her, Lilly ran out from the shadows calling Kyrel's name and grabbing his shoulder. The second she did, she too saw much of what he had. Only for her it was in a fraction of the time and almost immediately she was seeing along with him: a woman doubled over with both hands at her own throat. The great fear in her eyes was outweighed only by the betrayal as she watched another watching her die. Mordrel stood over the older woman with a chalice in one hand and a satisfied smirk on her lips.

A heavy thud brought Kyrel to his senses, and his hand drew back from the shraeka's neck. Immediately the form beneath him stopped convulsing, and shaking his head to clear it Kyrel turned to see Lilly on her back in the mud. Her eyelids fluttered as she clutched her head hissing.

"Shit, ouch, shit. Shit. Shit. Crap!"

"Ny dylur!" muttered Kyrel, his voice growing angry as he shook his head at her. "What are you doing? You could have been hurt!"

"Yeah well you looked like you *were* being hurt OK," Lilly groaned some more as she pushed herself up. "I was just.... aah fuck! My head! I was trying to help!"

"I did not request your help. I requested that you wait with the others." He nodded to the archway, and spotting Baxter lurking in the shadows waved for him to join them.

"Actually..." Lilly sat up slowly, still rubbing her head. "You didn't request anything. You ordered it! And as *I'm* the princess I figured I don't have to take orders. Anyway, what do you mean *could* have been hurt?" She moaned out a few more profanities before asking. "I'm pretty sure I just had at least one complete volume of the encyclopaedia Azeronia jammed into my skull, all right. It didn't exactly feel good!"

"Of course not," a hiss escaped Kyrel, "But you would rather be insolent, than recognise when another is trying to protect you. Well, see where it gets you. You have mud on your clothes and pain in your head. I hope the result is enlightening to you." He turned to Baxter, "And this one encourages you does he not?"

"Oh hey," Baxter shrugged, reaching down to help Lilly up, "if Slater wants to see what's-"

"I see the mischief in your eyes Robert Baxter."

"Yeah steady on mate, Baxter will do thanks."

"I may not yet know for what reason you meddle," Kyrel pointed a finger, "but do not think I do not see."

"Meddle!" Baxter's eyes rolled. "I'm stranded here just like Slater is OK. I have as much right to know how and when we're gonna get out of this place."

"And you believe sneaking around after me will answer this for you! How?"

"No see, the answers I want from *you* are along a different track. Goes a little something like who the hell do you think you are?"

"Hell?" Kyrel looked baffled.

"Yeah," nodded Baxter "Hell! Pretty much sums up this shitty world of yours OK. Now from what I see, you and these Da'ariel have a lot riding on Lilly, not something she asked for mind you. Just something you decided to plonk in her lap. So I'm thinking maybe she has a right to know what's going on."

"Then you think it is your place to decide what she needs to know?"

"You know *she's* standing right here guys," Lilly hissed through gritted teeth. Nonetheless her presence seemed forgotten.

"Actually," Baxter squared his shoulders taking a step forward. "I think I'd like to know how it's yours. I think she would too. You've been prancing around dishing out orders since back at the village. Telling the rest of us when we can and can't speak with her. You think just cos you can train her you have the right to -"

"Baxter," Lilly tried again to intercede. "Maybe you should back off."

"No maybe *he* should back off."

"You wish to declare a challenge on me?" Kyrel looked to the boy's stance.

"What?" Lilly glanced Baxter's way, the scowl on his face spoke volumes. "Whoa!" She signalled a T with her hands. "Time-out! No one's challenging anyone OK."

"I don't know," Baxter hissed through gritted teeth, "This declaring a challenge thing sounds spot on to me. Assuming the Deebanaarie can fight without his magicks of course."

Kyrel's eyebrow went up and glaring at Baxter Lilly asked,

"Are you insane?"

"No... I'm the hardest kid in Craven's Peak! I don't take shit from anyone in our world. Why should I stand here and take lip from this Tarzan, Robin Hood reject?"

"Stop it!" Dumbfounded she shook her head, "You're a school kid for crying out loud. Kyrel's a warrior."

"The princess is right," nodded Kyrel "a fight between us would be most unwise for you."

"Oh yeah..." Baxter jabbed his fists at the air in front of Kyrel's face and began bouncing back and forth. "Come on then. Let's have it!" Kyrel threw Lilly a puzzled look.

"How does he hope to defeat me when he has no weapons?"

"Err..." shrugging she opened her mouth to speak as Baxter said,

"Mano-a-mano you prick!" His eyes went to the dagger at Kyrel's belt, and he paused to shrug, "Obviously I... I was kind a hoping you'd be willing to drop your weapons."

"To do such a thing when you wish to fight me would be foolish would it not?"

"No," Baxter frowned, "we're not talking a fight to the death or anything."

"Then what purpose would this fight serve?"

Clearly aghast Baxter shook his head, "It's an honour thing OK!" sighing, he rolled his eyes and bouncing again began explaining. "One of us knocks the other down and-"

"My God would you just shut up!" Lilly shoved him backward almost toppling over. "This isn't the kind of place where you walk away from a fight." she told him. "Kyrel kills guys your age without batting an eyelid! You can't challenge him to a round of fisty-cuffs!"

"OK, yeah fine." Baxter relented with an indignant shrug. "No fighting, but he still needs to either back off or start dishing out some answers to go with all those orders he's been throwing around."

"Look... just..." Lilly shook her head, "Go wait with the others OK." It was Baxter's turn to throw her a puzzled look, "Go on," she told him. "Go be The Peak's hardest kid out there. Me and Kyrel need to talk."

"Sure," Baxter's hands went into his pockets. "You talk." He turned his back on them. "We'll see if you actually come out of here with anything resembling information."

As Lilly watched him leave, Kyrel kicked over the Da'ariel shraeka and bent to examine him.

"Hey I'm sorry about Baxter, he... well he can be a bit of an idiot, but for once I think his heart might actually be..."

Turning to see Kyrel poking a finger into the shraeka's shrivelled face; a gelatinous quality made it a distinctly disturbing sight for Lilly. Feeling bile rise in her throat, she turned away covering her mouth.

"OK, please stop doing that."

With a curious expression Kyrel stood to face her.

"He is gone. We will get nothing more through him."

"Yeah..." she turned back, glancing toward the body, "I... I see that. Do you think maybe you could you know... turn him back over."

Kyrel kicked the shraeka gently back on to his front before nodding, then waving a hand over it said, "Ta Varee." Together they watched both corpse and the grubby clothing it had worn dissolve in a bubbling heap until it was indistinguishable from the mud around them.

"Well, that was kinda gross." Lilly muttered.

"He is returned to the lands," said Kyrel, "no greater honour can be bestowed on the dead."

"Hey, however you want to look at it." She raised a hand. "I'm sticking with gross."

Unperturbed Kyrel glanced to the archway.

"You do realise we have no time to stand here talking? We have already remained too long. We must get into the forest."

"Fine," she shrugged, "then we'll talk and walk OK, just first... first you have to tell me one thing..."

Kyrel sighed, nodding, "You want to know what just happened. What it was you saw."

"So you're telling me that was what..." asked Lilly, "a part of your sister's mind?"

She and Kyrel were now at the front of the group and the treacherously muddy footing was finally giving way to a more densely packed ground beneath their feet.

"Yes," he nodded "what happens now and what's come before. Her desires, her intentions – all can be glimpsed when you know how."

"OK, but are we supposed to have a clue what any of it meant? Because personally I'm clueless. Shit I could barely tell one image from another, never mind figuring out her intentions from what's come before. I did see myself though so apparently she knows what I look like and I saw you!" She pointed his way, then wrinkling her nose shrugged, "at least I think it was you. You were younger."

"It has been much time since I was in Crizoleth," explained Kyrel. "You: she will have seen with quiesscence. Me: she is less interested in."

"Right," Lilly nodded, sucking in her lower lip as she shrugged. "I guess that makes... Hey, what about that other woman? She was... well I thought maybe she was dying. And that was your sister with her wasn't it? That was Mordrel... I think, actually no, I knew it was. She killed that woman, I know she did."

"My sister has killed many."

"Yeah but this was different. I felt it." With a shiver Lilly grimaced. "I felt relief! There was... I dunno... all this resentment and anger. I... I think I hated that woman. Then I felt, watching her die... I felt satis-"

"Perhaps you should let me decide the meanings of what was seen." Kyrel cut her off and looking up Lilly saw how his jaw had tensed. He forced his lips into a tentative smile and she sighed,

"Sure," then rubbing her temple added. "I guess I can do that. My head hurts too much for all this thinking anyway."

***

Slowly the mud thinned, giving way to hard dry ground. Up ahead a distant treeline could be seen. Though they spoke little, Lilly and Kyrel maintained a bubble of privacy by staying ahead of the group by several feet.

After lengthy discussion about Leyavanya, the other council members, and the power contained in the orbs, an almost as lengthy silence had weighed in on them. Kyrel sighed, keeping his eyes frontward as he finally spoke again.

"Had I known the orbs were present at the village I would surely have told you much of these things sooner." He shook his head "I had no knowledge of Mairiel's clan finding them and so no reason to consider doing so. The orbs have been lost to our peoples for many generations."

"It's OK." said Lilly. "I believe you."

"You are certain?"

"Oh come on," she shrugged. "I saw your face back in those tunnels, all right. You were well shocked."

Kyrel's eyes went to her for a brief sideways glance before he sighed, "Yet there are other things you believe me to be concealing?"

"Errm," she shoved her hands deep in her pockets. "Well there does seem to be a lot about the magicks that you're not telling me. And well I'm not saying it's intentional or anything but you have been kind of closed lipped on the whole... you know... *How* you fit into all this?"

"How I fit?" Kyrel frowned.

"Err... OK you knew my parents right... Or maybe just my mother... See I'm not even sure! Why are you here Kyrel? Why is my grandmother, who clearly detests you, allowing you to be so involved?"

Another far deeper sigh escaped Kyrel; Lilly sighed too.

"Maybe you could just teach me how to use that orb thingy."

His eyes snapped toward her, jaw tightening as he said, "You are to focus on the three forces we've-"

"See, now, that's part of the problem. You keep telling me Mordrel won't stop until I'm dead. Well I'm certain I don't wanna be dead. Easiest damn choice anyone's ever given me. Seriously: give this thing all I've got or wind up being a corpse... Well there's no contest, OK! And you can't honestly tell me you don't think I'm doing well? Bloody brilliant even... Cos everyone else here seems to think I'm pretty amazing!"

"Few of these Da'ariel ever saw the active magicks in use before you arrived. They do not possess the knowledge to correctly judge your abilities."

"Well, thanks... way to burst my bubble,"

"You ask for truth; that's truth. You are far from ready to wield the kind of power contained within an orb of Leyavanya."

"How can you know that, if you won't give me a chance?"

"You lack the will to focus on what I have already been teaching you. You cannot then expect to bend such ancient power to your will. I am far more practised, yet can barely control such magicks."

"Then teach me more of the other stuff!" she pleaded. "I mean not that thing you do with the ginats, OK! Tez and Vereena clued me in on the whole dres verfelt, forbidden magicks thing, and I don't think I'm ready to go there." As his eyebrows bounced up, she shrugged, "No matter though, right... you know other stuff too. What about what you did with that shreaka guy back there... the whole you know mind to mind thingy. Can't I learn that? Could be handy, right? I might need to do a little info gathering of my-"

"I will not be teaching you this."

"Why? Haven't I proved I can be a quick study? If you just show me how-"

"I cannot teach you what is not in your blood."

"Right, a little too Deebanaarie for me then," glum faced Lilly sighed. "You know, I'd love to know how come you guys got all the cool powers. All day I've been trying to figure out what the hell I'm gonna do if your sister catches up to us and so far I'm at zilch on ideas. She can do everything you can and is twice as powerful right? Well, the best I can do is stick a few trees in her way, or I dunno, put up a massive wall or something... what good is any of that gonna do when she can just demolish it again. Doesn't that pretty much make me screwed?"

"You are right to fear her Lilly. She has mastered many of the forces."

"Well cheers, that helps," she gave him a thumb's up before shaking her head. "Just how many is many anyway?"

Seeming to take an overly long time contemplating this, Kyrel eventually nodded, "Six."

"Six!" Lilly's eyes grew wide and her feet stopped moving, watching Kyrel pause also she watched him turn to face her, and gulped. "Your sister Mordrel can control *six* different forces?"

"At least that many," shrugged Kyrel, "as I said, it has been awhile since

I was last in Crizoleth."

"So maybe she can work more?" Lilly started walking again. "Aren't there like ten of these forces?"

Again he considered his words carefully only this time Lilly realised he was figuring out the translation of the numbers.

"Yes," he finally agreed, "but not since the days of the Tualavan has anyone been able to work them all."

"Yeah, well six is still way more than three. If you don't teach me more there's no way I can-"

"Lilly, after your Kalaareem, you will be so much-"

"What if I don't make it to my Kalaareem, Kyrel? Isn't that the big deal here? Isn't your sister gunning for me in a very real - this is probably the last day of my life kind of way?"

"I know how frightening this must-"

"You don't know anything," she shook her head. "I'm the one she wants dead, remember! I'm the one she's hunting. Me! And those funny glowing ball thingies, with all that power you won't even let me try and tap. You can walk away from this whenever you like. She doesn't even care that you exist."

"She would care if she knew," said Kyrel. Lilly threw him a questioning look and shrugging he added, "It is almost certain my sister believes I am dead."

"Well that's great for you, can't get much safer than already dead."

"It is true that she is not in pursuit of me but that does not keep me from risk. She had me banished to the plains of the Nihidi. Do not think you are the only one she wants dead."

"Is that the real reason we're running away?"

"Running away?"

"Sure, we could go face her, we probably should. Arteth and Toleth certainly could have done with our help, you saw everything I saw. You know how many of Mordrel's troops are out there. I don't see how they even stand a chance without us."

"It is unlikely that they do," said Kyrel. "Their plan is foolish and Mairiel would not want you involved."

"You know you're kind of a heartless bastard."

"The plan is to get you to safety." He shrugged, "There are more Da'ariel in Zanreal woods. Getting you safely to them is what Mairiel has charged me with. I gave my word. I will not break it."

"Well from what I saw when I touched you there isn't any safely anymore. I'm also pretty sure Mairiel's still alive and I think you know it."

"I know she wanted you kept safe until you're capable of protecting yourself."

"And that'll be tomorrow, right? On my Kalaareem?"

"Tomorrow will be a start," he told her. "Your powers should be greatly increased."

"*Should* be?"

"Times as they are, some Deebanaarie are getting little or no increase with the Kalaareem. So it was with the Da'ariel before us."

"And you're telling me this now!"

"I see no reason this should happen with you. Your power is already tremendous. Herrella was right to send you away when she saw the full mark upon you. It truly has brought you great power, more than I have ever seen in any as young as you. If you can only be patient, I will teach you many more things; all I can to make sure you can end Mordrel."

"Well sure, why not, I just live to be a tool for you. A spanner you can throw in your sister's works."

"I…" he shook his head, "I am unsure of your meaning."

"OK fine, let me put it this way: family or not… the Da'ariel brought me here to be a weapon, some way to fight back. For a while there, I actually thought you were different; like maybe you were helping me because you actually care." She shrugged, "But you came looking for me because you need a weapon too – something to use against your sister. Maybe you really do believe in a better Azeron. Or maybe you just want revenge because she banished you. I don't know, but I do know you're so busy trying to mould me into this perfect weapon you can't see the very real possibility that you might never get to use me if you don't allow me to use every bit of power I can muster." With a raised eyebrow he shook his head.

"You say you have been learning of the dres verfelt, surely you see how risky some of the forces can be."

"So what? The only other things you can teach me are forbidden?"

"There are no forbidden magicks anymore," he shrugged. "I break no laws when I use my powers. No matter what your Qin Am Ness may say. Using any magicks brought death to the Da'ariel for such a long time they learned how to mistrust over all else."

"But you don't want me to learn these wild magicks either. You were just saying how dangerous it can all be."

"Yes." Kyrel sighed. "It is dangerous and now is not the time for you to try, but I am not saying you can never learn. I am confident that with enough time and practice you can master a great deal more. For now we must concentrate on you being able to protect yourself. The forces you can best use to slow Mordrel down."

"Like growing trees?" It was Lilly's turn to raise an eyebrow. "Still not seeing how-"

"I had you work with the plants first because you had already shown a natural strength in it."

"Oh…" she bit her lip a moment before shrugging, "So then the mud manipulation and that wind stuff are…"

"Your true defences against Mordrel." He nodded. "But all the forces can be devastating if you simply learn to focus. You did so with Toleth earlier. That was the Laîoch was it not?"

"Err… yeah." Lilly shrugged. "I think so but I wasn't focused, I don't even know what I was thinking. I could have sent you both flying into that rock."

"Well I remain grateful that you did not." Kyrel nodded. "You saved my life and Toleth's. Had you spoken the Tuâoch, the result may have been different."

The briefest fear flashed in Lilly's eyes and she sighed. "Fine, when we stop again you can help me work on the focusing and I promise I'll stick with the right words, OK."

"This is a good decision you make." Kyrel smiled. "I am... pleased to hear it"

"Yeah, whatever, I still want to know how you knew my mother." The smile faded and his mouth slammed shut. "I want the truth…" insisted Lilly "why are you here?"

"This is… as you say… a long story."

"Yeah, well," Lilly gazed ahead to the distant tree-line. "That forest doesn't seem to be getting closer anytime soon."

"You are mistaken," Kyrel looked ahead with a frown, "it is closer with our every step."

Lilly's eyes rolled, and she shook her head. "Just tell me how you know the Avengturovs OK, Vereena also mentioned your banishment, so I'm guessing that had something to do with it."

"Yes…" he nodded. "It was a long time ago. I was not much older than you. My own Kalaareem had long passed leaving me strong, but escaping the Nihidi took much of that strength. I believed my death approached when I reached the forest, I fell and all became darkness. When I woke I did not know where I was. I could no longer see the trees. The damp ground had become soft straw and most of my clothing was gone."

***

Seconds after he'd used all his strength to pull himself to a seated position, Kyrel heard: "Your weapons have been removed." Upon turning, he a saw a young woman, possibly still in her late teens - was entering the small hut.

Glaring her way he stated, "Then I demand you return them to me; at once!" his eyes followed her every movement as he spoke.

In her hands was a tray from which a small flat-stone, piled high with chips of tellemi crystal, lit-up her face with their soft green hue. Alongside the flat-stone was a cup and a large bowl, each with slowly rising trails of steam above them. The girl set the tray down on a cut piece of tree stump.

"Oh I'm afraid mother would never allow that." She picked up the only other piece of furniture in the room, a small stool, and placed it beside him, then nodding as she sat added, "You are fortunate she allowed my troop to bring you inside the village at all."

"You are Da'ariel." He studied her clothes and face.

"And *you* are Deebanaarie." She smiled; her voice languid as she drank him in with her huge amber eyes. An overwhelming curiosity masked any other emotion she might be feeling as she followed up. "You must be an exceptional warrior to bear the insignia of a General so early in life." She pulled a steaming rag from the bowl and wrung it out.

"I will have my things returned to me now." Kyrel's paler yellow eyes darted from her to the door. "I must leave this place. It is not safe to-"

"From the look of you, this is the safest you have been in a long time." the girl said as she pulled the patchwork of animal skins off his dirty bruised chest. "Your people barely enter these woods and they have never found our village."

"I'm in the Shadowwood?" He scanned the room as if expecting to see something new.

"Yes," she said placing the hot damp cloth on his chest. Wincing he turned to face her again, and she told him, "We are many leagues from Deebanaarie territory."

"Then there really is a village out here?" He spoke with reverence. "My people searched for so many generations. How have you-"

Hissing he winced again as her cloth grazed an open wound on his shoulder.

"Sorry," she winced with him. "Your wounds, they… they go deep. They must be cleaned." Gritting his teeth he nodded and wiping more caked on muck away she shrugged, "Our village is protected: a barrier conceals all within from Deebanaarie eyes."

"Your people still use magicks?" His voice came out muted through his teeth. "How can that be possible? Da'ariel are not born with magicks anymore…" Kyrel shook his head, "And your barrier would have fallen during the Post-Hlledran raids."

"We relocated here after the raids, before that our clan held larger territories on the other side of the forest," nodded the girl. "And these magicks are not Da'ariel. They come from the many sprites who allow our people to remain in their forests. We have also learned many ways to draw essence from the land. None of which the Deebanaarie can detect."

"You should not be telling me these things," he shook his head. "You could be putting your people at risk."

"You asked." She shrugged, "Besides… I see no threat in your eyes," she gazed down into them, cloth pausing at a protruding rib. "Plenty of fear," she nodded, "but there isn't a speck of ill will in you."

"I am Deebanaarie!" Kyrel was aghast. "You *must* allow me to leave."

"I have no intention of stopping you," she mopped gently at the bruises down the side of his ribs. "But you will not be able to return and I would rather see you leave here with at least a chance of surviving the forests."

"Your belief in your safety here has robbed you of all sense. Why should you even want to help a Deebanaarie? I cannot have been away so long that we are not still your enemy? My people *hunt* yours! How can it serve you to ease my suffering? How does it not please you to see me so?"

"Odd that you ask such things when in doing so you *too* concern yourself with the fate of your enemy. I have lived among these trees all of my life General. When I was a child I played in them, enjoying what little beauty Azeron still had to offer. Suffering is not a thing I grew up knowing and it certainly is not a thing which pleases me." She dumped the cloth in the bowl and returning it to the tray picked up the cup.

"To get your strength up," she handed it to him, "Mother will not tolerate your presence here for long."

Kyrel sipped cautiously then, closing his eyes, began glugging hungrily. It had been so long since any liquid had passed his lips he couldn't help savouring every moment of the warm gaawa juice sliding down his parched throat.

His haste proved foolhardy however, as he was soon wracked with a coughing fit that had the girl snatching the cup from him and beating on his back as she pressed him forward.

Pushing her away Kyrel thanked her, through what he hoped were the last of the coughs, and handing him back the cup she smirked. "I was not suggesting you guzzle like a battle broken yimusa trundle. There is at least time for you to drink without choking."

When his only response was a grim look she picked up a poultice from the tray, and pressing it firmly against the open wound on his shoulder, watched his mouth clamp shut over gritted teeth, as she said, "You must not worry. I do have mother's word she will not make you leave before you are well enough."

Sipping more cautiously Kyrel swallowed as he nodded up at her.

"Do you and your mother usually take it on yourself to make decisions on behalf of your entire clan?" Hissing as another poultice went on he looked to it asking "Will your leaders not punish you both severely when they learn of you *taking me in* this way?"

With a chuckle the girl shrugged,

"We Da'ariel do not lead with fear as the Deebanaarie do." then nodding, she tilted her head to one side adding, "Still... your question has merit and some truth. I do lack experience deciding anything for the clan as a whole, but I've taken on many duties and my mother is-"

"Very much concerned with how much time her daughter has now been in here with this wounded Deebanaarie"

"Mai Mai." the girl bowed her head as her mother entered the hut.

"Mai Mai?" Kyrel's eyebrows bounced up, realisation creeping into his voice. "You're a clan mother." he also bowed his head. "I assure you I meant no harm by entering your territory. It was a mistake and I am thankful for the assistance given me. I must however insist that you return my things and allow me to leave."

With the movement of only his eyes, he gazed up at this older Da'ariel woman. Awaiting the slight nod she eventually afforded him; after a couple more seconds staring, before he fully raised his head.

"I would sooner spit on your corpse than offer assistance to any wearing the uniform of Mordrel's troops. Be grateful my daughter Herrella possesses more compassion. She alone has saved your life this day; she has begged for it in fact and has my word I'll let you live for the time being."

Kyrel dropped his eyes and the woman turned her invective on the daughter.

"As I have her word that doing so will in no way hinder her duties."

"But Mai Mai I completed my studies before today's hunt, and have personally inspected both ration huts, and the armoury since my return-"

"And now you are overdue in council are you not?" Herrella bit her lip, glancing Kyrel's way.

He respectfully kept his gaze locked on his lap. Nodding she turned back to her mother, head bowing once more as she said, "forgive me Mai Mai. I forgot the council was in attendance today. I shall make my way there immediately."

"See you do so." said Mai Mai before leaving.

"So much for not leading with fear." Kyrel muttered the second he and Herrella were alone again. Her gaze caught his and he smirked, "You seem pretty frightened to me… is your mother always so… so…"

"I admit your presence here has angered her some."

"Some?"

"In truth," sighed Herrella, "she is deeply angry with me for bringing you here and it would be wise if neither of us provoke her. But you heard for yourself, I do have her word you will be allowed to stay."

"For now," shrugged Kyrel "but to what end? Is either of us foolish enough to believe she would allow me… a Deebanaarie… to leave with knowledge of your village's whereabouts?"

"Perhaps we should concentrate on seeing you well before considering the outcome of your presence here." she reached for the tray but Kyrel caught her arm.

"You are Avengturov." For a moment she looked surprised but this subsided and smiling she nodded,

"So now you think you know who we are?"

"Lost village," shrugged Kyrel. "A *true* living clan mother! Your people hold council yet she makes decisions for all?" His eyebrow went up, "There can be no mistaking it. Your mother is the rightful Queen of all Azeron's Da'ariel."

"We both know the Deebanaarie acknowledge no such sovereignty." Herrella chided with a smile. "It surprises me you would even know the name Avengturov."

"Perhaps all Deebanaarie are not made up of the same ignorances…" sighed Kyrel. "You after all, seem much different from Mai Mai. Is it not equally possible that we Deebanaarie also have differences?"

It took Herrella a moment to contemplate him before she drew her arm gently from his feeble grasp. "Differences among your people matter not. Since the enthronement of Mordrel any changes that may have been with Queen Anniiada were made no more. Her offspring wilfully take up the role of your peoples ancestors. They use you and all who are subordinate to you, to raid our villages and destroy all that Azeron is and could be."

"This may be so…" Kyrel's gaze dropped momentarily then he asked "But you… are not you the heir to the Avengturov legacy?" He nodded to where Mai Mai had stood. "That is why she allows you the leniency with which you keep me here is it not?"

Herrella's eye's flitted to the doorway and she bit her lip before allowing her eyes to rest on him again, then leaned closer, whispering near his ear.

"Yes. I am the eldest daughter and rightful heir of the Avengturov line. Let us speak on it no further." Then she straightened up adding, "Now, I must attend council and you still require much rest."

"Wait!" croaked Kyrel as she left him for the door. "I do not yet understand; why are you doing this for me?"

"I do nothing for you that I would not do for any other." Herrella smiled. "Rest now. I will return."

True to her word she returned many times. Learning his name on her second visit, she brought him sustenance each day: a limited selection of fruits, nuts and dark sweet rolls accompanied a thin broth of Gaawa juice two times a day. She also checked, cleaned and – much to his chagrin at the time – re-poulticed his wounds daily, until he recovered enough to tend most of them himself.

At this point he was also able to hobble around the small room unassisted and though Herrella's duties kept her busy most of the day he would sit up on his cot of straw and the pair would talk the evenings away.

As time passed by, day's bled into weeks and Kyrel recovered enough of his strength to walk around the village. Most of the clan kept their distance at first, understandably wary of this young Deebanaarie in their midst, many would thumb their weapons as he passed by with the armed escort, which accompanied him everywhere.

If she had time Herrella would accompany him on these wanderings. Most areas had been deemed off limits to him, so they were never long and she would often return to her studies or some other duty when they were done. This did however allow them time to talk in slightly varied surroundings and the respect the clan had for her seemed to rub off as some warmed up to him.

The weeks became months and he was no longer eyed with only suspicion but had gained enough respect to receive the occasional nod or smile instead.

One day Herrella came to his hut in a flurry of excitement, informing him he'd been invited to dine with the rest of the Avengturov family. On hearing this news the stricken look on Kyrel's face made her burst out laughing.

"What?" He frowned, "Why do you laugh? I did nothing amusing."

"Except looking as if I just told you mother is feeding you to the village matfiac. This is not a bad thing. Kyrel, she bestows great honour on you."

"Sorry," he forced a smile "I meant no disrespect to Mairiel it is just…"

"What?"

"Herrella your brothers…they…" biting his lip he shook his head, "you must have seen the way Volesh looks at me."

"I know," she nodded, "he is troubled by your presence here."

"With good reason, we all know I should not-"

"Kyrel please, we have been over this… you are my guest. Mother herself has permitted you this sanctuary among us and it is she who bids you dine with us. You must know Volesh would not dare disrespect her by bringing such issues to the table."

"Even so I would rather stay out of his and everybody else's way."

"Well you cannot," her hands went to her hips as she nodded, "for that *would* be disrespectful and you know it."

Anger flashed in his eyes as they stared at each other, as always the battle of wills was brief. Kyrel had long resigned himself to the fact that his station in life had dramatically shifted. He was no longer saluted on sight and couldn't expect anyone to follow his orders to the letter; he no longer had anyone to give orders to and probably never would again. With a sigh he nodded.

"Very well Princess, you may... inform your mother her invitation is accepted."

Herrella unleashed a face splitting smile and, much to his surprise, flung her arms around him with a torrent of thanks. A moment later she remembered herself and disengaging with obvious embarrassment averted her eyes.

"I... I am sorry. That was..." slowly her eyes met his and nodding he said,

"You need not explain yourself to me." With a bow of his head he added, "As always I am glad to have pleased you." Keeping his eyes low he allowed her to escape his small hut without further indignity.

Awareness of the honour extended to him through Mai Mai's invitation, only served to make Kyrel more anxious. Determined not to show his fears he sat quietly through that meal, speaking only when spoken to and addressing everyone, including Herrella, by their rightful titles despite knowing all by given name.

Beside the eldest, Volesh, Herrella had two other brothers. Hay'n; also her elder appeared to be every bit as tough as his brother but when conversed with had a noticeably gentler manner. Lothar, being the youngest of Mairiel's offspring, was only two cycles from his Kalaareem and maintained a respectfully cheery disposition with everyone - except Kyrel, whom he rarely spoke to, but achieved an undertone of contempt every time he did.

There was also a sister: Niamma, younger than Herrella by one cycle of the sun, she'd been born to the duties of a Qin Am Ness and was generally afforded more leeway than her sister. Her studies certainly left more time to call her own, and she was fast approaching the birth of her first child.

Hay'n was the only one among them to have a life-mate: Terris Dian, a serious looking, reedy woman, whose entire face lit up on the rare occasions when she actually smiled. She was quicker with her Gaashmay than any Kyrel had seen previously and headed the two troop contingent which made up Mai Mai's personal guard. With her Hay'n had already provided Mai Mai two grandsons.

The first: a tall lean boy named Arteth, was but five cycles in age and already fancied himself a great warrior. Much to the irritation of his parents he would soon take to spending much of his time following Kyrel around. He would also ease the tension of subsequent dining experiences with his endless questions regarding the Deebanaarie army, from across the family table. Toleth: the second son of Hay'n was but an infant and often in attendance only to suckle at his mother's breast before dozing off in her arms.

Two weeks after this first dinner Herrella entered Kyrel's rooms in a similar flurry of excitement.

"I have such very good news for you," she announced as the dirty orange curtain fell shut behind her. "Mother has agreed to-"

A gasp escaped her at the sight of one of the lunti fruit he'd been sent that morning, bubbling and popping as its small yellow form melted into the ground.

Kyrel smushed it with the hand he'd held over it. Then throwing dirt over what remained, bounced to his feet snarling.

"Can you not afford me even the courtesy of announcing yourself before entering here?" Stepping to one side he placed himself between her and the mound he'd created.

Herrella's stunned gaze shifted to his face and remembering his place he bowed his head.

"Forgive me Princess. I...I meant only to-"

"What is that?" she tilted her head to see beyond him.

Kyrel took another step, obstructing her view farther.

"I...I...it is nothing. You need not concern yourself. I merely-"

"Stand aside."

"Herrella please... Let us not allow this to-"

"You *will* stand aside Kyrel."

Holding her gaze he sucked in his lips a moment then sighing closed his eyes and complied with a nod.

No words were said as he watched her kneel where he'd been and brush the top layer of dirt from the small mound. It had ceased its bubbling. All that remained was mush. Herrella plunged in a hand cringing at the sensation as it came out covered in the slick brown goo of what had once been edible.

Shaking her head she turned to glare at him.

"How can this be? We know enough of your people to know how scarce the active magicks now are in your lands." Her voice took on a higher pitch and Kyrel glanced warily to the door.

"Herrella I have wanted so much to tell you-"

"Tell me..." Getting up she shook her head. "Tell me what? Is it not true that only those of Royal descent still carry the Tuâoch in their blood?"

"I can explain."

"Then do so..." again his gaze fell to the ground and Herrella's voice became more a demand, "Be swift!" He looked up to see her intensified glare. "*Who* are you?"

"I am Kyrel," he nodded "The very same Deebanaarie you've come to know."

"I do not know *this*!" Shaking her head she gestured to the ground. "I know nothing of any Deebanaarie holding rank of a General with enough Tuâoch essence in the blood to work the ancient magicks." Watching him bite down on his lip, as his eyes drifted to the door her voice lowered to a near whisper.

"Kyrel please... tell me how this-"

"I have never lied to you Herrella."

"Deceit is deceit no matter which form it takes!"

He shook his head.

"I never once claimed to be one of Mordrel's generals."

"We found you in the uniform!"

"Did you?" Kyrel's gaze levelled with hers, his lip shaking between words. "Are you certain?"

"None other bears the insignia of the..." seeing his eyebrow rise, Herrella's breath seemed to stop in her throat. Shaking her head she gasped "Ny... Ny mech! It cannot be so."

"Herrella..." with splayed hands he took a slow step toward her nodding, "you know now that it is."

"I will not accept such a-"

"If I am not a General then how else did I wear the D'vey House crest among my insignia?" Herrella's gaze went to everywhere he wasn't.

"You cannot be of the D'vey line." She shook her head. "Queen Anniiada's offspring are all gone or busy bringing devastation to the lands. The movements and campaigns of Mordrel's clan siblings are well documented, her youngest brother obliterated one of our largest villages just this last..." before she could finish she was shaking her head, "How could you be-"

"Seems your clan is not as knowledgeable of my people's actions as you think." Kyrel, took another step toward her. "Did you not wander how I escaped the Nihidi? I am Kyrel D'vey? Youngest Brother to Mordrel D'vey."

"No," she shook her head. "Such a thing cannot be. Kyrel D'vey is his sister's strongest – most savage – hand. I have come to know you, you cannot be he-"

"I did no more than my family duty. Is not your brother Volesh your mother's strongest hand also? You too do all that is asked of you in the name of your line. You know what it is to live in servitude to the throne."

"The Da'ariel have no throne," her words came out a scathing hiss. "Your people deny us that right." Herrella's lip trembled as he approached, reaching for her arm. She pulled away, shaking her head. "You say such things then presume to touch me!"

"How many times have you spoken of my mother Herrella? With her things were different were they not?"

"Yet your claim makes you responsible for the death and enslavement of more of my people than any other Deebanaarie alive!"

"And if I had the least bit of pride in any of what I've done, in my sister's name, I would have told you sooner. My last campaign - to Endrandorn - was a failure. In the end duty did not matter, I could not do all she asked of me. I pressed my views too far; too publicly. I opposed her for the last time. She banished me because she wanted me dead."

"Her own First-Hand?" A strained laugh escaped Herrella, "You expect me to believe this?"

"Ny Princess I would rather if you did not, but you wanted the truth… you have it."

"What harm has the essence in you caused our lands? I sought only to do a fellow Azeronian good by bringing you here. Yet the Tuâoch in you may have done irreparable damage to the land of my clan."

"You have just seen for yourself the extent of my magicks. If you knew how long I worked on that Lunti." He gestured to the unearthed yellow mass with a shrug.

"Because you are weakened." She nodded, "but your powers will return won't they? And then I am putting my people in danger by keeping you here."

"There is no need to justify to me what we both know you must now do." He sighed. "I know you cannot keep this from your mother." His eyes wouldn't leave her and she couldn't tear hers from him.

"Do as you must," said Kyrel, "Tell Mai Mai. Your brother Volesh will be glad of the privilege to execute me."

"And what of me?" asked Herrella, "Should I be glad also?"

"You have your duty as I had mine." His back straightened in illustration of his resolve. "I shall not hold it against you. We both know what it is to be loyal to our clans and I was born into mine as you were yours. You have no reason to trust me. I accept this but I do ask one thing of you."

Herrella's lips tightened to a line but she nodded for him to go on.

"That you understand my loyalty has never been to my sister. I respected my mother too much to ever be capable of that. She alone is my Queen and she like her mother before did want to change things. Had I been known in her name your people would have seen a different Kyrel D'vey. Perhaps on standing face to face with me you would not tremble as you do now."

Herrella made a conscious effort to compose herself.

"Someday this entire clan will be my charge Kyrel, If I cannot protect them… if I am… not willing…"

"Then you are not fit." he nodded, offering a respectful bow. "I know this." Tentatively he reached for her again. Herrella watched his hand slip around her forearm. "Do not feel guilty for what you must do." Her eyes levelled to meet his as he added, "Know that nothing can ever change my gratitude of your continued compassion toward me. I owe you my life."

Day Three: Part Three

"So any guesses on what they're doing now?"

Harper nodded to a clearing, created by Kyrel's use of the Tuâoch, where he and Lilly now sat facing each other.

"We know what they're doing," said Tobias, his eyes on the fire that popped and hissed as he held a stick over it. "Training, training and more training."

"I don't know," Harper shook her head, "I think it's been more than that for a while. Slater's barely said two words to the rest of us since she came back out from under that bridge."

"Yeah I think she's a bit too preoccupied to worry about us right now." Terrence drew his own stick in from above the flames and examined the small creature on the end of it.

Vereena had shown them how to prepare and cook the creatures fished from the almost dried out riverbed under the bridge. Underneath their mud coating they were stark silver and smooth like fish, but the flesh was a deep purple and the texture and taste were meatier like pork.

"Who cares what they're doing?" Baxter sighed, "We have warm food and no one on our tail for the first time since the village was attacked. I for one don't need to be sitting here wasting my down time on Slater and her new fella."

"Well I care," Tobias grumbled, pulling in his own stick for a quick inspection before returning it to the flames. "I've had enough of these slippery little fuckers, I want some real food. Or at least some real flavour."

"They are kinda dry and tasteless." Terrence pulled his carefully off its stick and waved it at Vereena "What did you call these again."

"Pa'lellies." She glanced up from the binding they'd been studying.

"Yeah well whatever you wanna call them," huffed Tobias. "My brother's right; they're drier than a nun's crotch. Don't you guys do gravy?"

"Gravy?" The baffled expression on her face was answer enough and Tobias sighed, "That's what I thought," his gaze went to Lilly again as he added, "Maybe she can grow something to go with them."

"Sure," said Baxter "like herbs and a stick of butter. This ain't no gourmet restaurant you prat! We're refugees surviving the wilderness not guests at a five star meal. Quit your whingeing and eat your mud-fish."

"Hey just cos your poor-white-trash self can stomach anything, don't mean the rest of us have to sit here and pretend to like this shit, OK."

"My poor-white-trash self will come over there, kick your ass, and eat that little critter for you in a minute. *If* you don't shut up and let the rest of us eat in peace."

The slightest concern at losing the puny ration dished to him made Tobias tear a strip of flesh from the creature and stuff it in his mouth.

Harper's gaze was still on Lilly as she asked, "Hey Baxter, you really think there's something going on between them?"

"What?"

"You know," she turned to face him. "You keep making these cracks about him being her boyfriend and stuff, and well I know he's kinda old but now that I watch them…" Baxter's eyes followed hers and they both watched the animated gesturing of the pair for a moment. "They do seem kinda…"

"I seriously doubt it." Said Terrence. "Besides… from what I can tell Kyrel's quite a bit older than he looks."

"Why do you say that?" she turned to him.

"I don't know," Terrence shrugged, "I'm not sure physical appearance is as related to age here as it is to magicks."

"How could it have more to do with magicks if they're so rare?"

"Active magicks are rare in the people," Terrence explained. "But that stuff they're calling essence; that's 'thar' in the native tongue by the way…" He let them know with an air of smugness, which faded as swiftly as it had arose upon being met with looks of equal ire from his brother and Baxter alike. Terrence pushed on, "it's in pretty much everything here. We've seen the effect that drink has on Mairiel,"

"Yeah she goes from decrepit to middle aged in seconds." Tobias nodded between bites, "It's kind of creepy."

"It'd sell for a bomb back home," said Harper and ignoring them both Baxter turned to Terrence.

"We haven't seen Kyrel drink any of that stuff."

"Exactly," nodded Terrence "I don't think he needs it, see he has way more of the essence in him."

"You think that boiled root drink is some kinda substitute for this thar?" Baxter suggested.

"I think it's used to replace at least some important component… sure."

"A component that affects ageing?" Harper looked dubious but intrigued.

"And a few other things maybe. Haven't you noticed how much older he looks if he's been using his powers a lot? He seems older when he's… drained. Then there's times like now… you know since he's been carrying that orb thing around… he looks way younger."

"How much older you think he is exactly?" Baxter eyed the pair again. Lilly's hands were spread above the ground where a plant was slowly rising to meet them. "We're not talking hundreds of years like some elf in a Tolkein book right?"

"Because that would just be too bizarre?" Harper threw Baxter a sceptical look and holding her gaze he shrugged.

"No, because he doesn't have the pointy ears."

As she narrowed her eyes, Terrence interjected.

"I don't think we're talking about anything like that. I mean he looks what…" he also glanced over, "Mid-twenties at the moment?"

"Sure," Harper nodded as they all looked over. "I'll go along with that." Baxter and Tobias nodded with her.

"Yeah well I swear when we left the village he looked twice that."

The faces of the others glowed in the greenish fire-light, as they considered it.

"You know bro…" Tobias pulled another Pa'lellie off his stick. "I think you're right, he did look older yesterday"

"So what you think he's like in his forties?" Baxter was frowning now.

"I don't know maybe a little more, maybe less,"

"Well if he's in his fifties him and Slater would definitely be icky," said Harper.

"Yeah well that's just one reason I don't think that's what's going on here," agreed Terrence.

"Because older guys never go for pretty young blondes?" Baxter raised an eyebrow.

"Actually," Terrence glanced to where Vereena remained engrossed, his voice lowering by an iota. "Given the social structure of the people here I think it's fair to say the women make most of the... you know... choices when it comes to well... err... mating."

"What's that meant to mean?" Tobias stuffed another strip of meat into his mouth.

"What it means moron..." Baxter prodded the embers with a second stick. "...is your bro's trying to figure out how to make moves on this one," he nodded Vereena's way. "Without being branded 'easy'..."

Harper giggled, a hand going over her mouth as Tobias's eyes narrowed on his brother, who in turn cast a similar glare Baxter's way.

Vereena glanced up at them with a smile, before obliviously returning her attentions to the binding in her hands.

"Not exactly where I was going with that." A flustered chuckle escaped Terrence, as he added, "point is I don't think Kyrel's trying anything, OK. I doubt it would even occur to him. This is strictly a mentoring gig for him he's here for other reasons."

"Some deeply invested ones I'm thinking." Baxter's eyes were on the pair again.

"Yeah well I see the way he is with her." Harper's voice took on a suggestive lilt. "I don't care what you say about social structure, the women might do the chasing here but the need to possess; I'm thinking that's still a guy thing."

"Glad someone else sees it." Baxter muttered.

"He's responsible for her," shrugged Terrence. "Maybe all you're seeing is him being protective."

"Protective?" Said Baxter. "He behaves like he owns her! Like how many times has *he* decided she's out of bounds to us?"

"Well he does have a lot to teach her," said Terrence.

"Sure... except Lilly says he won't teach her any more forces than he already has."

"I think it's more that he doesn't want to yet. See, I figure it's like mastering basic maths before tackling algebra. Plus there are magicks she shouldn't learn, stuff that can be dangerous. If she does come up against Mordrel she'll need to be a surgical strike not an atom bomb."

"Well in this case," Baxter muttered "I'd have to say the atom bomb is highly underrated. Don't know about the rest of you guys but I'm still leaning towards getting out of this alive and if Lilly has to fight for that then I say she goes in packing all the punch she has."

"Definitely," said Tobias.

Harper also nodded her agreement.

"OK see you're not getting it," said Terrence "None of you are. All the punch Lilly has could very well be the thing that makes it game over with no continue for us. Kyrel might be kinda pushy but I think he has the right idea. I for one don't want to be the unintended victim of an attack on the enemy. I say Lilly should trust him, which for her sake, means we need to too."

"Sure," sighed Baxter, "I'll play along." done eating he stretched out, resting his head on his crossed arms. "Don't mean I have to like him."

***

"Try now." Kyrel watched the concentration on Lilly's face as she moved her hand slowly to the right and still growing, the small plant followed.

"I'm doing it." She smiled in triumph.

"Yes," he agreed. "Go higher."

Rising carefully, Lilly walked backward and more shoots appeared on the plant's stem; all growing toward her moving hand, as if seeking her out. They rose with her and more plants sprang from the ground.

"This is wicked!" She grinned as the trail became denser; the plants growing thicker and heavier.

"Don't lose it," instructed Kyrel as she picked up the pace to accommodate the speed with which the thick vines were now heading for her.

"I'm not losing any…" Lilly's face creased with strain and moving faster still she glanced backward; to see the tree-line approaching fast.

"Err Kyrel… there's a way to stop right?"

"You must focus on-"

"Shit!" Lilly hissed as she toppled over a fallen log. Lying on her back she raised her head and saw that despite her hands being at her sides, the plants growing with increased speed were at her feet and still going.

"Kyrel!" Lilly screamed as the rope-like foliage engulfed her. In seconds she was immobilised; her whole body being squeezed, and the dense mass blanketing her face began smothering her.

***

"Shit!" Baxter sat upright, watching as Kyrel sprang to his feet and raced toward where Lilly had been visible only seconds earlier.

The other classmates also watched as the Deebanaarie laid a hand on the first piece of vine in reach. Immediately it began breaking down into a mulch and he made his way to where Lilly was now re-appearing. When she made no attempt to move Baxter began to rise, but Kyrel had her upright in seconds and laying back down Baxter sighed.

"Some surgical strike; silly bitch just attacked her self."

"Yeah," chuckled Tobias "That was definitely an own goal."

"Hey you're the ones voting for the A-bomb," reminded Terrence.

"See now, why you must focus?" Kyrel watched Lilly brush the remaining mulch from her clothes.

"Don't start with me," she gasped through a scowl, Then waving a hand at the ground, muttered "Kiiat Vash." and plopped herself down on the small pedestal of earth that arose there.

Kyrel raised an eyebrow at the sight of her on top of it - doubled over and panting as she grasped her sides.

"Are you all right?"

"Do you care?" Looking up she rolled her eyes

"Lilly!" he held her gaze.

"Sure, I'm fine." She finally sighed, "Just taking a breather if that's OK."

"Of course," he nodded taking a seat alongside her.

They sat quietly a moment before he spoke. "The power in you *is* impressive Lilly. I am… you continue to surprise me." As she looked up, her expression a curious one he shrugged, "You were right before, I neglect to tell you how well you are doing. It is not because I do not see as the others do but because-"

"I know why you do it Kyrel." She straightened up.

"You do?" He looked dubious.

"Well yeah," Lilly nodded with a smirk. "Beyond the veil we call it tough love."

"Tough love?"

"Sure… you keep chucking me in at the deep end because you can't risk me sinking. Then every time I succeed you push even harder because you don't want me getting overconfident and slacking off."

"Then you understand," Kyrel nodded "This tough love; it is…"

"Useless on a kid like me," she watched his puzzled expression as he turned to face her. "I've had adults pushing me around all my life Kyrel." She shrugged, "The adoptives only packed me off to Craven's Peak because they gave up on trying to tell me what's best for me. I know what I can and can't do and I know what I *can* do is impressive to you. So push all you like, the reality is still written all over your face." Seeing him frown as his hand rose to his cheek she rolled her eyes sighing, "Chill out OK, there's nothing *on* your face… it's just a saying."

"Aaah," he smiled, "you do continue to confuse me with those."

"Yes I do," she nodded, "And you continue to keep me in suspense about my mother."

It was Kyrel's turn to sigh.

"You asked how I came to know her and the other Da'ariel," he shook his head, "have I not answered this-"

"Well yeah OK, but you can't seriously plan on leaving me guessing on how things turned out."

"Turned out?" He raised an eyebrow.

"Well obviously you weren't executed. So what happened? She didn't tell my grandmother did she? Why not?"

"Your mother may have been more fond of me than was wise."

"Yeah I got that, from her taking you in, in the first place. Still, she must have had guts: being willing to put that many noses out of joint; Mai Mai's included."

"Oh she did not lack for courage, but no: she did not tell your grandmother. I lay in my room waiting for the guards to arrive at my door. When I woke the next morning there was still none and I went in search of Herrella."

***

"What do you mean she takes the Taeleska? She said nothing of this to me."

"Do you fancy yourself my sister's keeper now Kyrel?" the Lady Niamma rose slowly from her seat; her growing belly almost brushing him as she signalled his armed escort to stay put as they both entered her hut.

"Never would I presume such a thing," Kyrel followed her. "It is just… In truth, I am surprised. She spoke nothing to me of a desire to mate."

"Strange words to hear from a male who does not presume." Niamma said while making her way to a small table on the far side of the hut. It was littered with wooden bowls and clay jars of varying sizes - the tools of her Qin Am Ness calling: sacred herbs, ointments and tinctures; many reserved only for use on those of the clan's noblest bloodlines.

Amidst the clutter sat a lidded metal jug and two sets of stacked wooden cups. Niamma retrieved one, and pouring juice for herself added, "Perhaps I heard wrong, you are after all Deebanaarie; and an outcast at that! The idea that you might think her choice to mate any business of yours would of course be absurd, and outright insulting to her-"

"I would never disgrace your sister with-"

"Of course you wouldn't," Niamma snapped a hand up at him, "You respect her too much for that; she put her honour on the line when she saved your life. She continues to risk her reputation here and among the other Da'ariel clans with every day that you are permitted to remain."

"I understand," Kyrel let his head bow. "I know the lengths to which she has gone to show me mercy and I assure you Lady Niamma, I meant no disrespect." He glanced up cautiously. "I apologise if my poor choice of words offended you."

Niamma contemplated him a moment before nodding. Kyrel straightened up. "I see that you are weary, I should take my leave of you."

Instead of dismissing him Niamma held up her cup.

"Herrella would offer you a drink would she not?"

Kyrel's gaze settled on the cup. On occasion he had drank with Herrella in her hut, less so since she'd accidentally hugged him, and realising this Kyrel dropped his eyes; reluctant to answer.

"There have been brief visits." He admitted.

"Such things should probably cease after the Taeleska, you understand it is for her own good. She will be a woman; it would not be proper."

"Yes," he nodded, "I understand."

"Now Kyrel... I *am* weary... leave me."

"Veyhi Qin Am Ness." He turned and left with a muddle of thoughts circling his mind.

A whole week went by before he again saw Herrella. He sat resting on top of a pile of firewood he'd volunteered to break up for distribution and almost dropped his cup of Gaawa when she appeared beside him.

"Princess," he hopped down from his perch, arm across his chest in greeting as he bowed his head.

"Be at rest Kyrel." She smiled as his arm fell to his side. Seeing him scan for the escort of two armed guards who still followed him everywhere outdoors, she added, "I dismissed them." Kyrel turned back to her, his top lip pinched between his teeth as she added, "I felt it time you were shown more trust-"

"But Mairiel-"

"Agrees." Stated Herrella.

As she held his gaze, Kyrel began shaking his head.

"I do not understand. I felt certain the next time I saw you it would be with more troops, not less. Exactly what did you say to your mother about my-"

"Mother cares not what is said any more. She is happy I have finally given in to her constant pestering."

"You speak of your Taeleska?" Seeing surprise in her eyes, he added "I meant not to pry. Your sister... she spoke with me."

"I see," said Herrella. "Then it is she who pries."

"She is your Qin Am Ness."

"I am many moons and more from being clan mother. I have no need of a Qin Am Ness."

"She is concerned for you, Princess. She does not want our friendship causing you problems." He forced a smile, "Neither do I... that is... if we still have a friendship?"

Herrella's lips pursed as she studied him a moment then she was nodding, "Yes," running her fingers idly along one section of the wood-pile and turning her back on him she said, "I would rather think we do, but I must ask something of you Kyrel and I know it may seem like a lot but I cannot-"

"I have not practised any magicks since we last spoke," watching her turn back to face him he nodded, "And you have my word I shall not again. Not for as long I remain your guest here. I would never shame you that way."

For a long moment they stared at each other; Herrella's lips pursing and un-pursing as she licked them fervently.

"No harm was ever meant." Kyrel shook his head, "I know how things must have looked but Herrella I swear, that life could not be further behind me."

"I believe you." she nodded, "I know now that my reaction was unfair, what I saw frightened me-"

"I am sorry," he shrugged. "I should have known better... your people have good reason to fear the Tuâoch. I never should have-"

"It was not *of* you that I was fearful Kyrel, but *for* you." He swallowed hard and she shook her head. "Had anyone else seen you... any but me..."

"I know," he nodded. "I was foolish and yet again am in your debt, but you need not protect me further. I will not have you sully your name over-"

"Just keep your word to me Kyrel, do not tap into the Tuâoch again and we shall forget it ever happened."

"Yes Princess. My word to you is a bond that shall not be broken. Still I…"

"What?" she asked as he looked to his feet. "What troubles you Kyrel?"

"Your sister said things… She raises concerns-"

"Niamma's concerns have no merit, she is young, and she is mistaken."

"She is a called Qin Am Ness who has been through the Taeleska." Stated Kyrel.

"And now, I will have also," Herrella blithely informed him. "Niamma is wrong and you will give her words no further thought. I have accepted that being long past my Kalaareem, it is only proper I show some willingness to continue the family line."

"Only some?" asked Kyrel, "Has your mother not been selecting suitable mates all this past week?"

"She has been doing so since I was born Kyrel," Herrella sighed, her hands going up with exasperation. "The truth is I do not feel ready to breed and I am not sure I will any time soon."

"Then I see why your sister worries."

"I bade you to give that no more thought," she insisted.

"Yes Princess." Kyrel dropped his gaze to the ground. "I am sorry."

Silence followed, until a moment later she was saying,

"Well I must take my leave of you. I am due in council."

"Yes Princess." He nodded, looking up only as she walked away, her verdant robe trailing behind her along the ground.

Mai Mai had indeed been selecting mates, and intent on keeping her happy, Herrella began meeting with them in her hut; entertaining two or sometimes three times a week; mostly to no end.

She did however strike up quite the friendship with one of the young men. S'ret: a member of her brother Volesh's troop. He was known well for his aim with a tellemi bow as well as his blade skills. Soon enough the pair could be seen taking regular walks around the village, or leaving it to hunt together, and speculation was rife in the air.

For Da'ariel and Deebanaarie alike, every birth was met with great reverence. A child born of royal blood couldn't have been farther from an exception, and the day Niamma went into labour an equally pregnant hush fell over the village.

No men were allowed inside the younger princess's hut during the many hours it took. The father, an accomplished hunter named Tovos, was however permitted to wait outside the door.

In the early hours of the next morning, the child was born: a girl – this doubled the rejoicing of the clan – and the next two days were dedicated to the celebration known as the naming: Niamma had settled on Serrelis in memory of a long gone Qin Am Ness she admired. Sitting back exhausted with the newborn face down on her lap the young princess used her Gaashmay to mark the baby's head with a Do'mass then allowed Tovos the honour of smearing the blood around the opening of the Eshron he'd spent months carving. Cheers filled the air when he closed the lid sealing it for a future the child would never know – Serrelis would die in her sleep, days later: a regular enough occurrence that couldn't be predicted - thus this possibility did nothing to dampen the spirit of the ceremony.

With her studies on hold Herrella insisted on dragging Kyrel out into the celebrations, and despite his initial reluctance he was soon drinking around the Tellemi pits, and dancing with her and other young women of the clan.

Herrella's oldest brother Volesh was one of the clan's strongest warriors. Being among the few permitted to travel regularly to other Da'ariel villages, he'd run into more than his fair share of Deebanaarie troops, allowing for frequent opportunities to hone his battle skills with or without a weapon.

More recently he'd become as equally known for his continued distrust of Kyrel's presence in their village, and for most of that first evening's revelry he made no secret of staring openly across at the young Deebanaarie, until long after Niamma had retired taking little Serrelis with her.

It was however an evening without incident.

The second evening appeared to be going the same way, until Volesh made it clear staring would no longer suffice by shoving Kyrel as they passed each other in the crowd.

"Watch where you step Deebanaarie. Get in the way of others too often and you might get squashed."

It could have been the copious amounts of rulocki grog Kyrel had downed since dusk that made him forget himself enough to sneer.

"Bigger warriors than you have tried."

"What was that?" Volesh turned to him with a thrilled sneer of his own. "Do you challenge me Deebanaarie?"

A lull fell over those nearest them; including S'ret and Terris Dian who, as was so often the case, maintained flanking positions from a couple of feet behind Mairiel's eldest son..

Kyrel swallowed hard. He knew, as Volesh clearly did, that Herrella had recently been called inside.

The stillness of those surrounding them was having a ripple effect. One by one those playing music set their instruments aside, and the giggling youths dancing around the fire also stopped to see what was happening.

"See this," Volesh addressed S'ret but spoke loud enough for most to hear. "Not content with getting in the way of your every opportunity to mate with my sister the Deebanaarie now challenges me."

Kyrel bit his lip. All eyes were on him now, and for a second he scanned the crowd. Herrella was pushing her way through to them, and he knew for her sake he could not accept any challenge.

"Ny." He muttered as he turned back to face Volesh. "You misunder-" A fierce jab of Volesh's elbow connected with Kyrel's left cheek bone: knocking him to the ground before he could finish.

Looking up through a watery stinging eye he suppressed the urge to bounce back up and retaliate. He could feel the essence inside him building, and knew he could not let the situation escalate.

"Ny." He heard Herrella's cry through the murmurs of the crowd. "Volesh Ny! Cat ya vac Volesh! Cat ya vac!"

If Volesh heard his sister he ignored her, and as Kyrel pulled himself up, mouth opening to speak, Volesh kicked him back to the ground.

Grinning he stomped toward Kyrel's crumpled form asking,

"This cannot be all you have for me Kyrel? Or are we to believe all Deebanaarie Generals are so weak without a battalion to command." He tore a dagger from his belt and threw it on the ground in front of Kyrel. "Get up Matfiack? Show at least *some* courage. You challenge me then lay there, what foolishness is this." He kicked Kyrel again. "Get up and fight!"

With blurred and doubling vision Kyrel looked to the blade inches from his hand. Volesh thumbed his broadsword in anticipation.

"Come on," his voice was a low steady growl of unmistakable intent. "You and me General... here and now."

Fuelled by emotion the essence boiled fervently in Kyrel's veins, his anger spurring him on. Then the dagger was kicked away and looking up he saw Herrella between them.

"Ny!" she faced her brother. "This stops now"

"The Deebanaarie challenges me," growled Volesh, he gestured to the crowd, "All here did see it. You cannot deny me the right to accept."

"I can and I am!" said Herrella, eyes narrowing on him. "You disrespect our sister and her new daughter with your disruption of these celebrations. Kyrel is still my guest here Volesh. I claim absolute responsibility for all of his actions and bid you bring any quarrel you have with him to me in council. As for any challenge there may have been here, you are the clear victor already. He is defeated and poses no threat to you or any other..." Lowering her voice she added, "now all any here see is you challenging a defenceless man. A sad feat for the clan's finest warrior, don't you think? So will you make me order you indoors Brother? Or can I trust you will stay out of my sight?"

A brief scan of the faces watching him had Volesh turning back to her with a nod as he spoke up for the benefit of the crowd.

"In light of such an *easy* defeat I offer mercy and accept the Deebanaarie's submission." Scowling down at Kyrel, he then spoke more for his sister: voice dropping to a hiss, as he added, "He would be wise to stay out of *my* way," and stalked off through the crowd.

Watching him go Kyrel shrugged out of Herrella's grasp the second she established it.

She looked down at his face, bloody and already bruising, yet his eyes pleaded for dignity and backing off she allowed him to get to his feet unaided.

A hubbub rose in the crowd as she followed him from the clearing, and the music picked back up as they disappeared around a corner of the nearest hut. Only then did Kyrel pause to lean back against the wall and crumpling up held his ribs.

"You are injured." Herrella hurried to support him.

"I will recover." He held her back with an arm and pushed himself off the wall with the other.

"I cannot believe Volesh. How dare he do this, and S'ret there at his side too... they are both-"

"He dares because he knows I do not belong here." Kyrel turned on her. "I asked you not to protect me further. One of these days you are going to have to see that your village is no place for me."

"Then where is it you should be Kyrel?" Herrella shook her head. "We both know your own people will not have you. As long as Mordrel lives you have no home in Deebanaarie occupied lands and it is doubtful any other Da'ariel village will offer you aid."

"I need no one's aid. Were it not for you I would have recovered in the woods and found-"

"Were it not for me you would have perished in the woods!"

"And if I had, would I not be better off?"

"Kyrel!" Disbelief flared in her eyes. "How can you-"

"You know how Princess. It is the same as the why in all Volesh does. I am a prisoner here among your people and he treats me accordingly. I am less than that even... lower than the village matfiack!"

"Nydrel Kyrel, that is not-"

"Yes!" he nodded. "Yes it is. Your people give me scraps and I give them obedience. Am I never to be respected as a man again? Is this why you saved me? To avenge the suffering your people endured at the hands of my ancestors by humiliating me for the rest of my days."

"You are upset," she reached for his arm. "Let me help you to your-"

"Don't," he slid swiftly along the wall to avoid her touch. "I told you: I need no aid. Stop helping me!"

She watched him walk away, hands clutching his ribs as he made his way to his hut.

That evening a mighty row was heard between the Princess and the Mai Mai. It ended with Herrella running from her mother's hut in tears. The next morning Kyrel's escort appeared to have abandoned their posts - they did not return.

A week later he was asked to attend the council chamber where, although Herrella barely looked his way, it was put forward he should find some way of making use of his skills if he was to stay within the village.

Thrilled at the prospect of being able to better contribute and thus prove his worth, Kyrel eagerly agreed. However, much as he appeared to have assimilated: dressing as most in the clan did, and being greeted wherever he went with considerably less of the ill-concealed hatred than he'd first encountered on walks around the village. He was soon deflated by the stark fact that: eager as he may be, few who had ever seen fit to spare him a smile were in anyway willing to work alongside him.

A second week had almost passed when Arteth, now a lanky child of six, found Kyrel gathering water at the village well and asked. "Has anyone offered you service yet General?"

"What's it to you boy?" Kyrel tied off the rope securing the bucket and dipped in a wooden ladle. "Don't you have studies? Training or something?"

He swigged back a mouthful of the water before shoving the ladle in the back of his belt and pouring the bucket into one he'd brought with him.

"I was training General, until father sent me to find you."

Kyrel narrowed his eyes to fix the boy with a stare, "What would your father want with me boy?" His eyebrows bounced in unison. "And why do you keep calling me General when you know I have been no such thing for as long as I've been here."

"Father says I must address you with respect if you are to be my new Shenti,"

"What did you-"

"He has an offer of service for you General, Mother dismissed another sword master today."

***

Kyrel stepped dubiously into the previously out-of-bounds Avengturov training room, with Arteth at his side.

"Aah," Hay'n waved when he spotted them. "Cat ya vac, cat ya vac… this way Kyrel, I have a proposal for you."

"So the boy tells me." Kyrel nodded Arteth's way, "and thankful as I am for the offer I must humbly inform you that while I do possess many skills, teaching is not among them. I regret, Prince Hay'n, that I am no Shenti."

"Nonsense Kyrel, would you truly ask I believe the rank of General is so easily come by in Mordrel's armies? You are a skilled fighter, besides, Arteth listens to you."

"But I have no experience of-"

"Have you not learnt swiftly to live among we Da'ariel?" Hay'n opened a large weapons chest. The contents, glistened in the eerie off-white light cast by several of the usual bright green torches. "From what I hear, you have even managed to competently use a Gaashmay." As Kyrel shifted uncomfortably Hay'n threw him a conspiratorial smirk before adding, "Surely what I ask now cannot be so far outside your abilities?"

Kyrel glanced down to see Arteth staring expectantly up at him as Hay'n made his way back to them. "Be assured he learns fast," said the Da'ariel Prince. "He also pledges to do all you say," he stopped to ruffle his son's hair adding, "Which will be an improvement on all his previous Shentis."

"And your shan'elek?" Kyrel raised a dubious eyebrow. "What does she make of such an arrangement?"

Hay'n's face split with a grin. "Stow your concern," he waved the question away "It was the boy's mother who saw fit to charge me with appointing a new Shenti - and I am appointing you. She's dismissed most who've taken the task within days so it will be no magnificent loss if she dismisses you also." he slapped Kyrel's shoulder and nodded to the chest adding, "I'll return before the sun sets to see how things are going."

"You're leaving me and the child alone in here... with these weapons?" asked Kyrel, more shock coming through in his voice than anticipated.

Hay'n was the one looking doubtful now, as he asked, "How else are you to train him if not with weapons?"

"I..." Kyrel looked from Arteth's beaming face to the well-equipped room then back to Hay'n, "You realise I am forbidden from this room by your mother?"

"Then you had better teach the boy something seriously impressive or we'll both be in trouble."

Hay'n slipped out through the curtain before any more could be said on the matter and looking down at Arteth, Kyrel sighed.

"So... the Gaashmay is what you're working with?"

"Veyhi General, it is."

"Shenti." Kyrel corrected with a reprimanding finger.

"In my studies I have learnt that General ranks higher than Shenti, and the higher rank always-"

"Not in this case."

Clearly baffled Arteth tried again, "But mother says-"

"Did your father not just assure me you will listen?" Kyrel cut the child off, his voice taking a sharp authoritative tone, which Arteth was most unused to from him. Yet immediately he respected it enough to pull back his shoulders and straighten up; meeting Kyrel's gaze square on as he nodded.

"Veyhi Shenti."

"Then we will have no more of this General nonsense, from now on you will address me only as Shenti, understood?"

"Veyhi Shenti"

"Good." Kyrel nodded "Now let's fetch your Gaashmay and see how far along you are."

"Veyhi Shenti." Eagerly the boy hurried to the chest his father had opened. Kyrel muttered, "This I can do..." before sighing a tacked on, "I think," and following Arteth across the room.

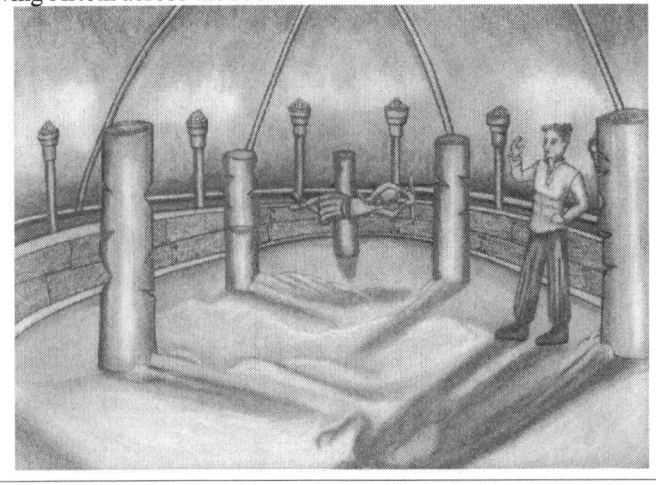

Two hours later, when Terris Dian arrived at the hut to put a stop to the lesson she had just learned to be in progress, she froze at the sight of her son spinning through the air, mastering moves which had previously been beyond him.

Hay'n returned at sunset as promised and discovering his shan'elek peeking in through the doorway curtain, too engrossed to notice him, he pulled back a snatch of it himself and watched a moment before whispering, "Admit it, you're impressed."

Terris Dian's hand fell from the curtain and turning to face him, she shook her head,

"You must know we cannot do this to your brother, Hay'n."

"What wrong do we do Volesh by choosing our son such a good teacher?"

"That teacher is the Deebanaarie!"

"And Arteth is *our* son! Please Terris… look how well he does. Do not take this away from him. Volesh has not been your superior for many a cycle. What he thinks should no longer matter."

"He is still Mai Mai's second."

"Veyhi, but it's doubtful he shall ever be my sister's."

"Your sister is not yet clan mother Hay'n."

"She has taken the taeleska and grows more into her role as our clan's next mother every day."

"Yet she puts off inviting S'ret to seed her," sighed Terris Dian. "How will she lead us when she is so easily distracted from her duties? Your brother is right, she spends too much time around the Deebanaarie. His acceptance here should not be encouraged."

"It is neither of our place to judge what develops between her and S'ret Terris. He should not even be speaking with you on such matters. Whom Herrella chooses as mate is her decision alone. Furthermore as we're talking about a future heir to the line, I think she does well to take time considering it."

"She should have considered it *before* her Taeleska."

"Why, because you did?" he smirked, "Maybe your options were more obvious; I *am* very well put together." Seeing her eyes begin to roll he slipped his arms around her waist. "Very well, I shall be serious. Did Mai Mai not say we must all show Herrella the respect of her position? That this quarrel Volesh has with her has gone on too long? He may be my mother's second hand but Herrella is still the first daughter. It is she we have a duty to support."

"That may be but we speak of trusting a Deebanaarie alone with our son each day."

"We have gone through every Shenti in the region already," sighed Hay'n "Our own duties allow neither of us the time to train Arteth ourselves, so it's the Deebanaarie or we pack him off to Tengiivek for next six cycles."

This was the comment which seemed to soften her resolve: unsurprising to either of them as both knew the rare privilege of an option had been a key in her taking him as life-mate.

"You realise that room contains many of the best weapons in this village?" She pointed out.

"Not all are as vigilant in their duties as you are shan'elek. Kyrel has been among us a whole cycle now. He has had ample time to turn on us, our son, or anyone else in the clan? I believe Herrella is right: he makes much effort to respect his place here. It is time we start trusting him."

"Then let her birth a son and the Deebanaarie can train him."

"Terris please... Herrella is now fully responsible for the Deebanaarie and she wants him given service. Should we not set an example to the rest of our people by giving him a chance? Consider the opportunity we would be denying our son. This Deebanaarie held a General's rank in Mordrel's armies. Who better to teach him the ways of the enemy? Since the loss of Volesh's oldest two our son is now set to be Herrella's second and maybe one day, her first! Think on the good he can do the clan with the training Kyrel can give him. Do not all Da'ariel think on that day when we might do more than survive...? Maybe Herrella is right. Maybe for things to change we need to be more willing to let them."

"Take care your sister's ideals do not make you as reckless as her. She devotes too much of her time to this Deebanaarie, it is not right."

"Well I am not devoted to him Terris. I ask only that you give him as much chance as you gave the other Shentis. If he ceases to impress you, you can dismiss him too but at least let him disappoint you first."

"Very well... but do not be surprised when he does disappoint me, it is not our enemies skills that defeat us but their numbers. I doubt there is really much even a Deebanaarie General can teach our son that his own people could not."

"Yes of course."

Hay'n knew not to argue with Terris Dian on a subject as important to her as their own troop's capabilities. All Da'ariel lived by the skills of their chosen weapon, but few showed her ferocity or cunning in combat. It was with good reason she'd been placed at the head of Mai Mai's personal guard. "You are to check in on them regularly Hay'n."

"You have my word on it." He nodded.

"And I am posting guards at this door."

"But Herrella expressly said-"

"I will clear it with Mai Mai myself. The Deebanaarie was denied access to this hut for good reason. My duties to the clan still come before your sister's wishes."

"Veyhi Terris, of course."

As Hay'n offered a respectful nod to his life-mate and she walked off to deal with other matters, Kyrel crept swiftly away from the other side of the doorway.

He had not meant to eavesdrop on Arteth's parents; had not even realised they were there, until the retrieval of fallen targets brought him close enough to hear their whispers.

Now as he made his way back to where the boy had just landed expertly back on his feet, Hay'n pushed the curtain aside and asked how the lesson had gone.

Thrilled to see the exertion on his son's face he let the boy show off a couple of moves before insisting it was time he go clean up in preparation for the evening's meal. Kyrel he dismissed on suggestion that the next day he start giving Arteth morning lessons and for almost an entire second cycle in the village that is exactly what Kyrel did.

More aware than ever before of all the Princess Herrella had staked on helping him, he decided it in her best interest to distance himself from her.

Two rotes after that first training session the entire clan rejoiced to learn their first Princess was with child and weeks later the villagers were still congratulating S'ret, whose ego had swelled with pride, on his successful seeding of the clan's first Princess and heir to what was left of the Avengturov legacy.

***

The great city of Crizoleth was as far removed from the verdant homelands of the Da'ariel as one thing could be from another. Had Lilly experienced it through more than the oily puddle of quiesscence she'd gawped into over Kyrel's shoulder, she might have thought herself transported to yet another realm far beyond Azeron.

Many hours had passed since that last communication between Mai Mai's grandsons and the other survivors of their clan. Clad now in the uniforms of Deebanaarie warriors, they made their way unhindered along the cobbled pathways that weaved their way between the many vast structures. Largest of all by far was the palace at the heart of the great city.

Far darker than the speckled greys and light browns of those buildings surrounding it, House D'vey; as it was colloquially known, loomed over all else. Its mere existence an imposing reminder of skills long lost to modern Azeronians. The six separate wings of the Palace spread like gnarly fingers across its massive stone courtyard, each topped at the end, with a watchtower.

Arteth paused, counting each of the smaller towers in relation to the imposing and well-guarded entrance of the building's main structure.

"There," pointed Arteth, "That one will lead us to the holding cells."

They made their way inside and marching their own men on as prisoners, passed the sentries on the entrance without event.

Everything was as Kyrel had assured them and with Arteth leading they made their way swiftly through the underground passages.

Another couple of corners and cell-doors were finally visible; as were another two guards posted at the same corridor's entrance. The brothers each singled out a guard. Creeping through the shadows, they worked in sync; slitting their throats then dragging their bloody carcasses back into the darkness.

Two more Da'ariel now dressed the part, leaving only two Da'ariel to remain in their own clothing. Deciding two fake prisoners, to four fake guards was a preposterous ratio, the brothers split from their troops. Scouting on ahead, with Toleth peering eagerly through the bars and view hatches of every door they passed.

After half a dozen he turned to Arteth frowning, "These cells are all empty brother."

Arteth gave the heavy black door in front of his younger brother a quick glance, before nodding

"And the doors contain milaratak'i, this must be where the shraeka are kept. Kyrel did say many crossed the bridge, Mordrel must have had them all released. Come..." he waved his brother on, "this way. There should be two more corridors at least before we will find Mai Mai and the others. Kyrel said Mordrel would keep them closer for interrogation."

"Closer..." sneered Toleth. "You continue to trust the words of this Deebanaarie?"

"And we continue to progress unhindered."

"Yes, but to what? For all we know an ambush awaits. Has he not betrayed our clan before? Are our parents not dead because of him?"

"He has no reason to betray us this day Toleth. He returned to our lands for one thing and he has her already,"

"Yes, another thing I do not like about any of this. Our parents were not the only ones to give their lives that day brother. Lilly should not be left with him."

They made their way around a wide bend with Arteth whispering, "She is safer with him than us at this moment Toleth. He was right to suggest Mai Mai would not want her with us."

"So we leave her with him? These are not good options."

"No," Arteth turned to his brother. "They are the *only* options. You campaigned more than any other to make this journey-"

"Then you think as he does: Mai Mai should be left to Mordrel?"

"Am I not here also? Do not suppose my seeing the merit in his reasoning, means I care any less for being here than you do. Still I know Kyrel was right: Mairiel would have preferred we follow her orders by getting Lilly to safety. This journey could be the end of us whether or not we accept his help. Mai Mai is likely lost to us already, the others too. Given what he saw from the shraeka Kyrel believes Mordrel knew of their capture, meaning she may well have the orb already. This could all be for nothing. We both know this,"

They reached a large set of steps, and embarking upward Arteth nodded, "As you also knew, we could not both have the princess with us *and* keep her safe. Your intentions are questionable brother, I fear your judgement impaired by your need to be as troublesome to Kyrel as possible."

"And so we have the reason for this anger I keep hearing in your voice. You accompany me yet agree with him."

"I agree you spoke on that which was not your place to speak."

"Place? You speak as if we owe him respect. Perhaps it is not my judgement that's impaired brother. It is after all, you who once had him as Shenti is it not?"

Halfway up the stairs, Arteth paused to look at his brother.

"Do not concern yourself with my loyalties Toleth. You were little more than a suckling babe when our village was Kyrel's home. I saw first-hand what came of those who trusted him. He brought more misery to our clan than you even think you remember."

"Yet you believe Aunt Herrella did no wrong in taking him in?"

"Times are different now, she grew up in a different Azeron; change seemed imminent. She could allow herself to trust. We have not had the luxury."

Arteth raised a hand to silence his brother as he took a quick peek around the bend at the top of the steps.

"Herrella was raised next in line to our family legacy during a time of reprieve." He pressed himself to the wall and gestured for Toleth to do the same. "Who are we to question her for hoping?" Arteth's voice dropped to lower than the previous whisper as he shrugged, "And we can know nothing of the pressures she faced. Ny brother, such things are not our business," Arteth shook his head, "Only Herrella, her Qin Am Ness or another clan mother can ever be fit to judge the actions she took. We are but men, we will never..."

Becoming silent, he raised a hand. Halfway up the corridor, footsteps marched.

"How many?" asked Toleth, he too was now pressed against the wall.

"Too many," sighed Arteth "if we wish to remain undetected, we must wait."

***

It hadn't taken long for Mairiel to realise the pulpustuem she'd accepted was little more than a ruse. If anything its potency was significantly understated. The persistent hot tingle in her veins should have been her first sign something was off. However with no other option available, she had pushed through that discomfort, and only gave it a second thought, when her vision began to blur.

This fresh impediment was but a minor hindrance to Mairiel; as a warrior of the Avengturov line, her other senses were already informing her movements. Relying on those senses a little more required only marginal adjustment and some squinting.

The crowd heaved gleefully to the ebb and flow of the battle's location, keeping both women enclosed without restricting the movements of either. Both Queens lunged and parried their way across the hall's polished floor.

For a while it seemed they would remain well matched despite Mordrel's many homeground advantages, until a sudden case of sensory overload, hopped on the bandwagon of Mairiel's growing list of unexpected side effects. Losing her grip on Drellaeleon's somewhat unwieldy long sword, she realised the true treachery of her opposition.

Forced to fight back with the shield alone she found it almost it impossible to focus and soon wound up clinging to its underside bracing herself against the blows.

All Mordrel's talk of Mairiel's condition and safe quantities, had been but a fraction of the narrative the Deebanaarie queen was spinning for her own people. It was, after all the cream of her noble crop whom she'd called on as an audience for this occasion. Loyal and honoured by the rarity of their invites, they would choose to see only an honourable bout fought here today and their influence would ensure the tales of it spread unhindered across the realm.

In reality the initial surge of strength they'd witnessed in Mairiel was both fleeting and the beginning of her end. The excessively strong pulpustuem brew did an excellent job of keeping her fresh faced and upright. It had also been more than sufficient to trigger the final stages of the exact condition Mordrel had so publicly alluded to: the withers.

Regardless of outward appearance, the older woman's body simply couldn't process the elixir as it would her normal dosage. After very little parrying, she began to feel the deep inner chill of an internal meltdown. Searing through her veins, the roots essence had gone far beyond rejuvenating her organs. It went straight to work pushing each one to their respective limits.

Subsequently, the entire time the two fought, Mairiel had also been subject to an unseen attack from within. A cascade of deep dull aches which worked their way erratically through her upper body, turning each lancet of fiery pain into a cold dead weight as one by one her organs were beginning to shut-down.

Eventually the ensuing numbness encompassed everything from the tops of her thighs to just behind her tongue. For a good deal of their fight she felt her entire torso throbbing from the weak thready beats of the only organ Mairiel could be sure remained functional.

With no option but to push on, Mairiel had dug in and pushed back with everything she had. Deriving fresh strength from the few scraps of faith she could still cling on to, it mattered not that this victory had already been stolen from her. She fought back all the more knowing every breath she took now, bought more time for Merly to escape this wretched Deebanaarie city. Assuring herself also, that her people would keep Lilliath alive long enough to master her powers. Trusting Vereena - now called to her duties as Qin Am Ness - would convince her cousin to take up her rightful place as head of House Avengturov; trusting also that she would guide her on her path as clan-mother over all the realm's Da'ariel.

Perhaps most importantly, and in spite of all that had transpired, Mairiel still believed Lilliath's powers could, and therefore would, eclipse those which Mordrel boasted. This belief allowed her to conclude her eldest granddaughter would one day avenge this stolen victory, along with the countless other injustices their people had endured through the ages: by finally bringing an end to Deebanaarie rule forever.

It had been difficult at first: putting any serious faith in that unruly waif her sprites had brought back from the human realm. Yet something had been niggling at Mairiel since the gates of Crizoleth had opened. Now the growing pulpustuem induced fog in her head brought with it a peculiar clarity of mind. Flooded with an array of memories - many including her own considerably older Qin Am Ness. Mairiel was struck by a realisation which immediately vexed her; while bringing with it an indescribable relief. With a grim and somewhat hazy determination, she decided: whatever the outcome of this battle, she was finally serving the purpose for which she had always been groomed. Lilliath would know, Mairiel told herself as she lunged again with the oversized sword. She would come to understand the treachery done this day.

The unavoidable fact that her granddaughter would also need to first learn how Da'ariel and Deebanaarie each follow distinct codes of honour, built on sacred traditions and written into their laws, as well as exactly how Mordrel was breaking them; was neither here nor there to the Da'ariel Queen by this point.

Mordrel had gone to great pains to ensure she put on a most honourable display in her Great Hall, filled with Deebanaarie clan mothers and warriors from some of the noblest Houses across her Maidom. Restoring her opponent to a more capable age and forgoing the use of her own magicks during the bout, were measures that carried their own weight and would make the inevitable storytelling all the more glorious.

Even their servants were caught up in the frenzy of excitement, roaring their approval, as Mairiel staved off relentless blows from their own Queen's matching short-swords. All the while, hearing those cheers, Mairiel knew most wouldn't realise she was being forced to battle on two fronts, unlike Mordrel who had obviously known exactly what effects the over-powered Pulpustuem would have on her: ensuring none could see the slow and painful deterioration from inside.

Mairiel fought through the noise. She pushed everything away including the unsteady thrumming of her own tired heart. Despite her acute awareness that each reverberating beat; sending fresh ripples of dull pain through the overwhelming numbness that her torso had become: rang out a clear, if not belaboured melody of her own imminent demise. As aware as she remained in her diminished state, she ignored it all. It simply couldn't matter that her heart insisted it wouldn't sustain her alone much longer. Or that it told her in no uncertain terms - when it gave out, she was going down with it. She told it out loud, she didn't care. With no time to dwell on her end being nigh, Mairiel resigned herself to the hope that Lilliath and the rest of her people would somehow learn what a charade this had all been; how she had still died with as much honour as was allowed to her, in order to ensure the future of her people.

Fully aware that the overarching effects of the pulpustuem were beginning to affect Mairiel's mind, Mordrel had enjoyed toying with her a while and would occasionally look to her gleeful audience with a smirk or chuckle in between a mad dash of jabs and slashes.

Precision had lost all consequence fairly early in the bout when the older queen had lost her grip on the long sword. Since then the already worked up crowd had erupted into a fresh frenzy every time the teetering Da'ariel queen was forced into a flurry of haphazard back steps. Somehow Mairiel managed to keep her balance time and again - all but hiding behind the huge Deebanaarie shield, while the larger, broader and significantly younger Queen went at her with repeated barrages of swipes and stabs from her own magnificently crafted pair of short swords.

Interspersed seemingly erratically between these violent forays, was the occasional monstrous kick or shove, right to the centre of the shield. However when each of these blows failed to knock Mairiel off her feet, Mordrel realised the other queen may be holding up better than expected.

If she didn't drop the Da'ariel queen soon, the outward appearance of her aged body would catch up to the reality of all that was truly occurring inside. It would be more than a reversion; all damage wrought by the overly potent elixir would inevitably reveal itself. Should that happen, Mordrel's neatly prepared ruse would lose all credibility, an outcome she wasn't inclined to risk given the innately competitive nature of her own people. Even as they cheered her on, Mordrel knew plenty among her audience would eagerly seek out any clear signs of weakness; in an attempt to elevate the status of their own lesser houses. Although it was widely agreed no force had successfully stood against House D'vey in near on a hundred cycles, attempts had been made - two fairly large Deebanaarie clans had all but ceased existing by the end of the last recorded conflict. Widely touted now as a most misguided rebellion; it was said to have been as sudden and messy as it was short-lived. Such events had occurred way back when Mordrel's grandmother was a youth, and were ingrained into Mordrel's childhood teachings. The ire of her own people was to be avoided at all costs, so she had learned to deceive them by any measure. Contrary to her teachings she had also learned rebellions could be quite exhilarating to crush, and if dealt with correctly, their repression echoed through her lands and brought others to heel on reputation alone.

Mordrel knew none would dare question the validity of this challenge, as long as most saw what they preferred. All had seen the older queen drink the very same elixir many among them relied upon daily. When her knees began to buckle, and a fatal blow seemed imminent, the subsequent roars confirmed exactly what outcome they preferred.

Mordrel slipped a subtle hand form in on her next offensive and Mairiel felt all remaining traces of air being sucked from her already impaired lungs. The hall began to dim and she had felt her grasp on the shield begin to weaken, a moment before fresh hot pain alerted her to the blade protruding from her abdomen.

***

Now, Mairiel and the rest of the captured Da'ariel were stuffed into two adjoining cages. By sheer luck Mordrel had lost interest in them, when her sprite, Neenia, had thumped the Deebanarie Queen's sceptre off the arm of her huge stone throne: alerting her to growing ripples in her spontaneously bubbling bowl.

Fully reverted to her elder state now - and then some - Mairiel lay on the dirt floor with her guard captain Lasaya kneeling at her side.

Lasaya's second had Mai Mai's head resting on his lap and every few minutes, when she was racked with a fit of coughs that shook her frail form, he would take a strip of cloth, torn from the sleeve of Lasaya's clothing, and press it gently to the aged lips of their trusted leader as blood spattered from her mouth.

"No more," Mai Mai gurgled out more blood and saliva, as she drew her hand slowly out of Lasaya's. "Your efforts to prolong my life only ensure I die at Mordrel's hands."

"Nydrel Mai Mai," Lasaya spoke softly. "You must not say such things. Allow us to help you. We will find a way out of this place."

"No child, we both know how doubtful that is," Mairiel coughed more with every word. "You are strong and still have much fight in you but my journey is ended."

"Ny!" Lasaya shook her head. "All you need is more pulpust-"

"Veyhi child. This body has been too weary too long. These wounds are too severe for even the pulpustuem to mend now."

"Please, Mai Mai," Lasaya shook her head. "Do not speak further, you must save your strength."

"Ny," coughed Mai Mai "Speaking is the only thing I have strength left in me to do, so speak I must. You have served me well and I ask now that you do me one final service-" more coughing had Lasaya pleading,

"Nydrel Mai Mai, please… you must hang on, speak no more."

A hubbub at the front of the cage caught their attention, and getting up Lasaya made her way through the other densely packed Da'ariel.

Guards approached – three of them – one pulled out a ring of keys as they neared the overcrowded cells.

"Cat ya vac!" he growled "All of you; step back. We come for the clan mother, bring her forth."

"Come in and get her," Lasaya glared through the bars. She lacked a weapon, but was fairly certain she could relieve him of his if he just stepped close enough.

The first guard almost took the bait. Unfortunately the female at their backs knew better. Snapping at them to not forget how wily these Da'ariel could be; she stepped forward shoving him aside and raising a couple of fingers threw a quick signal to the two male guards. Each immediately raised their tellemi bows, and aimed them through the bars. "We *can* come get her," the woman glared in at Lasaya, "but she will watch you all die first."

The Da'ariel guard captain didn't so much as bat an eyelid as she started an invective. "You think we fear you? You piece of Deeba-"

"Lasaya!" a fit of coughs and splutters followed Mai Mai's loud croak. "I tell you I am ended. Let it be! Others here still need you. Take me forth," she spoke to those around her. "I will allow no more to die for me. Take me forth I say."

With moans and wailing a path was made and the Da'ariel nearest Mai Mai began helping her up.

Few noticed the swish which parted the air but everyone, including the female guard noticed the thud of her two subordinates dropping either side of her. Their throats poured blood across the ground as Arteth landed at her back, and holding a Gaashmay to her throat hissed, "Open it!"

"Or you will kill me?" she asked. "Mordrel will do much worse if you do not."

"So shall it be." Arteth dragged his blade along the woman's throat in one swift motion and grabbed the ring of keys as she also fell to the floor.

"Siem tae! Arteth!" Lasaya hurried to the bars. "You must hurry, Mai Mai is in a bad way."

It took several tries to find the right key, and Toleth was at Arteth's side by the time he felt it click. Everyone backed up as the princes entered. Handing the keys to Lasaya Arteth ordered her to unlock the other cell and start getting their people out of there.

Mai Mai had been re-settled onto the lap of Lasaya's second and though her eyes were barely open she scowled at the sight of her grandsons.

"You should not be here," she rasped as Toleth took her hand in his. "Where is Lilliath? You did not-"

"She is safe," Arteth said as he too knelt beside her; assessing her injuries with a quick scan as he added "She and the others continue on to Zanreal, Veer and Kyrel remain with her."

"And the orb?" coughed Mai Mai.

"They have it," Arteth's eyes went to a large tear at the side of her inner gown where a steady flow of blood oozed into a puddle on the floor. A makeshift bandage had been applied but her clothing was soaked through - she'd obviously been bleeding for much time.

"What of the one you kept?"

"Safe… for now. Merly. She has-"

"You are badly wounded." Toleth said as he followed his brother's gaze.

"Veyhi," Mai Mai coughed up more blood. Taking the rag from Lasaya's second, Arteth nodded for him to follow the others. "Mordrel has seen to my end."

"No," Toleth shook his head. "We are here now, we will get you out.'"

"Veyhi," agreed Arteth. "We only need get you up Mai Mai. We can find you pulpustuem in the forest."

"Ny," Mairiel told her grandsons. "The root can preserve me no longer," holding back her next cough she wheezed "and in this state you would be fortunate to get me free of these catacombs. I will not hinder your escape; your journey here must not be all a loss."

Her sentence was punctuated with another fit of coughing, forcing Arteth to wait on them subsiding before he could then ask,

"What will you have us do Mai Mai?" his eyes showed sorrow but his voice remained steady.

"Our people need Lilly now more than ever. And Mordrel cannot be allowed to get anymore of the orbs. You must find Merly. Get her to your cousin; ensure our next clan mother has their-"

"Do not speak this way," Toleth cut her off with a hiss. "We are getting you out of here…" he put an arm under hers, but with no semblance of assistance from Arteth stopped to look at him. "Will you not aid me brother? We can get her out of here."

"I am ended boy!" the gentle rasp of Mai Mai's voice was firm, and immediately Toleth was shaking his head, as he returned her arm to her side. "That's right," she told him. "You must let me be. Other things are more important now. Mordrel has other orbs. Two! She must have had them some time. They're all but drained of their power. Still…" coughed Mai Mai. "There was enough essence within them for her sprite to locate us with the ginaten."

"And if she did so once she can do so again." Arteth's voice was grave.

"Yes," agreed Mai Mai "If she hasn't already done so it is only because she waits for her orbs to regain their full strength, but she will not wait much longer Arteth. You must get word to-"

"Do not concern yourself." He pressed the rag against her lips as she coughed and spluttered some more.

Toleth held Mai Mai closer, stroking her wispy white hair as he cradled her head on his lap. "We have quiesscence," said Arteth. "We will see Kyrel knows more ginaten are on the way."

"It is more than this, hear me Arteth. Mordrel knows Lilly's Kalaareem is close, her troops have failed her too many times she will not rely on them or the ginaten again."

"Veyhi," he nodded. "She sent her shraeka. No harm was done."

"A distraction," Mai Mai's words whistled through her blood soaked teeth as her voice became more of a wheeze. "She knows they can be avoided. Their purpose was only to slow the others down. She knows her troops will not be able to locate Lilly and bring her here to Crizoleth before her Kalaareem has taken full effect. Instead they now seek the orbs, while Mordrel makes ready to receive your cousin. It is this you must warn Kyrel of: he must be ready to face his sister. The T'karas seeks them out."

The next coughing fit which racked Mai Mai ended only when her body was lifeless.

"Ny," Toleth gazed down at his grandmother, his hand moving from her silky white hair to her cold pale cheek. He tapped lightly with the back of his hand, "Mai Mai. Speak to us. Say something… Mai Mai please... please… you must tell us what to do."

"She already has," Arteth swallowed back a hard lump as he placed a hand slowly over his brothers. "We must leave this place and get word to Kyrel of all we've learnt. He must be ready for Mordrel and so must our new clan mother."

***

At least two dozen Da'ariel with youngsters among them, now made their way through the wide but dark, winding corridors of Palace D'vey's huge underground detention wing. They were definitely too large a group to move undetected and needed to split up again if there was truly any chance of escaping. Weapons were in short supply so instructing the others to arm themselves however possible, Arteth saw to it each small group had at least one of the armed warriors who had accompanied him and his brother into the Deebanaarie heartland.

They would also remain close; one small group always in sight of another, in the hopes they could aid each other if it became necessary. He and Toleth took point, and all of the youths with them.

Though his brother had barely spoken since they'd left Mai Mai's body behind, he appeared alert if not a little distant, and thumbing the hilt of his weapon, nodded his agreement to every suggestion Arteth made.

Only when they approached the exit and Toleth dashed forward, tearing his Gaashmay from his hip, did Arteth see the true depth of his brother's grief.

The younger prince had spied two guards and leaping into the air, he spun at the first, slicing him to bloody ribbons before there was chance for surprise.

The second man turned around with barely enough time to let out a startled yelp as Toleth landed behind him.

He slammed his Gaashmay into the side of this one's partially exposed neck; all but severing his head as he wrenched his arm forward in a flicking motion which tore the blade out through the front of his throat.

Arteth and the younger Da'ariel watched the guard's body crumple as the knees buckled and the head lolled backward before the entire corpse fell on its side.

Toleth panted, staring down at it; too engrossed by the sight of arterial blood spraying the ground, to notice the third warrior of the troop come running around the corner.

With broad sword unsheathed he raced at Toleth as a second troop came around the opposite corner, each guard unsheathing their weapon when they spotted the fallen men. One raised a tellemi bow, aiming for the younger prince's back.

Arteth whipped out his dagger, hurling it full force. It flew swiftly across the short distance, and lodged itself in the exposed pit of the man's raised arm. The bow clattered to the ground. As the Deebanaarie fell also, rolling in agony beside his bow, Arteth was already in the air hurtling towards the guard nearest his brother; whose sword was now inches from the back of Toleth's head.

Arteth did a back-flip: his Gaashmay running through the man's arm, just below the elbow. Crying out, the guard watched it dangle a second, before a kick in the back, also from Arteth, sent him crashing to the ground. He rolled over, trying in vain to retrieve his sword from the hand of his damaged arm.

Toleth span around, almost losing his footing, as his brother landed beside him.

Arteth crouched at the guard's arm, grabbing the sword before rising to plunge it deep into the man's chest, pinning him to the ground.

Only now did he afford his brother the briefest of glances before he was off again; leaping into the air and letting his Gaashmay carry him toward the remainder of the other troop.

Toleth swallowed hard, on his guard now. He watched Arteth come out of his spin with a flying kick that toppled both men. Landing a couple of feet from their heads he doubled back, pulling his sword from his belt.

The man on Arteth's left was rising. Lunging for him first the older prince stamped a foot down on his back, then grabbed the rim of his helmet. Pulling up his head, he ran his sword along the man's throat.

The second man had just turned over when Arteth reached him. They looked momentarily into each other's eyes as Arteth's sword came down again.

With both hands and all his might he forced the blade through the guard's armoured chest. Glancing back to his face, Arteth saw the blood welling up in his mouth. He gave his sword a quick twist and yanked it free then doubling back to the previously felled guard and kneeling to retrieve his dagger. Jabbing it into the man's throat for good measure, before he wiped it on the sleeve of the lifeless arm and stood to wave the youngsters over.

Seeing those most capable equipping themselves with the weapons of the dead guards he made his way back to Toleth.

"I know," Toleth averted his eyes as his brother reached him. "That was foolish."

"It lacked caution." Arteth nodded. "We were after all charged with final orders. It will surely be difficult to find a place from which we can contact the others if we-"

"Do not lecture me brother!" Toleth afforded him a brief sideways glance. "It will not happen again, that is all that need be said."

Arteth stared at him a moment, studying the tension apparent in every inch of him, then he was nodding.

"Help get these bodies stripped and hidden. The more we have in the uniform of Mordrel's troops the more likely we are to get everyone out of here."

By the time the rest of the small groups were all also with them, the uniforms had all been taken and they were back to viable numbers for passing as a bunch of Deebanaarie guards, escorting prisoners through the great city.

Arteth took point, hurrying the group away from the palace and off through Crizoleth's spaghetti of streets.

The night sky's pink hue was fading, it would be daybreak within hours and Kyrel would be waiting to hear from them. Arteth hoped it would be in time.

They were but a league from the entrance of the ancient tunnels and so far remained undetected. There was as of yet no sign of their Grandmother's youngest sprite, Merly, but entrusted with an orb or not Arteth knew searching couldn't be an option. More than anything else now he must focus on keeping everyone, and his brother, together, if there was any chance of them making it back to the safety of Tualavan's tunnels.

Day Four: Part One

Tossing and turning, Lilly woke to find Kyrel, Vereena and the other Craven's Peak kids watching her.

They all sat in the same semi-circle they'd settled to rest in and the expression on their faces was of pure awe.

"OK." Lilly pushed herself up on her elbows. "What's going on? Why are we all looking at me like that?"

"Err…" this came from Harper, but it soon became apparent she had no more to add and raising both eyebrows Baxter nodded beyond Lilly. Turning to look over her shoulder she saw the clearing they were in seemed to have closed in around them while she'd slept. Dozens of new trees had sprouted up where only earlier Kyrel had removed others. Nearer the ground many more were in various stages of growth, all could be seen slowly rising skyward.

"Whoa," she turned back to look at them "am I… is that…"

"Yeah," Baxter nodded again. "Our thoughts exactly." Looking to Kyrel she caught the faint smile on his face and shook her head.

"But I was sleeping! How is that even-"

"It is your Kalaareem." said Vereena, she too was smiling – unreservedly. "It is begun…" her eyes drifted to the patch of growing trees. "…and you are going to be *very* powerful."

Kyrel's smile disappeared.

"It has begun yes," he agreed with a nod. "Still… what power Lilly has when it is through remains unclear."

"Ny Kyrel," Vereena gasped as she turned to him, "Do you not see as we do?"

"I see a Qin Am Ness who should know better. Have you not studied the effects of the Kalaareem in those with active magicks? Surely you know what we see now need not indicate what we see later?" For a moment Vereena's mouth snapped shut, her eyes darting as she considered his words. The others watched until finally she turned back to Lilly, nodding.

"It is true. Your powers will be changeable this day." She shook her head, eyes drifting to Kyrel. "But from what I… what we all witness, I do *believe* you are going to be very powerful cousin." She turned to Kyrel. "Not in all the ancient writings have I seen anything to make me believe otherwise."

"Well, we shall see," sighed Kyrel "as I said the end result of the Kalaareem remains unclear."

Again Lilly looked back at the new trees. Their growth had stopped now, with many of the smaller shoots no higher than an inch or two out of the ground. There were so many they gave that section of the forest floor a grassy appearance. To Lilly this was as eerie to look upon as it was beautiful.

She turned back to Kyrel.

"Well, unclear or not, this is a good thing right? If my Kalaareem has started already then you can teach me some of the other-"

"Nydrel," he shook his head, "There will be no learning of anything this day, other than what you've already taken on."

"What?" Lilly's face scrunched into a tight frown. "But you said you couldn't teach me because I hadn't had my Kalaareem yet"

"And you still have not," he shrugged.

"But..." she gestured behind her with a hand, "these... you just said..."

"What we see now is the beginning, nothing more. Your powers will change often this day. There is no control over that."

"OK, but this does mean I finally have the strength to work some of the other magicks right, and you did say-"

"I said you could learn more *after* your Kalaareem, not that you should attempt to do so while it is happening."

Lilly's jaw dropped, her own eyes slowly roaming the faces of the others as they found various ways of averting theirs. Only Baxter held her gaze and he did so in silence with his lower lip sucked in.

"How can there be any point in waiting now?" Lilly returned her attention to Kyrel. "If this is it: my Kalaareem, then your sister definitely won't be waiting. She's going to make her move Kyrel. You know she is. More than ever this whole thing just became a now or never situation."

"Nothing has changed. Mordrel has no way of knowing your Kalaareem has begun already and she cannot make a move on that which she cannot find."

"Like she couldn't find the village?" Lilly's eyebrow bobbed upward. "You thought I was safe there too remember?"

"Mairiel's orders remain the same," insisted Kyrel, "Until this day is over I am to keep you from my sister's troops and aid you in furthering your ability to defend yourself according to the instruction of your grandmother."

"Oh come on Kyrel, again with the orders? Ain't like her instruction has steered us right so far. Your sister's been like a step ahead of us this entire time. She didn't just find the village; her troops brought it down in minutes. Then they managed to capture Mai Mai and the others even after you went back and got them out."

"You will not change my answer by reminding me of what I already know Lilly." Kyrel got to his feet. "Today you practice your use of the Gaashmay and those forces you have already learned. Nothing more need be said on this matter."

"Hey now wait a minute..." as she rose so did her voice.

"I will not," Kyrel turned his back on her adding, "And neither shall you. Everyone is rested. If we move now we may still make it to Zanreal before the sky is fully light."

"And what good is that going to do us?" she grabbed her backpack. "Didn't we already see Mordrel's troops heading in the exact same direction?"

"Hey wait," Terrence got up as Lilly passed him - the others did the same. "I know it's a bitch but maybe Kyrel's right." Added Terrence, "If your powers are unstable you probably shouldn't-"

"There's nothing unstable about me!" she snarled at him.

"Lilly, you just grew back that forest in half the time it took Kyrel to clear it and you were asleep!"

"Yeah, exactly," her arms went up with exasperation. "The word for that is powerful!" she sighed. "Powerful Tez, not unstable! I'm in control OK and I'm sick of being wet-nursed; I'm not some freaking baby."

"Cousin please…" Vereena put a hand to Lilly's arm, but dropped it quickly in response to the glare she received. "It is not right that you be angered by Kyrel's actions." Her voice came out placating. "He follows Mai Mai's orders as do the rest of us. He must do as he pledged in words. This is the way of our world. To do otherwise would be… well it would-"

"Be dishonourable," suggested Terrence, getting a nod from Vereena he added, "Veer's right… times two if you factor in that Mai Mai's a Queen and Kyrel's… well… a man."

"If you ask me he's a pussy," interjected Baxter. The others turned to him, with varying expressions of curiosity on their faces. He stuffed his hands in his pockets and nodded after Kyrel. "He isn't just *some* man is he? He's a prince."

"Yeah," agreed Terrence, "of the enemy camp. Where he's considered a traitor and thought to be dead."

"Yeah and I'm betting the last thing he wants is that to change," said Baxter. "Look at him…"

They all watched Kyrel make his way through the thinly spread clusters of Da'ariel, waking any who slept, as he gave word they were to depart.

"He's been so long in hiding from his sister he doesn't know how to do anything else," shrugged Baxter. "Lilly's right, neither of them should be taking the orders here. They're the only ones with any real-"

"Hey, hiding is plenty good enough for me." Tobias thumbed his own chest. "Till we can get home it's still the plan I'm voting on."

"Definitely," Harper agreed. "And hey... who better to see we're successful than a guy who's managed to stay hidden for years from the exact same enemy we're trying to avoid?" she looked from Baxter to Lilly. "You're the one who wanted us to trust him Slater. So far so good," she shrugged, "he's kept us alive, no offence but maybe you ought to practice what you preach."

"And maybe you're all missing the point," sighed Lilly "Hiding is fine but it's not a guarantee. Mordrel's already found us once, she can do it again."

"Yeah," agreed Baxter "We don't know this Zanreal place is any safer than the village was. As Slater says: all we know for sure is Mordrel's troops went that way yesterday."

"It is unlikely their destination is the same as ours," frowned Vereena. "Many other places lie beyond the bridge. Mordrel has no reason to seek us out in Zanreal. The Da'ariel were driven from there long before even she was born. Like much of Azeron those lands were consumed by the Tuâoch soon after the wars began."

"Oh great," sighed Baxter "Our full-proof plan B is hiding out in a spot that's already fallen to the enemy."

"Err I think you mean fool-proof," offered Terrence. Then receiving a cutting look from Baxter, he averted his gaze and lowering his voice added, "Kyrel can't just go against the word of Lilly's grandmother." He nodded her way. "You said it yourself: this clan took him in. They cared for him when his own people wouldn't. He owes all of them a great-"

"Whatever he owes them obviously didn't stop him betraying them before," snapped Baxter.

"Exactly," Lilly nodded. "Why should it stop him from teaching me what I need to know now?"

"He obviously doesn't think you need to know any of that other stuff right now." said Harper.

"Oh come on." Baxter's eyes rolled as he spoke, "If that's the best you's can do, you might as well tell her the truth."

"What truth?" Lilly looked to each of them in turn until her gaze rested back on Baxter.

"Tez here has concerns about your powers." He nodded to the eldest twin and Lilly followed his gaze.

"Concerns?" she raised an eyebrow.

"Err... well you wanted me to find out everything I could about your powers so me and Veer have been going over as many of these-"

"Yeah blah blah..." Baxter cut him off. "Get to the point, tell her why you bunch of losers are all freaking over this Kalaareem thing. Tell her that crap you were telling us about atom bombs and shit."

"Err..." Lilly's gaze swung to Terrence. "Atom bombs?"

"Not real ones," Tobias stepped forward in defence of his brother. "Tez was just... you know... comparing you and-"

"Actually," Terrence gently pulled his brother back and offered Lilly a smile. "This is something I wanted to talk to you about," he shrugged, "Thing is it's sort of complicated."

"Simplify it!" Lilly's harsh tone came out through gritted teeth and the look on her face had Terrence nodding.

"Simplify it... right."

***

"So you are in here." Kyrel looked up to the doorway and the now familiar pregnant form creating an ample silhouette there.

"Princess Herrella." He stepped away from the reading stand he'd been hunched over, his eyes going immediately to the ground as the curtain fell back behind her. "This is... I was not..."

"Niamma tells me you spend much of your time in here these days." She stepped slowly toward him. "She says you're in here most every evening." Her eyes passed over the dozens of small crevices in the writing room's walls before falling to the bindings he'd piled on top of the stand.

"I did not realise keeping record of my whereabouts had become one of her daily duties." Kyrel stepped aside as Herrella moved closer.

Taking his place at the stand she lifted the top sheet from the pile and scanned its contents.

"I am familiar with this one," he watched her frown. "These are ancient Laîoch core words."

"You're surprised," he sighed at the fact. "Perhaps you expected to find me practising my-"

"My surprise lies only in your ability to understand these writings enough to find them of interest, Kyrel."

With an apologetic nod he glanced around.

"I find many things in here of interest."

"Of course," Herrella placed the sheet back on the pile and sighed. "Anniiada's interest in the ancient scripts was known to us. My surprise must seem foolish given the standing you once had among-"

"Forgive me Princess…" Kyrel's gaze edged toward the door as she looked up at him. "…but I have no desire to discuss my life before your village or the lives of any other Deebanaarie."

The trepidation in his voice had her glancing to the door also.

"Yes," she nodded when turning back to him. "You are right. We should not dwell on a past you can never return to. Your place is here now; among the people of this village."

"True enough," agreed Kyrel. "I do have obligations among your people. Ties I never expected." He shrugged "Your nephew's training being one of them. The fighting style of your people is formidable yet solitary. I have petitioned your brother for more students so I may teach Arteth the value of combining his skills with others."

"Yes," Herrella beamed. "Hay'n extended your offer to the council. He and Terris both speak highly of your progress with the boy. Many are eager to see what you will teach once the extra students are selected."

"The triumph is not mine alone Princess," nodded Kyrel. "Your brother and his life-mate have much to be proud of. Arteth is a swift learner. Still, there is much I believe I can teach him *if* these extra students can be found."

"Oh I'm certain there is," said Herrella "And do not worry, they will be found. Hay'n was right to appoint you." She patted her protruding belly. "Perhaps when this one reaches age you could take up the mantle of Shenti again. After all, every future clan mother should have the best teachers available."

The unease in his eyes caused her to chuckle,

"Relax, Kyrel," she shook her head. "There is nothing untoward in what I ask of you. Even if there were," she glanced pointedly around. "Who do you believe to be listening?"

"Perhaps Princess… if it were your blood your brother Volesh was so eager to spill you could better appreciate the need for caution."

"Kyrel that is not fair." Herrella's smile waned. "I appreciate the need… how could you think-"

"Do you?" he held her gaze. "Were you the one he sought to challenge at the naming of Niamma's first-born? Because I thought that was me."

"Then you continue to hold events of that evening against me." When he dropped his gaze she sighed. "Do you think me so naive… so blinded to the difficulties you face here? Is that it Kyrel? The truth of why we speak so little since we-"

"We do not speak little enough!" his voice cut through hers with a sharpness that surprised even him. Swallowing hard he shook his head, "I believed we understood each other. That the reasons for us keeping our distance were as obvious to you as they are to me."

Silence followed as they eyed each other a moment, then he was shaking his head again. "You can't truly believe me oblivious of your continuous interference in my life here. You speak of Hay'n and the council as if you don't continue to plead on my behalf... As if I don't know you promise favours for me."

"You misunderstand."

"Oh no..." Kyrel shook his head. "I understand perfectly. I let Volesh get to me and I let you see it. I confessed to feeling despair here among your people. That was wrong of me and I'm sorry you felt the need to fix it."

"Kyrel..."

"No," he shook his head, "you must hear me Princess. You must hear me because we must not have this conversation again." Herrella said nothing, but he saw her swallow hard as she sucked in her bottom lip. "To some extent," Kyrel nodded, "I must also confess finding myself glad of your efforts. Keeping busy has...." he eyed her a moment studying her entire form before his eyes came to rest again at her face. "It has helped. I have things to keep my mind on and that's good. But tell me Princess... How many of your clan now await your enthronement with thoughts of reaping rewards for offering me service?"

"I brought you here Kyrel. I'm responsible for you..."

"Of course... and when further situations arise with Volesh or his men I can count on you to handle them."

"Yes," she nodded "yes you can. Of course I would-"

"I don't need to be handled by you Herrella!" His voice rose enough that she too glanced to the curtain. Seeing this he consciously lowered his volume. "I don't need to be handled by anyone!"

Again a heavy silence fell and aware he'd crossed a line he felt a longing to take back his words. This was however, accompanied by the knowledge that he'd said too many of them for that to be possible.

"Perhaps it is you who is naive," said Herrella. Looking up he saw her shrug, "Mai Mai sees this... distance you wish us to keep from each other Kyrel. Have you forgotten she lets you stay here only because I petitioned for it? Even now she and Terris Dian are discussing the oddness of our behaviour. Don't you see? The course you choose will bring neither of us peace. If you desire difficult questions you are treading just the right path."

"Is that why you're here... to warn me that yet more of your kin grow increasingly suspicious of me? Should I treat this as new information?"

Herrella considered him a second before letting out a deep breath.

"No," she told him. "While it does seem you need informing, I am here to see you will be attending the naming of the child when it is born."

Seeing him open his mouth to speak she waved a hand. "Before you waste both our time protesting let me point out that nothing will raise more questions now than your not attending this naming, when all know you were in attendance for the naming of Serrelis."

"Well thank you Princess. I shall take your words under advisement."

"Kyrel please..." Herrella took a tentative step toward him, shaking her head as she asked, "How long must we do this?" Refusing to budge he held her gaze as she took another step. "Has there not been enough anger aimed our way without contribution from us? Is it not enough that we agree mistakes were made? It's true we've both been at fault..."

Another step brought them face to face but keeping his gaze locked on hers Kyrel refused to relent.

"Things don't have to be this way." Herrella smiled. "We can work together on coming to a resolution?"

"The resolution is already come to, Princess. You need to let me be. That is how-"

"That's your resolution not mine!"

"It is what's best for both of us."

"Why? Why does it have to be Kyrel?" her hand rose to touch his face. "Why should all we had be reduced to-"

"Because...." he caught her arm. "I am what I am and that will never change."

"What does that...?" Herrella shook her head, pulling her arm away. "What are you saying?"

Pushing his face close enough to hers that their noses almost touched, Kyrel lowered his voice.

"It means I cannot take much more."

"Much more of what? I don't under-"

"Don't you see? I am already repaying so many of your kindnesses. I deny everything of myself with every step I take in this village and I do so only for you."

"But I-"

"For *you*... Princess!"

For a moment her tongue was stilled by the intensity of his stare. Then she was shaking her head.

"Not once have I ever asked you to repay any-"

"Then you left me a choice?" his eyebrows went up. "Or perhaps you suppose I am without honour? That the debt of my life is something I could turn my back on."

"Kyrel that is not why-"

"Do you honestly not see that disappointing you is the last thing I desire?" As she sucked in her lips he shrugged. "You saved me Herrella... from so much more than you realise. Everyday I'm here I strive to do right by you, but there are things I cannot do to please you. Things about myself, I cannot change. The next time Volesh sees fit to confront me I fear he will find that out."

"Careful Kyrel," her words came out a gasp. "What you say is-"

"The truth!" he nodded. "Your brother *will* challenge me again. We both know this. If only I could be as certain of my ability to deny a second challenge from him."

"Kyrel please... you cannot engage-"

"But we both know I can! One way or another Volesh will find out the truth of me."

"He does not have to," she shook her head. "No one does. Just let me help. I can speak-"

"He will not be appeased until he and I have met in arms. I know you see this as I do. And believe me Princess, when it happens... I *will* disappoint you. Which is why you must leave me be, so that day stays as far from us as possible." His gaze drifted to her belly. "If you do not there is no chance of me ever being shenti... or... anything else to this child."

***

"Hey..." called out Lilly as she hurried to Kyrel's side. "Hey wait up, didn't you hear me?" Her words came out a breathless panting, she'd been calling to him for as long as it had taken her to reach his side from back in the middle of their caravan of people.

"Sorry I..." Kyrel shook his head, "I was thinking."

"Yeah I'll say..." shrugged Lilly "You looked a million miles away." Ignoring the lack of comprehension in his distant gaze, she increased her pace to keep up with his long stride and sighed, "Look... about earlier... I'm sorry if I came off kind of pushy." Spotting the brief sideways glance he gave her Lilly added, "Tez told me some of the other stuff he's learned about the magicks. He agrees with you by the way; says my powers are unstable during the Kalaareem."

"And he is right."

"Yeah well, I wanted to make sure you know... That I get it."

"Get it?"

"Yes. You have a plan, a... a good plan. This Zanreal place, Vereena says the Da'ariel there are concealed - like the village was. She also told me your people have no clue there are any Da'ariel in that area so I do get why you must be thinking we'll be safer there but what if-"

"Lilly-".

"No wait... just hear me out OK. I have like a couple of questions... tops. You answer those and I swear I will totally drop the subject." This time when Kyrel's eyebrows bounced up it was with a measure of recognition that had her nodding, "Seriously... I'm giving you my word we'll do things your way. No more argument."

Kyrel contemplated her a moment before sighing.

"As you wish... ask your questions."

"OK." She grinned. "So tell me this... all the crazy shit I've seen here."

"Crazy shit?"

"You know what I mean," she rolled her eyes. "There's the Ginaten and that shiny water stuff you poured out to speak to Arteth in. In fact from what I'm being told everything in Azeron has some of this... this essence in it. Now according to Tez... well Vereena I guess... Any living thing here, with enough of it, has some inherent magical ability or another right? That's how the sprites brought me here, how the ginats have power, it's how me and you can do the things we do."

"Yes." agreed Kyrel, "All things in Azeron have essence within and therefore the potential for as you say... magickal ability."

"Right," nodded Lilly "And your sister, she has way more of it than you right?" seeing his jaw tense she shrugged. "I mean you're good... Obviously! But well... being a woman does mean she's naturally better right... that she will probably always be more powerful than you?"

"Right," Kyrel nodded his whole body now as rigid as his jaw. "Exactly the reason we must keep on moving."

"Oh totally... like I said... I get it. I mean as things stand if she does somehow catch up to us we're pretty much screwed... right?"

Kyrel afforded her a brief glance.

"You have not yet asked your true questions have you Lilly?"

Shrugging she smiled.

"Well see I was wondering... with all the magic here, and your sister having... well... what seems like unlimited resources. How sure can you be that Zanreal hasn't been compromised?"

"Compromised?"

"Yeah, you know like... just maybe it's not as hidden as Mai Mai thinks."

As he considered the idea Lilly shook her head, "Can you honestly say there's a hundred per cent no way Mordrel could have learned the location of the Da'ariel there?" Kyrel's gaze on her didn't falter but he sucked in his bottom lip and taking that as a cue to go on she shrugged, "She's always going to be better than you... that is what you said right? So what if she has found out about Zanreal. What if somehow she does catch up to us...?"

Taking a moment he paused to look at her and behind them the others slowed to a halt.

"Well..." Lilly raised an eyebrow.

The feeling of multiple pairs of eyes staring her way made her lower her voice. "What if instead of running from danger, we're running into an ambush... running straight to your sister... Course she could just catch up to us before we even get there... either way if this run and hide plan turns out to be a bust, what are you going to do about it?"

"Whatever it takes."

"Yeah OK and what if it takes more than you've got? You just agreed your magicks can't beat hers. You can't take her Kyrel, you know that."

When his only response was to maintain eye contact and suck his lips into a pucker Lilly shrugged, "Compared to her you're powerless aren't you? But there's a real chance at least for today... that I'm not."

"We must trust it will not come to that."

"See now that sounds a lot like having no plan to me." Kyrel's mouth opened but Lilly was the one who spoke. "It also sounds bloody stupid!" she told him. "So maybe my magicks are unstable. If those trees were anything to go by that's a good thing. I'm powerful Kyrel. I felt it when I woke. I feel it now. I am the one who stands the best chance of beating-"

"Kyrel!" the shrill whisper came from Vereena. "Levilshd cat ya vac," she added as they each turned to look at her.

Immediately Kyrel's stance changed to that of a man on his guard. Lilly didn't notice, she was busy watching the younger girl who'd just unhooked her Gaashmay from her belt – and was now holding it aloft, but only for a second before she spun upward, disappearing into the trees.

At the same instant Lilly was yanked aside.

"Hey what the…" was all she had time to say before Kyrel had her pressed against the nearest tree with one arm across her chest and his free hand pulling his sword from his waist.

"Stay here!" he whispered pushing her down to a crouch before dipping around the tree and disappearing from sight also.

"Shit!" Lilly muttered as she thumbed the Gaashmay in her jacket pocket, miserably aware it was her only weapon.

Beside her a twig snapped and something brushed against her shoulder. Lilly spun around, raising a hand and saying "Kims-"

"Whoa!" Baxter slapped her arm aside before she could finish. "Easy there Slater, it's only me." Crouching next to her he pressed himself against the tree also, "Looks like you were right about the enemy catching up to us."

As he nodded toward where the rest of their group had been, she followed his gaze to the now empty forest floor.

"Where did everyone…"

"Shhh!" Baxter's finger went to his lips, "I think this is the part where we hide."

"Right," Lilly muttered, her eyes darting as she repeatedly scanned their surroundings. "Is it Mordrel's army? What if they find us? What do we do?"

"Don't freak out OK." Pulling a Da'ariel dagger from his waist Baxter turned to her. "It's probably nothing, and anyway's these guys have your back, don't they. Kyrel might be a prick but you're like his golden child. He isn't going to let anything happen to you."

As he finished speaking the air was filled with the whistling of dozens upon dozens of tellemi darts; their bright greenish white glow, lighting up the foliage, as they flew through the forest, passing by the pair with enough speed to resemble mini lightning strikes.

"Holy shit!" Hissed Lilly as several feet to their right one of the Da'ariel fell to the ground with a thud.

Caught by a dart he'd fallen from a nearby tree and like Sandra Morris was dead before he hit the ground.

"Holy shit! Holy shit!" Lilly's hissing grew more frantic as a second Da'ariel hit the ground less than three feet ahead of them.

This one had been caught on the front of his left shoulder. Singed bone was bared by the wound and with agonised groans he reached for it with both hands, repeatedly drawing them back each time he made contact with the seared flesh and gasping as he kicked up dirt with his continued writhing.

"All the same…" Baxter muttered as Lilly and he stared on with equally aghast expressions. "You might wanna be ready with some a that hand waving stuff."

"Right," she nodded as the unmistakable sound of their approaching aggressors grew nearer. Baxter's face now told her he'd also made out the now familiar thudding of the many trundles heading toward them.

A chance glance told her these were accompanied by the hasty advance of a squadron of men on foot. Each seemed to have a bow raised.

"Shit!" Lilly hissed as she ducked her head back and several feet away another of the Da'ariel fell to the ground. A woman this time; she landed as dead as the first.

With this Lilly knew the continued whistle of the darts would be the least of their worries.

This was the enemy they had persevered so hard to avoid. The arduous journey and three - nearly four days - of hiding to escape confronting Mordrel's forces had taken them smack dab into that exact enemy.

This was going to be a battle with considerably more bloodshed before it was over and with much to still learn, she had serious doubts about herself or any of the classmates surviving it

The sounds of galloping and footfalls grew as the distance between them and the enemy shrank. Scanning their surroundings she asked. "You didn't see where Kyrel went did you?"

"Sure, he disappeared into the trees like the rest of them."

"Great," muttered Lilly, "fat lot of good he's doing me from up there."

"Fat lot of good it seems to be doing any of them." Baxter nodded to the nearest man who continued to writhe and groan in front of them.

Before Lilly could respond a trundle of the deepest blue appeared in the forest ahead of them.

"Err... Baxter..." she muttered as others appeared by the second, until they swiftly seemed to outnumber the trees themselves. "If Mordrel's army are up ahead who the hell are..."

"Oh Fuck!" Baxter said as he followed her gaze.

The armoured rider who'd first appeared was raising his bow and both their mouths fell open.

A second later a wave of green fire tore across the forest. Sweeping from right to left, it took mere seconds to engulf the entire line of men at the front of the group and sent those behind skittering as they lost control of their equine beasts.

The fire died out where it had begun and Lilly glanced over to see a deathly pale Kyrel, swaying on his feet with his eyes closed and both arms outstretched. His hands remained pressed together in a form he was yet to teach her: his thumbs back to back against each other, and his pinkies meeting them in a pair of O's, while the tips of his other fingers created a point with which he'd aimed at their opponents. Both harnessing, and focusing the destructive powers of fire with enough might to send those who survived it fleeing.

"Well, fuck me sideways on a Sunday afternoon!" muttered Baxter, his gaze also fixed on Kyrel. "I didn't know he could that. Did you know he could do that?" he asked as he turned back to Lilly, "Can you do-"

"Sorry," she shook her head. "Don't think I know that move."

Kyrel opened his eyes, unsheathed his broadsword and somersaulting high into the air, flew at a handful of the remaining men - unseated by their trundles in their efforts to escape the flames - they scrambled to defend themselves as their once fellow Deebanaarie cut them down.

Hacking at two on his first pass he caught one across the back and the other on the face and neck. His blade made short work of both, sending a spray of blood which splattered the ground and surrounding foliage, while the men fell in a heap.

Then Kyrel's body stiffened and spinning full circle he kicked down two more men, before a fourth swiped through the air with his thick navy shield making an arc wide enough to catch their assailant in the back, sending him hurtling backward into the nearest tree.

Winded, Kyrel panted where he lay, as sword held high the other Deebanaarie ran at him. The sword rose higher as he drew nearer and only at the last possible second did Kyrel swing out a foot kicking the man's legs out from under him.

Lilly and Baxter watched him extend an arm and as he created the hand form she recognised as Ta varee the man - already getting to his feet - disappeared. It was impossible to see from their no-vantage point but having just witnessed the true strength of Kyrel's powers and seeing he was pulling no punches, Lilly knew the warrior had been swallowed deep into the bowels of Azeron.

Grabbing his sword Kyrel clambered to his feet, then taking a moment to bend his knees, sprang up into the trees; disappearing from sight again.

Uncertain how long Baxter had been pulling on her arm Lilly turned back to see him pointing into the distance as he yelled.

"You have to get us out of here."

"What?" she asked, only to see what he'd seen, and know he was right. The blue uniforms of Mordrel's troops permeated the forest, clashing with the greens and browns at an alarming rate. "How the hell am I supposed to get us out of here?" she yelled back at Baxter.

He grabbed the hand she'd forgotten held her Gaashmay and lifted it above their heads.

"You're Da'ariel remember!" he shouted louder over the increased whistling of the darts. "No sense holding onto this thing, if you ain't gonna use it." He pulled her to her feet.

"Right," Lilly nodded as Baxter locked both arms over her shoulders. "Here goes nothing." She closed her eyes tight.

"Oi!" he snapped. "Nuh ah, Slater," he shook his head as her eyes opened. "Don't you dare close your eyes, I ain't flying this thing."

"Right," she nodded again, "Sorry. Kinda nervous."

"Just go already!" he shouted as darts whistled by within inches of their heads.

The next second they were airborne and Baxter let out a shrill scream as they ascended toward the top of the forest with a speed he hadn't anticipated.

The bright lights of the darts followed them a significant way but the main barrage was soon left behind.

"You did learn how to stop this thing right?" yelled Baxter as they soared higher.

It turned out to be a short lived concern. They came to an abrupt halt several feet above the tree-line. The pair had just enough time to see the fear in each other's eyes before their ascent became a descent and, both screaming now, they lost hold of one another and crashed back down into the tree-tops.

Losing sight of Baxter, Lilly tumbled many feet before losing momentum.

She collided with branches, crashing through them at an alarming rate; bashing her head and ribs repeatedly; and tearing open the flesh on the palm of her free hand in an effort to catch hold of at least one branch thick enough to support her weight.

When it eventually happened it was accidental. The stubby remainder of a previously broken branch snagged her leather jacket. It tore violently at the seam yet miraculously held fast on the corner of its lower left side. Groaning, Lilly dangled, flailing in her effort to achieve some sort of footing and screaming for Baxter or anyone else nearby to help.

Only realising her mistake after she'd called out several times: that her shouts could indeed alert *anyone* nearby.

"Shit!" hissed Lilly, gazing around frantically.

***

On the ground the other classmates, as concealed as they could be in a thicket, cowered low in the foliage. With a terrified fascination they watched Kyrel and the Da'ariel zip between the trunks of the trees; slicing men down with as much speed as the tellemi darts around them.

Others dropped from the trees snatching up the armoured men. The speed with which they moved gave the impression they were ricocheting off the ground when they took off again. Straight up they disappeared with the men in their grasp, only to drop them from high, allowing the fall to extinguish their lives or cripple them enough that death would not be far.

Despite their prowess in the forest the Da'ariel continued to take casualties. Sometimes the men lifted away struggled so hard both they and their assailant would come crashing to the ground. Others on the forest floor, continued to fight back, lashing out at those Da'ariel whose bodies had become extensions of their Gaashmay.

All around was carnage as Da'ariel and Deebanaarie clashed. Hoping the fighting kept its distance seemed to be all the classmates could do to ensure their own safety, A hope which faded when a couple of feet from their position a Da'ariel was knocked from the air and they were forced to leap out of the way and scurry off in opposite directions as he came rolling through the centre of their thicket.

Terrence stumbled a few feet out and found himself in a clearing, with the same Deebanaarie who'd disturbed their hiding place now bearing down on him with a raised sword.

Tobias wasted no time picking up the nearest rock, and hurled it at his brother's would be attacker. Athletic ability had long been his one redeeming factor in school, but even for him this was a lucky shot. The Deebanaarie had lost his helmet at some point in the battle and the rock struck him square on the back of his head.

Though this wasn't enough to drop him, it diverted his attention from Terrence, allowing him the time to get to his feet.

However, seeing Tobias turn and run when the Deebanaarie ran at him, his sword going every which way, Terrence didn't hesitate in repaying the favour. He grabbed a huge branch from the forest floor, and running at the Deebanaarie whacked him hard up the side of his head. With a roar the soldier turned back to where the first twin was now backing away. Then a second rock hit him between the shoulder blades. Eyes bulging with confusion he turned to see Harper gathering more rocks by the base of the tree she'd been using as cover.

As Terrence backed off to a safer distance a third rock whistled through the air, it was Tobias again. This shot clipped the left side of the Deebanaarie's face and as blood sprayed from his bottom lip, Terrence re-joined the offensive.

The three classmates hurled a steady barrage of rocks until this would be assailant toppled to the ground. Still they continued to stone him, adrenaline drawing them closer as his movements slowed. Eventually they were all stood less than two feet from his prone body, which had ceased moving altogether.

A brief moment of staring at the panting sweaty sight of each other was enough to bring them to their senses, and with their eyes doing all the talking, they fled the scene.

Running through the forest with no sense of direction they knew only to head away from the fighting.

Yet still they managed to encounter more Deebanaarie - the first stepped out from behind a tree, catching Tobias by the collar. He lifted the twin high in the air and slammed him right side first into the tree's thick trunk. Harper screamed with terrified surprise while Terrence, seeing his brother crumple to the floor, ran toward him screaming. "Nooo!" only to have his path blocked by two more Deebanaarie soldiers. One whacked him down to the ground with the back of his shield and the other one kicked him in the ribs when he struggled to get up.

Harper backed away, arms out stretched and waving in an effort to identify the nearest tree she could hide behind.

Instead of bark her hand found smooth metal and eyes wide with dread she turned to see a fourth Deebanaarie directly behind her.

His sword was already raised. His bloodshot eyes glared beneath his helmet and his lips were pulled back in a snarl as he brought the sword down in a wide arc. It tore into her left arm, bringing with it an excruciating sting as it sliced through the flesh under her clothing.

Screaming, she stumbled backward, her hand going to the wounded bicep. Falling to the ground she walloped her head off the forest floor and tears flooded her eyes.

Her vision became a watery blur as, hissing on the ground, she watched the soldier raise his sword a second time. It went up above his head and Harper screamed again as he brought it down for the kill.

The blade's tip was inches from her chest when a Da'ariel sized projectile collided with the soldier's head.

A loud grinding, not unlike a buzz-saw, rent the air as blood spattered Harper's face in a fine spray and the soldier disappeared before her eyes. Gasping she turned to see him spreadeagled on the floor several feet from her in a pool of his own blood. Scattered through that blood were a handful of reddish blobs which had Harper momentarily confused.

Then she saw a large portion of his skull was gone, along with the greyish pink brain matter it revealed and she was left no doubts what those blobs were. Turning the other way, she threw up the meagre contents of her stomach.

When she looked up again the other three Deebanaarie soldiers had also been taken out of the fight. Tobias and one of the Da'ariel men were helping Terrence to his feet. Vereena was also with them, but only for a second before turning to face Harper. She raised the arm in which she held her Gaashmay, and after a short spin through the air, was in front of Harper, looking down at her.

"You are injured?"

"Err... yeah." Harper sucked in a sharp breath "my arm," she nodded to it, while tilting her hand forward so the other girl could see the blood oozing through her clothing.

"Is that all?"

"All!" the alarm in Harper's voice rivalled the lack of it in Vereena's. "Just look at this mess," she gestured to the bloody gash "Do you have any idea how much this top cost?"

"I do not." shrugged Vereena, "But you remain alive, so things could be worse."

"OK, OK." Nodded Harper "I should be counting my blessings, I get it."

Vereena reached down, grasping Harper's uninjured arm and helping her to her feet.

All about them the fighting continued, but now that she was neither running nor hiding Harper was able to see only handfuls of Deebanaarie remained.

The Da'ariel had them drastically out-numbered. So much so that she frowned adding, "Or maybe what I should be counting is you guys."

The Da'ariel all seemed to have come down from the trees now. Instead of whizzing their way through the forest on their Gaashmays they met their enemy face on; clustering together, with sword, dagger and Gaashmay, to take out the men on the ground.

"Either I hit my head way harder than I thought." muttered Harper, her hand going to the back of her skull as she added, "and I'm now seeing double. Or there are like twice as many Da'ariel here than there were before." She turned to see Vereena's face alight with a smile of triumph as nodding, she said,

"You are not seeing double, Sandra Harper."

Day Four: Part Two

Once she realised calling for help was not her best idea, Lilly knew she would have to help herself. She also knew time was a factor. The lack of response she'd received from Baxter, along with the awareness that she may have already alerted Mordrel's troops to her position, meant every minute she dangled on that tree was her life on the line.

The injuries she'd sustained in her fall had weakened her and it took considerable time for her to summon enough strength to call on her powers.

Her first thought was to bring the ground up to meet her. The convenience of the idea was tempting. She had, after all, had great success manipulating soil back at the village.

The ground however was now very far away, and if by some chance she did succeed, a large enough column of the forest floor rising up to meet her would undoubtedly alert everyone in the immediate vicinity.

Both for ease and discretion she required a smaller solution. Directing her attention to the tree she reached out, making the hand-form she'd grown most used to and hissing, "Kiiat Vash."

When nothing happened she remembered Kyrel's instruction to make her words a command and, tried again.

Still there was nothing. Lilly sighed, disappointment conspiring with despair to tie her stomach into unseen knots. She'd been trying to ignore the dread creeping up on her, bringing her closer every second to a useless state of hysteria.

Pushing away all thoughts of her powers being unstable, she closed her eyes and took in a slow deep breath.

Now as she reopened her eyes and told the tree: "Kiiat Vash!" she saw a new stem begin to grow. It was barely a twig and remained so for another couple of tries. Lilly was soon concentrating so hard her head hurt and through sheer frustration she spat the words, "Ta Varee," at the tree.

Again the stem grew, but very slowly, and squinting with the effort, she watched the delicate sprig increase in length and girth, its strength also growing as it reached out to meet her, its progress painfully slow.

Only when the branch held many smaller ones of its own, complete with enough foliage to blend in with the rest of the tree, did she consider it strong enough climb down onto.

The multitude of scrapes and bangs she'd already acquired made the task all the more difficult, nonetheless - trying not to think of how much easier she could have made things by growing the new branch just a few inches closer – Lilly huffed, and groaned in agony as she struggled to pull herself over on to it.

Finally across, she clung on spreading her weight along the newly grown branch. Gasping for breath she lay still a moment, before sliding slowly down toward the tree's trunk.

A couple of metres down she spotted Baxter, he was caught in the branches of the tree directly in front of her; his body flopped limp over a thick branch, arms dangling on one side, legs on the other.

"Oh God," muttered Lilly, her whispered words coming out as a hissing through her clenched teeth. "Please don't be dead." She descended faster.

"Baxter..." she called quietly out to him as she got closer, getting no response, she tried again - still nothing.

Lilly began considering ways to wake him without raising her voice. Looking around she saw a bunch of smaller branches. They were less than an arm's length from her, but with her injuries, reaching them was a gruelling task.

In her haste she slipped, nearly losing her footing completely. When she eventually managed to snap off one of the branches - she took aim and chucked it across the space between her and Baxter. It fell short, losing forward momentum a good foot and a half from the other tree and plummeting to the ground below. Lilly's eyes rolled as she tipped her head back with a sigh.

Several branches later she got a second hit and seeing Baxter's fingers twitch, began calling out to him again as she threw more branches.

***

Harper stared up at the forest's vast ceiling of leaves, her teeth tightly gritted as she leant up against the trunk of a huge tree trying not to look, or worse: cry out, as Vereena cleaned and patched up the wound on her arm.

As much as it hurt, the twins seemed to have come out worse off. Terrence was black and blue all over and both boys sat at the base of the same tree, each holding their chests in a way that had her suspecting broken ribs.

"So what..." wheezed Tobias, "These guys are reinforcements?"

Terrence followed the gaze of his twin. To the right of them in a nearby clearing several Da'ariel clamoured to greet each other. With their fists pressed up against their chests, they bowed their heads and eyed one another with obvious reverence. Those eyes told a thousand tales of distant but deep seated mutual respect.

"I don't care who they are..." shrugged Terrence before doubling over in a fit of coughs. Coming to a gradual stop, he sat up again and nodded, "They saved our asses. That's plenty good enough for me"

"And they're not trying to kill us," hissed Harper "That's the part I especially li- iiiiiike!" her words ended in a shriek as the tourniquet being applied to her arm was tightened in one swift tug.

Both boys looked up, as patting Harper's other shoulder Vereena said. "You shall be fine." Harper threw her a distinctly frosty look. The younger girl appeared not to notice. She was already nodding toward the new faces among them, as these less familiar Da'ariel approached her and the classmates. "These are the warriors of Zanreal," she spoke with a faint smile.

"Zanreal?" Terrence's head tipped back for the sake of eye contact. "Then we're here? We made it?"

"Made it!" Tobias frowned "Made it to where? We're still in the exact same woods we've been in all ni-"

"Yes." Vereena nodded, "we are here." Her eyes remained on the approaching group as a tall, muscular Da'ariel male stepped forward; his arm already across his chest. Bowing in sync with him Vereena spoke first.

Though they used only the native Azeron language it was obvious they were previously acquainted and held one another in high regard. It was also obvious when their fast paced conversation went from gratitude and other pleasantries to more serious matters.

The stricken looks passing between them had the twins riveted. Harper was less capable of quiet; one close brush with the business end of a broad sword was more than enough for her. The last thing she wanted was to stand around waiting for Mordrel's troops to come at them again. If this was Zanreal: the sanctuary they'd travelled two nights to reach, then she wanted in – out of the open.

A tap on the shoulder returned Vereena's attentions to her. Harper shrugged, her hand going back to her arm. "Is there a reason we're not getting out of here?"

"Yes," her gaze swept over the three of them. "We are as yet unable to locate Kyrel or cousin Lilly."

"OK," nodded Harper, "that can't be good"

"No," the Da'ariel man looked to the three classmates now. "It is not good."

"Hey…" Tobias was the first to point out the obvious. "He speaks… I… I mean *You*… you speak…"

"Yes," nodded the man. "I speak the language of our future Queen."

He turned back to Vereena and they continued their foreign chatter. A minute later the girl was nodding, and calling to his troops the warrior hurried away. Breaking into a run he pulled out his gaashmay and leaping into the air, disappeared. Those he'd called on followed suit, while other Zanreal warriors began ushering their fellow Da'ariel off in another direction.

"S'ret was once Mai Mai's third hand," Vereena turned back to the classmates. "He moved to be with his life-mate, but he grew up in our village and served alongside my father when my brothers were younger."

"And now him and his troops have gone looking for Slater?" Harper nodded after them.

"No," said Vereena "They are looking for Kyrel, without him we would have been overpowered in this battle from the beginning."

"Yeah, we saw him flambé the first wave." nodded Terrence. "Neat trick,"

"Definitely," muttered Tobias.

"Sure," agreed Harper, "bet he's real fun at a barbecue."

"Wielding the forces in such a way takes much effort," said Vereena.

"You're thinking it was too much for him…" Terrence pulled himself slowly up on to his feet. "That… maybe he's lying around here somewhere needing our help."

"Whoa, hang on!" Tobias shot his brother an incredulous look. "I know I didn't just hear you volunteering us for search and rescue in the forest of sword wielding bad guys?"

"No," Terrence's gaze skimmed Harper's wounded arm, "of course not." He nodded to her. "You should go in with the others, *both* of you."

"Go *in*! Where are we meant to…" as Terrence gestured behind them with a wave Tobias turned, looking over his own shoulder, immediately agape he got quickly to his feet.

Not far from them many of the Da'ariel had gathered together and one at a time, right before his eyes, they were disappearing through some unseen barrier. "Holy cow!" muttered Tobias, "How in the… what in the-"

"Explanations later," said Vereena. "For now your brother is right: going inside with the others would be best for all of you."

"Yeah…" Tobias glared at his twin "…Best for *all* of us!"

"Tobe's is right," nodded Harper, "these guys aren't messing about Tez, staying out here is crazy… if it's safe in there we should-"

"They are right," Vereena offered a hasty smile before turning to walk away and adding, "Mordrel's troops could be back at any time and none of you is equipped to-"

"No, OK!" pushing himself off the tree Terrence grabbed her arm. "I can't just sit around doing nothing. It isn't just your people out there. Lilly and Baxter both need to be found too. One of us should be here for them."

"And what," Tobias pulled himself up also. "That's automatically you? You can't be here for them inside? Together we were barely a match for one of those Deebanaarie guys. What the hell do you expect to do on your own?"

"Look, don't worry OK." Terrence shrugged. "I won't do anything stupid. If they come back I'll be the first one hiding." Turning back to Vereena he added, "You might not need my help but you could sure as hell use it. The sooner we find the others the sooner we can all get in out of sight, and I don't care how badass you are, you can't want to die today any more than I do."

Vereena contemplated him a second longer before nodding.

"Very well, Terrence Emerson. You may accompany me on the ground, while my people search the trees. Just know if Mordrel's troops do return you are to do exactly as you have vowed: you must stay well hidden."

"Not a problem," shrugged Terrence.

As she again turned to leave, he took a step to follow and Tobias grabbed his shoulder.

"Seriously bro?" he shook his head as both Vereena and Terrence turned to face him. "Not a problem? You really think I'm going to just let you do this?"

"Tobes…" he smiled, "You can't stop me. Besides, we both know if it was me out here you'd want all the help you could get looking for me."

"Then I'm coming with you-"

"What!" Harper's voice was all alarm. "What's the matter with you two? All this way to reach safety and you wanna hang around out here?"

"No." Terrence looked to her wounded arm. "Harper's right, she's injured. One of us should stay-"

"Then you can be the one to play gentleman," Tobias pushed off from the tree's trunk, and attempting to slip past his brother added, "and I'll be the one too-"

"This isn't some stupid pissing contest!" Terrence slammed him back against the tree. "You're staying here… Got it?"

"No, OK. I don't got it. What's it to be Tez, Gentleman or Hero because either way I'm not letting you wander back out into this fight without me."

Terrence stared at him a moment, lips scrunched inward as he held back a scowl. Finally he rolled his eyes and sighing turned to offer Harper a shrug.

"I'm sure we won't be long you'll be fine here with-"

"You've got to be kidding!" both her eyebrows went up. "I've seen enough movies to know splitting up is never a good idea, there's no way I'm staying here without yous, besides if you think I'm going to be the only one facing all those difficult questions back home if I'm the only one those sprite things can send home tomorrow morning..."

"You can't be serious!" Terrence shook his head.

"What, because I'm the girl I gotta be the one that runs to safety?"

"No," with a frown he glared pointedly down at her arm, "Because you're already down one limb and I figured it could be something of a hindrance!"

"Oh right, a hindrance," nodded Harper, her eyes narrowing to slits as she asked, "to all that hiding you just swore you'd be doing?"

"Harper, come on..." rolling his eyes his Tez tried again. "...You really wanna-"

"Yeah OK, you want to stand here arguing with me..." gesturing beyond him with a wave she added "or we going to get moving before little Miss Jab-Happy over there, is completely out of our sight?"

Turning to see Vereena already quite some distance away, Terrence mumbled "Ah crap!" and limping into action he gave chase.

Harper turned to see Tobias smirking her way, and took a second to respond in kind before they set off together after the other two.

***

"So err..." Terrence kept his voice low, "...that fire thing Kyrel did - you ever see something like that before?"

He and Vereena had been shoulder to shoulder since he'd caught up with her, while Harper and his brother seemed content to remain a few feet behind. All four of them weaved through the trees, straining their eyes for any sign of their missing companions.

"Until he brought Cousin Lilly to our village I had never seen any but our sprites use the active magicks before," Vereena told him.

"Right," nodded Terrence. "Of course."

"Still," she paused to hold back a cluster of branches for him, her eyes on the forest the whole time. "Power over the Kratack was once a common trait among the Deebanaarie."

"The Kratack?" Terrence glanced over his shoulder. "And that's what... like your word for fire or something?"

"Yes..." she turned to give him a brief nod, "It *is* 'or something.'"

"So then – no." He smiled as she turned to look at him.

"Kratack is the force that produces fire," shrugged Vereena. "The word is more like your word: flame."

"Well where I'm from, that was definitely more a fire than a flame. In fact by most people's standards, I'd go as far as to say it was a raging inferno."

"Yes," nodded Vereena. "Kyrel possesses exceptional abilities for a male, but then the D'vey family line was always among the strongest."

"Exceptional," muttered Terrence.

"Oh yes," said Vereena. "Unlike many of our time, he has not let his being male limit his knowledge of the magicks. Mai Mai believes he had mastered many of the forces, and was already powerful when he stayed with our clan all those cycles ago."

"You mean when Lilly's mother was alive?" Harper interjected from behind.

"Yes…" Vereena glanced over her shoulder to the other two. "He caused much destruction to our clan. Two troops worth of Mai Mai's guard were killed; my parents among them."

"Sorry," said Terrence, then seeing her raise an eyebrow, he shrugged. "You know… that you lost your parents. I didn't mean to… well… err… dredge up the past."

"Aah, you believe I may need consoling for the loss?"

"Err… well…"

"Those days are many cycles gone Terrence Emerson. There is not much about them of which I have personal memories, I was but a child."

"Yeah, but still." Tobias spoke up from behind them. "To grow up without parents… I mean well…"

"I have always had all the parents I needed in Mai Mai and my cousins," said Vereena, "Not to mention our clan Douleks, Shentis, and the head guards on each of the royal troops." She sighed. "I am the youngest offspring in the Avengturov House, and born to be Qin Am Ness, believe me, I have never lacked parenting."

"So teen angst does exist in Azeron," quipped Harper.

Catching the puzzled expression on her face as she turned to ask Harper's meaning, Terrence shook his head telling her, "Don't worry about it; totally not important."

"So…" asked Harper, "Are there any others in Kyrel's family who have the err… that can use the active magics? I mean you know… besides Mordrel? Is there anyone else Lilly should probably know about?"

"In line for the throne there are none," shrugged Vereena "still, others of the Deebanaarie noble blood lines can wield the forces."

"Others like who… are there brothers? Are we talking a bunch more Kyrel's out there who aren't on our side?"

"No," said Vereena. "To my knowledge none of Kyrel's other siblings were born with the mark; although Talyaal the eldest brother was said to be a great warrior."

"Was?" asked Terrence "What happened to him?"

"He perished."

"Right," muttered Tobias "Course he di-"

"Shh…" putting one of her delicate fingers to her lips, Vereena turned to

Terrence whispering, "I hear something," closing her eyes, she cocked her head to one side. Tobias and Harper began looking around, each straining their ears in vain but only for a second before the young Da'ariel girl's eyes flickered open and waving them onward, she whispered, "This way, stay close."

Terrence was again the first to give chase; although attempting to catch up proved a pointless endeavour for all of them. There was no chance of any of them matching her speed, but the prospect of encountering the enemy again without her nearby was more than enough impetus for all three to keep moving.

With the other two close behind him, Terrence had dashed through several clearings, before he heard the clashing of swords in the distance. Barely managing to keep Vereena in sight, he saw her finally slowing to a halt near the edge of the next clearing.

Keeping low, she sidled up to a huge tree and facing him with her back against it, signalled again for quiet.

Terrence nodded, keeping low as he crept as swiftly as he dared toward her.

She was already sneaking toward another tree as he reached the one she'd been at; he watched her peer around its trunk.

Through the foliage he could just about make out shapes. At least three swords were bared and the men swinging them advanced on Kyrel; flanking him, they closed in. His own sword lay glinting in the early morning sun not much farther than a foot away from his position. However every attempt he made to retrieve it was thwarted with a near miss from a blade.

Terrence reached the tree Vereena had her back against, as she unsheathed her long sword with an impatient scowl. Only now, as he took a second glance did Terrence notice Kyrel's aggressors were not in the uniform dark blue of Mordrel's troops.

"Hey, those are…" he pointed to the men but speaking over him Vereena said,

"Wait here for your friends," and darted out into the clearing, at which point he realised she had already identified these troops as Da'ariel - a fact that did nothing to stop her leaping to Kyrel's defence.

Terrence hugged the tree, watching as this young girl brought her blade down just in time to stop a blow aimed for the back of Kyrel's neck. In an instant she had flicked her own sword back up in a wide arc that sent the armed Da'ariel at the other end of it flying.

Turning around, the Deebanaarie caught a glimpse of his defender before she spun around to deflect several more blows from the men at his front. With no time wasted he made use of the diversion; rolling across the ground, he snatched up his sword, and flicked himself back up on to his feet, weapon at the ready.

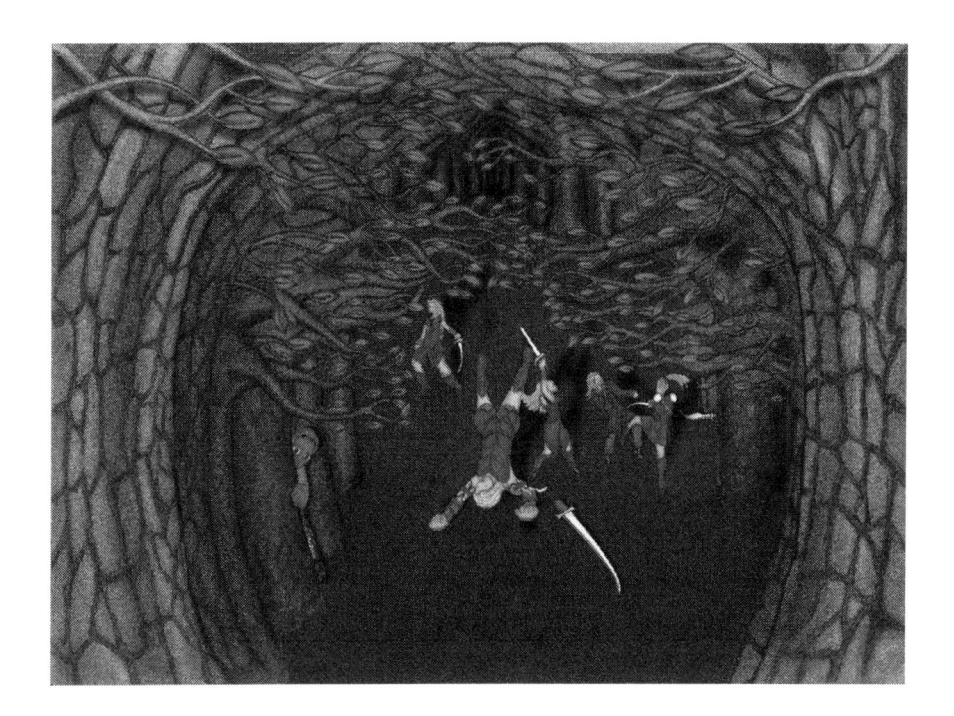

Harper and Tobias joined Terrence in cowering behind the tree, as the third man, now back on his feet, took a flying leap at Kyrel, Terrence stepped out, about to yell a warning.

"What the fuck are you doing?" Tobias hissed as he pulled him back. "We're supposed to be hiding remember!"

Before Terrence could respond Kyrel was in the air again, his blade met the flying Da'ariel halfway, knocking him to the ground and disarming him.

The man rolled over, reaching out to retrieve his weapon. It was a futile effort. Kyrel dived atop him, one knee coming down on the man's chest to pin him in place. He pressed the tip of his blade against his victim's jugular before shouting something across to where Vereena stood grasping her blade at an angle which enabled her to hold off the other two men as she and they exchanged words.

They conversed only in the native tongue but body language and tone made it clear that things could be going better.

***

"You come defending this Deebanaarie, then presume to give us orders!" sneered one of the men.

"Step aside," the other demanded as he brought his sword up for another swing. "For what reason do you fight to keep him alive?" he asked as their blades clashed. "When he is dead we will let you keep whichever piece of him you wish. A Deebanaarie ear is sure to impress the other youths of your clan."

"Yes," laughed the first. "We wish only to pay homage to the ancestors, to smear his blood across the forest's floor, and celebrate the passing of yet another Deebanaarie. You can say you alone made the kill." He grinned.

"I have no need of such a false triumph." Vereena glared at them.

"Then what is meant by this treachery? You betray our people with your actions. Tell us now why we should not cut you down with him."

"Has not enough blood been spilled in the name of our ancestors this morning?" she told them.

"You are confused young one." The second Da'ariel took a step closer, his narrowed eyes telling all on where he believed that confusion lay. "There can never be enough Deebanaarie blood on the ground. Now move aside!" With a lunge he unleashed a fierce display of swordsmanship, throwing Vereena into a dance of continuous parrying. The attack was intended to topple and disarm her while giving his comrade, whose step back had been nothing more than a feint, the chance to manoeuvre around her and aid the other from their troop.

Vereena was not caught off guard. She gave as good as she got and when the first Da'ariel attempted to slip past her, she spun around. Flooring him with a flying kick to the ribs, she landed back on her feet in time to block another blow from the first warrior. Her blade clashed with his several more times; the pair of them going at it a few more seconds until he was the one disarmed. Leaning forward with her blade at his throat she said, "One more move... and you will have only one hand on which to bear the needless deaths of your companions. For once their throats are slit, I shall personally be removing the other from you."

Beside her the Da'riel she'd kicked down froze; his threatened hand mere inches from the dagger he kept in his boot.

"Can you not see we are Zanreal warriors?" his confusion was unmistakable now. "I am Liath, third under the command of S'ret. We have orders to eradicate all Deeba-."

"I know who you are," Vereena turned to face him. "As I know your orders. Now have your men set aside their weapons for I will not order them, or you, to stand down another time."

"This is our territory to protect as we wish young one," hissed the soldier at the end of Vereena's blade. "Cease this impudence. Who are you to command us?"

"You do see that you will be the first to have his throat slit?" She tapped the tip of her blade up under his chin. "Your lack of insight astounds me *warrior*. It is not my wish to injure one of my own but if you must continue your refusal to recognise the superiority of my skills over yours, look to my braid..." she tapped him again nodding, "and know that I too have my orders, and I will do all needed to carry them out." With a slight tilting of her head and gritting of her teeth, Vereena added, "that does include spilling your insides where you stand, if you insist on forcing my hand."

"Well Veer..." Laughter came from the trees as S'ret and his men stepped out from behind them. "You certainly grew up with a formidable tongue on you."

Glancing his way, a faint smile rippled its way across her lips as the man on the ground nearest her looked quickly to the long clan-braid hanging down the side of her head, then muttered, "Veer... Princess Vereena!" He drew his hand back from the top of his boot and bowed his head. "Oh gracious Lady, forgive us our ignorance. We did not know-"

"What?" sneered Vereena. "That I am above your station? Given the ineffective use you made of your weapon, I find that difficult to believe. Unless of course you're claiming it's always this easy for we *'impudent young ones'* to best you and your men in battle."

"Ny Lady Vereena, I assure you, my men and myself are all worthy fighters."

"This is true," S'ret said as he approached the group. "What my men lack in reasoning abilities they make up for in vigour. Still... Liath and his men might well have recognised your braid - if they had been given half a chance to, before you so effectively disarmed them."

"I can make no use of the awe of your men S'ret. I require only their obedience in the name of my line."

"And you shall have it," he placed his hand over her sword and slowly pressed it down. "Liath's troop was hunting, when we received word you were due. Their ignorance is as true as your blade."

Behind them Kyrel got to his feet, dragging his captive Da'ariel with him. The edge of his sword remained against the warrior's prone throat. Gesturing to them with a nod Vereena addressed Liath and his men. "This Deebanaarie is an ally of our people. You will all treat him accordingly."

The warrior nearest Vereena turned to glare at S'ret.

"First she defends him, now she suggests we work with him as an equal, would not doing so be akin to treachery! Does the Lady Vereena seek to amuse us, Sir?"

A deep scowl tightened the edges of S'ret's face as he stepped forward hissing, "Still your tongue! That you would even dare to question-"

"S'ret!" Vereena's hand went up and sucking in his lips he backed up as she stepped forward.

The young girl's studious glare was more than a match for the defiant one she was receiving from the hot tempered warrior before her. "Name?" she asked, her tone making it clear she was addressing S'ret while her eyes remained locked on his subordinate.

"Rishlek," S'ret told her. "A little fresh in his boots perhaps, but while he is apparently unaware that we have no need of his mouth, he is an otherwise fine fighter. I assure you Veer, there is much promise in this one."

"Clearly, that remains to be seen." She stepped closer to Rishlek, watching as her scrutiny caused his eyes to dip slightly and the lines of his jaw began to tighten. "It does seem he has much to learn," she added while closing the gap between them. "I can only imagine how pleased my grandmother will be to learn that her orders, given for the good of all Da'ariel, have been deemed treacherous." With her face now inches from his, she watched him force down a gulp, and nodded. "That's right Rishlek, you hear me clearly now don't you?"

He barely managed a nod before stepping back; she was glancing around at the others. "Listen carefully because I only have time to clarify this once and misunderstandings will not be tolerated." Her gaze returned to Rishlek. "There were no *suggestions*! Nor did I say anything of you and the Deebanaarie working together as *equals*. As named guardian of the Princess Lilliath, he is here in service of our Mai Mai. Until she re-joins us his station is my second." Ignoring the wide eyed glances she received from both S'ret and Kyrel she added, "You will all do everything in your power to assist with whatever he asks of you... Understood?"

In unison Liath and his troop nodded their heads; with Rishlek muttering an accompanying "Yes, Lady Vereena," as he bowed and backed away.

Switching from the native language Vereena glanced toward the tree line calling "It is safe to come out."

The three classmates poked their heads out around the tree, as she turned back to Kyrel, with a raised eyebrow, and seeing this he let loose his grip on the other warrior, who immediately stalked away rubbing his neck and muttering something under his breath.

"Qin Am Ness Vereena," Kyrel slid his sword back into its sheath, "The assistance is appreciated. Now I must return to your cousin. Take me to-"

"Where are they?" Terrence asked as he and the other two ran toward them. "Where are Slater and Baxter?"

Again Kyrel's eyes grew wide, as he also switched from their native language.

"She is not with you?" he glared at Vereena.

"Nydrel," she shook her head, with a growing hint of desperation in her eyes. "My hope was to find her with you."

"And so you would, had she remained where I left her," anger and frustration seemed about equal in his voice, his face however was all concern. "You!" he turned to Terrence "You say the other boy is missing also... are they together?"

"Err..." momentarily flummoxed, Terrence's mouth flapped has he shook his head saying, "I... I don't know." Nodding and looking to his classmates for support, he added, "I... I mean, he did leave us to go to her. But that was way back when-"

"You were still with her then." Harper cut in, shoving her hands in her pockets as she muttered. "Baxter was headed over to both of you... was kind of itching to give you a piece of his mind."

"Of his mind?" Kyrel's confusion was clear and Tobias stepped forward to clear things up,

"You kind of grabbed her..." explained the younger twin. "Baxter didn't like it."

Though there was still confusion in Kyrel's eyes, there was at least enough understanding for him to raise an irked eyebrow at the three children. A look, which seemed to leave only Tobias unfazed – as his brother and Harper each averted their eyes – he shrugged. "After that we couldn't really tell you where either of them went. All hell was breaking loose out here... we were kinda busy finding a place to hide."

"Hide!" S'ret spat his words out with disgust. "If there is no fight in these off-worlders why did they not remain within the sanctuary with the rest of the low born?"

"Hey, who you calling a low…" Tobias was quickly cut off by a curt glare from Vereena before she turned back to S'ret, asking "Am I to also have my orders questioned by you now too?" Vereena stared at S'ret.

"Ny Veer, nydrel." His arm went across his chest as he switched to the native language. "I would never dishonour your-"

"These humans are companions of the Princess Lilliath." Kyrel interjected, he'd also switched language, leaving Harper and the twins clueless as to what was being said.

They watched the Deebanaarie nod Terrence's way as he added something, that had S'ret affording him a second more intrigued glance.

However the glances became less distinguishable as the pair went on and the urgency with which they spoke, became the only constant.

"Can you spare me more than this troop?" Kyrel was asking S'ret. "The Princess must be found before my sister's forces return with reinforcements."

"By the Lady Leyavanya! He is the Prince!" Rishlek's surprise was as obvious in his tone as it was in the glance he chanced at S'ret when adding, "There is truth in the stories."

S'ret stared pointedly at Kyrel, his face a blank canvas as he said, "Yes, I can spare more troops. I also know exactly *who* to send for them." Without the slightest glance in Rishlek's direction, they all knew that would be him - Harper and the twins being the obvious exception - with no one showing any inclination to switch languages again, they were still unable to follow the conversation.

Hence, moments later, when Rishlek hurried off in the direction they'd come from; only Harper and the twins had no idea why. Neither was an explanation forthcoming, as Kyrel lead the other two Deebanaarie away in the opposite direction.

"What's going on?" Harper muttered to Terrence.

Throwing her a brief I-don't-know look, he turned back to Vereena; tapping her shoulder and saying, "Err guys…" Vereena however, was in the thick of some all engrossing conversation with S'ret. The flow of their words increased with vehemence that revealed anger, as did the prolonged stares they were soon giving each other.

"Err, Veer," Terrence tried the shoulder tapping a second time, but was unable to get her attention before S'ret was speaking again.

The warrior's tone now carried enough warning to make Tobias yank Terrence backward muttering, "Yeah, I think we should leave them to it."

Harper nodded her agreement and unnoticed by the two Da'ariel, the three of them backed up a few feet; picking out a spot from which they could sit watching the incomprehensible yet obvious argument unfold. Though Tobias spent most of this time gazing about them with thoughts of how safe their immediate surroundings were.

A minute more however, and even his attention was drawn back to the argument when Vereena drew her dagger and pressed its tip to S'ret's throat.

"Whoa!" Terrence leapt to his feet. "Hang on… hang on! I thought we were all friends here?"

"Tez!" Tobias jumped also, his warning tone escaping through gritted teeth.

Terrence waved a hand at him. "Just gimme a sec here, OK bro?" Reluctantly hanging back, Tobias watched his brother wave that same hand at Vereena and adding "same side remember?"

Without looking his way, Veerena switched language and also speaking through tightly gritted teeth said. "Not content with insulting the Qin Am Ness of our next Mai Mai, this Matfiack now insults our current Queen. For his first offence alone I have the right to take his life."

"Or..." Terrence raised a finger. "... You could, you know, seeing as you *are* the Qin Am Ness of the next Mai Mai... you could just... forgive him."

"And what of the insult to my grandmother?" She pressed the tip of her blade a little more against S'ret's throat. "It is not my place to forgive in her name."

"Well no, OK maybe not. But hey... is it your place to kill in her name? Is it?"

"Yes," Vereena's tone was brusque. "To do so is my duty," glaring at S'ret she added, "An honour."

"Alright then," a slight, and somewhat nervous, chuckle escaped Terrence. "Should have probably seen that coming." He rolled his eyes before speaking up again, "But we do need every able body we can get right now, don't we? I mean... well aren't things very much all-hands-on-deck at the moment?"

"On deck?" Vereena's eyes remained locked with S'ret's.

"Yeah, you know..." called out Harper; without her injured arm for support, getting off the ground had been a strain and the effort rang clear in her voice. "Possible huge fight scene coming up and all that." She panted out her words as if recovering from a short run. "Is depleting your people's numbers now really such a good idea?"

"Exactly," Terrence agreed, "everything Harper just said."

In silence they watched Vereena suck in her bottom lip, affording Terrence the briefest of sideways glances; during which he offered what he hoped to be a winning smile.

"You may be right." Her gaze returned to S'ret.

"See..." grinned Terrence, "now that's what I'm talking ab-"

"Perhaps I shall simply cut out his disloyal tongue instead."

Though there was no reaction from S'ret, Harper and Tobias developed a similar wide eyed look of horror, while Terrence gave voice to their thoughts; his disgust as evident in his words as it was on all three of their faces.

"Seriously?" he grimaced. "You'd do that?" the look Vereena shot his way was answer enough. "Ick!" he shivered. "Come on! What the hell is the matter with you people? Is a simple court martial so much to ask? Why's everything gotta be death, and blood, a-and tongues getting cut out! Look..." he reached out, slowly grasping Vereena's blade hand as he gestured to S'ret with a nod. "...Whatever he said about your granny..." seeing the Da'ariel girl's eyebrow bounce upward, his eyes did a quick roll. "Sorry, your... your grandmother: Mairiel! Whatever…err… S'ret?" he glanced to the older warrior for confirmation and receiving it in the form of a cautious – for obvious reasons – nod he added, "Whatever he said about her; I'm sure he didn't mean it."

"That is untrue," insisted S'ret, "I would not speak words to Veer that I do not mean…" though he'd also switched language to accommodate Terrence, S'ret's eyes remained on Vereena and the nature of his next statement made it clearly for her benefit. "The Doloch Ty should be considered if only to ensure the full co-operation of my troops."

"If your troops are so unruly, then your appointment here was a mistake I am willing to correct." Vereena hissed in response.

"They are not unruly Veer. They are confused! As am I – how many generations have we avoided the Deebanaarie? Now finally we're ordered into battle against them, yet expected to take orders from one."

"My cousin does not only possess the active magicks S'ret, she is the only living heir of the Avengturov line. Protecting her should offer no confusion for any of us."

"But *Kyrel*, Veer! He is the reason Herrella died before your grandmother could pass on that birth-right to her."

"Then perhaps you are needlessly concerned S'ret. Guilt could be his only motivation for his now protecting her daughter."

"As if that would be reason enough for Mairiel's appoint-"

"The reasons do not matter. If anything holds true since the days of my parents it is that our people have no defence against Deebanaarie magicks. That alone makes keeping Kyrel an ally, far favourable over again making him a foe. Mai Mai knows this and I do not need the wisdom of a thousand generations in my head to know what this opportunity means to our people. Too long have we waited to reclaim all that is ours. Now the task of seeing this chance is not lost falls on me until Mai Mai is again with us. And I will not allow that to happen because your troops could not let go of the old hatreds and do their duties." As S'ret's mouth opened she raised a hand. "There is no more to be said on this matter, we both have our orders, if you will not follow yours-"

"I did not say I would not do my duty Veer. I would never disobey the orders of our rightful Mai Mai. I question only whether that is still Mairiel. You must know she may already be lost to us."

"Say that again," growled Vereena, her eyes narrowing to slits as the tempo of her words became menacingly slow. "See if I do not cut you down where you stand."

"Hey!" snapped Terrence, attempting to push her hand down, failing mostly through fear of causing her blade to slip.

Instead he glared S'ret's way, hissing, "Not… helping!" before he turned back to Vereena and sighed. "Look… I - I'm sure he's sorry. Or, you know… he will be later on when he comes to his-"

"As Qin Am Ness to the next able heir, declaring Doloch Ty is a right you hold." S'ret spoke over Terrence.

His gaze had shifted to Vereena's blade the moment she'd pulled it on him. Yet even now - with the tip piercing his skin and a thin trickle of blood running down the centre of his throat - he made no attempt to escape it. He did however close his eyes, at least appearing to take a moment composing his thoughts - or possibly working on his resolve. Then he had them open again, his voice every bit as steady as before "Do it, Veer. Take my life if you truly believe my words to be ill founded. I would rather die knowing I remain loyal to our people than live with you thinking me capable of any treachery against them."

"Then you do forget yourself S'ret," her scowl was deep; forbidding. "Even your place as Herrella's mate did not make you worthy of suggesting I consider usurping my grandmother."

With growing comprehension Terrence and the others watched as S'ret chuckled, "You speak as if such words should still bear truth for me."

"I know not of what you spea-"

"Veer please. Must you also treat me as a fool? Have I not just seen the truth with my own eyes? Heard it with my own ears?"

His glare proved enough to make her gaze shift; while watching them Harper and Tobias exchanged wary glances and Terrence, feeling Vereena's hand slacken decided to try again on playing the voice of reason.

"OK... this sounds a lot like an issue for another-"

"I have held command here in Zanreal for nearly four cycles," S'ret cut him short again, practically spitting out his words in anger, "yet you appoint *him* over me."

"The appointment was not mine to make. He is guardian of our people's next Mai Mai."

"He is Kyrel D'vey!"

"I have not forgotten his name S'ret."

"Then perhaps you have forgotten that he alone is responsible for the deaths of so many of our clan."

"That is not-"

"Both your parents and Herrella among them," S'ret spoke over her now. "Is it not insult enough that he again walks among us? Now by seeing himself named protector and guide to our next Mai Mai-"

"That is enough S'ret!" seeing his eyes grow wide and his mouth snap shut, she nodded. "You go too far!"

"Do I?" he raised an eyebrow.

"Truly Veer... tell me these things do not insult you. That they do not *sicken* you! Tell me and I shall never again speak of your grandmother being far beyond her days."

"Perhaps it is you who is beyond his days."

"Vereena please..." Terrence hissed as he felt her pressing on the blade again.

Her and S'ret's eyes remained locked on each other.

"And so it is..." nodded the warrior. "New duties or not, you *are* still the princess I know. So make me take orders from that Deebanaarie moolach in front of my own troops if you must, but do not speak to me as if I am a fool."

Terrence watched as her lips tightened, realising as he did, that each time he garnered some fresh understanding of their discussion it took new turns and he was left more confused than before. All he knew for certain was an intense desire to end the situation and return to the search. With that in mind he forced an end to their staring by shoving S'ret back and pushing himself between them.

"Tez!" Tobias came closer as he again called out with warning. This time Terrence ignored him outright.

"I know you're pissed," he nodded Veerena's way "but this guy's one of you lot, we *need* him."

"Need?" she sneered, "there are many other able warriors of the Zanreal, Terrence Emerson."

"Yes," he nodded "and we need every one of them!" All too aware that she was yet to lower her blade, despite his now being on the receiving end of it, he shrugged. "Come on... be smart about this. The odds aren't exactly in our favour. You said yourself Mordrel's forces outnumber your own, like five to one or something. You seriously telling me all that ancient knowledge you're carrying around has you thinking this is your best course of action right now? Slater and Baxter need us, remember! Your princess, Veer! Your... Lady! She could be out here all alone, isn't getting to her your most important duty?"

Vereena's gaze went beyond him to S'ret but only for a moment before she closed her eyes, took a deep breath and let her arm drop to her side.

Terrence and the others breathed quiet sighs of relief as her eyelids fluttered open and she nodded.

"Cousin Lilly is right about you, Terrence Emerson. You are swift in learning our ways." Then she was turning back to S'ret, "This entire conversation is a distraction we can ill afford. But make no mistake; you keep your life this day only that you may serve Mai Mai. Speak again of Doloch Ty and it is you who will be lost to us."

"As you will it, Qin Am Ness." With the customary bow he backed away before stepping back and running the back of his hand across his throat then glancing down at the blood it left smeared there.

It was a brief, almost dismissive glance, one in which Terrence could read no emotion.

"Come..." Veerena turned to him, then on to where Harper and Tobias stood watching, "There is still much of the forest to search before we re-join Kyrel and the others. Let us not waste what little time we have."

"Sure," agreed Terrence; he threw his friends a weary glance as he added, "Let us... not."

Vereena nodded S'ret's way, and without another word he took the lead and they all set off again.

With the other two still hanging back; Harper half listening to Tobias complaining in whispers of what he saw as his brother's stupidity, Terrence remained alongside Veerena, his voice as quiet as it was cautious.

"Not that I want to lose my tongue or anything, but isn't there a chance," he nodded to where S'ret weaved through the trees ahead of them. "This warrior friend of yours... couldn't he be on to something?"

"*On* to something?" Vereena's eyebrows dipped a moment. "You're suggesting S'ret may be right about Mai Mai?"

"Well no... Of course not! I... I just... well I'm-"

"Do not be concerned Terrence Emerson," She gave him another of her frank glances. "Like you, I am my cousin's servant..."

"Hey now," he began to protest. "I'd hardly say I'm-"

"Taking my blade to your tongue would seem - for now at least - to be very much against her wishes."

"Right," nodded Terrence. "Of course. I totally serve Lilly a...and my tongue – totally important for my telling her all the stuff I'm learning."

Hearing the undeniable relief in his voice Vereena let her hand drop to her waist, resting it on the hilt of her short sword, as she shrugged,

"There are of course other less important parts to you. A finger or two maybe."

"Say what now..." he came to a dead stop, gaze shifting momentarily from her to where the other two were out of hearing range.

Vereena turned to him with a smirk of such obvious amusement, it proved infectious. "You're messing with me!" He pointed her way, shaking his head, and forcing words out through his partial chuckle, "and thank God for that because the alternative... had me scared enough to be needing a clean pair of pants." Seeing her frown as she set about divining his meaning, he grinned, clapping his palms together before waving both hands at her. "So... terrifying... and funny. Good to know."

Day Four: Part Three

"He's always like this…" Tobias was telling Harper. "gotta be the freaking hero."

"So what…" she frowned. "You'd rather he left it to you?"

"Unnecessary peril… not really one of my things."

"Yeah, I think I got that."

"Hey, I'm good with no one playing hero OK."

"Hey, I get it…" Harper shrugged "honest, before I knew Morris I was all about that every gal for herself thing, course she was you know… way tougher than me, so I guess she could afford to: be the first 'right in there' if she saw someone getting hassled."

"Yeah," sighed Tobes, "that sounds like Tez." Then he was frowning, "Not that I'm saying he's way tougher than me or anything."

"Course not," Harper smirked.

"Hey come on," said Tobias "Just cos he has this whole big brother thing going on… you know he is only four minutes older than me, and if anything, I've got the better physique. He's not tougher or braver OK, just idealistic and less cautious." Sighing again he shrugged, "Course he has stepped in and saved my ass more times than I know too… and obviously I'm grateful but… well…" he shook his head and Harper added.

"It can get a little annoying when it's other people he's sticking his neck out for?"

"Yeah! I mean, no! It's just-"

"Your brother's a stand-up guy Tobes, maybe you should cut him some lack. Ain't such a bad thing to wanna do the right thing."

"Yeah well, if being a stand-up guy means not giving a shit about being the fan that the shit hits… well… I can't cut him slack there OK. What was I supposed to do if what's her face there…" he nodded ahead to where his brother and Vereena walked, adding. "Like you said: Miss Jab Happy… what if she'd turned around and sliced his throat back there or something? What good would slack have done him?"

"Not much I guess," Harper sighed. "But you know… I really don't think Tez stayed with this search because of some hero thing."

"Well, no, course not," Tobias shrugged "he's got the hots for," again he nodded ahead and seeing Harper's gaze follow added, "He's barely left her side since we got here."

"There you go then," Harper nudged him with her good arm. "She sure ain't no damsel in distress."

"No," grumbled Tobias. "She's an exotic, sword wielding babe; can't see that being a problem."

"Problem," Harper gave them a second more quizzical glance before nodding, "Oh," as her eyes rolled. "Now I get it."

"Get what?"

"You."

"What about me?" Tobias raised an eyebrow.

"You know what!" She shook her head, "You're worried your brother likes it here, that maybe he isn't going to want to come back with us."

"What? That's just…" Tobias began but Harper's brow dipped and sighing he shrugged. "Actually I'm hoping it isn't an option."

"You don't really think he'd stay? I mean seriously… over a girl? She's like what, two years younger than us? That's like year nine or eight man. Come on!"

"You haven't heard him talk about her. Or all the stuff he's learning from her."

"Err Tobes… everybody's heard him talk about the stuff he's learning off her."

"Yeah OK, I take that back. And trust me; I know it sounds crazy. I mean any of us thinking of staying here should get our heads examined right? Even Lilly shouldn't be thinking about it. I don't care if that is pretty much why she was brought here. She doesn't belong in this place any more than the rest of us."

"She was born here. I'd call that a pretty good argument for sticking around."

"I don't care!" he shook his head. "She's one of us. She didn't grow up here. She has to come back."

For a moment they were both silent, then Harper was asking,

"You're serious about this? You really do think Tez would stay cos of a girl?" turning to see her watching him Tobias shrugged.

"I don't know. There's more to it than that. Tez never belonged at The Peak."

"Nobody belongs at the Peak."

"Well no," agreed Tobias "But it's different for Tez. He ain't really like the rest of us. We all fucked up, we stole and we lied, we made life hell for our parents and everyone else around us-"

"Oh… So Tez is a saint?"

"If you like… all he ever did wrong was take the fall for me."

"What do you mean?"

"Like I said, OK. He's always gotta play the hero"

"Yeah but-"

"He's always gotta step in when he don't need to."

"Are you saying -"

"Yeah, I am," nodded Tobias. "I'm the one who fucked up." Seeing her suck in her bottom lip as she stared at him, he shrugged. "I was hanging with some real assholes and he knew it OK. When things got heavy he knew that too. He saw I was in way over my head and he did what he's always done: he stepped up so I didn't have to."

"So if it wasn't for you then-"

"He never would have been at The Peak." Tobias shook his head and waved toward the door, "He sure as hell wouldn't be out here, risking life and limb in search of an asshole and a long lost Princess."

Hearing Harper snigger he turned to her with a sombre smirk and shrugging she said,

"Look, I'm no expert, but this doesn't seem like the place for regrets. I mean none of us knew any of this was going to happen. How could we? I don't know about you but this whole 'other world thing' the forest dwelling folk, and us landing smack dab in the middle of some great ancient war; definitely not something that came up in my weekly horoscope."

"Well no, I don't suppose it would."

"None of us was prepared for this. If I was I might not have freaked when we got here."

"Hey I was fine when we lost the bus," Tobias shook his head. "We were out of there so fast I had no idea how serious it all was till Lilly told us."

"Maybe not, but you still weren't any more prepared than I was and I tell you something now: if I'd known Sunday night, what Monday morning had in store... well there's a few things I'd a done a little differently."

"Yeah I feel you there," agreed Tobias. "Like refusing to get on that damn bus!"

"Yeah," chuckled Harper. "So maybe it's best if we just forget the 'what ifs' and 'maybes'. Because hey - we start in on those and I'm a have to be considering whether or not Morris being gone is my fault."

"Don't be a dumbass!" he threw her a frank look. "That can't be what you really think? I saw you when Lilly and Kyrel brought you in. She wasn't lying when she said there was nothing you could have done. You were totally out of it..."

"And if I hadn't been?" She gave him a stern look.

"Oh come on, what's that supposed to-"

"You saw Kyrel's power today, we all did. You have to know if he hadn't been carrying me that first day he could have fought back."

"That's just silly," Tobias shook his head. "Prepared or not, you can't go blaming yourself for what happened to Morris"

"No," she shrugged, her eyebrows rising. "And you can't blame yourself for Tez being here with the rest of us. He knew exactly what he was doing when he saw the good ship Tobias was sinking and decided to hop on board."

"Great! Now you got me seeing my brother in a Sailor suit... cheers for that." Harper managed a straight face for all of a second before her shoulders began to convulse, which precipitated sniggering from Tobias.

"Hey!" Terrence whispered back at them, as loudly as he dared, before putting a finger to his lips and shushing them with a glare.

"Sorry," mouthed Harper. Tobias merely narrowed his eyes, then turning back to her whispered,

"See what I mean, four minutes earlier and he thinks he gets to call all the shots."

"Yeah I know," Harper sighed "But come on, he's your brother; being at your side is what matters to him. Not where you wind up, or what happens there, just... you know... being at your side so he can tell everyone how he saved your butt."

"At my side, he didn't even want us along!"

"Yeah because he wants to make sure you get home in one piece." With a glance to her arm she sighed "or you know... as intact as possible." Then she was smiling again, "Like you said he's stepping up so you don't have to."

"I guess," he sighed, offering a weak smile; it was the bravest face he could muster. Fortunately for him Harper wasn't having any of it.

"So... Tez in a sailor suit hey. Isn't that kinda like: you in a sailor suit?"

"Yeah, like I said," Tobias favoured her with a more genuine smile. "Cheers for that!"

***

Lilly's branch throwing had finally paid off. With a deep groan Baxter had done more than stir: he'd shifted on his branch, enough to make her think he was about to fall off it.

Instead the gasp which escaped her had him asking, "Slater? Slater is that you?"

"Yes," she'd cried with an excitement so obvious it was almost inappropriate. "Thank God!" she whispered then realising he was still face down asked, "Are you OK?"

"I might be if you stop throwing things at me." Baxter raised his head enough to throw her a pained glance.

"Sorry," Lilly's face tingled letting her know she was going bright pink. "My powers are on the fritz," she added. "I thought you were dead."

"So you decided to throw stuff at me, that's nice Slater... real respectful!"

"Oh shut up!" she hissed, slithering on her belly along the limb she was on. "I couldn't reach you, OK. I was worried."

"About me," raising his head again he smirked. "Really Slater, I didn't know you cared."

"For crying out loud," she rolled her eyes. "Do you always have to be such an Assho..." seeing him grimace her words petered out.

She was suddenly aware of his whitewashed pallor and the film of perspiration moistening his hairline so the short dark curls stuck to his forehead. "You're not OK at all are you?" Lilly shook her head.

"I've had better days." Baxter wheezed before coughing out a fine spray of blood, most of which splattered the branch beneath him.

"Oh shit!" hissed Lilly as he groaned again; the sound was weaker now and she realised there was agony in it; as there was in his every strained movement, and deep within his eyes, which were swiftly welling up. "What is it?" she crawled out closer to him. "Tell me what's wrong? What I can do?"

"You can stop moving," muttered Baxter.

Although she did so immediately, Lilly's voice filled with indignation as she asked, "Then how the hell am I supposed to get to you? I can't help you if I can't get to you?"

"Then you'd better not help me."

"What the fuck are you-"

"Slater," Baxter coughed, fixing her with a stare. "You want the truth?

Really?" Seeing her nod he forced himself to speak through his wheezing. "I'm seriously fucked OK. So unless you think both of us being seriously fucked sounds better, then please... *please...*" he spoke through gritted teeth "Don't be a fucking idiot! For the sake of... of everything: back the fuck up and leave me the fuck alone, because if you fall, we are... both... *fucked*!" When her only response was to bite her lip he prompted with an "All right?"

Nodding she mumbled, "Yeah. Yeah sure..." His head flopped a moment as he lay still, closing his eyes. After staring at him a moment she began saying "but if I can just-"

"What?" Baxter cut her off. "What are you gonna do? Fall on me? Cos I don't see that helping."

"No OK, I was just gonna say maybe if I can scootch a little furth-"

"No!" his voice cracked as it rose. "Unless your powers are working, and Kyrel taught you a whole bunch of mad skills I don't know about, you're staying put. Got it?"

"I can't just leave you to-"

"No arguments, Slater! And definitely no fucking scootching OK?"

"Right," she nodded, "No... no scootching. I'll stay put." She watched him rest his head against the tree's gnarly trunk again.

Wind swished through the leaves around them but the only sound Lilly could hear was Baxter gasping, wheezing and occasionally coughing beneath her. When his next cough gave way to whimpers, she shook her head, muttered "Fuck," and tried her powers again.

"Ta Varee!" She stretched out an arm and told the branch nearest Baxter. "Ta Varee!" she told it again before reaching back and trying her own. Nothing happened and giving in to tears she let her head flop.

"Please don't." Baxter sobbed with her. "Someone will come OK. I'll be fine."

"No one's been around for ages," Lilly wiped her eyes, unable to stop the tears. "Nobody has a clue where we are. Shit for all we know, everyone else is dead."

"No," said Baxter. "They'll be here. They'll find you. Kyrel will come or your powers will come back. Or even that girl Vereena, don't worry... You're gonna be fine."

"I'll be fine?" Lilly's tears became more profuse as she pushed herself up asking, "What about you? Why won't you tell me what's wrong? Why you can't move?"

"Slater..."

"What Baxter? Why won't you tell me? There might be something I can do. I could know, OK... I could know what to do. I know plenty of things."

"Sla-"

"Is it a leg? An arm? Is something broken? We're in a tree... Maybe we can make splints"

"I already know what to do."

"What... nothing?"

"Exactly!"

"And that's going to help?"

"Well back home it might save my life."

"And here?"

"Well..." he forced his head up once more to smirk through his tears. "I ain't too sure they have hospitals. You seen any?"

Slowly Lilly sucked in both her lips, running a finger along them, before sucking that in too, and chewing on it. Baxter watched her eyes darting over his body until eventually she was nodding.

"You're impaled on that thing aren't you?"

"Maybe," he mumbled, then as she opened her mouth he pre-empted her next question with its answer, "My thigh's caught something wicked," coughing up more blood as he finished, he saw her raise an eyebrow at the splatters and sighing let his head drop. "Oh yeah... maybe also my chest."

"Oh fucking hell," whispered Lilly, her hand going to her mouth, covering it to stem her otherwise uncontrollable sobbing. Again she tried her powers but getting nothing after several attempts resorted to hitting the limb she was on and crying "I'm so sorry Baxter... This is all my fault... If I hadn't been such an idiot about learning to use my Gaashmay. Or, listened to Kyrel about my magicks being unstable. Fuck!" She hit the tree again. You shouldn't even be here. None of you should have been..." Only when she realised her sobs had become the only sound did Lilly become aware that Baxter, now lying motionless, was yet to respond. "Baxter?" she called but still there was nothing. "Baxter? Baxter do you hear me?" Her voice rose to cracking point. "Answer me damn it! Robert! please... please answer me!"

He didn't, and hoping he'd merely passed out again was little comfort. Lilly knew now that he'd been as right about her being in no position to help him as he had about the likelihood of there being hospitals in Azeron. Like him she knew now that all she could do was watch him die.

***

Liath and his second landed on the ground a few feet ahead of Kyrel. Approaching them the Deebanaarie asked, "Have you found Drelga?"

"Ny." Liath shook his head, "It seems the few patches we knew of have been harvested recently."

"Then for what reason do you return with empty hands?" Kyrel made no attempt to hide his annoyance. "Were your orders so unclear?"

"Sir, I believed it prudent to inform you that shraeka approach your position," he pointed to Kyrel's left adding "less than half a league that way... there are many... possibly more than even you can avoid." With a sigh Kyrel shook his head, "and this news requires both of you to give up the search? Get back into the trees. Do not return again without-"

"Kathor also believes a T'karas to be upon us," said Liath.

The reprimand died on Kyrel's lips as he looked to the skies above, his eyes filling with obvious alarm as he turned to the man he'd held at the point of his blade less than an hour earlier asking, "You saw this T'karas?"

"No... Sir," he shook his head, "but the trees; they bend and break without reason."

"Where?"

"Less than a league behind us." Kathor pointed back the way they'd come.

"Nydrel!" hissed Kyrel as he glanced back that way, speaking mostly to himself he added. "Are you so desperate sister?"

"Then it is true..." said Liath terror flitting briefly through his eyes. "Mordrel commands these beasts?"

"Ny," Kyrel shook his head at both men. "Such a thing is way beyond her abilities."

"But you just said-."

"It is not she," Kyrel cut Liath off with a raised hand, "and we cannot afford to give up our search now."

"But we should find cover," insisted Kathor. "Such a creature cannot be fought. If we are discovered it will-"

"No T'karas would wander this far over Zanreal of its own accord," insisted Kyrel, "If there is one here it also searches for the Princess. And if she is captured you had better hope we are too."

With obvious trepidation Liath's second looked to him. No reprieve was offered, nodding Liath said.

"You have your orders... Go! Keep looking."

"Yes Sir." Arm across his chest the man bowed his head to Kyrel before raising his Gaashmay and spinning upward out of sight again.

"With respect, you're eminen...." a sharp look from Kyrel conveyed enough to make the Da'ariel rethink his words "I... I... Sir... we have many searching above now? Would I not be of more use to you here on the ground? If the shraeka reach your-"

"Ny," Kyrel cut him off. "My needs remain the same. Bring me word of the princess or the root of a drelga so I am better able to search for myself."

"Yes Sir," Liath raised his Gaashmay ready to spin away as he added, "as you will it Liege."

But before he could take off Kyrel hissed, "Wait!"

His hand snapped up, and watching him tilt his head to one side the Zanreal warrior asked.

"You sense something. The T'karas perhaps? Should we find cover?"

"Quiet!" Kyrel shot him an impatient look, listening a moment longer, before his gaze shifted to the right and his eyes grew wide, as filled with relief as they were with anxiety. "She is nearby and in much pain... this way." He dashed off through the forest. "I may have need of you yet."

Left to bring up the rear Liath curled back his tongue and unleashed a fierce whistle, alerting other Da'ariel in the vicinity of their discovery, before chasing after the Deebanaarie Prince.

***

"But if S'ret was right?" Terrence passed Vereena by as she held back branches for him. "That would change things for Lilly big time right? I mean like you said: she's the heir; next in line to lead your people. If your cousins don't make it back with Mai Mai-"

"If Mai Mai has perished then much has already changed for all of us." Vereena's voice was sullen.

"All of us?" asked Terrence, his own tone filled with apprehension. "Like for me and the others too?"

"Perhaps," She nodded as he turned to look at her. "I know you and your friends have concerns about returning home. And I should like very much to have good news on the matter. The truth however may not be so. Two of the clan's sprites are now missing to us and one of them: Merly, was last seen with Mairiel-"

"And it took all three of them to get us here." Terrence glanced over his shoulder, checking his brother and Harper were still out of hearing range.

"Yes," Vereena was nodding as he turned back, "I am sorry, Terrence Emerson, but if my grandmother fails to return to us it is unlikely her sprites will do so and T'vor does not have the strength alone."

"Great," muttered Terrence, his gaze skimming every tree in sight before his eyes settled again on the willowy form of S'ret up ahead and pushing on he added. "Well you probably shouldn't tell the others that just yet."

"Should I not have told you 'just yet' either?"

"Nah, that's cool, I'm glad you did. It's just… Well…"

"You do not wish to see the concerns of the others increase needlessly," said Vereena. "Your intentions are commendable, I shall do my best to comply. I am however duty bound to inform my Lady of any-"

"Your… Oh you mean Slater. Sure, no worries," he shrugged. "I just… Well I'd really rather my brother doesn't know just yet."

"You do not believe he will receive such news well then."

"I believe the thought of us getting home is about all that's holding him together right now. He's not really the best under pressure if you get my meaning."

"I'm not certain that I do." She ducked under a low hanging branch.

"Your world's real strange to us," Terrence told her "Very new, Tobes isn't what one might call a fan of the strange…" he sighed. "Or the new for that matter. Guess he's kind of like our Pops that way. Likes things best when they stay exactly how he's used to them."

"What are... your pops?"

"Oh sorry, that's... it's what we call our grandfather. And like Tobes, he's no fan of change."

"You know of your grandfather!" Remarked Vereena, there was intrigue in her voice. "I did not realise you were of such a prominent lineage Terrence Emerson."

"A prominent lin-... Oh!" Wide eyed he grinned back at her. "You think... No, no I'm not like nobility or something."

"Oh... Then he was a great warrior." She sounded yet more impressed.

"No, no," Terrence shook his head. "I'm not important like you are. Pops is just... Well he's Pops. See the people of my world, we don't really go about the whole 'Mating thing' in quite the same way as yours."

"So I have seen. With the thing you call marriage it does seem a more common thing to take a life-mate."

"Yeah, OK. But see there's way more to it than that. For starters, there's no *taking* a life-mate." Frowning he added, "Well not where I hail from anyway. We try not to pick each other out based on... on breeding potential. Both parents and their families are seen as equally important... At least we like to think they are." Then he sighed. "Guess you'd find things pretty strange in our world too. All our ideals of love and-"

"Oh I'm aware of the love," Vereena nodded, "Lilly watched much of this in the quiesscence box she kept in her room."

"The Quiess... err..." Terrence's brow dipped again. "She didn't happen to call it a TV did she? Or maybe a telly?"

"Yes..." said Veerena. "The telly-box. That is what I speak of. In truth the magicks of your world have always been a fascination to me." Excitement crept into Veerena's voice. "To be able to look in on so many other worlds with such ease!"

"Yeah," he shrugged "That would be pretty cool."

"Then you did not possess one of these telly-boxes?"

"It's called a TV?" He nodded back at her, "and sure we have a few in our house. But there's really nothing magical about them; no quiesscence, no other worlds. TV's just tales we like to tell ourselves and the technology we use for that."

"Tales," her confusion was obvious. "Technology? I... I don't...."

"Well you see...." with his hands now doing much of the talking he nodded her way again, "We errm..." he gave it further thought before adding. "The people of my world are inventors; creators of great things! We take what's around us and we... we shape it. To meet our needs."

"Oh." Nodded Vereena, "Like the ancients! Well that is yet more fascinating. I should like to know more of this invent-"

"What?" reading the bewildered concern that crossed her face Terrence spun around. "Hey where'd S'ret go," shaking his head he muttered, "Just a second ago, he was there. I had my eye on him. He was there!" Then spinning around he saw Tobias and Harper were nowhere to be seen either, turning back to

Vereena he watched her cast her eyes skyward with a grimace; giving him just enough time to whisper, "What's going on?" before a brownish-pink mass descended from above like a lead balloon and engulfed her. Its movement and appearance were much like the end of a giant lizard's tongue, but instead of sticking to the young Da'ariel Princess it had swallowed her whole.

Though it happened swifter than Terrence could exclaim, he felt he'd seen the entire event in great detail: The huge blob had closed over Vereena, it's outside slick and veiny. Strong enough to lift her, yet thin enough to show arms and legs protruding, as it retracted; disappearing before his eyes.

"Ho - oh shit!" Terrence muttered; his eyes following the vast elasticated blob upward only to spot a smudge on the sky directly above his head. Mouth falling open, he turned to run, but at that very second he was swallowed up too.

***

Having retreated back along the limb she was on Lilly had curled into a tight ball halfway up the huge tree, and was still in tears, when something large whooshed up from the ground, startling her into gazing up as the leaves parted in its wake. She sat watching, her eyes wide as an unfamiliar Da'ariel landed on the limb nearest her, clinging to his back, Kyrel climbed carefully down before leaping across to her.

"Oh thank God," sobbed Lilly as he began checking her over.

"You are hurt?"

"No," she shook her head, "I'm OK. I'll be fine." she nodded across to where Baxter lay caught in the opposite tree. "Help him! He's hurt… please… you have to do something."

Kyrel's eyes followed her gaze, his expression turning grim as he spotted Baxter's motionless form.

"Liath…." he looked to the Da'ariel. "Neelust t'tait. Cat ya vac inst!" Turning back to Lilly he shook his head. "Can you move? It is not safe here. We must go."

"Not without Baxter," her lip quivered as she spoke. "I won't leave him."

"You must." Kyrel attempted to pull her up.

"No!" she fought him off: hands waving frantically as her tears increased. "We already left Morris." Lilly shook her head. "I won't leave him too. You help him, damn you! Help him or I'm staying right here."

Kyrel's expression was a pained one as he turned to Liath. The Da'ariel had perched himself on a branch near the boy and his expression was grim as he checked for signs of life.

"Keilest vel?" asked Kyrel. "Nish t'alet tai't neelus?"

"Nydrel," Liath shook his head. "Distaya tai't. Ny inst nish neelus."

Unable to understand a word Lilly gulped, biting her lip as Kyrel turned back to her. "Liath will–"

A scream from Lilly froze the words on Kyrel's lips and he turned around in time to see the thick pinkish-brown blob that had engulfed both the boy and the Da'ariel warrior, retracting upward, snapping the branch they'd been on and taking a huge portion of it with them.

"Nydrel!" He threw himself on Lilly, his arms going around her a split second before they too were swallowed by a second gelatinous blob and pulled away from the tree they'd been on.

Day Four: Part Four

The sickening squelch which had expelled Terrence back into the world was reproduced again and again by the flying creatures - known as T'karas - their appearance similar to ray fish except for their vast size, and the fact they were airborne. Another clear difference was the way they seemed to wink in and out of existence; their huge bodies constantly working at blending them with their surroundings like chameleons.

They hovered overhead, letting down humongous, sticky, proboscis-like tongues. One after another, wet warm lumps of steaming Da'ariel were deposited with both an appearance and regularity that reminded Terrence of an ant queen's back end.

Most of the expelled Da'ariel took a moment to regain enough equilibrium to stand up. A few attempted to crawl, their limbs broken by the indelicate means of transport. Others remained motionless: unconscious or in some cases dead, their mucus drenched corpses cluttering what little space remained in the enclosure.

Obsidian in appearance, its stalagmite-like columns protruded from the ground around them, Irregular in height but each tall enough for the lack of a ceiling to prove meaningless for all those trapped inside.

The area was also littered with clusters of boulders; or as close to boulders as such jagged forms could be considered; made up of various sizes, they were mostly the same dark crystalline rock as the cage itself. The few that weren't, bore more resemblance to the boulders they'd passed after leaving the tunnels of

Tualavan, and stood out starkly against the tarry black stone.

Before he had time to consider the nature of their presence another sticky proboscis tongue touched down a few metres from Terrence. Hitting harder than those before, it shook the ground, releasing two more of the misplaced boulders as it retracted.

Da'ariel scattered as the huge rocks hurtled along at a bone-crushing pace, allowing Terrence precisely enough time to realise the largest one was headed straight for him and scream with the gusto of a horror movie blonde, before Vereena – previously conferring with S'ret, and other warriors on the opposite side of the enclosure – hearing his terrified wail, came spinning at him with a speed that sent them both flying into a couple of the tall dark pillars.

The result was a cascade of electrical red sparks, setting the entire cage momentarily aglow, before the pair thudded to the ground. Vereena's Gaashmay tumbled from her hand, clattering across the hard floor.

Gasping for air Terrence watched the boulder thump to a stop.

Only when he looked down did he realise he'd landed on top of the young Da'ariel girl.

"Err... thanks... I..."

"You owe her one..." said Tobias, as he pulled his brother to his feet, "now quit flirting." Grinning as they laid eyes on each other, they hugged, with Terrence muttering, "Thank fuck you're OK," before he stepped back asking, "Where's Harper? Is she..." Tobias pointed across the cage, to where she was slowly making her way toward them.

Vereena, now on her feet, dusted herself off and nodding curiously at Tobias asked, "What is this flirting and what exactly does your brother owe me?"

"Err..." he raised an eyebrow at her. Then shaking his head Terrence cleared his throat and glaring at his brother said,

"Never mind that... what was with the light show?"

"Light show?"

Terrence waved a hand at the same black stalagmite like column they'd bounced off, adding, "The red lightning stuff." A deepening concern crept onto his face. Tilting his head to one side he asked, "and why does my head suddenly feel like smoke is about to come out of my ears?" while patting his ear as if trying to drain the other of water.

"Aaah," sighed Vereena. "drakstorl t'fambroch."

"Err, I thought you devoted your life to learning our language," Tobias narrowed his eyes at her "You wanna run that one by us again... in English."

"The red lightning," explained Vereena as Terrence began patting his other ear. "It's quite deadly."

"Deadly!" the twins exclaimed in sync as Terrence's hand froze near his ear and he snapped his head around to face her.

"We were fortunate," said Vereena.

"We were?"

"Yes," she assured him while getting to her feet "My Gaashmay was repelled before any real harm could be done."

"Right." He began patting his ear again, "and this burning in my-"

"It will pass."

"You're sure?" Tobias frowned as he watched Harper picking up the fallen Gaashmay.

"Yes," nodded Vereena "t'fambroch brings a quick death but only as long as contact is made."

"You should probably hang on to this," Harper held out the Gaashmay as she reached them adding "never know when Tez might need you saving his bacon again."

"Thank you," smiled Vereena then she was raising her eyebrow, "Bacon?" but before any of them could say more another T'karas tongue lashed the ground a couple of metres from them.

This time the sticky heap left steaming alongside them was such an irregular shape it claimed all of their attention. Almost immediately a third of it began pulling away and got shakily to its feet.

"Liath!" Vereena gasped as the warrior wiped the clinging goo from his face and breathed in deep breaths.

"Oh crap!" Terrence hurried to the side of the larger portion of the regurgitated blob. "It's Baxter!" With both hands he scraped the slimy gunk off the other boy's face. Clearing most of it away from the nose, mouth and eyes before he realised how unresponsive Baxter was. "Oh man..." mumbled Terrence "No, no, no!" he glanced over his shoulder. "Guy's... I...I think he's hurt. Shit man...." he shook his head "I-I think he's hurt real bad."

Preoccupied with uncovering the rest of Baxter's face, Terence barely noticed when another T'karas tongue slapped down across the other side of the cage. He did however, notice that no one was responding and turning back he asked, "Didn't you guys..." his words slowed as he registered the hush which had fallen over the crowded stone cage. Following the many gazes he mumbled, "hear... me?" and stared in wonder at the freshest steaming lump.

The slimy outer skin of T'karas mucus was changing colour as it dried, the pinkish brown fading to an off white, which promptly crumbled to a fine dust, powdering the hard black floor or being carried away on the wind.

In the end Kyrel, lay clean and dry on the floor. He was curled into a ball with his arms wrapped tight around another person.

"Cousin Lilly..." Vereena ran across the enclosure.

Hearing her, the Deebanaarie glanced up before carefully uncurling himself. The way he cradled Lilly's head in the crook of his arm, pulling them both into a sitting position, had Terrence thinking she too must be incapacitated.

Then he noticed her shoulders heaving: she was distraught but alive. "Thank God," muttered Terrence.

Awash with relief he turned his attention back to Baxter as Tobias came along and knelt at his side. A second later Harper was also with them, and though it took maybe a couple of minutes Lilly had soon limped over and was kneeling on Baxter's other side.

"What the hell happened?" Harper shook her head, "Where were you guys?" Sniffing back tears Lilly opened her mouth to speak but scraping out more slime from underneath Baxter, Terrence frowned "Fuck! What is this? There's like a whole tree here!"

This was apparently too much for Lilly to bear; hearing her whimper, he looked up as she broke down in a fresh sobbing fit.

***

"Oh please just go away..." Lilly sniffed, wiping at her face as she glanced up at Kyrel standing over her. "...Just leave me alone." she shook her head.

"I cannot," Kyrel crouched before her. "It is my duty to-"

"How do you not get it?" she shrugged as Harper and the twins appeared behind him. "I've had enough OK. I'm not doing this anymore. Screw duty. I want to go home!"

"You ask for that which you have already received." Kyrel shook his head.

"No." she looked him squarely in the eyes. "I want... to go... home! To my world: the place where people aren't dying because of me. Send me back there-"

"Princess Lillia-"

"Now!" she shrieked in his face.

"This is not something within my-"

"Now damn you! You send me back right now!" A hush fell over those nearest them and spread like wildfire among the cage's other occupants as she continued screaming. "Send me home Kyrel... you send me home right now. Right! Now!"

Tobias pushed the Deebanaarie aside, crouching in his place, and as Lilly started in on another batch of obscenely high pitched 'Now's' he slapped her hard across the face.

Immediately every able bodied Da'ariel within a five foot radius surged forward. It was an unspoken yet collective agreement, of first come first served on who would put an end to the life of the off-worlder who had dared to lay a hand on their next Queen.

"Slater..." Terrence cried out as the momentum of so many rushing by him sent him crashing to the ground, noticing as he landed that Tobias was nowhere to be seen amidst the throng, he screamed for her again. "Slater! Slater snap out of it!" His pleas were drowned out by the frenzied din of the riot his brother had incited, but a second later she was up on her feet.

"Cat ya vac!" she yelled as she ran at the crowd. "Cat ya vac! Cat ya fucking vac you assholes!"

As swiftly as they'd converged, the Da'ariel moved aside; none willing to be party to injuring her and all showing at least a modicum of confusion.

Afforded no such privilege, Kyrel was still pushing his way through those who'd gathered before him. Arms up over his head, Tobias peeked out from the foetal ball he'd curled into and cast a wary eye on the crowd.

"Nice work Moses." He grumbled as Lilly helped him to his feet. Terrence came up on her other side adding.

"Yeah maybe for your next trick you can try parting the bars of this giant man-traption we've landed in"

"Sorry," she sighed, "Doubt I could part mud with a shovel right now."

Seeing his eyebrow rise she shrugged. "You remember there was an incy little question of stability."

"You're shitting me," said Tobias as he looked pointedly around at their surroundings, "Now Slater? Seriously?"

"Actually," she muttered through her teeth. "It's been a couple of hours."

"Fuck!" hissed Terrence before taking in the anxiety on her face and adding, "Oh well… might not have worked anyway. There's some sort of force-field over these bars, and I'm guessing that's no coincidence."

"But hey…" Tobias grimaced, raising a fist to the air. "Score one for pack mentality. We might be in the belly of the beast but at least you've got loyalty on your side. If nothing else, these guys *definitely* have your back." He rubbed at the small of his own back adding, "Seems a few of them got my back too," then offering a weak yet grateful smile he sighed, "Still, maybe if the magicks are out you should try for a rousing speech."

Lilly threw him a disheartened look as Kyrel, with Harper at his heels, pushed aside the last of the Da'ariel to reach them. "Works in the movies." Terrence shrugged as the Deebanaarie re-joined them asking, "Movies?"

"Don't worry about it." Lilly's eyes rolled. "These guys were just trying to lighten the mood."

"With movies?" Harper sounded as confused as the Deebanaarie.

"No, OK, they were being funny." Seeing Kyrel raise an eyebrow she explained "It's something people do in a crisis…" but his obvious lack of comprehension had her sighing when Tobias chimed in with "You know… we were joking."

"So first you strike at those who are not your enemy," Kyrel stated with obvious perplexity, "then you attempt to make them laugh. Even for a world such as yours that seems a strange way to behave in a crisis,"

"It's a morale thing," sighed Terrence. "Well the joke part is anyway." when Kyrel's face remained a blank he nodded "just call it a quaint custom from-"

"No," Lilly glared at Terrence, "Call it a waste of time because it doesn't matter. Look around." she waved her arms. "All the morale in the world ain't gonna do squat in here is it? Even if my powers were working: You just said there's some sort of force-field on-"

"Your powers have retreated?" asked Kyrel "When? How long ago?"

"I don't know," Lilly mumbled "Most of the time I was in that tree."

"What were you doing in a tree?" Harper's nose wrinkled.

Lilly merely shook her head and shrugged, "What does it matter? No powers is as no powers does. All that training and I'm no use to anyone."

"Ny," said Kyrel. "You are in the ka'aam shareê." He spoke as though this answer should be obvious to her.

"The ka'aam share," whispered Terrence.

"Oh don't you start," grumbled Lilly, her eyes rolling as clicking his fingers, he added.

"No, no I know this, Veer told me about it," he pointed at Kyrel. "The final stage of the kalaareem right?"

"Yes," nodded Kyrel.

"That's why you lost your powers." Terrence grinned. "They could come back any minute."

"Ny," Kyrel shook his head at her. "Your wounds are much, you must rest."

"Well sure why not, I'll just take on Mordrel in my sleep."

"Hey Kyrel still has powers!" said Harper, "he can like whip us up another one of those tunnels."

"Yeah," added Tobias "this guy's been holding out on us Slater. You should see how many Deebanaarie he can torch with a wave of his hand. Can't you mate?" he turned to Kyrel.

"I can do nothing," he shook his head.

"What?" asked Tobias.

"Why the hell not?" asked Harper.

"Because magicks are not possible." Kyrel told them.

"Err...When you say... not possible?" Terrence chimed in and coming up behind him Vereena said.

"He means his magicks will not work in here."

"But he used them when he and Slater landed," Tobias shook his head, "how else did he get all this..." he grimaced - pulling at the sticky gunk still clinging to his own clothes - while adding, "Off of them?"

"You saw the magicks I used as the T'karas captured me and Lilly. This... stuff..." Kyrel nodded to Tobias's clothes "brings all time to a stop for that which is within it until released by the T'karas."

"That's why everything seemed so swift," nodded Terrence "Being inside this stuff is pretty much like being put to sleep."

"Like being in some kind of cocoon?" asked Harper.

"Exactly!" he nodded, "Those things could have carried us for hours and we wouldn't know it."

"Yes," agreed Kyrel. "I used my magicks as we were captured, that is why they were effective even within this thing."

"Yeah I still don't get it," Tobias raised an eyebrow. "Why won't the magicks work?"

"Because this is solid milaratak'i." Kyrel gestured to the floor and bars.

"The black rock?" Terrence glanced to the floor.

"No," Kyrel shook his head. "Milaratak'i is not rock."

"Looks like rock to me." Tobias mumbled to Harper.

"In your tongue," went on Kyrel "it would be..." uncertain he shook his head turning to Vereena.

"Err..." with a small non-committal shrug she suggested "Dead... blood... hard."

"Dead blood hard?" Tobias spoke up, his tone more than a little disdainful.

"Yes," she nodded "I am almost certain of the translation; that is how your people would say it."

"Then you're wrong," he told her. "Because our people don't say dumb shit like-"

"Actually," said Terrence, his tone far the kinder. "Veer is probably right."

"What?" asked Harper, "Who the hell names something a dead blood hard? That's just... stupid."

"No," Terrence shook his head. "Differences in grammatical rule and structure would make a lot of sentences shake up correct word placement when directly translated to..." seeing both theirs and Lilly's expressions glaze over he rolled his eyes, sighing, then turned to Vereena asking, "Perhaps a better translation would be... hard dead blood?"

Nodding with him she said, "Perhaps."

"Whatever," snorted Tobias "Like that's a better name for anything."

"Yeah really," Harper stuffed her hands in her pockets, "And how exactly is it not a rock anyway." She glanced around, "Sure looks like a shit load of rock to me."

"The milaratak'i is far harder than any rock," said Kyrel "It flows as blood from the Ata'ki tree, then hardens."

"Oh... OK," Terrence thumbed his chin, taking a fresh look at the pillars. "Then it's a sap!"

"Sap..." Vereena let the word slither slowly from her tongue before beaming a wide smile at him and nodding, "Thank you Terrence Emerson. As he grinned back at her she nodded. "The T'karas use this... sap... in the building of their nests." With a dubious look around she added, "Prey are dropped in as we were, to feed their young..."

"Great," Tobias muttered. "So now we know why those things... brought us here." He looked hastily up to the sky where the T'karas had not been visible for some time.

"We're lunch!" As Harper's eyes grew wider and she looked dismally about them, Vereena shook her head,

"There are no young here." She threw Kyrel a dubious glance.

"Because this is no T'karas nest," he looked around at the dark rock walls beyond the bars and shook his head. "This place is cho'odzi,"

"Cho'odzi?" Harper turned to Vereena, "Why do I get the feeling that isn't much better?"

"Cho'odzi are four mountains; known best for spraying a liquid fire in the days of the ancestors," explained Veerena.

Lilly's eyebrows went up as she and Terrence caught sight of one another, and shaking his head Tobias stepped forward grabbing his brothers arm as he asked, "Did she just say we're in a fucking volcano?"

Shrugging Terrence gulped, "Err yeah... I...I think so."

"We are on the outer edges of my sisters territories; a few leagues from Endrandorn," Kyrel spoke directly to Lilly. "...inside the cho'odzi. The T'karas would never come so far to nest." He glanced around again. "This Milaratk'i is here by Deebanaarie hands alone. Its structure is... like that of the creatures' nests only to fool them. No…" he shook his head. "These beasts, they bring us here under the command of another, and there are not many with the powers to command them."

"What do you wanna bet Mordrel's one of the few?" Harper muttered.

"Ny…." Kyrel shook his head. "My sister does not have this ability… but there are others of our blood-line, cousins and such, who also consort with geshurian sprites that do."

"Brilliant…" Lilly's arms went up.

"Wait hang on…" Tobias cut in. "You're saying there are more of those nasty little-"

An elbow to the ribs from Terrence had him gasping before rephrasing with, "I-I mean those... very friendly furry... little creatures out there?"

"Geshurian Sprites are not furry," said Vereena.

"And they are not friendly," scowled Kyrel.

"Then they're some other type?" asked Terrence.

"Da'ariel keep company only with Tekurian sprites," explained Vereena. "They are very… very different and so are their magicks."

"Control over the various lesser beings of our realm is a common power with the geshurian sprites."

"That's why the ginaten came after the village," said Terrence.

"Yes," nodded Kyrel. "My sister's sprite Neenia has power over them. If I had known of the orbs…" his gaze drifted to Lilly who gave a despondent shrug.

"So now I'm supposed to fight off even more evil Deebanaarie," she sighed, "as well as their evil sprites; from the inside of a cage where I couldn't use my powers even if I did still have them... Like I said... Brilliant!"

"Ny," Kyrel shook his head. "Whoever controls the T'karas will remain in the palace, there is more power to draw from there, by now my sister will have been informed of your capture." He nodded at Lilly adding, "With so little time she is sure to come for you personally."

"This must a taken a lot of trees." Terrence was gazing about them with obvious awe, as he thumbed his chin, oblivious of the raised eyebrows of his brother and the two girls.

"Yes," nodded Vereena, her voice solemn as she also looked around at the dark bars, adding, "Far from here, in the land where the T'karas come from. Our people speak of-"

"Deeb glena kal'shoree," said Kyrel, as slowly turning to look at him she added.

"The forest that is no more," then nodded, "You knew of this! So much Milaratak'i… How could you not speak-"

"Nydrel," he shook his head at her. "The idea of this is as ancient as the wars between our peoples," his arms went up. "But I could not know this would be here. It is little more than a forgotten impossibility! The magicks required to create it have been lost to the Deebanaarie for many generations."

"Yeah well," Harper shrugged, "looks to me like someone found them."

"So…" Terrence turned to Kyrel. "Why would your people build this? What's so special about this sap exactly?"

"It is said to be the strongest substance in all Azeron," said Kyrel. "It yields not to any weapons…"

"And tames the magicks," added Vereena.

"OK, when you say tames?" asked Terrence.

"It has long been believed that the Milaratak'i works against our magicks," said Kyrel, "That its very essence opposes ours; Tuâoch and Lâioch alike." He shook his head. "Many Deebanaarie no longer believe this to be true. All life in Azeron bears its own essence yes, but any essence strong enough to create the active magicks is dependent upon those things around it. It is possible the essence of the Atak'i tree is lost as the sap hardens and that this, its final form, is simply impenetrable to the active magicks."

"And how do these Deebanaarie explain the drakstorl t'fambroch?" Vereena raised a curious eyebrow at him?"

"It is the beasts above us," Kyrel glanced upward. "It has long been known that they're drawn to the Milaratak'i. It is their essence, which works against ours. Their very presence here conspires with the Milarataki to create the barrier."

"The red lightning," muttered Terrence.

"OK, wait? What are we talking about now?" asked Lilly.

"The force-field around this thing." Terence nodded her way then, seeing her brow dip as she looked to the bars, he added, "You can't see it but trust me…" he grimaced rubbing at his collar bone. "You don't wanna mess with it." After a quick look up at the seemingly empty sky he nodded Kyrel's way, adding, "If he's right, those T'karas things are somehow generating it. Something about their proximity to this dead blood stuff… that and maybe the fact that there's so much of it down here."

"The reasons are many," Kyrel assured them, "even the shape and size of this structure… With no end point the strength of the force-field only increases." He waved both arms, gesturing at their prison in a way that made Harper glance around them asking,

"You mean because it's a circle?"

"Yes," nodded Kyrel "Circle… Above us the T'karas also fly this way… a circle. As long as they remain up there, the force-field remains active and we remain cut off from the essence of what little life there is inside the cho'odzi." He shook his head at Lilly, "You were never going to be able to use your powers in here. We will both have to make do without."

"Isn't there something we can do about it?" Terrence shook his head at Kyrel but it was Lilly who responded first.

"Do?" She glared at him, her hands going up in exasperation. "Didn't you just hear? We're inside a goddamn forgotten impossibility! Exactly which part of that doesn't sound bad to you?"

"So that's it…" Harper shrugged, "you're just gonna give up… because things sound bad?"

"*Sound* bad?" Lilly's hands dropped to her hips as she threw the other girl an incredulous glare. "Things don't just sound bad OK. Our weapons and magicks are all useless on this thing; I'd say that qualifies as looking, smelling, and tasting pretty fucking shitty!"

"OK sure…" Tobias shrugged "things *are* bad but since when does that mean impossible?"

"Fine," she raised an eyebrow, one hand leaving her hip to gesture, as she said, "Then you go on and tell me something about all this that doesn't sound *impossible?*"

Tobias gave it a moment's thought before he rolled his eyes, sighing "Yeah OK fine, it does all *sound* kind of impossible, but we can't let that matter right now."

"*Let it matter*! You say that as if we have any-"

"I'm saying it because somebody has to... and oh I don't know… maybe… Because I feel a certain obligation to talk some frigging sense into you. Look around Slater," he waved a hand at the various faces, so many Da'ariel looking expectantly to where this smaller group discussed the situation.

"Most of these Da'ariel already made it to safety. Every one of us had the chance to hide away in their Zanreal sanctuary."

"Then why the hell aren't you-"

"What?" he screwed up his face, "Still back there? Don't be a moron Slater. You and Baxter were still out here. What were we going to do… leave this world without you?"

"Well this is much better." She rolled her eyes. "Now we all get to die together!"

"What is with you?" hissed Tobias.

"Me? What about you? You saw Baxter. He's impaled on a fucking tree Tobes! He's dead over there because of me."

"Lilly no," reaching for her arm Terrence shook his head. "Whatever happened to Baxter was-"

"Completely my fault!" she growled, pulling away. "These Da'ariel are looking for some fearless leader but when the fighting broke out I was terrified. I flew up there without even thinking about how I was going to stop. Don't you get it?" her hand went to her chest. "I'm supposed to have all this power but all I could do was sit there watching him hack up blood and cry like a baby. And why… because I dropped him; that's why!" she sniffed. "He fell because of me!" Turning back to Tobias she added, "So yeah maybe I do think you all should have done the *smart* thing and hid in that sanctuary"

"And again you're being a moron." Tobias shook his head. "The smart thing to do is watch each other's backs. We came here together, that's how we're leaving."

"Oh and also…" Terrence chimed in, "Baxter's not dead!" Seeing her eyes grow wide he nodded, "Yeah, that's what I was just trying to tell you. He's in a bad way, but he's alive. I managed to get enough of that crap off his neck to check for a pulse; if we can get him out of here-"

"Get him out of here?" Lilly laughed a dry humourless laugh, and shaking his head Terrence said,

"Tobes is right! This isn't the time for quitting."

"No?" she looked pointedly around them, her arms waving as she added,

"We passed quitting time days ago... How many Da'ariel do you really think died at that village? She looked from one twin to the other. "What about in our school bus... how many of our classmates did we lose? I watched Morris die," her lips trembled as her eyes flittered over Harper before she dropped them adding, "and now I'm going to watch Baxter die too."

"So giving up is the solution..." Harper shook her head, "You keep saying this is a mistake..." she cocked her head to one side, "...that you shouldn't be here and you know what Slater... I ain't arguing with you OK, but... I'm not the one who needs convincing am I? You want to prove something..." she nodded at the crowd, "Whether you're one of them or you're one of us. Well I don't know about them but we're just not the curl up and die type, OK."

"That's right," shrugged Tobias "We're kids from the Peak. We don't take any shit lying down. We fight back."

"He's right," said Terrence. "That's why we were on that bus isn't it? We're the ones who fight back!"

"Yeah," agreed Harper "Our parents, the system,"

"An evil queen," added Tobias, "we fight hard and we fight dirty,"

"Hell," said Harper, "The lives most of us have back home, you know we're survivors! We're the ones who squirm around till the bitter end, which all things considered... may seem kind a dumb, but we do it anyway because we're hoping to squirm right off the damn hook, and because fighting to survive sure beats standing around arguing over whether or not it's possible."

Seeing her chomp down on her lip Terrence nodded at Kyrel, adding,

"Come on Slater, if he's right and this dead blood thingy we're in is so impossible then there has to be something we're not seeing. Maybe if we put our heads together, we can figure it out."

For a moment her gaze drifted over them as she contemplated their words; finally she stuffed her hands in her pockets, shrugging, "Sorry guys but enough's enough..." Turning on her heel she stalked off calling back, "I'm done OK. You all go ahead and figure it out without me..."

"Slater..." Harper called after her, she was about to give chase, but immediately Kyrel's hand was at her shoulder.

"Leave her now," he nodded. "Your words are spoken, she alone must think on them."

"But we don't have time for-"

"Time has yet to be any friend of ours." Kyrel's eyes went to Vereena and nodding for her to follow Lilly, he turned back to the three classmates adding, "Let us speak more of the surviving and the..." he looked to Harper with a raised eyebrow "...Squirming?"

***

With her arms wrapped around her legs, and her back pressed against the same boulder that had almost crushed Terrence, Lilly felt her desire to be left alone had been made abundantly clear. So when she heard footsteps approach she didn't bother to look up, but instead mumbled miserably into her knees. "Oh come on then... let's have it?"

"It?" asked Vereena, "Was I to bring you something cousin?" Looking up in time to see the Da'ariel girl look back the way she'd come; scanning for some object Lilly might require, she rolled her eyes.

"God you're a dozy lot," Lilly let her head drop back onto her knees. "No wonder you think I have potential."

"Potential," Vereena sat beside Lilly, tucking her legs up beneath her. "This is not a word I know yet."

"Doesn't matter," shrugged Lilly "Point is: you're wrong, but that don't matter either... because barring a miracle, I don't see either of us getting to use the language of my world for much longer. Sorry you wasted your life and stuff."

"Now it is you who is wrong."

"Oh?" Lilly peeked up over her forearms.

"Yes," insisted Vereena "It is true: much of my life has been spent learning how best to serve you Cousin, like all Qin Am Ness before me I eagerly awaited the day I would be called. But never before has a Qin Am Ness done so with such an uncertain future ahead. There were those among the Da'ariel who did not believe we would ever see you return. Yet more who did not believe you to be blessed with the powers of our ancestors. No amount of study is much burden for a Qin Am Ness, we are bred for it... you understand this yes?"

"I dunno," shrugged Lilly, "Kyrel's told me a bit, but well... the way he puts it; you kind of sound like a bunch of racehorses"

"Racehorses?"

"Yeah they're errm... well oddly: like you lot, they're all bred for a specific purpose, from the best stock available."

"Then the idea is not unfamiliar to you."

"Well... no..." stretching the words out, Lilly raised her head fixing Vereena with a curious stare. "Bit on the cold side though ain't it?"

"I'm uncertain of your meaning."

"Course you are," Lilly sighed before shrugging, "OK look, don't get me wrong... this thing you've got going: the women calling the shots; having the final say on whether or not there'll even be any...." her hands began to flail.

"You do still speak of the mating?"

"Huh?"

"That is what you call it, yes?" Vereena nodded. "When a woman chooses to take a man into her-"

"Yes, yes, yes." Lilly raised a hand. "The err... the mating, let's err... Let's just skip the details shall we."

"As you will it Cousin... please... continue."

"OK look," Lilly straightened up, her eyes rolling, as she muttered. "I cannot believe I'm about to say this... but..." again she was shrugging, her eyebrows rising in time with her shoulders. "Well... You do kind of treat your men like... meat."

The way Vereena screwed up her face and tipped her head slightly to one side, was enough to let Lilly know her meaning had fallen short and sighing again she asked, "Look from what I hear the Da'ariel idea of a long term relationship amounts to 'well he's given me a good healthy baby maybe I'll call on him again." Waving her hands she added, "I do *not* want to ruin a good thing OK, but seriously - Where's the love?"

"Aah." Nodded Vereena. "Of course… this… human concept, it seems to form the basis of so many of their ideas. Though you, I believe, speak mostly on the bond of affection formed between two persons, do you not?"

"Yeah," Lilly's hands went up again as she also nodded, "Love and all the other feelings that come with it. Heat! Passion! Occasional bouts of crazy! How can this whole world be without it?"

"Perhaps we are not," Vereena shook her head. "Perhaps we have simply gotten by without the need to name it," responding to Lilly's frown she shrugged. "Can you honestly say these are a people without passion?" She gestured with an outstretched arm to where the other Da'ariel gathered around Kyrel and Lilly's classmates.

Each was listening intently to everything the Deebanaarie was telling them. Lilly had no idea what that might be nor did she care but she could not deny the rapt attention on the faces of those who did.

"Every one of them is here for you," said Vereena, "See their readiness to fight?" On cue Lilly noticed most kept their hands on their weapons. "Is this not the heat you speak of cousin? When the blood rushes through the body compelling that action is taken. They would all give up their lives to protect you. Is that not passion?"

"Well yeah sure." Nodded Lilly. "That's… a type… of passion." Then she was rolling her eyes again adding, "Exactly the type this place could do with a little less of if you ask me. Enough people have already died because of me… Baxter *is* dying because of me."

"It is not *because* of you we Da'ariel are willing to give up our lives cousin, but *for* you. So that you may live on: because after today Mordrel will not be able to touch you. Her hunger will count for nothing in the face of your power. Within you is enough essence to finally bring about healing to Azeron and all its people. Is this continued loyalty to our people, the service these few do both you and all the remaining clans of the Da'ariel: are these things not covered by the human idea of love?"

"I guess they are." Lilly sighed, resting her head on the boulder at their backs.

"Then you see," Vereena smiled. "We do have love. Our world is filled with it." Nodding she added, "You are right; we do not choose our mates with the same affections the humans do. But we also do not breed as abundantly. While their world groans under the weight of so much life, ours has the opposite problem. Without the magicks of the Laîoch this world does not replenish as it did in the days of the ancestors. As our essence fades from these lands - so does all life here, Da'ariel and Deebanaarie included."

"Seriously?" Lilly's eyebrows bobbed upward, and nodding Vereena said.

"Yes cousin. Seriously. With every cycle that passes our clans suffer increased difficulty in bearing healthy young. We cannot afford the debate of emotional bonds. What is it to us when our true needs are producing as many strong, healthy Da'ariel as possible?"

"But that's a horrible way of looking at things…" Lilly's mouth fell open and also resting her head back against the boulder Vereena sighed.

"It is what it is. We have no time for that concept of love, which the humans linger over most. Like all living things here in Azeron we Da'ariel spend our passion on existing." With a sideways glance Vereena caught sight of Lilly's solemn expression and turning her head just enough to smile her way added. "But through that need we do have a bond. We do all we can in the name of the clans and unlike the many smaller bonds of the humans; this one *is* unbreakable."

The Da'ariel had split into groups now, several working together on pushing the largest boulders they could toward the only visible entrance - other than the open top of big black cage. Kyrel and everyone else were doing more of an every man for themselves kind of thing: walking around with their eyes to the ground and occasionally kicking at the floor or crouching for closer inspection.

"What are they doing now?" muttered Lilly.

"Whatever they can to ensure you live on," said Vereena.

As the two girls watched, one of the Da'ariel called out something, and seeing Kyrel hurry over Harper and the twins did also.

However after a few seconds poring over the ground there they were all shaking their heads and returning to their solitary searches.

"They believe you vital to the survival of the clans," said Vereena. "As do I and though you may not like it we will all fight to the last breath to see you survive."

"I could order you not to though right? I'm your princess."

"But not yet our Mai Mai," Vereena offered a brief smile. "When you are you can give whatever orders you choose and we will do our best to follow them. Until that day arrives even your wishes must bow to those of another. Everyone in here knows their orders cousin. We will not abandon you no matter how much you think you want it."

Biting down on her lip Lilly stared out across the cage, until Vereena said, "You know cousin, you say I have wasted my life… learning your language and the ways of the people of the human world. I say you are wrong. You see the more I did learn of you and that world… the more I knew your coming home… here… to us, that it was going to be more difficult than Mai Mai believed."

"Oh?" Lilly turned her head slightly, raising an eyebrow at the other girl.

"Perhaps as your Qin Am Ness I should not say such things…"

"No that's OK," Lilly shook her head. "I don't mind… really… tell me the truth-"

"The truth cousin?"

"Yes," nodded Lilly "The truth, go on."

"As you will it…" Vereena nodded, her arm going across her chest, before she again raised her eyes. "As our sprites became fewer and many among our people were concerned of your survival in that realm, others doubted we would ever see your return. Myself: I worried mostly of the day that you did return."

"Really?" Lilly frowned "You worried about me?"

"But of course cousin; watching you growing up without us: your family, learning all you know from the humans. The more I learned of your life there, the more aware I became of the weaknesses growing in you. The humans surround themselves with comfort and fret over fineries. They agonise over luxuries they do not yet possess, instead of ever truly enjoying the abundance at their fingertips." A puzzled expression settled on her face as she added, "They also appear to spend unthinkable amounts of their time decorating themselves and their homes. Oh and those homes…"she gasped, her eyes growing; all puzzlement gone. "By the Lady herself!" Vereena's hands flapped in time with her words. "Why they are the grandest I have ever seen! With so many strange and wonderful things inside: the thing you call a fridge; with its never-ending bounty of fine foods. And the water; how it flows into the cup, by nothing more than a simple turning of that… that…"

"Tap," Lilly smirked. "We call it a tap."

"Yes," she nodded "The tap; a wonderful thing is it not? To pour out water on command like that."

"Sure," shrugged Lilly "I guess it is."

"Oh it is cousin… Even in the days of the ancestors, when these lands were filled with life, why such things are unheard of here. Yet…" she gave Lilly a frank look. "it is because of things such as these that I have spent my life fearing who you would become."

"Fearing? You said you were eager to meet me!"

"Yes," nodded Vereena "But in a world where they so value making even their simplest daily tasks simpler, where a day's learning for a child is little more than sitting and listening. So many times I watched you take part in those studies that are considered physical. Those lessons the adults of the schools had you do as part of your studies."

"You mean P.E?"

"Yes," Vereena waved a hand "The PeeeEeee…"

Lilly smirked again at the sight of her new found cousin struggling to pronounce the simple acronym. "It is games yes?"

"Sure, it's sometimes called that too."

"Sorry cousin, but you misunderstand." Vereena nodded. "I speak of how it *is* games. All of it… You played games: with the humans."

"Oh! Yes," nodded Lilly. "You mean like netball and rounders and stuff… with like teams? And balls."

"Veyhi. Yes." Vereena cupped an imaginary ball in her hands, smiling as she nodded, "those things!" Then she was shaking her head, "So many strange games." She leaned back against the boulder again. "The only real training I have ever seen you endure, seems no more than a pointless indulging of the senses."

"The point is fun," nodded Lilly. "And you know… exercise… but who cares about that."

"Then it is… this *fun*… which most benefits the humans when they meet their enemies in battle?"

"Err… well… See the humans don't…." Lilly sat forward biting down on her lower lip, "… I mean we don't…The people of that world…."

The sight of one of Vereena's eyebrows rising increased her stammering.

"o - of – m – '*my*' world." and hearing her own tone become overly insistent Lilly sighed. "That's just not what schools are for OK!"

"That is where the next generation are taught, is it not?"

"Well yeah, sure but armed combat; not generally in the curriculum."

"Curric…" Vereena began shaking her head.

"It just isn't something we teach kids all right! Violence and the prospect of a bloody death: those are exactly the kinds of things children of the human world are generally shielded from."

"Yes," Vereena gave a knowing nod. "And this cousin Lilly, this is why I did fear your return."

"Aah," Lilly also sat back. "I guess I can understand that."

"Then it would seem we each understand the other." Vereena turned to look at her. "To be Qin Am Ness to a Mai Mai who knows nothing of our world. To have seen what you came from, and know the burdens you must now carry? I believe you are right cousin, a lot… maybe too much… is being asked of you."

Feeling tears sting her eyes Lilly gulped, turning away to look at the empty ground beside her, and sniffing them back she mumbled,

"Way too much."

"As is also being asked of me," said Vereena and when Lilly threw her a curious glance she shrugged. "You ask for truth," she nodded, "the idea that you: so long in the realm of the humans, softened by their teachings, their ways… That you would have power enough to end an enemy such as Mordrel… and bring about the change our lands have needed since the Deebanaarie seized control. To think that I… as your Qin Am Ness, should be the one to guide you through all this; to aid you in ending so many cycles of fear. Our clan has lived in hiding too long and I do know that. But the idea that you cousin Lilly, may actually bring about peace - real lasting peace. Why it is… as you would say: stupid."

"Yes," nodded Lilly "That's exactly what I've *been* saying, totally flipping stupid!"

"Yes," Vereena agreed. "That is as I too have always believed…Yet now you are here and I have seen the strength of your magicks. And that cousin, that is why I am now without fear." Seeing Lilly turn to face her Vereena nodded. "Even before your Kalaareem began: you could have stood well against any Deebanaarie alive who still bears the active magicks."

"Like Mordrel and these other relatives of Kyrel's?" asked Lilly.

"I would not mention it otherwise." Vereena shrugged. "You may not have been raised here, but I was and I know when your Kalaareem is over there is no Deebanaarie living this day with the power to stand against you."

"Well if we weren't already in the belly of the beast; stuck inside a magic proof cage, and I actually still had my powers, I'm sure that'd be a great comfort."

"You know cousin, I did not understand everything your friends said to you over there, but I am certain they are correct on at least one thing: we must fight until we cannot fight any longer. I know you believe us at fault for hiding from the Deebanaarie so long but we have always done what was necessary to ensure our survival. You have seen now that we can fight and that we do when necessary. Never have the Deebanaarie found our camps and taken even one of our people without a fight. You are Da'ariel Lilly, and most of us still have our weapons. Even from in here-"

"It doesn't matter Veer," Lilly snapped at her, "even if we did somehow manage to get out of here and my powers came back just in time for me to take Mordrel down, I'm obviously not cut out for this shit. If you've seen so much of my life then you know I'm no Princess, and I'm definitely not ready to be anyone's queen! Not in the human world or this place. I don't know the first thing about leading folks into battle."

"No," agreed Vereena "Maybe not but you do know many other things, things which I believe could greatly benefit all of Azeron if you would but allow yourself the chance-"

"The chance to what? Show you all what a disaster I am? Look if you're thinking I can teach your clans how to rig up taps, or start making fridges or something…" Lilly waved her hands. "… You couldn't be more wrong."

"No," Vereena shook her head. "Our people have no need of such things, but the human world is not all about ease and indulgence is it… they have their strengths: the things you call ideals, things such as the Love. I believe many things such as this have been lost to us through so many cycles of war."

"You just don't get it," Lilly's voice became a mumbled pleading, "I might be a princess to the Da'ariel, but back in the human world: the only world I know! I'm just that pain in the neck kid: the one the other kids cross the street to avoid. Even the adoptives regret ever laying eyes on me. I'm selfish OK, a total bitch. Definitely not known for mixing well with others, never mind leading them to victory. And anyway… if today's anything to go by," she nodded to where Baxter lay. "Which… I think we can safely say it is; I'm *certainly* never going to be any good to any of you in a fight. Like you said I have no weapon skills. I was raised by the humans, in their world. Da'ariel or not I'm every bit as soft as they are and you know it."

"What I know cousin is that while you may not know your people or how to fight, I do. And being at your side to see you get things right is exactly the life I was raised for. I cannot make you stay any more than I can say we will get out of here." She glanced pointedly around their giant cell. "But for as long as I am at your side cousin I *can* say that I will do my duty," watching Lilly bite her lip she smiled, "for this is the way of your people."

Looking around again she watched as a female troop leader raised a hand, calling out to Kyrel. This time only Terrence rushed to follow and crouching low they examined the ground together. "Mordrel will not have you without a fight," said Vereena. "And whether we are successful or not, I will remain honoured to have served you."

"Yeah well," Lilly sighed, "let's just wait and see how the getting-out-of-here goes before we start planning for other eventualities."

"Of course cousin as you will it," said Vereena, her eyes still on Terrence and Kyrel. Following her gaze Lilly saw others gathering around them now, with Tobias and Harper on their way, as conversations became more animated with each new Da'ariel who joined the throng.

"What is it now?" she mumbled.

"It appears they have found what they were looking for." Vereena got to her feet.

"And what were they looking for?" Lilly looked up at the other girl.

"Come," she nodded toward the growing crowd. "Is it not best to find out for yourself?"

"Like there's any point?" huffed Lilly. "Seriously…" she raised an eyebrow. "What's with you people? Is there really no time when Da'ariel are allowed to just admit defeat and quietly stop trying?"

"If we stop trying we are already dead." said Vereena. "And if *you* are already dead then this has all been for nothing, and every life already lost in this fight will never have been any more than a waste. If that is truly your will, then it shall no doubt come to pass whether I aid you in it or not." With a solemn shrug she added, "For now cousin, I ask respectfully that I be allowed the humble privilege of continuing to believe I have *not* wasted my life."

"What… like I'm gonna stop you?" Lilly rolled her eyes, and sighing dropped her head onto her knees again, not bothering to watch as Vereena turned to leave – her brief walk back to the others set to be a determined, but lonely one.

***

A minute later, however, when Vereena did re-join the group Lilly appeared at her side.

Without another word on the matter the younger girl offered a faint smile and waved the crowd aside.

"So what are we looking at?" Lilly asked, as she shuffled up to where Kyrel and Terrence were crouched at the centre of the amassed Da'ariel.

Tobias and Harper had also just re-joined them and meeting her gaze Harper offered a smile.

"Are your magicks returned?" Kyrel looked up at Lilly.

"Err no…" she shook her head, eyes going to Terrence who was running a hand along the ground, brushing aside the thick layer of grime – a combination of mucous from the T'karas and dust from the boulders they dropped into the cage – which had accumulated across most of the ground.

"Slater," he glanced up. "Come look at this."

As she and Vereena crouched beside him and Kyrel they all saw the thick ridge Terrence had uncovered; a narrow, wavy sliver barely noticeable beneath them.

"What is it?" Vereena looked to Terrence.

"A seam." He continued uncovering more, a pensive look on his face.

Lilly's expression was similar as she also started slopping off the thick grime. Moving with it she followed the line, standing up to skip gaps and barely noticing the Da'ariel who watched with eager interested faces while slowly parting to let her through.

Only when she reached the centre of the cage did she call out.

"Err guys… over here."

As Kyrel and the classmates all moved to join her, so too did the mob of Da'ariel.

"That will probably do it." Terrence grinned down on the patch of ground where Lilly had discovered the line met up with several others, creating a wavy star at their feet.

"Do what?" she asked, "What is this? Can we use it?"

"This," Terrence threw Lilly a cursory glance, "I think anyway... is how Mordrel made the impossible – possible."

"Oh OK," Lilly gave him a mocking look. "Could you be maybe a little vaguer?" she said as Harper and Tobias joined them in looking down on the nexus.

"Well it seems this stuff is real quick drying, Kyrel says the only way to keep it liquid long enough for transport is by keeping it boiling, and that's so difficult it's almost never done." He knelt carefully down on one knee as she asked,

"So?"

"So... I think you just found the sweet spot"

"The sweet spot. You do know you're still being vague right?"

Looking up he grinned,

"This thing didn't come here in one piece Slater... it was put together here like flat pack furniture," gazing studiously down at the star of lines he thumbed his chin adding. "From the looks of this a small amount of the sap was kept heated and used for gluing on site, all the pieces meet up here so this is probably the weakest spot."

"Yeah," shrugged Lilly. "The weakest spot on the hardest substance in all of Azeron?"

"Hey even diamond can be cut." Harper offered a hasty smile "you just need to have more diamond right... well," holding up a softball sized chunk of the Milaratak'i she added, "*This* is also the hardest substance in all of Azeron."

"Seriously?" Lilly's eyebrow went up as Terrence took the chunk of sap and raised it high above his head. "This is the plan? This stuff's impenetrable by magicks and you wanna break through it with a frigging rock!"

"Sap!" Terrence stopped to wave it at her. "Not a rock remember! And no we're not gonna dig with it OK. This stuff may be essence-free but the ground beneath it isn't and Kyrel's pretty sure nothing beneath the surface will be affected by the effect the T'karas are having on this stuff so yeah; I figure maybe if we can get it to crack... shouldn't take much, the tiniest sliver might be enough for Kyrel to get the magicks through."

As he started beating on the ground, not making so much as a dent but wincing each time he made contact, Lilly turned to Kyrel.

"Is he right... cracking that will give you back the use of your magicks?"

"It is possible," said Kyrel.

"Then you really think this can work?" Lilly began to sound hopeful. "Is there anything I can do?"

"I think he is right to try," shrugged Kyrel, then he was shaking his head adding, "Had you done as I instructed and practised more with your Gaashmay, there may now be things you could do..."

Terrence paused looking up to see Lilly glaring at Kyrel, Tobias and Harper also noticed - as did Vereena; who actually bit down hard on her lip while watching the pair.

Oblivious of the looks he was receiving Kyrel added, "Mordrel could be upon us at any moment; yet your injuries make your powers return more slowly. For now the best you can do is rest."

That said he walked off shouting Azeronian commands, spurring others into helping move whichever boulders they could toward the gates. A seemingly pointless task; with the first boulder only now being rolled into place by the handful of Da'ariel originally appointed.

Day Four: Part Five

"Cousin..." Vereena came up behind Lily, an apprehensive look on her face, and a small clay bottle in her hand. "Kyrel is right that you must rest but I do believe there is more you could do to help."

"Yeah?" Lilly raised an eyebrow at the bottle and nodding Vereena held it out to her saying.

"We have wounded here who may be revived. Three drops is all it takes." Seeing Lilly's gaze go to Baxter she shook her head, "He is beyond the help of the tonic as are many here," she looked around sadly adding, "But if you choose wisely others here may still aid us in this fight."

"Choose wisely!" Lilly glared at her now. "You're telling me to pick out who lives and who dies..." she shook her head. "That's not the kind of decision-"

"I can help!" Harper appeared at Vereena's side and snatching the bottle, waved her away, adding, "Don't worry we've got this." The Da'ariel girl raised an eyebrow, looking from her to Lilly. "It's OK," shrugged Harper, "We've got this! You can go!" Glancing beyond Vereena to where Kyrel was still dishing out orders she added, "Go see to your troops or something, the princess is fine with me."

Vereena turned to Lilly and receiving a nod responded in kind, her eyes going back to Harper as she added, "Remember, you must give only drops, no more than three. And only to those who may still-"

"We got it!" Harper shooed her away with another wave, before turning back to Lilly and shrugging, "Come on then, let's get some of these dead men walking."

Deciding where to start was the hard part, but after reviving a couple of Da'ariel and losing a couple, the two girls soon worked out a satisfactory system of triage; with Harper shaking the near motionless bodies to see if they could be roused before holding their mouths open for Lilly to administer the tonic one careful drop at a time.

"About before..." Harper held open the mouth of a young Da'ariel male and nodded for Lilly to try the tonic on him. "We weren't trying to give you a hard time," she said as she watched the translucent brown liquid drop from the bottle.

"Yes you were," Lilly pressed the tiny bung back into the bottle as Harper shook the youth a second time saying, "Hey! Wake up! Wake up! Come on! Cat ya vac!" as his eyes opened and he regained focus, she and Lilly got back on their feet and resuming the conversation she shrugged, "Well, yeah OK, maybe we did mean to give you a hard time, but only because we thought we had to, still..." she nodded after Kyrel as he joined the Da'ariel in, very slowly, rolling a boulder along. "I'm pretty sure *he* doesn't mean to."

"Maybe not," Lilly turned to watch him; a curious expression on her face, "Doesn't matter," she sighed, "A big fat I-told-you-so was in order, I get that. He's allowed to rub it in."

"True as that may be, I ain't sure that's what he was doing... in fact if you ask me, he's just not used to feeling responsible for someone, like he does for you right now. I mean sure he mighta looked in on you from time to time, but other than that he's led this solitary nomadic existence right? Hiding from the Da'ariel, and his sister, no one to care about, or argue with; now here you are this upstart from another world in serious need of a kick up the ass." Lilly's brow rose higher as they paused at the next incapacitated Da'ariel, and shrugging Harper grinned, "From his point of view... obviously."

"Obviously." Lilly's eyes narrowed.

"Look I'm just glad you're back in this," she shook the woman between them. Seeing her slowly open her eyes Harper grabbed her jaw, pulling it open and nodding for Lilly to proceed as she added, "For a minute there we really thought you were throwing in the towel."

"Ain't too sure I'm not yet..." muttered Lilly then seeing the stricken look on the other girl's face she sighed. "Let's just see how this little plan of Tez's pans out." Turning to glance at where Terrence was now taking a break and Tobias was trying to crack a hole in the ground's hard surface – his face etched with determination, brow already coated with a thin film of sweat. Lilly sighed and dripped the first drop of tonic into the Da'ariel's open mouth, adding, "Course we don't actually have any way of knowing how long it'll take Mordrel to show up do we."

"According to Kyrel, we're pretty far from the palace, and he's sure she won't have left until she knew you were captured."

"Funny how much that sounds like wishful thinking," mumbled Lilly.

"No really," nodded Harper. "What he told us made sense, at least Vereena and Tez seemed to think so," seeing Lilly frown, she shrugged, "There were quite a few references to stuff I'm clueless on, but I got the gist OK. Something about how wide a net Mordrel's cast in her search for you and..." shaking her head she said, "Look it made sense at the time. Besides... I don't think wishful thinking is something these people do a lot of."

"No, I guess not," Lilly sighed, pressing the bung back into the bottle again. "This place is pretty bleak right, kinda makes you wonder what the point is. I mean really, why are we even trying any more. Nothing we've done has made a diff-."

"Yeah I think you'll find the point is us getting out of here and going home." Harper turned to check another Da'ariel behind her.

"Home..." Lilly's voice became distant. "Guess there's still plenty to hope for back there. I'm kinda jealous that you all still have that-"

"*You all!*" Harper turned back with a raised eyebrow. "What do you mean *'you-'*"

"You know what I mean," Lilly's gaze drifted over to the twins, then on to the blob that was Baxter. "If by some miracle we do manage to '*squirm*' our way out of this I'm still the next heir to the-"

"You don't have to stay here just because the Da'ariel have you pegged as some all-powerful leader Slater," Harper got to her feet. Shaking her head as she watched Lilly do the same with a solemn look on her face, Harper grabbed her by the arm, forcing her to look up. "You do know that right? You know they can't make you do-"

"I saw the tear in the veil Harper; that first day we got here."

"Yeah so… we all did, that doesn't mean anything."

"Except I'm pretty sure I felt it too… as we passed through into this world… I felt…" she shook her head, "Well I didn't know what it was at the time, but I swear I knew… Somehow, at that moment, I knew things were never going to be the same again."

"You just think that," Harper shook her head. "You gotta know you couldn't have actually known any such thing. You can't even know it now."

"Now," Lilly scowled. "After everything I've seen here… after everything I know? How can I go back to-"

"You can do whatever you want OK, you heard Tobe: we came here together; we leave together. We can all still go back, and when we do you can forget this place ever existed just like the rest of us."

"Seriously," Lilly looked doubtful. "I'm not even human!"

"Yeah, well you look human enough to me," Harper shoved her hands in her pockets. "No one ever noticed before, what makes you think they would now? Any ways…" she glanced around at the cage full of Da'ariel. Zanreal warriors - or not; the hardened facial expressions and rugged overall appearance were universal among them, and all - women, men and youths - were kitted out with weaponry. All pitched in: doing their part to give their Princess one last fighting chance, regardless of the odds. "…you sure as hell don't fit in around here," smirked Harper.

"You think I don't know that?" Lilly sighed "Or how crazy this whole thing is? When we got here I didn't want to believe anything they told me, Kyrel or the Da'ariel… I just… getting back was all I could think about. The things they were saying were too much…" Lilly's eyes glistened as they welled up. "I walked away from the bus telling myself I'd been imagining things. Smoke inhalation, stress… doesn't matter I knew I could find a way to explain away what I'd seen. There was more than the tear, there was this fog only I could see and before that, when we were all trapped in the bus the door was somehow ripped off its hinges."

"Yeah, Tobes told me about that, I can't believe I don't remember."

"Did he tell you how it was all caught up in the bushes?"

"You think it was you!"

"I wanted off that bus!"

"Yeah but you didn't even know about the words," Harper crouched at the next body, "Or those hand signal thingys. How could you have-"

"I don't know OK…" Lilly shook her head, "But when I was so hungry I couldn't make my mind up, I grew that every-fruit tree that wrecked most of the village reading room. When I was angry and I wanted Tobes and Baxter out of my hair I sent them sky high. And both times I used the Deebanaarie words. Ain't like that really makes more sense?"

"I don't know about this one," Harper gazed down at the Da'ariel she'd been shaking. Lilly crouched with her and shook him again; his eyelids fluttered slightly and nodding for Harper to open his mouth, she carefully uncorked the tonic.

"Slater…" there was a gentle caution in the other girl's voice.

"Just open his mouth," snapped Lilly.

In went the three drops, "Cat ya vac." Lilly shook him some more "Cat ya vac!" Eventually, roused enough to blink up at the two girls, the Da'ariel muttered,

"Siiem tae, Siiem tae, dir lishka! Lek tek Mai."

"Err... sure." Lilly nodded before shrugging and waving a hand, "Up now. Up! Cat ya vac!" The Da'ariel nodded with her, pushing himself unsteadily up on one arm, then his eyes rolled back in his head and before either girl could stop him, he'd fallen back against the hard ground with a sickening crack that had them both wincing. "Shit!" hissed Lilly, her eyes going to Harper as she sucked in a sharp breath.

"Hey," Harper nodded. "We're not going to save them all OK, you can't expect to."

"I know," Lilly muttered as they got to their feet again.

"So…" Harper nodded toward another likely candidate, then asked, "Are you saying you think the intention's more important than the words when it comes to your magicks?" as they made their way over.

"I really don't know," Lilly shook her head. "Kyrel doesn't want me using the Tuâoch; the Deebanaarie words. He says it's too unpredictable, that I should stick to the words of my own ancestors, and all this other crap I don't get but… I swear when I do…" Lilly shook her head.

"You get way better results," shrugged Harper. "I know, Tez told us." Her eyes sought him out as she added, "Actually it's kind of scary how much he's learnt about this place already. Has Tobes pretty freaked out over-"

"Harper what if they're right about me?" Lilly paused, waiting for Harper to stop and face her before adding, "If this mark on my head… If the powers I have are… You know even after Kyrel found us, after we met Mairiel and all the other Da'ariel, even after we stayed in their village and saw it fall to the Deebanaarie, all I could think about was making it home, but now…" as they knelt beside another fallen Da'ariel Lilly looked around the cage, her expression dark as a brewing storm. "Well now," she sighed, "all I can think about is how many more of these people are going to die because I can't possibly live up to their expectations."

"This feud started long before you got here Slater, long before anyone here now was even born. You can't possibly take responsibility for the lives lost during the course of it."

"No… maybe not."

"No, of course not!" Harper's nose wrinkled. "That's just-"

"And if I walk away…" Lilly cut her off. "If I really am the best chance this world has at peace and I leave…What about those who die after I'm gone?" Scanning the crowd again she sighed, "Did you know this whole world is dying?"

"Yeah," Harper rocked on her heels. "I heard jab-happy over there," she nodded to where Vereena was ordering one of the few bulkier Da'ariel to take over from the twins. "Something about the magicks being all out of whack right?" she asked. "I didn't get much of it, was a bit over my head, but I know they think the lack of Da'ariel magicks… the Tuâoch?"

"Laîoch," corrected Lilly.

The Da'ariel between them was already opening his eyes, and pouring three drops of tonic into his mouth she added. "Tuâoch is the Deebanaarie magick."

"Right," nodded Harper "that one. The Laîoch, they think it's because there's been so little of it here for so long, which I guess makes sense," she shrugged. "I mean our world isn't that different is it. Every living thing has its purpose. Nature has all these ways of keeping things in balance. We screw with that balance and all sorts of shit starts fucking up, right? Seems to me this is the same kind of deal. A bit more direct sure, but not all that different."

"Yeah, but we're not talking climate change here are we?" Lilly got up and they made their way across the cage to the next clump of bodies. "The slow part of this process is already long over," said Lilly. "If someone doesn't put things right here soon this world doesn't get a not-too-distant future."

"Look… I know all that, OK," Harper paused to give Lilly a frank stare. "I get it already: Mordrel's worse than all the queens that came before her. She captures and kills countless Da'ariel with no regard for the effect it's having on this world, or even her own people, and yada, yada, yada… but you know what…" she shrugged "Boo hoo for them. Our world has its problems too, it can be every bit as cruel as this one is, and these Da'ariel abandoned you to it. The way I see it Slater… Princess or not; Powers or not, they gave up their right to call on you for anything the day they sent you away."

"But that was my mother," Lilly shook her head as they moved on. "She did it to protect me and… Well I kind of get the impression she was working alone."

"So maybe she was, but the others: the old lady, your cousins, they've been watching you for how long? They've always known where you were, they could have whipped you back here and given you a real chance to learn all this crap they're expecting you to be capable of way before now."

"They left me where they thought I was safest."

"Yeah I heard that version," nodded Harper.

"Version?" Lilly's eyebrow went up.

"What," shrugged Harper, "Like you haven't considered that maybe there's a little more to it than that… Or you know less."

"What do you mean?"

"Slater come on… You telling me that back home you never wondered about your real family?"

"Yeah, course I did."

"And if you'd known there was a way to meet them?"

"Well I probably would have jumped at it, but there were extenuating circumstances. I didn't know what was going on here."

"Mmm hmm…" nodded Harper, "extenuating circumstances. Well then maybe I reckon there's still a few of those that you don't know about."

"You think they're hiding stuff from me?"

"I think trusting someone just because they say they're family is always a dumb move." She followed Lilly's gaze out across the cage.

Amidst the Da'ariel, Kyrel was busy giving fresh orders; checking all were equipped with weapons and pointing out positions for them to defend.

"Sometimes I do kind of get the impression there's stuff Kyrel wants to say to me. Like I dunno maybe he knows more about my mother or something." Turning back to Harper she added, "Sometimes I think I see... I don't know... glances," her eyes went to Vereena and nodding Harper said, "Then you do see it too."

"I don't know what I see..." sighed Lilly, "You know I wasn't 'successfully placed' with the Slater's till I was like seven OK, and if that councillor they had me seeing over the summer was right then I have issues up the wazoo: trust pretty much at the top of the list so..."

"So what... You're thinking maybe you can't see the woods for the trees here? That your view can only be tainted? No, OK..." Harper shook her head. "I don't trust these people either and I've always known exactly who my folks are. It's not just you. There's more going on here than they're letting you in on and you know it."

"I don't know anything," Lilly's gaze was still on Vereena. "In fact I'm pretty sure the whole Qin Am Ness thing includes being honest."

"Well sure maybe, but does it also include volunteering information? If you don't ask about something, is she going to go out of her way to tell you?"

"Maybe not," Lilly muttered as she watched her cousin join Kyrel, and the Da'ariel she'd already pegged as leader of the Zanreal warriors.

The pair had been caught up in a somewhat hostile looking conversation and Vereena wasted no time getting between them. "Course it's not important now, is it," Lilly held out both hands mimicking a scale as she said, "Potential deep dark family secrets; evil Queen on her way to kill me. I think you can see where my priorities lie."

"Oh hey," Harper nodded, "Obviously Mordrel's the bigger worry here," she glanced around at the frantically busy Da'ariel. The twins were also hard at work again, only now they were amongst a large group rolling along a boulder. "But... well..." Harper shrugged "...there's nothing like the threat of impending death to loosen people's tongues is there? Whether we come out of this or not, you probably won't be getting another chance like this later."

"If there is a later," Lilly sighed, shaking her head as her gaze went back to Vereena – still trying to police the argument between Kyrel and the taller Da'ariel male – she stood firm between the pair, a hand on each of their chests.

"Anyway... they're obviously busy, and I don't even know what to ask."

"Well I'd probably start with S'ret over there..." she nodded toward the argument adding, "for being such a good and loyal warrior, he seems to constantly be at loggerheads with Kyrel and your cousin."

"S'ret?" Lilly raised an eyebrow. "That's him? That's his name?"

"Yeah," nodded Harper "Why, you know of him?"

Lilly bit her lip, watching the group of three a moment longer before nodding, "My mother chose a mate named S'ret, but well... I guess I assumed he died with her and the others."

"You don't think...." Harper's eyebrow went up as a thoughtful look crossed her face. "Vereena did say he used to live in the village."

"She did?"

"Yeah," nodded Harper "used to be part of Mai Mai's like personal guard or some shit, even speaks our language a little, learned it before being reassigned." Seeing Lilly's lip tremble she asked, "You really think he could be your father don't you?"

"Dunno," shrugged Lilly, "seems a lot like the kind of thing someone should have mentioned when we got here right? Like maybe an introduction would have been-"

"I think you're forgetting who we're talking about," frowned Harper. "Far as these Da'ariel are concerned a father doesn't matter remember? Guys here ain't much more than sperm donors."

Lilly grimaced at the reference then nodding said, "You're right, these people don't care about any of that stuff; I don't even know why we're talking about it; wouldn't make a blind bit of difference to him anyway."

"What does it matter if he cares?" asked Harper "You care don't you?"

"No." Lilly shook her head, "Not really," then seeing the disbelief on the other girl's face she shrugged. "OK yeah, so maybe I care a little, but come on… even if it did mean something what am I meant to say? I wouldn't know where to start."

She stared out across the cage, watching the three of them again.

Kyrel's hand was on the butt of his sword, and he was obviously itching for a shot at S'ret - whose scowl matched his own in fierceness. Neither they nor Vereena appeared to be backing down, and as the two girls watched, she dealt S'ret a mighty backhander, causing him to stumble backward.

***

"Damn!" Lilly's eyes grew wide as she watched S'ret recovering his equilibrium with a defiant glare that went straight past Vereena, to Kyrel.

"Yeah," Harper mumbled as she also watched them. A slap was apparently not enough for S'ret. Though neither of the girls could hear a word, it was clear many were being exchanged. From the determined stance of both men: shoulders back and chests jutting, each was eager to pounce. Yet they remained at bay, held back by Vereena, who was now yelling relentlessly in S'ret's face forcing him to give her his full attention.

"Well there's definitely something going on with him and Kyrel..." Harper gave an oh-so-slight nod of her head, "You should go over there and find out what it is."

"I... I can't..." Lilly gulped, her gaze going to the tiny bottle in her hand. "We have other things to be-"

"No worries." Harper snatched the bottle away from her. "I have this covered."

"What? No," Lilly began, with a shake of her head, "I can't leave you to..."

"Yes you can," Harper cut her off. "You're kinda crappy at the triage stuff anyways. Seriously," she shrugged, "I can manage."

"But... I... I can't just-"

"What can't you just?"

Both girls looked up to find Terrence staring down at them. They had been so engrossed in their conversation neither had noticed the twins were now taking a well-earned break.

Straggling behind came Tobias, with his head tipped back, and a near empty animal skin pressed up against his lips; while Terrence stood over them with a curious frown and his hands deep in his pockets.

Lilly opened her mouth to speak but before anything came out Harper jumped in with.

"We think S'ret might be Slater's father!"

Tobias choked on his next mouthful of water; almost losing the lot in a splutter of coughs that had the girls squinting with disgust, each ducking for cover underneath their own arms, as he sprayed them with a less than fine mist; before he managed to turn away and cover his mouth, gulping back all he'd retained.

Lilly turned to Harper with a scowl.

"Oh... sorry!" shrugged the other girl "Were we keeping that a secret?"

With a quick roll of her eyes Lilly sighed, "No, it's OK."

"You're serious?" asked Terrence.

"Totally," Harper grinned up at the twins, nodding over to where S'ret and the other two continued glaring at each other. "Lilly's mother chose a mate with the same name. Oh and we also think they're hiding something about her."

Seeing Lilly's scowl refresh, Harper chuckled,

"Sorry I guess I should say *I* think they're hiding something," she threw Lilly a quick smirk, adding, "Slater thinks she might not be seeing things too clearly cos some councillor told her she has issues." Then raising her brow at the boys as coughing once more Tobias turned back to face them, she asked, "She should go talk to him right?"

"And say what exactly?" Tobias wiped his mouth on his sleeve, his words laced with sarcasm, "Hey don't you owe me sixteen years' worth of birthday and Christmas presents."

"Yeah," Harper chuckled. "Not to mention CSA cheques."

"Err... not sure this is really the best time for that..." Terrence's face screwed up as he watched S'ret and the other two glaring at each other.

"Exactly!" Lilly scowled Harper's way again as she spoke through her teeth. "We don't have time for a paternity debate in a world where fathers are barely recognised-"

"Actually I just meant the sixteen years back-pay thing." Terrence turned back to them. "That idea aside, I'm with Harper, you should totally go speak with him." Seeing Lilly glare up at him he shrugged, "Hey if someone doesn't go break up whatever the hell's going on over there," he raised an eyebrow to where the two men, each a good foot taller than Vereena, were now ignoring her in favour of yelling at one another over her head while she struggled to keep Kyrel under control, holding him back and yelling in his face much the same way she'd done with S'ret.

Around them the rest of the Da'ariel, having all continued working as ordered up until this point, were inevitably slowing down to watch - many reaching for their own weapons as they edged closer.

Then S'ret bared his teeth, gesturing to Kyrel with a dismissive wave as he shook his head, and said something else Lilly and the others couldn't hear.

Apparently it was more provocative than he'd intended because Vereena whirled around, unsheathing her dagger and waving it at him, before Kyrel had time to respond.

S'ret stepped back, waving both hands as the young Da'ariel girl approached him with a menacing scowl.

Harper raised an eyebrow as she turned to Lilly nodding, "OK seriously... if they kill each other, I'm fairly certain we're screwed."

"Hey," Terrence's hands went up and shaking his head he said, "I've already done my part to stop that pair slicing out each other's tongues." Then seeing Lilly throw him a bewildered look, he nodded, "Yeah exactly... and Kyrel wasn't even around then so I think you'll understand when I say I'd really rather stay out of whatever..." pointing to the trio he added, "...this is," before shrugging. "You on the other hand... do seem to have the perfect excuse."

"And authority," smirked Harper, "you're the Princess, right? They have to answer your questions!"

"Unless her granny, The Queen, has ordered them not to," shrugged Tobias, "if they're hiding something, I bet you she's behind it."

"See!" Harper glared at Lilly, "It's not just you. None of us trust these guys." Then seeing Lilly suck in her lower lip, she smiled, "Oh go on, you know you totally want to. Besides if you're seriously thinking about staying to save this world, a place you know next to nothing about, you should at least get a better idea of your own family's politics, right?"

"Staying?" Tobias raised an eyebrow. "You're thinking of staying? When the hell did you lose your mind?"

Again, Lilly turned to Harper with a scowl, and again she responded with, "Sorry. Were we keeping *that* a secret?" There was more sincerity this time, and rolling her eyes, Lilly sighed, "You know I think maybe I *will* go talk to them..."

"Or..." Terrence grabbed her arm, as she got up, his gaze locking in place on the large gates as his eyes grew wide and he added, "You could just jump in with an I told you so on the whole this not being the time thing..."

"Being the..." seeing fear in his eyes, Lilly glanced at Tobias. He had an identical expression on his face. Then she heard it: stomp, stomp, stomp.

Lilly spun around to see troop after troop of Mordrel's forces, gradually filling the enclosed space beyond the black bars. They came marching in through the two large doorways, hewn into the rock outside it.

The four school kids were not the only ones to notice, within seconds Vereena and Kyrel were at Lilly's side – moving her to the cage's centre where the lump formerly known as Baxter had already been relocated and the Da'ariel warrior Vereena had ordered to take over from the twins was getting to his feet.

Most of the Da'ariel ran to take up fighting stances near the gates, while others flocked around Lilly and the others, forming a protective ring, their weapons at the ready.

Terrence dropped to his knees, retrieving the discarded chunk of milaratak'i and bashing it against the ground again.

Tobias threw him a fresh look of disbelief.

"Seriously bro! There's no give in that shit. Shouldn't we just stay out of the way and let these Zanreal warriors do their thing?"

"They're warriors! Terrence glared up at him, "fighting *is* their thing, and if we wanna get out of here alive we need to help even the odds."

"But we're sitting ducks out here in the centre of this cage."

"Maybe Tobes is right..." Harper's eyes were on Mordrel's troops, her face pale, and her lower lip trembling as she watched the enemy amass. "We should just stay out of the way..."

"In case you missed it there's no trees in this thing for all that fancy flying about," Terrence looked up at them. "These guys pretty much left their edge back in the forest, OK."

"He is right." Kyrel appeared at Lilly's side. "Without the magicks we *are,* as you humans say, screwed!"

"They're right." Lilly turned to Harper as Terrence set about beating the ground. "If anyone's gonna crack this thing open it's gonna have to be us."

"I don't know..." Harper frowned, biting her lip. "There's a heck of a lot of those guys. Maybe a corner to hide in is-"

"We're in a circular cage." Terrence paused to look up at them again. There aren't any corners!"

He slammed the chunk of sap into the ground again.

"There isn't anywhere to hide in here," agreed Lilly. "And between us we don't have half the skills of even one of these Da'ariel, but if we can make a crack in this we can at least have Kyrel's powers on our side."

"Exactly," Terrence looked up again, glancing around at the Da'ariel now encircling them and gesturing with a nod he added. "Besides, centre of the cage or not, it seems the safest place to be right now is wherever Lilly's at, and her and Kyrel both need to stay here for the best chance of getting their powers back."

"Then you're gonna need some help," nodded Tobias, "There's like a bunch more of those pieces next to a boulder over there. Don't look like these Deebanaarie are making a move yet. If I run for it I can be back in a few seconds."

"Good idea." Lilly nodded. "Bring enough for all of us."

"I'm going with him." Harper said as Tobias slipped through the wall of Da'ariel backs. She disappeared too.

"This 'sweet spot' of yours..." Lilly looked down at Terrence as he raised the milaratak'i chunk again.

"Yeah?" he looked up, wincing as he brought it down again.

"It better be real fucking sweet, because I'm getting a real nasty taste in my mouth!" Tiptoeing she gazed out beyond the bars to where more and more of the Deebanaarie soldiers were filing in. With their hands on the hilts of their ubiquitous short swords, they marched swiftly; filling the limited space between the cage and the walls of the vast crater.

Terrence got in a few more hefty whacks before a sharp gasp escaped him and looking up to Lilly with a grimace he sighed, "Do you see them coming back yet? Because I'm definitely going to be needing that hand."

On tiptoes again Lilly shook her head, before dropping to her knees beside him and snatching up the hardened sap. Using both hands she took one hard smack at the ground before Kyrel dropped beside her and grabbing her arm said, "Ny! You must not do this." He tore the chunk from her hands.

"What?" she glared at him. "What now? Is the Princess not allowed to help save her own ass?"

"You are in the ka'aam shareê." He shook his head, as though this answer should make obvious sense to her. All around them the Da'ariel clamoured in ever tighter, forcing them to duck their heads and crouch in closer to one another.

"Kyrel's right." Terrence's voice rose to compensate for the growing hubbub at their backs. "Your body's already coping with too much," he told her. "You should be resting."

"Resting!" she glared at each of them in turn. "What am I meant to do: go tell Mordrel I'm calling a time-out on account of just not being ready yet?"

"That is unlikely to help," Kyrel frowned. "Even if my sister did speak your tongue, she is not known for-"

"OK, you know what... if we do get through this..." Lilly glowered at him, "Remind me to instruct you all about the wonders of a little thing called sarcasm."

"It's OK," Terrence flexed his wrist a couple of times. "Just a cramp, is all. I can manage."

"You sure?" Lilly didn't look convinced and there was obvious irritation in her voice.

"Course I am," Terrence smiled, holding out his other hand, he added. "Will you just for once do as he tells you." His eyes went to Kyrel and he nodded, "Come on. Hand it over."

There was obvious trepidation on Terrence's face as Kyrel complied, and knowing Lilly saw it he forced another smile and quickly set about pounding the ground again. Fortunately there was just enough time for her to shoot Kyrel an angry glare before Tobias and Harper reappeared; forcing their way through the tightly packed Da'ariel.

Immediately Tobias knelt beside his twin and joined the endeavour while Harper crouched next to Lilly offering her one of the milaratak'i chunks they'd retrieved. Lilly shot a pleading look at Kyrel. The only response was a staunch rising of his eyebrows and sighing she shook her head.

"Seriously" There was an ill-disguised disgust in Harper's voice. "We kinda need all the help we can get."

Seeing Lilly drop her eyes Terrence spoke up for her.

"She should probably just rest."

"This is hardly the locale for a bit of R & R," Harper raised an eyebrow. "Ain't like she can just curl up and take a power nap."

"She's got a point there," Tobias glanced up, wincing as his brother had done, each time the milaratak'i chunk in his hand ricocheted off the floor.

"Well no..." agreed Terrence, rubbing at his wrist "... But there's more to it than that." With a questioning look in Kyrel's direction he added, "Before the wars there were rituals; to end the Kalaareem sooner?"

"Yes!" nodded Kyrel, "Diun Sela Lekaa."

Nodding with him Terrence asked. "Diun…That's like words right? The repeating and rhyming of certain words."

"Veyhi…" nodded Kyrel. "Words that..." He waved a hand gently through the air and raising her own hand as if in class, Harper nearly jumped back onto her feet.

"Song!" she shouted over the din. "You want Slater to sing a song!" Then she was frowning, "No wait, that can't be right." Shaking her head, she asked in a more doubtful voice. "You want Slater to *sing* a song?"

"Yes," Vereena appeared behind Kyrel, crouching at Lilly's side, she nodded "The Sela Lekaa is like song."

"OK you know what, just let me help with this," Lilly snatched up one of the milaratak'i chunks; sounding more disgusted than Harper looked bewildered as she added, "because I am *not* singing a song!"

"Nyrdel!" Kyrel snatched it from her again as he yelled in her face, "Vrelgest Dylur! Tolori, hishlivt matfiac!"

"Oh yeah!" hissed Lilly, "Well, fuck you too!" Though his words had meant little to her, his tone could not have been clearer and they glared at each other.

"Lilly please!" Terrence said, "We don't have time to argue about this. We'll do what we can," His eyes went to Harper and without any further protest she slid closer to Tobias and joined him in beating at the ground. "Just hear him out," added Terrence. "I really think this could help."

"Seriously!" Lilly raised an eyebrow at Kyrel. "First I should rest, now I should sing! He's fucking crazy!"

"It matters not," Vereena shook her head at Lilly. "You cannot perform Sela Lekaa, this is a wisdom of the ancestors; lost to our people almost as long as we have been without magicks."

"My people have not been without magicks!" Kyrel turned his glare on Vereena. "I can guide her through."

"Nydrel," hissed Vereena "You cannot!" slipping into their native language they were soon in the thick of an argument none of the classmates could understand.

Though the lack of comprehension did little to stop them watching avidly; as the words Mai Mai, Tuâoch, and Laîoch, were thrown back and forth, along with a couple more mentions of the Diun Sela Lekaa; it did give rise to an anger in Lilly, which she was about to put into some choice words of her own when a woman's voice cut through the tirade.

Mordrel spoke more of the same incomprehensible Azeronian, however the sudden stillness of the bodies pressed up against their backs and the stricken look on Vereena's face in the deathly silence that followed, was enough to make the hairs rise on the back of Lilly's neck as Terrence still massaging his wrist, asked, "What? What is it? What did she say?"

The marching from beyond the cage had ceased, and all about them became quieter. Nodding at Lilly, Kyrel whispered.

"Diun Sela Lekaa may be your only way of getting your powers back while you still have the chance to use them."

"I don't have the chance to use them!" Lilly whispered back through gritted teeth, nodding pointedly to the ground. "We haven't even made a mark on this damn stuff and I don't think me hitting the high notes is really going to cut it. Think of something else. I ain't singing no damn song!"

"Cut it…" muttered Terrence.

"You what?" she glared angrily at him.

"Not you," he shrugged "It! Cut… It!" he waved the chunk at the ground. "This stuff might be hard but it ain't very heavy…"

"Oh for crying out loud," complained Harper. "Doesn't anyone have something useful to say?"

"This *is* useful!" insisted Terrence. "At least I hope it is. And so is what Kyrel's saying," his gaze flittered over Lilly now.

"He's saying I have to sing!" she hissed. "I *don't* sing!"

"It's not really singing, OK," he shook his head, "think more of... a chant." Nudging his brother, Terrence nodded to the milaratak'i chunk adding,"like a mantra..." as he dragged the hardened sap.

Following his brother's lead Tobias began grinding his chunk back and forth along one of the lines on the ground. Looking up at Lilly, Terrence added, "Like you know... for meditation."

Seeing her raise an eyebrow, her entire face seeming to tighten, Harper sighed, "Slater please," as she joined the boys in scratching her own chunk of milaratak'i hard against a third line on the ground. "If it can make your powers come back then-"

"Oh flipping hell," Lilly rolled her eyes.

"Shh!" Terrence raised a finger to his lips. "I don't think she's done."

He was right, Mordrel was still speaking, and around them the Da'ariel seemed to bristle more with her every word.

Lilly looked to Kyrel, his face now void of expression as he also listened.

For a moment she listened intently too, but unable to glean anything, turned to see Terrence running a finger along the ground.

"Is it working?" she asked, crawling over to him.

"Yeah, I think maybe it is." He dipped his head down to blow away a thin sheet of dust which had formed there, beneath it was a groove - about the width of his finger.

"Yes!" he grinned up at her, then the others. "We can do this!"

"Good!" nodded Lilly - another glance at Vereena and Kyrel told her a translation wasn't forthcoming any time soon. "Keep going..." she turned back to Terrence and the others. "...faster would be good." Then, before Kyrel could see her to stop her, she crawled away.

Determined to at least get a look at the enemy she couldn't understand, Lilly was about to poke her head out through the throng of legs when the hairs on the back of her neck rose again - Mordrel's words were no longer foreign to her. The Deebanaarie queen's voice rang out in clear English, and still on all fours, Lilly froze.

"I know you hear me girl. I speak for you now so these Da'ariel will know my words are truth. Mairiel spent much time learning your tongue. Not an easy task at her age. For such a long time her mind and body were failing her. Did she tell you that girl? Did she tell you how forcing herself to hold on for you after your mother's death was one of the hardest things she ever did? I know this as well as she experienced it, for it is her essence within me, which allows me to speak your tongue now."

Peering out between a pair of Da'ariel legs, Lilly scanned for a glimpse of the woman speaking.

Instead, from her vantage point so near to the floor, the first thing she was able to single out was the body of Mairiel: a tangled heap on the floor. Though she faced the cage with open eyes, they were little more than a yellowish orange goo which had dribbled down her face, which had once again reverted to its elderly state, with a soundless scream etched onto it.

"What are you doing?"

Lilly turned to face Kyrel as his hand landed on her shoulder.

"I... err... I... I was going to... Mairiel's dead!"

"Yes," still his face lacked expression. "That *is* what my sister just said." He shrugged "Now if we do not get you out of here the Da'ariel will truly be without a Queen. Come," he nodded back toward the others. "We must return..." he insisted "Your friends make good progress, we must-"

"Lilliath Avengturov!" continued Mordrel. "That is what they named you isn't it child? Or should I call you Lilly as the humans do? You see I know so much about you. Thanks to your grandmother, I know of much she did not tell you."

"Lilly..." Kyrel shook his head at her. "...nothing she says is of any importance to you now. If she reaches you before your magicks return she will end you to take them. The Diun Sela Lekaa must be started before-"

"In truth, I meant only to take a little of her essence," said Mordrel. "I had so much more planned for Mairiel; she has been an annoyance to me for such a long time - the woman these Da'ariel insist on calling their Queen. If she had not fought so hard... Still... that is the way of the Da'ariel, is it not Lilly? They are a people who do not know when they are defeated. Your grandmother forced me to push harder." Breaking off momentarily, she switched languages, issuing orders to someone nearer her, and quick to take the opportunity, Kyrel pushed his face up to Lilly's.

"We must begin Diun Sela Lekaa before it is too late."

"Right," she nodded, "I'm with you." Lilly crawled after him through the mass of Da'ariel legs as Mordrel continued.

"In the end she gave up so much more than I had wanted."

Lilly paused, staring at the ground; listening without wanting to as Mordrel added, "You do not know she also wanted you dead do you girl? That she would have prevented your birth if doing so would not have meant the death of her precious Herrella."

"Cousin Lilly..." the urgency in Vereena's voice cut through Mordrel's. "Please!" she called out as the clashing of swords signalled Deebanaarie troops entering the cage.

"Lilly!" insisted Kyrel. "We must begin now."

He sat beside Vereena, crossing his legs and raising his palms as Lilly rejoined them.

Copying the way he sat down exactly, she heard Mordrel's voice rise over the fighting.

"She did not tell you anything of the true nature of your powers did she girl? Oh yes, she knew what you were... a symptom of a sickness that like her, I once thought removed from these lands."

"Focus!" Kyrel took hold of Lilly's wrists, pulling her arms down to her sides and placing her palms flat on the shiny black floor. "Listen to me!" he insisted, "Not to her!"

While Lilly nodded for him to go on, Mordrel added, "Mairiel may have foolishly pledged to keep you safe, girl - after she lost her daughter, you were her only hope - but my words are truth… on first seeing you all she felt was disgust, and more fear than she had ever known before your birth."

"Me!" Kyrel hit Lilly hard in the side of her head. "Listen *only*… to me!"

"OK, OK!" she frowned, rubbing at her head then placing her hand back on the ground. "I'm listening already."

"Close your eyes," he instructed, as he placed his fingertips gently against the sides of her head. "Think only of your powers. Remember how it feels to use them."

As the clashing of blades increased, and near the gates, howls of agony could be heard amid the fervent cries of battle, Mordrel's voice grew louder.

"Unlike Mairiel *I* do *not* fear you," she said as all about them Deebanaarie and Da'ariel collided, each side attempting to out-hack, out-slash, and out-stab the other.

"To me you are a gift." Mordrel was saying now. "A ripe fruit I shall enjoy plucking-"

"Ta esta, ta'at…" said Kyrel. *"…ta tuatha vorok…"*

"And when I have all of your essence," his sister went on. "The Avengturov line shall be over and these Da'ariel will finally…"

"I cannot do this for you!" Kyrel growled at Lilly, his voice all urgency and frustration. "You must speak as I speak, or this cannot work."

"She's messing with you Slater," Harper nodded over at them. "She knows she hasn't won yet."

"Yeah," agreed Terrence "which means we can still do this."

"Right," Lilly opened her eyes long enough to tell Kyrel "Sorry," and nod. "Let's try again."

"Ta esta, ta'at, ta tuatha vorok," Kyrel said again.

"So much of the Lady's power, in one so weak," said Mordrel, "Soon there will be no Da'ariel left in there to protect you girl. Your essence shall be…"

"Ta esta, ta'at, ta, tuatha vorok." Lilly forced herself to do as Kyrel had instructed: echoing him, and thinking of her powers; she repeated everything he said.

"Thev-levath… risth ta… risth vak."
"Thev-levath… risth ta… risth vak."

"No more blood need be spilled this day girl…" Mordrel's incessant baiting became more distant as the warmth of Kyrel's fingers, pressed against Lilly's temples, felt as though it were seeping into her; flooding her mind, and bringing with it a steady flow of images.

All at once she was back to unintentionally growing that first tree in the forest; an instant later it was the plant, which had become an assorted fruit tree; then she was losing her temper with Tobias and Baxter, sending them skyward in another gigantic tree.

"*Lathaa tuatha vorok inst.*" said Kyrel.
"Lathaa tuatha vorok inst." Lilly repeated.

"Mairiel is no more, but all need not be lost," Mordrel was saying as the gates clattered open a second time and more of her forces stormed into the cage. "At your command these Da'ariel can lay down their weapons." She went on. "Come to me willingly girl, and many lives can be spared. As the only true Queen of these lands you have my word - I will spare any who are not your blood-"

"*Ta esta, ta'at, ta tuatha vorok.*" Kyrel's voice cut in.
"Ta esta, ta'at, ta tuatha vorok." Lilly said again.

Around them the Da'ariel were gradually thinning. One after another those on the outer-circle were drawn into the fight; while those on the inner, seemed to sway and rock as one, moving constantly to close each new gap.

"*Thev-levath... risth ta... risth... vak.*"
"Thev-levath... risth ta... risth vak."

"Any idea how long this is gonna take them?" Harper asked Terrence. He looked to Vereena, and she shook her head.

"My people's knowledge of these magicks is... limited."

"Not too limited for you to look real worried." Tobias gave a quick nod. "He's right," agreed Terrence. "Is there something we need to know?" For a moment longer she continued to look troubled then she nodded.

"Kyrel is right. We are out of options."

"OK, is it just me...?" Tobias turned to his brother asking, "Or did that sound very *not* promising?"

"How will we know when it's working?" asked Harper.

"Lilly will know," nodded Vereena "If Kyrel can truly do this," her eyes went back to the pair: both lost deep now in the grip of the words. "It should not be long." She looked to the ground. "What of this? Do you still think you can break through?"

"I don't know," Terrence looked grim. He'd been rubbing so hard, his arms were going dead again, yet each time he blew away more dust his progress seemed less than the time before. "A little more and I'm hoping we can crack it, but that's going to be difficult with this," he stopped his rubbing to wave the milaratak'i chunk at her; its size had diminished significantly.

"Yeah," Harper held hers up, it too had diminished to a fraction of its original size. "They're not exactly holding up well; getting kinda difficult to keep up the pace with such a small piece."

After a quick scan around them Vereena nodded, "I shall get more. Do not stop."

"Right," Terrence called after her as they watched her crawl out the back of their Da'ariel circle.

Day Four: Part Six

    Mordrel continued her baiting but Lilly was no longer aware of it.
    Although somewhere in the deepest recesses of her mind she knew a battle raged on around her, in the foreground – as she echoed Kyrel – she knew only a vibrant outpouring of memories.
    Over the past four days she had begun getting acquainted with her powers and now every moment of that was racing through her mind.
    This was more than memory: it was a Technicolor dreamscape that went by at a dizzying pace. Every sensation Lilly had felt at the time of these past events was repeated on her now with each fresh image.
    The time Kyrel had sunk her repeatedly into the ground, forcing her to use her power over the earth to free herself; the time she'd raised an entire wall between him and her; the time she had disregarded his instruction, and using the Tuâoch command: katat, had blasted him halfway across the village training ground.
    As the warmth radiating from his fingertips relaxed her entire body and she grew more comfortable repeating his words, Kyrel kicked it up a notch. Together they were soon reciting at a speed that gave the words cadence and proved Terrence right: it really was more a chant than a song.

    "Ta esta, ta'at, ta tuatha vorok."
    "Ta esta, ta'at, ta tuatha vorok."

    "Thev-levath... risth ta... risth... vak."
    "Thev-levath... risth ta... risth vak."

    "Lathaa tuatha vorok inst."
    "Lathaa tuatha vorok inst."

    Lilly was no longer aware of the words leaving her own mouth. She was fully immersed in her memories; like daydreaming in surround sound, she re-lived those moments in which she had exerted her powers. As each event had been accompanied by an array of sensations – from the physical five to those which could be deemed purely emotional – so too was each memory. And for Lilly, feeling all this the second time around was every bit as intense as those first times. Only now, much like under the bridge when she had touched Kyrel as he'd performed the Dres Verfelt upon the shraeka, she experienced it all in a fraction of the time it had truly taken.

    "Ta esta, ta'at, ta tuatha vorok."

    She and Kyrel were speaking as one now, their lips moving in perfect sync with each other's.

"Thev-levath… risth ta… risth vak."

The many fears and anxieties Lilly had felt through using her powers returned, pouring into her with each memory.

"Lathaa tuatha vorok inst."

The loneliness and confusion her entire situation had engulfed her in gushed in too, as did the rage she'd been feeling each time she had used her powers in anger.
Faster and faster she and Kyrel spoke together.

"Ta esta, ta'at, ta tuatha vorok."

"Thev-levath… risth ta… risth vak."

"Lathaa tuatha vorok inst."

Again she felt the pride and triumph of her every magickal accomplishment. Again she felt the rush of strength which surged through her each time she'd used her powers.

"Ta esta, ta'at, ta tuatha vorok."

"Thev-levath… risth ta… risth vak."

"Lathaa tuatha vorok inst."

Lilly remembered using her powers to save Kyrel when Toleth, under the control of a young ginat, had attacked without due cause.

While Harper kept an eye on their surroundings: scanning and re-scanning for fresh dangers or any sign of Vereena's return, she and the twins kept up their grinding; pausing every few seconds to blow away the accumulating dust, and rub at the floor's hard surface with their fingertips.
Despite the abundance of the dust, her groove seemed no different from the last few times she'd checked it, and fresh doubts sprang to mind: was it really getting any deeper? Did the surface really feel any thinner?
Terrence was also wondering if he was about to be proved wrong by his own untimely death.
As much as he told himself the dust was proof, the chunk of sap growing smaller in his hand made this fact debatable. It was also clear that with every Da'ariel who pulled away from the group surrounding them, time was running out.
Unlike Lilly, he was very much aware of the battle inside the cage, as

were his brother and Harper, and as he looked over to them, he saw from the engrossed looks on their faces that they were both still listening intently to Mordrel.

"Do you not see this fighting is foolish?" she was asking. "I do know you are without your powers, girl. Anything the Da'ariel could have taught you is no use to you now, in here. See, when I learned you still lived... How Herrella had saved your life by sending you to the human world, I decided it would be wise to take precautions. So you see... Even if the ka'aam shareê is not yet upon you, this cage will contain you until it is."

While Lilly appeared entranced in her chanting, Mordrel's voice made it clear that the more she said the more worked up she was becoming. "You cannot truly think to defeat me!" she yelled, "Your birth was unsanctioned, your essence is rightfully mine, and as the head of House D'vey – as the rightful ruler of all Azeron – I am here to claim it."

The second wave of troops who'd entered the cage were slowly decimating the pitiful amount of able bodied Da'ariel who stood against them. Looking around, Tobias saw enough of the warriors had left the circle now for him to have a decent view of most of the battle raging beyond this small, and for the moment, slightly safer spot.

Unfortunately his brother was definitely right about one thing: skilled as the Da'ariel were with their weapons, the forest was their terrain; without the trees to weave between they had indeed lost their edge.

Not that they were doing badly, they'd taken from Mordrel's forces at least as many as they themselves had lost, but with her having countless more troops outside the cage, their efforts obviously weren't going to be enough. The dead and the dying littered the ground, while any able remained in the fray.

As they ground their milaratak'i chunks against the floor, Tobias found his eyes drawn to a Da'ariel woman with a gash down the length of her back, and a dagger protruding from the back of her right thigh - an injury, which slowed, but far from stopped her. She took most of her body weight onto her arms; crawling to help a companion, who was pinned down by a Deebanaarie with a short sword less than an inch from his jugular.

Eyes bulging with strain, the woman made it in the nick of time, pulling the dagger from her own thigh, she plunged it deep between the Deebanaarie's shoulder blades.

They both went limp, and the previously pinned down Da'ariel male pushed away both their bodies; retrieving his weapon without a second glance, he leapt back into the fight.

As a shiver ran down his spine, Tobias turned to look at his brother; he had been watching too and for a second their eyes locked. Then two of the Da'ariel behind Terrence fell backwards on to him and Tobias leapt to his feet as Harper crawled to safety.

For a moment the wind was knocked out of Terrence and the weight of two bodies had him pinned to the hard floor at such awkward angles he was certain something would snap before he could get back up, but seconds later they were both up again and racing out into the main fight.

Tobias crouched over him offering a hand, and taking it Terrence gasped. "I'm OK, I'm OK." He checked himself over, before running the back of his wrist across his brow and taking several deep breaths, as he watched what was left of their Da'ariel enclosure close back up around them.

"I don't think we have much longer." Tobias shook his head. "The Da'ariel are losing too many too quickly."

"I know," nodded Terrence, his tone as reassuring as he could make it. "But Veer will be back here any second with more of this sap stuff, OK." He picked up the piece originally meant for Lilly and crawled back to his 'sweet spot' going back to his grinding as he added, "Then I'm pretty sure we'll be able to crack-"

"Pretty sure!" Tobias crawled over to him. "What if she doesn't even make it back here? Can you see what's going on in here? For all we know she's already de-"

"She'll get back here!" snapped Terrence, and biting his lip Tobias looked over to Lilly and Kyrel, neither appeared affected by the brief intrusion. They each seemed as entranced as the other in their continued chanting.

Mordrel on the other hand, was apparently done with words altogether. That or the din within the crystal cage was now too much to hear anything more from her.

Still scratching away, Harper glanced up to see the gates opening a third time, and watching more of the Deebanaarie rushing inside, their swords at the ready, she knew Tobias was right: the Da'ariel would soon be overpowered.

A hand on Terrence's shoulder gave him a start. Turning around he saw Vereena. Tobias and Harper turned around too. Panting like a dog on a hot day, the Da'ariel girl held one fresh lump of milaratak'i out to Terrence.

A deep slice across her left cheek which poured blood down her face, and an equally nasty gash on her arm, a couple of inches below her shoulder on the same side, had Terrence asking, "You OK?" as he took the sap.

"I shall be fine." Vereena placed her dagger between her teeth and pressing her hand against her arm, assessed the damage before she pulled a rag from one of the pouches at her waist and began wrapping it around the wound.

One handed, it was proving tricky and handing the milaratak'i she had retrieved over to his brother, Terrence reached for the rag.

"Here, let me help with…"

Vereena pulled away with a confused look.

"I have no need of-"

"Trust me OK, I can do this faster," he snatched the rag from her hand adding, "The last thing we want, when more of those Deebanaarie come crashing through your pals here, is you not ready to kick their asses." Then he was tying it into a tourniquet, and seeing her wince as he tightened it, smirked, "So you do feel pain then… that's good to know."

Hearing Harper snigger Vereena turned to catch her also smirking and glared pointedly down to where her hands remained motionless.

"Right," Harper looked down at the small but totally usable piece of sap in hand and shrugged. "I should probably-"

But before she could finish, the circle was breached again, and pushing Terrence aside Vereena bounced up.

Wrapping the crook of her injured arm around the face of the first Deebanaarie to make it through, she snapped the man's head back, and spinning him - backward - against her chest, jabbed her dagger deep into his windpipe, arterial blood spraying as she wrenched the blade free.

As he sagged, she spun him again and kicked his body back out onto the next approaching Deebanaarie.

This one was a woman and as the body of her companion sent her tumbling to the ground, another Da'ariel forced his blade through her armoured chest pinning her to the ground. That same Da'ariel twisted his blade for good measure before pulling it back out and turning on another approaching Deebanaarie.

The three kids grimaced, turning away but in every direction similar sights of bloody violence were occurring around them.

Turning back, Terrence saw a third Deebanaarie come crashing through on the opposite side of the not-so-protective circle, less than a metre from where Lilly and Kyrel remained deep in their trance-like state.

"There!" he pointed, yelling for Vereena's attention. A second later the young girl was at her cousin's side beating back several Deebanaarie with the help of her fellow Da'ariel.

Tobias and Harper glanced about, realising as they did that the last shreds of Da'ariel enclosing them were rapidly falling away. There was little more anyone could do to keep the barrier of bodies effective.

A second later Vereena was yelling, "You two! Down!" as she leapt over their heads, her short-sword already at mid-swing.

Looking over his shoulder Terrence saw she had downed another Deebanaarie, probably saving his life yet again. "Thanks," he called out as he watched her bounce to her feet.

"Break the milaratak'i!" she shouted back at him, her blade already locked fiercely in battle with another. "We must have access to the essence!" she told him. "Break the ground, break it now!"

"Right," he picked up the second chunk of sap and got back to work, scraping the floor. A few seconds later however and all three of the classmates were ducking from another attack.

Again, Vereena reacted swiftly enough to save them. Tobias watched as she offered his brother a helping hand. In spite of their situation Terrence smiled gratefully up at her as she began reiterating what she had already said.

"There is no more time; you must try again to crack-"

Then all at once her mouth and eyes grew wide and she took in a short, sharp breath. Instead of getting Terrence upright she slumped forward onto him. Feeling a warm trickle run down his right leg he pressed his hand to it, it came away smeared with blood. Terrence craned his neck, seeing the shiny bluish butt of a dagger sticking out of Vereena's back.

Grasping her shoulders, Terrence, held her out at arm's length. "Shit!" he hissed as he watched her lower jaw trembling and the colour leaving her already pale face. "No," he mumbled, staring into her wide, watering eyes. "No, no, no!"

Harper and Tobias crawled over to him, and amidst a confusing array of questions, all of which could be summed up by 'what the hell are we going to do now?', they began pulling the young Da'ariel girl off him, then Terrence glanced up; seeing their side of the Da'ariel barrier was now as good as dispersed, and that two Deebanaarie were running at them with raised swords, his next "Oh Shit!" came out as a scream. Startled, Harper and Tobias let go of Vereena, dropping her back onto his chest as they scrambled about with Harper turning around to see the same two Deebanaarie and also screaming.

Tobias looked over too. Only he did so just in time to see S'ret dive in between them, fending both Deebanaarie off with several vicious lashes of his short-sword.

Gasping for air, Terrence slithered out from under Vereena, and sitting up, pulled her onto his lap. Despite the obvious agony in them, he was relieved to see her eyes re-open.

"The magicks are our only chance now," she gasped the words at him. "You must.... crack.... the surface."

"You're hurt," he gulped "It looks real bad. If I don't-"

"Terrence... Emerson," she grabbed his hand, pulling him closer as she strained to keep her voice audible. "Without the magicks," she struggled for air. "We are all dead. Do it now! Break the..." her eyes drooped shut again.

"Veer..." Terrence tried to rouse her. "Veer? Vereena!" Gulping again as tears sprang to his eyes, he turned to see his brother watching him, a distraught yet pitying look on his face, and nodding Terrence muttered, "We... We have to-"

"Break the surface," Tobias nodded, his expression instantly becoming one of abject determination, as he added, "I'm on it," then crawled away, retrieving the larger chunk of sap Vereena had brought them.

Harper was the next to speak up, her hand burrowing deep inside her jeans pocket.

"It's OK," she pulled out the tiny clay bottle Vereena had given her and Lilly earlier. "I've got this," she prised out its minute bung and carefully administered three drops.

As the third drop went in, Tobias was calling for her and Terrence to get down, and with a quick glance up they saw a Da'ariel youth obliviously backing into them as he fought off three Deebanaarie.

Terrence stretched himself over Vereena; his first instinct, to keep her from further injury. Harper on the other hand, realising the Deebanaarie were equally as oblivious of their presence; kicked out her foot tripping the first to come close enough.

He toppled over, helmet clattering to the ground, and also caught unawares, the Deebanaarie directly behind him went flying too. The third saw what was happening and already a slave to momentum, was forced to take a flying leap over them.

He landed on his feet but only just and before he could fully recover his wits, a broad swipe from the youth's sword separated his head from his neck.

In spite of the triumphant relief they felt on seeing the Deebanaarie's body fall to the floor and his head roll across the cage before landing amidst a scuffle of feet and disappearing from sight – a mutually disgusted "Ewww!" came from both Terrence and Harper: bringing with it a synchronised need to avert their eyes.

The two Deebanaarie felled by Harper's initial intrusion were already untangling from one another. The first, having lost his helmet, glowered angrily over at her as he reached for his weapon.

Fortunately for Harper, her help turned out to be all the advantage the Da'ariel youth required.

The second the glowering Deebanaarie was up, he leapt forward, diving at him and thrusting the length of his short-sword deep into his gut.

As he accomplished this, the third Deebanaarie, also on his feet, and missing his short-sword since going flying, pulled out what looked to Harper like a small wooden mace; it's long gnarled handle appeared little more than a thick branch torn from a bush or some other minor foliage. Its multi-pronged barbs were tipped the vile yellow of pus though many had already picked up a hefty coating of crimson.

Seeing him seize on the opportunity presented by having the Da'ariel's back to him as he raised the weapon high above his head, Harper screamed. "Behind you!" Spinning around, the youth plunged his dagger up into the Deebanaarie's left armpit, making his mouth spring open for a silent shriek, as the grisly looking weapon dropped to the ground.

At this point he pulled his dagger out of the Deebanaarie's armpit and plunged it into him again. This time he jabbed it up behind the chin; taking a moment to twist and grind before pulling it out again and kicking the now limp corpse down onto the ground. After this, he whirled around, threw a grateful smile Harper's way, and running off, leaped back into the fray.

Turning back, she saw Terrence watching her, a miserable glint in his eye.

The friendship he'd struck up with Vereena was obvious to everyone. Now his inability to stop her bleeding out as he held her in his arms was – to Harper at least – a heart-wrenching sight.

Meanwhile, Tobias, having adopted what appeared to be a permanent scowl, had gone back to rubbing at the floor again and was so busy giving it his all he barely seemed to notice his brother's distress.

Harper knew better: if nothing else, his grinding at that sap as hard and fast as he was, served mostly to distract from the many discomfiting things going on around him. Every few seconds he would try again to crack it. Several more times the Deebanaarie got near him and each time S'ret or another nearby Da'ariel fought them off.

When one of these attacks forced him to roll out of the way, he was back up again on all fours in seconds, muttering something Harper couldn't quite make out, under his breath.

"Who the hell am I kidding?" Tobias muttered as he crawled back into position and began – again – to scrape and bash at it, "I can't do this," he told himself. "Stupid plan. Stupid fucking plan!" He kept scraping, before bashing on each word as he added, "Fuck! Fuck! Fuck! We're. All. Gonna. Die."

Never before had he doubted his brother so much, but he couldn't help it. There was no real sign of this super hard flooring giving way any time soon. Now as he was sent flying across it again, he was about ready to give up. However this time the arm held out to him was Harper's. "Come on," she urged and together they crawled back to the cage's centre again, and each with a chunk of the milaratak'i in hand began bashing at it together.

***

A second later Kyrel joined them and glancing over to where he had been sitting moments earlier, Tobias saw Lilly seated exactly as she had been; her legs crossed and her palms pressed down flat either side of her; only now a feint, but deep orange glow was emanating from her lap.

Terrence and Harper were also watching her as looking down on Tobias, Kyrel scanned the cage as if returning to it from a distant land, and said, "Lilly no longer requires my assistance," before nodding to the floor and asking, "You do?"

"Err... yeah." Tobias shook his head, "I'm beginning to think Slater was right about this plan," he shrugged, his gaze skirting his brother as he added; "We can't break this stuff. We're screwed!"

"Nydrel!" Kyrel dropped to his knees and snatching the chunk away from Harper set about pounding it against the ground himself. "We cannot let her be right." He added, "She must have access to essence, now!"

"What do you think we've been doing?" Harper snarled at him. "It's not working, OK. We have to find another way."

"There is no other way," Kyrel hissed through tightly gritted teeth, wincing as he bashed repeatedly at the floor. "We must make this work!"

As if conceding to the desperation of his words, the next time he slammed down the chunk, small shards flew up from the ground beneath it. Though not enough to see beneath, or even through the Milaratak'i, it was proof the plan could work and caused Kyrel to pause a second as he and the others stared at it, then at one another, with dumbfounded expressions. Then Tobias was grinning down at the thin sliver which had appeared.

"Well come on then!" he nodded. "What are we waiting on? Permission from the Queen?" Duly spurred on, he and Kyrel brought their chunks down again, faster and faster, each blow now coming down harder than the last.

"The Diun Sela Lekaa is begun," said Kyrel as they beat at the ground. "To bring the ka'aam shareê to a close now Lilly *must* have access to essence," he explained "If she cannot draw it from the ground here all other essence is forfeit."

"But you said no essence can pass through this thing," Harper spoke up, as if on a loop, her gaze shifting between Vereena's body, inert in Terrence's arms; Lilly zoned out and glowing; and Kyrel with his determined bashing. "What other essence is..." her words petered out, her eyes following Terrence's to Vereena; as he remembered so many of the things she'd told him: regardless of magickal ability *all* living beings in Azeron had essence. In some way it was an essential part of the very fibre of their being; something in their blood and vital to them.

Looking up, he scanned the cage to the best of his understanding, the mark they called the full Do'mass - on the back of Lilly's head - would make her the most powerful sentient being conceived in Azeron since their ancestors, the Tualavan, disappeared from the lands. Yet, it was the gradual diminishing of essence in the Da'ariel, which had ultimately caused their inherent lack of active magicks.

Just how much essence did they have to spare? And how much could a being as powerful as they hoped Lilly was about to become require to finish the Kalaareem by way of the Diun Sela Lekaa?

Seeing the glow in her lap begin to expand he turned slowly back to Kyrel.

"Can it be stopped?"

"Nydrel," the Deebanaarie spoke without looking up, "The Ka'aam Sharee is begun. It will finish only on its own."

Terrence looked down to the floor. Now that its surface had been breached, it was coming away relatively easily. Small as they were, pieces flew up with each fresh whack.

Another look Lilly's way showed the glow was still expanding; already encompassing most of her thighs and waist. Its brightness increasing as it spread through her body, growing at a slow, but steady pace.

Again Terrence's gaze fell to the ground, where shard after shard flew up as Kyrel and the others continued to work at it.

"It's not coming away fast enough is it?" he asked.

Kyrel's only response was to keep on beating,

"What have you done?"

Terrence shook his head and the obvious reprimand in his voice had Tobias asking, "What's the matter?" as Kyrel, still bashing, glanced up saying, "Only what I had to."

"How many of these Da'ariel have you put at risk?" asked Terrence.

"At risk?" Harper and Tobias paused in synch.

"These Da'ariel are not the only ones at risk," Kyrel smashed away more of the floor. "As the only other being of active magicks within the milaratak'i," he slammed his piece ever harder against the ground. "I am the first she will take from."

"Are you crazy?" Harper's eyes grew wide as she too began to understand. "What if she drains you all completely?"

"Then every Deebanaarie in here will also meet their end," he smacked the chunk down again. "And Lilly will have all the essence she needs to defeat my sister."

"At a cost of everyone in this cage?" Tobias shook his head.

"At a cost of your own life!" added Harper. "Slater wouldn't have wanted that. You should have told her-"

"Lilly will learn to understand my actions here today." Kyrel bashed and bashed but all any of them saw was more milaratak'i underneath what he smashed away. "As Azeron's rightful leader; she was born to make sacrifices."

"Sacrifices?" Tobias frowned as he looked around the cage.

Terrence was looking Lilly's way again; the glow had reached her ankles and two thirds of the way up her chest.

Outside the bars Mordrel could see it too. Her words were all native now, and the more she spoke the more agitated her voice became. Soon she was screaming at her troops, "Liensh ven! Liensh ven inst! Cat ya vac inst!" again the gates opened.

"Err... guys..." Harper shook her head as she watched the remaining Deebanaarie pouring into the cage. "Guys!" she raised her voice to get their attention. "Kyrel! I'm pretty sure your sister's done waiting on our surrender."

"Surren..." One look at the hordes now clashing with the remaining Da'ariel, and Kyrel dropped his piece of milaratak'i back in front of Tobias as he said, "Finish it!" Then bouncing up, he drew his sword, and ran to help defend Lilly.

"Oh hey sure," Tobias shouted after him. "Ain't like we weren't trying before or anything."

Kyrel wasn't listening - he couldn't - he, Liath and two others were presently all that stood between Lilly's incandescent form and a growing number of Deebanaarie converging on her position.

Despite his ill-timed sarcasm Tobias and Harper went back to beating at the ground again and it continued to shatter.

Tobias took another quick look Lilly's way; the glow, now bright enough to make him squint, had travelled down her arms as far as her wrists, and already encompassed everything else below her neck. Terrence was right: whatever was happening to her was happening too fast. It didn't matter how thick the milaratak'i was, it simply wasn't coming away in large enough pieces.

Yet the Ka'aam shareê was also taking too long. Unable to keep her eyes off the fight, Harper was looking every few seconds to Kyrel and the three Da'ariel warriors still surrounding Lilly. It took the four of them a great deal of slicing and hacking to keep the immediate area around her clear. It was a continuous melee; with each of them ducking, diving and leaping out of the way of the blades swinging at them.

The Da'ariel on the left of Liath took a hit: a Deebanaarie blade cut a deep slice into the top of his left thigh, forcing him to slump on one knee. This however, barely seemed to slow him down. Turning the momentary disadvantage into an advantage; he continued to fight from that lowered position. Chopping at the legs of two more Deebanaarie with his sword before he swung it backwards, a diagonal slice seemingly aimed at the ground, which tore through the ankle of the one who had wounded him.

Suddenly footless, the Deebanaarie howled, falling forward, and the same Da'ariel then swung his blade upward, running almost its entire length across his throat before he hit the ground. The Da'ariel bounced up and dived back into the fray with the others.

"Liensh ven! Liensh ven!" Mordrel continued her shrieking. "Cat ya vac inst!" More of her troops poured inside the cage.

Catching sight of the despair on his brother's face – as Terrence gazed down at the young Da'ariel girl, his lips moving continuously as he talked to her, despite her apparent lack of consciousness – Tobias beat harder at the ground.

The milaratak'i continued to give, but still it wasn't enough. Another look to Lilly, and he saw no part of her was now without the glow; all the way to its tips, her platinum blonde hair was significantly more brilliant than usual. Her hands remained either side of her, as good as glued to the floor, where Kyrel had placed them. Though her eyes were closed, her head was tipped back far enough that she faced the sky. It seemed she was also done chanting, as her mouth, now motionless, hung open to its widest.

"Crap!" Tobias let loose a fervent string of obscenities, as he continued bashing.

"Nydrel!" cried Mordrel. Realising too late what was happening within the cage, she ran for the gates herself; throwing her own troops aside. However, before she had a foot across the threshold Lilly let loose a heart stopping shriek. Aided by the unending stone wall of the vast crater it echoed around them and all other sound came to a stop.

This was no scream of fear, or pain, but of release, and both Da'ariel and Deebanaarie alike were compelled to stop all they were doing. Some were caught mid-leap and falling short of their targets landed hard on the ground yet even they hurried to roll over and stare at Lilly as the hot white light she had become, shot straight up in one solid beam.

For the longest few seconds, that beam maintained a length that went from Lilly to the height of the cage; one narrow, almost blinding pillar of light. Mesmerising was an understatement. From the way everyone stared up at it; it was clear no one present had seen any such a thing before.

After a few seconds, the pillar of light seemed to disperse, becoming instead billions of tiny sparks of yellow, each bouncing about amidst the top of the bars. Not only were they setting off the red sparks of the drakstorl t'fambroch, they appeared to be locked in a fierce dance with them.

Then all the sparks dived to the ground, yellow and red combined. Cries of terror rent the air from Da'ariel, Deebanaarie and classmates alike, all except Tobias ducked instinctively, arms raised over their heads.

About half-way down, the sparks re-converged; becoming one solid beam again only now - tainted by the red – it was considerably thicker and more a burning orange than the hot white light Lilly had released.

Mesmerising a sight as all this was, Tobias gave that beam of light little more than a cursory glance. Instead he beat harder and faster at the ground, smashing away shard after shard, his sights set on only one thing: easing his brother's pain.

The next thing he knew he was sent flying by a gasping Terrence and looking up as they rolled to a stop, they watched the butt of the light's beam come crashing down. It collided with the ground, right where he'd been bashing, then became stationary. One thick iridescent pillar swaying, as if influenced by the gentlest summer breeze.

Both brothers looked over at Lilly. It was difficult to tell beneath the vibrant glow that still clung to her but she also seemed to be swaying.

A loud crack rent the air and their attention was immediately drawn back to the ground, where, being the only ones close enough to see such detail, they, Kyrel, and Harper all watched as a mesh of hairline cracks began to light up in the milaratak'i floor.

These cracks quickly worked their way outward until their circumference was at least a metre wide.

Thin whip-like strands leapt out of the main beam, lacking its orange hue they were the same hot white as before.

Their movement appeared sentient: huge tentacles each lashing out and clamping onto separate bodies; striking Da'ariel and Deebanaarie without discrimination.

One swooped down and latched onto Kyrel. Catching him in the small of his back it lit him up and held him as if in suspended animation. Another lunged down beside Harper, causing Vereena to jerk as it plunged in through her midriff inches from where the dagger had entered.

"No!" screamed Terrence as she also lit up.

Then a louder cracking could be heard, and on the move again, the dazzling pillar of light roared down into the ground.

The fine cracks beneath the milarataki's surface faded, and with a series of thunderclaps from the ground, many larger cracks opened in their place.

Though there were considerably less of them, these new fissures ran to twice the length of those before, but only until the thick whip-like strands retracted from their victims, becoming one with the beams main body again, as it disappeared into the ground.

Complete silence followed and with it came a stillness, which seemed to weigh down the air itself. From Deebanaarie to Da'ariel, puzzled glances abounded.

In an instant Mordrel was yelling commands at her troops again, and as everyone remembered their weapons, scuffles began to break out.

However, few managed to do more than start something before Lilly expelled a second scream and the electric red of the drakstorl t'fambroch burst from her mouth just as the first light had. This time, instead of stopping at the top of the bars, it shot straight through them and kept ascending till it disappeared.

Seconds later, from far above them, a deep sad wailing could be heard. It reminded Harper of every recording she'd ever heard of the under-water cries from whales.

A huge shadow appeared over the cage, growing in seconds to encompass most of the cho'odzi's crater. All at once, everyone inside it realised one of the T'karas was falling. The frenzied scrambling that followed was unanimous.

Most of the Da'ariel ran toward Lilly; each intent on somehow protecting her, while the Deebanaarie almost trampled Mordrel in their efforts to exit the cage.

All of these actions were in vain. There was no time for escape and the creature's magnificent size made defending against its imminent collision a futile endeavour.

Fortunately, for all, its size also saved them. It smacked down on its back, directly over the top of the huge cage; the outer edges of one of its wings pierced by several of the thick milaratak'i bars.

Not yet dead, the T'karas continued its wailing. Its proximity and the acoustics within the crater made the sound painful; everyone covered their ears, while the few still standing, dropped to their knees, as others doubled over in agony.

Not that this stopped most from watching with rapt attention as the creature's other wing came down with a loud slap. It covered a vast section of the cage, plunging most of the area beneath it into darkness.

Finally the death moans stopped. Mordrel was the first on her feet. Kicking bodies, both dead and injured, from her path, she made her way toward the centre of the cage where Lilly remained motionless, her head still tipped back and her eyes still closed.

Others began clambering to their feet; many of the Da'ariel running at Mordrel, they swung their blades at her. She had only to wave them on, and following the motion of her hand, they flew across the cage, some skidding across the floor others slamming into the thick bars.

Liath rose as Mordrel passed him by and wasted no time leaping at her back. Spinning around she kicked him out of the air, then using the same force she had used on the other Da'ariel, pulled him against her hand shouting for everyone else to hear.

Although she spoke only the native language now and no one was immediately available to interpret, the three classmates got the gist as well as anyone else when Liath dropped to the ground; screaming as he rolled around in agony, until he stopped moving altogether and a burnt orange mush dribbled from his eye sockets and down his face.

Tobias turned away, grimacing as he fought the urge to regurgitate. As he did, he noticed Kyrel, barely recovered from the light's whip-lash at his back, slowly rising from the ground.

One of the fissures had opened next to him, and reaching out, he placed a hand across it, his other going out toward his sister, a line of fire shooting out of it.

Mordrel swung around, quelling the flames with an instinctive wave of her hand. Pausing to stare at it in stunned silence, she watched it fizzle out, then turning fully caught sight of Kyrel - barely up on all fours – her brother's pained expression told the truth of his weakened state.

An instant scowl formed on Mordrel's face and she unleashed yet another string of Azeronian that didn't need interpreting.

This family re-union was only ever going to go one of two ways: One of these siblings wasn't coming out alive, and given that Kyrel could barely achieve an upright position, it was easy to see why Mordrel began chuckling as she made her way toward him.

Shaking her head as she made her approach she switched languages again.

"How pitiful you have become brother. Do you know this word? It is one the humans use to describe a chorosh k'bar like you." Kyrel was too busy gasping to answer, and tilting her head Mordrel's expression became contemplative as she said, "Mairiel spent a lot of time learning words to describe you. That's right," she nodded in response to the doubt in his eyes. "She always intended to tell the girl of you, had some fine words picked out too. Then of course you made an appearance and well..." Mordrel shrugged, "ruined all of her plans... you are good at that, are you not brother?"

Again Kyrel raised his hand, shooting a second jet of flame after her. This time it barely reached to within a foot of her dark blue shoe before fizzling out on its own. Again Mordrel laughed, drawing closer with every word as she added. "Was she really worth it brother: filthying yourself up against the Da'ariel?"

The sight of him straining as he forced himself up on to shaky legs had her laughing more; guffawing the words. "Worse still, it seems their foolish persistence has grown upon you. You know you cannot protect this child, still you try. And for what brother? Is it because she too is pitiful? She cannot even contain her own essence! Is this really the best your filthy Da'ariel could bring into the world?" She gestured beyond him to where Lilly remained seated. "To think I would have let you return," Mordrel shook her head. "That you could have stood here at my side all these cycles past; all you had to do was bring me the girl Kyrel, had you the strength, you could have killed her yourself. All would have been forgiven."

Taking a moment to move a couple more bodies from her path with her powers she glared over at him.

"That you should think our people could ever know how you deigned to taint the D'vey bloodline…"

For Terrence, Mordrel's reason for switching from her language was made clear in that one sentence. She had things to say to her brother that she did not want her own troops to know.

Whether or not Kyrel was listening was another matter. From the way he swayed it was obvious a lot of concentration was already going into simply staying on his feet. Somehow he did manage, keeping his vaguely protective stance as he kept his back to Lilly, obscuring his sister's view of her, and the others. Seeing Vereena begin to stir, her eyes opening and her bleary gaze settling almost immediately on him, Terrence put a finger to his mouth, and keeping low crawled back to her as Mordrel was telling Kyrel, "The very idea that you still live sickens me."

With a grimace the young Da'ariel girl looked up at Terrence, her voice coming out in a raspy whisper.

"Ny Mech! It is so dark!"

"I know," he whispered as she attempted to push herself up with a wince. "You probably shouldn't," he pressed her gently back down. "You err… took a dagger in the back." Watching her reach around to feel it he gulped, nodding, "looks pretty bad. You err... you probably…"

With a deep groan she pulled out the blade, and nodding Terrence added, "…shouldn't pull it out..." before sighing. "Never mind," he finished, as she dropped it to the floor.

"If I do not move," Vereena hissed through her teeth. "I cannot protect cousin Lilly." Keeping one hand pressed against her wound, she tried a second time to get up, and again he pushed her back down.

"Don't you know what 'looks bad' means?" he glared to her side. "You've already lost a heap of blood. Now you've gone and pulled out the-"

"I cannot just lay here," she grabbed hold of his arm, using it to pull herself up before he could object further. "Mairiel is dead." Vereena's voice, wavered slightly but no other sign of emotion showed as she asked. "You do know what that means?"

"Err…" Terrence's eyebrow bobbed up as he somewhat dubiously asked, "that Lilly just made Queen?"

"I should be at her side." nodded Vereena.

"No," He shook his head holding her back. "Kyrel has magicks, what can you do that he-"

"You do not understand." She attempted to wriggle free of his grasp, but her wound proved too much of a hindrance, and instead she ended up clinging to him as Tobias and Harper appeared either side of them.

"Is she going to be OK?" asked Harper.

"No," Terrence shook his head as he held Vereena close. "Not if I can't stop her from getting back in the fight."

"Kyrel is already weakened." Vereena pulled away again.

"And you're not?" Terrence glared at her.

"Terrence Emerson," she shook her head at him. "At his strongest Kyrel is little match for his sister. Here within this much milaratak'i… within the cho'odzi… where there is already so little life," she shook her head. "Too few of his powers can be called on for him to hold her off much longer.

"Least he has powers!" shrugged Harper. "What the crap have we got?"

With an awesome effort Vereena managed to push herself off Terrence, wincing as she took a second to steady herself, clinging to his arm for support again; a sharp hiss escaping her tightly gritted teeth. "Kyrel cannot protect Lilly alone. He *must* have help!"

Mordrel was still goading Kyrel. "You could still return home," she was telling him now. "You are my brother Kyrel; take her life yourself and we shall see how generous I feel."

Still shaky on his feet he finally spoke up, his voice barely above a whispered wheeze. "I will not… allow you to do-"

"Allow!" Mordrel glared at him. "*You*… will not 'allow'… *me*!" she shook her head, "Mother truly was a fool: letting you spend so much time in study, when you should have been in training as my first. See now how you do not know your place… As if the wisdoms of the ancestors could ever be truly understood by you: A male… Ha! Your head is too full of moolach, Kyrel. You can barely sustain the Kratack, yet I have grown far stronger in your absence. You should have stayed away brother…" she grinned, "what could I possibly have to fear from you now?"

Less than a metre from him now, she could barely contain herself for laughter. "Perhaps… you intend to fall on me… that is about all you look capable of." Turning around she spoke to her troops, translating something of similar effect to them.

A rumble of skittish laughter went through those few still physically capable of showing amusement and turning back to Kyrel she smirked.

"You think you taste victory now? That in preventing me from reclaiming the girl's thar you have somehow won? What a fool you are. Powers or not I will still have her essence." A scowl crossed Mordrel's face as she added, "If only to see that victory become rot in your mouth brother - when you watch me do as you should have done so long ago."

"Nydrel," Kyrel shook his head, "As long as I still have the breath to stan-"

"Then you shall have no breath!" Mordrel's hand went up, and so did Kyrel's, though he was immediately pulled toward her; the heels of his boots squeaking across the smooth ground, his demise seemingly imminent; a stalemate of wills followed. With each of them creating a vacuum: a reverse of Lilly's ability to create gusts – they were caught up in a tug-o-war without a rope.

"You really want to do this brother? You are already so weak…" Mordrel spoke through gritted teeth, a slight but obvious strain in her voice. "You know you cannot stop me," she told him. "End this now and I shall make your death a swift one."

There was no response from Kyrel, he was concentrating every iota of his strength on not being sucked across to her. But that strength was failing fast. Taking a chance he tilted his palm away, and quickly raised his other hand, again a line of fire blasted toward Mordrel. Only this time her powers lent it strength, and unable to outmanoeuvre herself, she was soon a shrieking fireball.

The brightness of the blaze lit up the entire crater and everybody watching was again forced to shield their eyes.

Kyrel was no exception, having toppled onto his rear, he sat watching his sister hop and whirl, tearing off her outer garments and hurling them to the ground.

Extinguishing the flames with a wave of her hand, she stood a moment, swathed in a halo of thick smoke that remained visible as the area re-darkened, then she fell to her knees coughing.

The long blonde hair, which had adorned her head, was now a crisp black lump on the top of her scalp, her brows and lashes had suffered the same and the skin of her cheeks, nose and her forehead were mottled with seared red patches.

The acrid stink of cooked meat and singed hair assailed the nostrils of everybody close enough.

"Nice!" Tobias muttered, as he paused from crawling to appreciate the spectacle. However, seeing Mordrel reach for the nearest living body; a semi-conscious Deebanaarie with a badly twisted leg and a run of stab wounds going diagonally across his chest, they watched as she lay a hand across that lacerated chest and grimacing Harper said, "Not so nice for him." as a murky orange glow began seeping from the soldier into Mordrel. It snaked its way up her arm fading just past the shoulder. Beneath her hand the soldier convulsed, as the skin on his face began sagging, before bubbling and dribbling into a thick blancmange-like puddle on the floor.

Watching with grim fascination, Terrence was thankful he'd had so little to eat over the past few days. Although he and the other classmates could barely believe their eyes, as the black lump of charred hair slid off Mordrel's head and new hair began growing in, he knew she was sapping the Deebanaarie of his life-force.

Though the process happened swiftly, it gave Kyrel the chance to get back on his feet - a mighty effort with grunts, gasps, and the odd hiss of pain. Yet somehow he managed to be up and back in his fighting stance a second before she too was on her feet.

Mordrel turned to face him, her hair back to at least a quarter of its previous length, and her burns completely gone.

When she spoke again her voice carried with it all the vehemence of the flames which had burnt her.

"That... brother... was your biggest mistake yet!" Again she made her approach, shaking her head as she added. "A swift death would have been too good for you. No... you shall join the ranks of my shraeka, so your agonies can be as endless as they shall be boundless."

"Always you have had more words than sense, Sister," wincing Kyrel spoke in short gasps. "You plan with more ambition than wisdom." He shook his head. "You remain as cut off in here as I. If anything my powers give me the advantage," shaking with exhaustion he pulled his sword from his belt, "the dres verfelt can only give back so much. Eventually you will be losing more than you gain if you continue to try your magicks on me. "Ny," he shook his head. "To end this you shall have to try another method."

For a moment Mordrel glared at him, her eyes hot shards of anger which few could see in the darkened cage. Then she said, "as you wish brother," it was clear from her voice that she spoke through a smirk and as she did, she used her power to raise a nearby sword from the ground.

Kyrel squinted, watching its blade glint in the darkness as it travelled butt first toward her. However, with his and everyone else's attention diverted, Mordrel swung out her other arm and a magnesium-white flash, crackled from her hand, briefly abolishing the dark.

Kyrel turned in time to pull a stunned face as the brunt of the strike caught him across the left side of his cheek and forked off to dance down that side of his body.

It was he who shrieked now, shocked in more ways than one, he dropped to his knees. His sword clattering to the ground as his hands flew to his face; in a vain attempt to subdue the immense pain there.

"You think I would lower myself by locking blades with you?" Mordrel asked through an escalating chuckle.

"Shit!" gasped Terrence, "Come on." He set off crawling toward them again.

"Seriously bro," Tobias caught hold of his ankle. "You did just see that right? What the hell are we supposed to do against somebody who shoots lightning from their hands?"

"I don't know," Terrence shook his head as he turned back to Tobias adding, "But Veer's right, if Kyrel falls…" the sentence didn't require finishing, instead they both began scanning the immediate area for a solution.

The sword Mordrel had used as her ruse lay on the ground again. Oblivious of it now, she raised both hands, separate strikes leapt from the fingertips of each, zapping her brother a second time.

While one caught Kyrel on the chest, just below his left shoulder, the other hit the top of his right leg. Crying out, he jittered violently at the end of each stream of lightning. Revelling in her power, Mordrel kept these on him far longer than the initial strike. When she finally released him, he toppled onto his side; charred, smoking and undeniably crippled. "You arrogant fool!" she made her way toward him. "Do you truly think yourself the only D'vey still capable of developing new magicks?" Kyrel rolled onto his front, trying in vain to push himself up. His head got no higher than an inch off the ground before his sister was standing over him.

Placing a foot on the back of his neck she pressed his blackened face against the ground. Kyrel couldn't even whimper; he was too weak to do anything but lay there as she gazed down at him.

"Now you will see," said Mordrel "I shall leave you just enough essence to understand what is happening when the girl dies at my hands."

Terrence was just grabbing hold of the twice-discarded short-sword, when Tobias grabbed hold of his ankle again.

"Hey wait," he pointed. "Look," From their position they had a clear view of Lilly. Until now she had been statuesque: frozen in the exact position she'd been in when the first pillar of light had lurched from her mouth.

Now as the twins watched, her head began lowering, stopping only when she faced a more normal, forward angle.

Mordrel was too preoccupied with tormenting her brother to notice that just off to the side of her, Lilly was awakening.

Abruptly she rose from the ground, her movement reminiscent of a silk handkerchief being tugged upward on a thread. To the twins it appeared to happen in a blink, and though they couldn't be certain in the darkness; she seemed a lot like she was floating.

"I don't think this is down to Kyrel anymore." Tobias told his brother.

"Right," muttered Terrence, "I don't think it's down to any of us anymore."

Together they watched as Lilly; definitely floating, glided silently towards Mordrel's back.

"Even if our people knew the truth," she was telling Kyrel. "You truly believe they would ever allow you to defile our line? That your tainted blood could ever take the place of their true Queen? Your life is given up for nothing brother…" Removing her foot from his neck, she waved a hand over him, immediately his body was rising from the ground to meet her. "What would you have me do…" she asked as he hovered ever higher "submit to the Doloch Ty of a deserter? Ny," she shook her head. "It is you who has more ambition than sense …and now you shall have the full reward of that ambi-"

Coming in from the left; Lilly tapped Mordrel's right shoulder. The Deebanaarie queen turned to glance behind. Unfamiliar with this common schoolyard prank, she scowled at finding no one there; her confusion as inevitable as her next move, and the second she looked the other way, Lilly socked her one: square in the jaw.

Kyrel's blackened body thudded to the ground, forgotten by his sister, as she raised a hand to her startled face and Lilly said.

"A little something new for you to learn from the human world… Karma's a bitch – Bitch!" a second blow knocked Mordrel clear off her feet.

"Yes!" Tobias punched the air and not daring to take his eyes off the action, Terrence, raised an uncertain eyebrow.

Lilly raised a hand, waving it at Mordrel and sent a gust strong enough to send her flying backwards across the cage and into its thick bars.

This knocked the wind out of the Deebanaarie Queen, and while she clawed the ground, struggling to get up, Lilly glanced down at Kyrel.

The sight of him hit her hard and her immediate thought was to help him, but alarm rang out in the form of a call from Terrence.

"Slater! Watch out!"

Whirling around she saw Mordrel's hand aimed at her. Lilly found herself moving aside with such unexpected ease that she was several feet out of the way when the lighting lurched from Mordrel's palm.

"Whoa!" muttered Tobias; his voice echoing the surprise of everyone present; including Lilly, whose bizarrely peaceful facial expression now seemed as perplexed as the Deebanaarie queen was outraged.

Again Mordrel struck out at Lilly, and again she was out of the way before the white hot sparks reached within feet of where she'd been; the only difference being that this time she moved in the opposite direction.

A growl of frustration escaped Mordrel, her lips a snarl, as her eyes darted about and she began yelling in Azeronian.

All at once those of her troops not incapacitated seemed to shake off their own stunned demeanours and getting back on their feet began running at Lilly with their weapons drawn.

"Oh crap!" hissed Terrence, as the Da'ariel also came out of their stupor, and scuffles broke out around them.

A Deebanaarie near the twins turned, catching sight of them and seeing the blade in Terrence's hand, ran at them swinging his sword. Rolling aside Terrence screamed as the blade came down where he'd been.

Dropping his sword, he scurried away as fast as all four of his limbs would carry him. He was so focused on getting out of the situation, he only realised Tobias wasn't with him as he got to within a few feet of the girls.

Vereena's tonic appeared to be working; despite her injury she was back on her feet, with her dagger in hand, and a determined scowl on her face; she positioned herself somewhat unsteadily between Harper and a handful of Deebanaarie.

Like her, the few other remaining Da'ariel were also occupied in combat. Realising none of them would be coming to aid him, Terrence glanced up over his shoulder, and seeing the same Deebanaarie still pursuing him - sword raised high for a second lunge - he rolled aside again, landing on his back in time to watch the blood smeared blade come down inches from his ear.

Relentless as he was terrifying, the Deebanaarie warrior wasted no time raising his sword a third time, and trying to roll back the other way. Terrence knew he was moving too slow.

There just wasn't anyway he could outmanoeuvre this snarling warrior above him, screaming, he watched the sword coming down toward his face. However, before it reached him, the Deebanaarie's face crumpled and toppling to the right he went down hard.

Terrence's gaze went with him: he watched the warrior grimace more with anger than pain as he pressed a hand to the huge gash spurting blood out the top of his left thigh. Stunned, Terrence glanced up, catching a look of similar surprise on his brother's face. While there had been no real skill in his attack, the element of surprise had made it effective enough, affording them at least a moment's respite.

Tobias doubled over, panting for breath, with the twice discarded short-sword now grasped firmly in both hands.

This was however all he had time for before Terrence saw the Deebanaarie attempting to get up and yelled out his brother's name. With a look of panic and an absolute lack of hesitation; Tobias ran forward. He brought the sword down hard, lopping off three fingers on the hand the warrior had been using for support.

Letting out a howl, the Deebanaarie fell flat on his face, then growling with anger, began getting up again. Seeing Tobias take another few swings at him - the force of each blow being enough to make him hit the ground afresh, with the blade ricocheting off the back of his armour – Terrence realised no real damage was being done, and fearing the Deebanaarie may regain his equilibrium any second, began yelling.

"His neck Tobes, get the neck! Go for the throat!"

Shifting on one foot, Tobias swung around, and jabbing downward with all his might, put a significant portion of the blade through the side of the warrior's neck. A fountain of blood sprayed upward, splattering him all over – face included – and leaving the short-sword sticking out of the dead Deebanaarie's neck like a garish blood soaked cocktail stick, he stumbled backward staring at the corpse.

Getting up, Terrence caught his brother before he could fall over, and hearing a voice boom out above them they looked up to see Lilly floating high above the heads of everyone present. "Diam lutor, di ti enkart, durst Mai Leyavanya," said Lilly with that same bright yellow glow which had ensconced her entire body before, now confined to her eyes.

Whatever she'd said put an immediate stop to all the fighting as everyone turned to gaze up at her. "Divula lanasta kator?" she shook her head at them, her words carrying more than a hint of reprimand. "Nuath lienth d'lor ki ti!" She smiled down at Deebanaarie and Da'ariel alike.

As Tobias and Terrence looked around at them; all mesmerised by the awesome sight that Lilly had become, Harper poked her head out from behind Vereena so she could watch also.

"Ti durst lek ti Mai." Lilly added, "Viesh di ti lek ensha Mai Mai. Ek tanak ek lavuck di inst Doloch ty-"

A horrific shriek came from Mordrel and again she lashed out. Another streak of magnesium white blazed across at Lilly.

Despite the suddenness of the attack Lilly seemed the only one not taken by surprise. Her movements remaining as fluid as before, she whooshed through the air, moving aside faster than Mordrel could aim. Along came a second strike, then a third and fourth; with Mordrel letting loose further angry shrieks, as she tried several more times to catch Lilly with those same fearsome bolts she'd used on Kyrel; so demoralising the Da'ariel hopes: hopes, which Lilly was now returning to them three-fold as she glided aside avoiding them effortlessly.

"I don't get it?" Tobias straightened up and gazed around muttering. "What happened? Why did they all stop attacking? They're not even trying to help Mordrel… why not?"

"Because she is unworthy…" Vereena's voice came out as a tight little gasp from behind the twins. They spun around to find her wincing; one hand pressed to her injured side, her other arm slung over Harper for support.

Immediately Terrence was at their side, taking her weight on to him, his voice all concern as he asked "What do you mean unworthy?"

"Does it matter?" asked Harper "The fighting's stopped, that's good enough for me."

"I ain't complaining. But she's their Queen; shouldn't she be pretty damn worthy?"

Gazing around at the mesmerised faces Tobias shook his head.

"Nevermind that... when did Slater learn Azeronian?" Together the four of them stared up at the trailing yellow light that was Lilly circling the cage, easily evading the shots Mordrel was still taking at her.

Suddenly she stopped, and turned to fully face Mordrel.

Vereena and the classmates gasped as she was buffeted by the full strength of Mordrel's next lightning blast. Lilly wavered in mid-air for a second, before leaning into the waves of electricity, steadying herself like someone facing a heavy wind. The power crackled across her skin, seeming to flow through her body. The glow in her eyes blazed even brighter as she drew strength from Mordrel's attack.

"What in the fuck..." muttered Tobias.

Lilly raised her palm, and everyone – including Mordrel – looked on in confusion as a cloud of thick vapour accumulated before it. Then, muttering something none of them could hear, she waved her hand directing the mist. In an instant the vapour solidified into dozens of fine shards and a light flick of her hand sent those shards hurtling toward Mordrel. Again the 'unworthy' queen was shrieking, only this time there was considerably more fear in it.

Several shards shattered against the bars and floor around her but a great majority hit home; embedding themselves deep into her body, and extracting a scream of agony in the process.

"Holy Shit!" squeaked Tobias, "What was that?"

All at once he and Harper seemed to be hopping with excitement, as they talked over each other, asking a flurry of questions.

"Was that water?" Harper was frowning; whereas Tobias, apparently having difficulty finishing the simplest of thoughts asked, "What just... Did she just... Was that..."

"Yes." Vereena gave the one answer to each of their questions, as like them she stared on in amazement.

"When did she learn that?" Terrence was asking now, "I don't remember her learn-"

Vereena placed a hand over his, conveying all she needed with a look, and they both turned back to see Mordrel looking around for the nearest living body to drain, as she had done after Kyrel's attack on her.

This time however, she was not as fortunate. Having been flung to the edge of the cage she was now several feet from any bodies, living or otherwise.

Lilly waved a hand her way and a heavy gust lifted Mordrel off the ground.

With a second wave she brought her slamming back down, and with a third; she sent her flying up so hard, that upon hitting the carcass of the T'karas above them, the Deebanaarie queen burst through its thick flesh, sending large splatters of blood and mucous down on a significant number of the onlookers.

"Eww!" Harper's mouth fell open as a large splodge landed on her shoulder.

When she looked up again Lilly was no longer floating; she was kneeling at Kyrel's side, apparently oblivious of everyone else watching her and each other with uncertain expressions on their faces.

With Terrence's continued support, Vereena and the other two headed for the pair. Watching, as turning Kyrel over, Lilly cradled him in her arms, and proceeded to lay a hand on his forehead.

On reaching them, Vereena dropped to her knees.

"Cousin you truly are-"

Lilly turned to face her and seeing Lilly's eyes still glowed yellow, both Terence and the Da'ariel girl gasped.

"Ny dilur!" muttered Vereena.

"Timur Am Ness Vereena, velair d'tat. Siiem tae," smiled Lilly.

"OK, seriously," Harper shook her head as she and Tobias reached them also. "What's with you speaking native all of a sudden? When the fuck did that happen?"

"When my people lent me their essence." Lilly glanced her way, the yellow behind her eyes making them seem oddly distant. "I am sorry you were injured." She turned back to Vereena, and reaching out pressed a hand to her cousin's back where the dagger had gone in.

Despite all they'd seen, the classmates stared in amazement as that same light that persisted in Lilly's eyes began glowing there too.

Vereena looked down, her mouth falling open as a deep warmth brought with it an odd but distinct sensation. The second Lilly removed her hand the younger girl was pulling aside her tunic and shaking her head.

"This cannot..." her eyes followed Lilly's hand back to Kyrel's forehead, and looking every bit as stunned as the others, she watched that same glow seep into the Deebanaarie. It gradually filled his body, changing his skin - mottled with charred patches - back to its former healthy state.

As the light reached the tips of Kyrel's toes he opened his eyes, and echoing Vereena murmured, "Ny Dilur!"

Gulping, he pushed himself up into a sitting position so he could better stare into Lilly's iridescent eyes.

"Timur Fai lek Kyrel," She smiled, "velair d'tat. Siiem tae."

"Quim an," Kyrel shook his head. His lower lip trembled and his eyes welled up, "nassana d'elth," he added "ta'taa lisk mina. K'tek vota-"

"Ny." Lilly's smile grew as she put a finger to his lips. "T'tait d'elth vieenst kathor." Holding his gaze she nodded, "Diesh ven Fai lek Kyrel."

"What's going on?" Keeping his voice low Tobias tugged on his brother's arm, "Why isn't anyone speaking English anymore?"

"Err..." Terrence whispered into Vereena's ear. "What are they saying?"

Vereena could barely take her eyes from Lilly, as she answered in a confused whisper of her own. "These words... they are... Tualavan..."

"Tualavan?" Harper raised an eyebrow. "As in the huge mess of tunnels we went through to escape the village?"

"Not exactly," Terrence shook his head, his gaze fixed on Lilly. His mind reeled with all he'd learned about Azeron's history. "Tualavan wasn't the tunnels, it was the capitol, it's also what the Da'ariel call their Ancestors who lived there."

"Yes," agreed Vereena in an awe filled whisper. "It seems cousin Lilly now speaks the language of our ancestors..."

"How is that even possible?" asked Harper.

"I... I cannot..." Vereena shook her head. "I am sorry." She finally tore her gaze from Lilly, turning instead to Terrence. "I am unsure how to completely translate."

"Then just give us the gist," shrugged Harper.

"Gist?" she shook her head, eyes flitting over Lilly and Kyrel before returning to Terrence. "I do not think I-"

"Just tell us what's been said so far," interjected Tobias. Terrence's tone was more apologetic.

"We're kind of out of the loop since no one's speaking our language anymore."

"Yes," nodded Vereena "yes, of course... err." turning back to keep watching she added, "Cousin Lilly thanked us, for the essence we each gave to her."

"And that's why Kyrel looks like he might break down any second?" Harper sounded dubious. "Must a been some thank you."

"Ny, ny..." Vereena shook her head. "He does not believe he did enough. He says he failed her, that he is unworthy of her thanks."

"Failed her!" Harper shook her head. "How much more does he think he could have..."

"Kel ven yath lek," Lilly was saying now as she pressed a hand to Kyrel's chest. Foreign as the language was, compassion was clear in her words. "Tes vai, shan lek." She placed the same hand at her own chest, in a fist, giving him the customary head bow.

"Ny, ny!" Alarm was obvious in Kyrel's voice as he glanced nervously about them, clearly aware of the intrigued audience. "Nydrel!"

All near enough were watching with avid fascination - their faces an equal measure of awe and uncertainty. "D'mousk kel t'vey," Kyrel shook his head, and reaching out, gently closed a hand over Lilly's fist,

"Siiem tae, Mai Lilliath. Vor lesh ka kel kek t'vey."

"He thanks her..." whispered Vereena. "...and says she belittles herself in bowing to him."

"Ny," Lilly was shaking her head again; gently pushing Kyrel's hand away, so she could put hers to her chest again, "Dirlisk kek, t'vey... Fai lek Kyrel."

Terrence watched him nod, a grateful yet fearful look in his eyes as he again looked around them.

"Fai lek?" Harper's face screwed up. "What's Fai lek? Why does she keep saying that?" Seeing Vereena's gaze shift as she bit down on her lip, Tobias shrugged, "What? You don't know or you don't want to tell us?"

"This is... not for me to say..." Vereena spoke with obvious embarrassment, then she was bowing her head as Lilly turned their way. Lilly's hot yellow gaze moved slowly over all of them before settling on Vereena as she said,

"There is no wrong in what they ask you cousin."

Moving with that same fluid grace she had before, she rose from the ground and made her way to where Baxter and the branch remained fused within

305

their globule of mucus.

"Such simple creatures these humans are," she knelt at his side, staring curiously down at him. "So frail. So easily damaged."

"Hey!" Harper raised an eyebrow. "Who's she calling frail and..." her words trailed off as Lilly added, "Yet they experience…" realisation seemed to dawn on her and turning Vereena's way she frowned, "Their world has affected me."

"Yes," nodded Vereena, "A risk that needed to be taken… will you still be able-"

"Veyhi!" Lilly stated, with the certainty of freshly confirmed facts. "I am not diminished. There is so much... so many… emotions within this body…" she let her head tip slightly to look down on Baxter again. "For this one, we feel... regret, loss." Her eyes closed and her face became the picture of sadness. "So much sorrow."

"Grief," suggested Terrence, and again he was facing that eerie yellow stare of hers. With a gulp he shrugged "Lilly was…Well I... I guess we all kind of figured he was a goner, so yeah, I'm pretty sure grief is what you're feeling"

"Grief," Lilly's head tilted to one side. "You are right… this is…" gasping she swayed, then closing her eyes again steadied herself before opening them. "It infuses our essence." Looking back down at Baxter she nodded, "There is much feeling for this one. His suffering... it is too much."

Seeing her push a hand in through the thick pinkish brown goo, that still covered Baxter; Harper almost dived on them both.

"Hey, hey wait..." She stepped forward, "what're you-"

"Please no…" Vereena put a hand to the other girl's chest, as did Terrence nodding, "I think we have to trust her."

In spite of his words there was similar concern on his face, and seeing this Vereena nodded. "You must *all* trust her," before turning back to watch as yet again light poured out of Lilly.

"But Baxter's not even from this world," insisted Harper, "How do we know that's even gonna..."

"I think it's OK," Terrence put a hand on her shoulder and she followed his gaze to where the entire sack of mucous was now glowing, the light seeming to pulse as it increased in brightness.

Seconds later, when it was almost too bright to look at, it dissolved into a fine dust, each speck glowing individually as they fell down around Baxter, or swirled away on the slight breeze that wafted about inside the cho'odzi.

The huge chunk of tree was also gone, and as Vereena dropped her arm, Harper and Terrence both rushed forward, falling to their knees beside Lilly; Terrence immediately set about checking Baxter over.

Finding torn clothes and patches of damp blood, but no sign of any actual injury he couldn't help grinning when Baxter's eyelids fluttered open, and he grumbled; "Yeah, you can quit groping me now mate." Then he caught sight of Lilly watching him; her face serene and her eyes glowing and blinking profusely. Baxter pushed himself up to get a better look at her as he whispered, "Holy shit! All of that really just happened… you took out Mordrel."

"Welcome back Robert."

"Robert?" Harper's nose wrinkled as if offended on Baxter's behalf.

"How can you know about Mordrel..." asked Terrence, "You were," he frowned, shaking his head as he muttered. "At least I thought you were unconscious."

"I was," nodded Baxter. "At least I *think* I was." Biting his lip, he stared down at the floor, shaking his head as he added. "I remember being stuck in a tree... then everything went dark... I... I guess I passed out but then..." he shook his head again. "Then there was light, the most amazing fucking light."

"What, like... the-end-of-the-tunnel kinda light?" Harper looked doubtful. "Did you hear voices too, or see a long dead relative beckoning to you?"

"No." Narrowing one eye at her, Baxter shook his head, "It wasn't anything like that, alright. This light was... it was everywhere and frightening but real beautiful," his brow dipped. "a-and I saw fire... and I think there was ice."

"So you woke up during the fight?" asked Terrence.

"No." Baxter looked up, glancing his way. "I was unconscious right here," Baxter patted the floor. "I saw that too."

Equally confused Tobias asked, "Saw that too? So what, you had an out-of-body experience?"

"No!" Baxter turned to stare at Lilly, unperturbed by the glow in her eyes, "It was you..." he nodded, his lower lip trembling, in much the same way Kyrel's had. "You came to me, I... I... I saw..."

"What you saw was-"

"The things you'd seen!" Baxter finished the sentence for her.

"What?" Terrence's gaze shifted between them. "How did you-"

"Yes," Lilly nodded at Baxter, "We shared our essence with you."

"OK, that just sounds dirty." Harper's hands went up and she threw the twins a dubious look. Neither Lilly nor Baxter was listening.

"It was necessary to heal your wounds." Lilly was saying.

"I know," Baxter nodded "I... I more than saw things. I think... I think I knew things too... like you were telling me stuff as you... as you fixed me... too much for me to remember now," he shook his head, frowning again. "But I think I knew that too."

"Mmm hmm," nodded Lilly, "Do you remember that we would not have shared the essence with you if it were not-"

"Yes," said Baxter, his voice cracking slightly as he raised it. "I remember," he nodded. "It's OK. I understand. I still know enough, to know I'm OK with this... really, i... it's fine. Actually it's kind of amazing. Thank you."

"What's fine?" asked Tobias, "What's amazing?"

Lilly was already shaking her head, her smile as comforting as that of a mother offering her child warm milk and a cookie.

"No thanks necessary Robert," she said before floating up onto her feet again.

"Yeah, well, I'm still confused here," said Harper. "Someone wanna tell me what the hell just happened?"

"Oh hey," it was Baxter's turn to raise both hands. "If I understood," he shrugged, "I would."

"But you just said you understand."

"Sure," agreed Baxter "A few things, but not everything!"

Seeing Terrence raise a quizzical eyebrow, he shrugged. "Look, all I'm certain of is I was at death's door and on the losing side of a bloody battle." His gaze remained on Lilly as she neared Vereena, "Now I'm all patched up and somehow I know Slater single-handedly won this war while I was out of it! It's kinda confusing actually, but I'm not gonna knock it."

"Won the war?" Again Terrence was raising an eyebrow as Harper got up shrugging.

"Well I just hope you can walk," she offered Baxter a hand adding, "cos I don't think we're getting a taxi out of here."

Pushing her hand away he got to his feet grinning, "I'm a hundred and ten percent."

Giving Lilly a wary look, Terrence asked, "So do you know anything else?"

"Like what?" they watched her float Kyrel's way, nodding for him to get up.

Lowering her voice, Harper whispered from behind her hand,

"Like why all of a sudden she's speaking the language of the ancients and referring to herself as we?"

"She is?" asked Baxter a bemused look on his face, "I don't think I noticed."

"Mmm hmm," Tobias nodded, "It's kind of odd."

The classmates watched her speaking with Kyrel, who continued to look humbled. A second later Baxter was saying, "Hey, far as I'm concerned... them that go around performing miracles can talk however the hell they want."

"Miracles..." Lilly turned to look at them, her expression thoughtful. "...Is not the entire existence of this world a miracle by the standards of the human world?"

"Well, yeah," he shrugged "You've got me there." Stuffing his hands in his pockets he nodded, "It's just that these guys are a little-"

"We are aware of their concerns." Lilly eyed each of them in turn, her eyes settling on Tobias: standing a short ways off from the others, with his hands stuffed deep in his pockets and a desolate look on his face. "Even those concerns which are not voiced are known to us."

As the others looked his way, Tobias averted his eyes, and turning back to them she said, "Whispering works only for those forced to rely upon hearing."

"Right," Baxter nodded, "Of course... they didn't mean to-"

"What do you mean, of course?" Harper scowled. "Like that made any sense!" She shook her head, "Look, I don't mean to be rude, but what the hell have you done with Slater?"

Lilly's smile widened as she said, "Isn't that just like the humans?" She turned her smile on Vereena. "My last Qin Am Ness. You alone know the truth of what we are. How we came to be."

"Yes," nodded Vereena, her arm going across her chest. "I am Qin Am

Ness. To carry the knowledge of you is my duty."

"Knowledge of?" Terrence shook his head. "You mean knowledge *for* right?"

Lilly turned to him, the glow in her eyes making the hairs on his neck rise. "There has always been more to the duties of a Qin Am Ness than any but they have ever known…" she explained.

"Duties like what?" asked Harper. "Who… or…what the hell are you?"

"I'm still the girl you knew," she nodded, and Tobias mumbled, "Yeah… well your eyes beg to differ."

Lilly's next smile was all amusement as she closed her eyes then reopened them. There was no sign of the light and looking to him she asked. "Is this more to your liking?" Instead of answering he looked back down at the ground and turning back to Harper, Lilly said, "You see… I'm still she."

"But you're more now too aren't you?" asked Terrence. "You're speaking some ancient Azeronian language a…and… you took out Mordrel with magicks Kyrel hasn't even taught Slater yet."

"I am different," agreed Lilly.

"Because of that light, right… that was your essence… the real you… and those other lights, the ones that came out of it those were…"

"You know what they were," she told him. "And I see that you do not approve, but I required more strength to break through the milaratak'i. Taking what I needed from my people was a necessary measure."

"Necessary!" Anger flashed in Terrence's eyes. "Veer was already injured when you *'borrowed'* her essence. You could have-"

"Ny diesh ver!" hissed Kyrel, his intention to spring obvious enough to make Terrence cringe away, an arm going up over his face.

"Nydrel!" said Lilly, her hand rising to halt the Deebanaarie - although the calm in her voice was apparently enough.

Not for Baxter though - he took Terrence completely by surprise: slapping him hard up the side of the head and literally spitting with rage as he yelled, "You watch your fucking mouth!"

"Hey! What the fuck?" Terrence dropped his arm as he turned to glare at Baxter, "Seriously? I'm looking out for all of us here… how the hell is that a problem for-"

"It's a problem if you're gonna be talking to her that way!" Baxter squared up to him. "Show some fucking respect or I'll-"

"What…" Tobias joined his brother. Shoving Baxter backward as he added, "… Come on then. Tell us what you'll do!"

"I'll show you what I'm gonna…" he drew his arm back with a mighty swing, his hand balling into a fist, aimed squarely at Tobias's face.

"Robert!" The harsh disapproval in Lilly's voice stopped him instantly; his arm hovering mid-way between himself and Tobias; his face a mixture of determination and confusion.

Sucking in his lips he glared at the twins a moment longer, eyes flitting from one to the other - both stared at him as though he'd gone crazy. "No!" Lilly told him; her tone softer but every bit as stern. Baxter shook his head, arm returning slowly to his side.

"No one should be talking to you like that…" he turned to look at her. "It's… it's… I won't let them! I can't!"

"You can and you will," said Lilly, her voice commanding yet soothing.

"What the hell has she done to him?" Harper whispered near Tobias's ear as she sidled closer to the twins.

"Dunno," he shook his head, "Some kind of mind control?" he suggested, with a glance to his brother.

"Couldn't tell you," Terrence shrugged "Maybe it's-"

"There is no need for concern." Lilly assured them. "Robert remains influenced by the essence I shared with him. His loyalty and the desire to defend me are little more than unavoidable side effects, most of which should pass soon enough." She looked from Baxter to Vereena and on to Kyrel. "Must I remind you of their efforts? The milaratak'i would not have been weakened were it not for these three," she turned back to smile at them. "They have not been touched, they have no way to know who they address… but they *have* earned the right to ask questions," She nodded Vereena's way, and taking a step back the young girl bowed her head. Lilly's gaze moved on, landing next on Kyrel as she said, "And you will have to learn tolerance Fai Lek. It is true the ways of the humans are very different from those of our world. However their help will be most valuable if your daughter is to carry on what has begun this day."

Kyrel also stepped back, bowing his head as Vereena had done. Lilly turned to Baxter, smiling as she shook her head. "You *know* we have no desire to see any of you harm each other…" taking a moment she looked out across the crowd. Every eye was on her; the Da'ariel and Deebanaarie all listening as intently as if they could still understand her words. "Everybody here means a great deal to us," said Lilly as she turned back to Baxter. She raised an eyebrow at him.

"Yeah…" he mumbled with genuine remorse as he stepped aside, and she made her way toward them, "I… I'm sorry," added Baxter, "I didn't mean-"

"It is OK." Lilly said as she came to a stop in front of Harper and the twins. Tobias kept his eyes low, a disgruntled wary look on his face, whereas Terrence, attempting to focus on her, showed a whole different kind of apprehension: his eyes drawn consistently to Baxter for cautious glances.

"He will not strike you again."

"So what; until your essence wears off he's like your lap dog?" asked Harper as she threw Baxter a wary glance shrugging, "Sorry to be the one to say it but: That's a little too weird."

"Am I to understand that you would have preferred I let Robert die?"

"No!" Harper shook her head. "Of course not I… I just…"

"We're just a little confused," said Terrence.

"Ain't that the understatement of the year," agreed Harper.

"And you…" Lilly floated up to Tobias, her face inches from his, compelling him to look up. "… so full of concerns."

"W-well yeah," he muttered. "Maybe I am."

"Hey, we all have concerns," Terrence spoke up. "I mean sure, we're real glad you can do the healing thing and that you took out Mordrel, but nobody said anything about you being like this... about you being..."

"All über powerful and floaty light..." Harper nodded to where Lilly's feet weren't quite touching the floor. "Plus..." she shrugged "you do seem to have lost a little something called your mind." Getting a sharp look from Baxter, she glared back at him pointing, "Don't you even think of starting with me Baxter! I don't care where she's been putting her essence, or how loopy it's made you. She says she's still Slater: I say I'll talk to her any way I please."

Again Baxter's lips pulled back into a scowl, but the second Lilly raised a hand he was sucking them in and averting his gaze. Harper turned back to Lilly, "So what's with all the, you know... 'we' and 'us' malarkey? Do *you* even know who you are anymore? Because I don't know about anyone else here, but I'm definitely getting a Slater's left-the-building kinda vibe."

The bemused smile that broke up Lilly's face had Harper raising a hand as she added. "Don't get me wrong OK; Baxter the lap dog, I can learn to live with that." She glanced his way with a shrug, "I think we can all learn to live with that. But seriously, just tell us what's really going on here? What's really happened to Slater... Who... What are you?"

Lilly continued to float as if no longer capable of walking. She paused in front of Terrence, looking him in the eyes as she said, "You are the one charged with finding answers."

"Well, yeah," he frowned "But nothing about this, those scrolls were way old. It was all ancient history."

"You sure bro?" Tobias sounded dubious as he turned to Terrence. "Maybe you're forgetting something?"

"You have been through an awful lot of them," Harper shrugged his way. "Surely it wasn't *all*-"

"Seriously?" He raised an eyebrow and glaring from her to his brother added, "If anything Veer translated for me had been titled "*So You've Come Into Your Powers and Ended Thousands of Years of War, What Happens Next?* I'm pretty sure I'd have shared with the class already."

"Tez is right," Tobias nodded. "There's no way he could have kept something like whatever the hell is going on here to himself."

"Good point." shrugged Harper "He's been boring us all with the details for days now."

Lilly was not so easily appeased; her eyes narrowed as she stared deeper into Terrence's, then she was shaking her head.

"You learnt so much more than you believe. I see it; the buried truths inside of you."

There was a smirk as she turned to Vereena. Immediately the younger girl dropped her eyes. It was the first time she'd shown any difficulty looking at Lilly since the transformation.

"What is it?" Terrence asked her. "Veer what's wrong? What is she talking about?" Slowly she looked up and for the first time he could remember he saw a fearfulness in her eyes as she looked from him to Lilly then back again.

"I had an oath to keep." As if that was all the explanation needed; apparently for Lilly it was.

"I know," she nodded, "and I'm sorry." Reaching out a hand; the tips of her fingers touched Terrence's left temple and before he could pull away or protest with more than, "Sorry for-" his body went rigid, his head snapped backward, and his eyes glowed bright yellow. For everyone watching it was over in a split second with Terrence sent flying to land on his ass as if knocked down in a fight.

***

For Terrence himself, the experience lasted far longer. His mind was flooded with an array of imagery all jumbled up at first.

He and Vereena reading, and talking, and learning from each other, he and Vereena sipping juice from wooden mugs, or water from animal skins. He and Vereena laughing as he shared jokes from home with her, or regaled her with tales of the many splendid, and not so splendid, things he'd done in the name of brotherhood. Eventually the mess of memories began untangling into a linear sequence of events.

He and Vereena were back at the village, poring over scrolls in what was left of the room of writings. As she translated aloud he dug deeper into the shelves, pulling more and more scrolls from the wall. When he thought he heard her read something of possible importance he took the time to sit and scribble down notes.

It was at one of these scribbling moments that she read out a section neither of them could comprehend so Terrence had asked her to repeat it.

"*... only the mother of all mothers can pacify her young and heal the ills of our Azeron, and only if a child of both is mother of mother, will all that was return of the mother.*"

"Man, did your Ancestors know how to talk in riddles." Terrence had scoffed. "I mean no offence, but come on: mother of mothers of mothers of mothers! And I mean seriously... Last I checked it pretty much always takes two to tango right so this whole 'child of both' thing... well talk about redundant." Looking up to see the pensive look on her face he'd asked, "It makes more sense to you?"

The young Da'ariel girl had bitten down hard on her bottom lip, obvious apprehension in her eyes as she raised an eyebrow. Terrence added, "It does! You totally get it! Well come on then... What are we talking about exactly? Is it important? Should we tell Lilly?"

"Nydrel," Vereena shook her head, "These writings, they are so old. The language mostly forgotten; you were correct the first time, Terrence Emerson. None of this makes any sense. Even my knowledge as Qin Am Ness cannot help me decipher a meaning from this." Seeing his disappointment she sighed, "Perhaps I read it wron-"

"No wait," he insisted with a raised hand. "A mother of mothers is basically what Mai Mai means right?"

"Mmm hmm," Vereena nodded, watching a moment as he scratched his head, mulling the words over with more careful consideration. As he started to scribble on his notepad again she turned the binding over in her hands taking in for the first time the few etched lines and the faded Do'mass on its otherwise plain sepia outer skin.

By the time he glanced back up at her, shaking his head and saying, "Nope, sorry, but I got nothing." Vereena had already rolled up the binding, and moved on to another.

"Perhaps there will be something more useful in this," she smiled, rolling open the new binding and set about translating its contents.

***

A second memory flooded Terrence's psyche: later that same day when he'd sought Vereena out, after a meeting she'd had to attend with her Grandmother, he'd hardly been able to contain his excitement.

Convinced he'd figured out a viable meaning to what he'd had her repeat earlier, he followed her back to her hut, to where she told him she'd brought the binding for further study.

Once inside Vereena had handed it to him as she set about making them drinks and he set about explaining his theory.

"See I was thinking about the wording, and well, maybe it isn't so redundant after all. I mean, sure, a Mother of mothers is a Mai Mai right? Any Mai Mai and Every Mai Mai, so that part's clear, but what about this mother of *all* mothers? That's not even the same thing."

"It isn't?" asked Vereena, as she ground a handful of dried berries into a fine powder.

"No," said Terrence, "you read it! The exact words were: only the mother of *all* mothers can pacify her young and heal the ills of our Azeron... right?"

"That is what I read," she nodded.

"Well that seems like a pretty significant difference to me. I mean why would your ancestors slip that *'All'* in there if it wasn't important?"

"I do not know that they would." Vereena let him continue as she scraped the berries into two wooden mugs and poured on a watery yellowish liquid.

"Then the only explanation is that it *was* intentional." Terrence told her. "Because the Mother of *all* mothers which that scroll speaks about is not just any Mai Mai. She's more than a figurehead."

"Figurehead?" Vereena's eyebrow went up as she carried their drinks to the small table.

"Yeah," Terrence's hands went everywhere as he explained. "A symbol, a monarch with very little real powers."

"Then this Mother of all mothers has powers?" suggested Vereena. "Do you believe the binding speaks of Cousin Lilly?"

"God, I sure hope that tastes a lot better than it looks." Terrence frowned as she put the drink down in front of him. Then looking up to see her gazing down at him he shrugged, "No offence," and receiving a smile added, "but no, not Lilly," reading disappointment in the young girl's eyes before she turned her back on him and made her way back across the room he nodded, "I mean Lilly is important, I didn't get it before, but after you read from this." He ran a hand down the rolled out scroll. "And then I saw her and Kyrel training today, well then it all made sense, at least it does if I'm right."

"Go on," Vereena prompted as she returned, sipping her own drink.

"Well you spoke before of the Lady Leyavanya," said Terrence. "The first Queen of the Da'ariel right?" he nodded. "You told me yourself that to your people she's sometimes known as the Mother of *all* mothers." As Vereena reached his side Terrence sipped his own drink and looking up at her smiled, "Wow, that's not half-"

Before he could finish a fine powder was blown into his face. It whooshed up his nose and clogged his throat, preventing him from making a sound. Immediately his eyes were watering, throbbing and bulging in their sockets. He feared they may explode. Then everything became foggy, including Vereena's face, so close to his but almost impossible to make out.

"I'm sorry, Terrence Emerson." Her voice was sad and distant. "This knowledge is not for sharing yet."

***

"What the fuck?" Tobias shot Lilly a fierce glare from his brother's side.

"You OK?" Harper was at his other side staring down at him, her face all concern as he blinked profusely, trying to clear the mists from his mind.

"I...I'm fine," he shrugged off their efforts to help him up adding, "I'm OK." Struggling to get his bearings, he looked up, scanning the faces of the others; all staring back at him. His eyes settled on Vereena, she alone still had her back to him, but feeling his eyes on her, she slowly turned around, her expression solemn, yet proud.

"Why would you..." he shook his head, gazing up at her from the hard black floor. "I... I thought we were friends?"

Dropping her eyes, Vereena turned to Lilly.

"Niesk vey taag taal Mai Lilliath, Dimsh un Cat ya vac."

Lilly nodded, and Vereena strode off without another word.

For a moment, watching her go, Terrence looked as though he might cry.

"What was that all about?" Tobias glared after the younger girl, "Where is she going?"

"To ready our people," nodded Lilly. "It is time we left this place."

"But what about Tez?" he turned to his brother. "What did she do to you Bro?"

"She is my Qin Am Ness," said Lilly "She did what she must."

"Not exactly an explanation!" growled Tobias but Lilly barely seemed to notice his growing anger. Instead she turned her gaze back on Terrence.

"You must know you cannot blame her. The duties of a Qin Am Ness go above that of any friendship."

Swallowing down an acrid lump of nothing, he clambered onto his feet.

"I do know who you are." He nodded, "I figured it out. All of it, but she made me forget. A-and now I remember. I... I..." for a moment there was confusion in his eyes then he was nodding again, "I know who *both* of you are."

"What do you mean?" asked Tobias "What did Jab-Happy do to you bro?

Who is she? What did she make you forget?"

"Vereena is exactly who you have always known her to be," Lilly told them. "A fine warrior and a worthy Qin Am Ness. It was never her intention to deceive any of you."

"But she did!" insisted Terrence.

"And because you do remember, you know why she had to," insisted Lilly. "You know how important it was that the truth of me remain hidden until now."

"Just because I get it, doesn't mean I'm OK with it," his voice rose enough to make both Kyrel and Baxter step forward. Though Lilly's hand went up, Terrence seemed not to notice, instead his eyes remained fixed on her as he added, "She screwed with my head! Blew that crap in my face and made me forget, when all I was doing was trying to help. Don't you think for even a moment that I'm OK with that! I thought we were friends. That, *that* meant something to her. But she..." his voice became solemn. "She didn't even hesitate!"

"Do not allow anger to blind you Terrence. The last Qin Am Ness faced with such a decision chose a much more final solution to keeping my secret. Generations may have come and gone since then, but things do not change as swiftly in Azeron as they do in the human world. Had a Qin Am Ness chosen to execute you, none of my people would have questioned it." Seeing him gulp she added, "Stripping you of your memories *was* a hesitation for Vereena and it happened only because of how much your friendship has come to mean to her."

"If that's true then why even make me remember? Why not just leave things how they were? You still know everything Lilly knows and she had to know how much I'd hate feeling this way? Why didn't you just leave things the way they-"

"Because," Lilly's feet finally touched ground and she stepped closer to him. "You deserve the truth Terrence." Scanning the faces of Harper and Tobias she nodded, "because you all deserve the truth and I know of none better suited to explaining that which has transpired here."

"What about you?" He shook his head, "I'm no servant of yours. Why the hell should I do what you can just as easily do yourself? Probably easier I reckon," he shrugged. "You're the one who started this whole damn thing. No one has a better idea what's going on than..."

Despite the obvious vehemence of his words they trailed off the second she raised a hand.

"This Kalaareem is all but ended," she smiled. "And with it my link to this vessel fades. When all that remains is the last daughter of my line, she will not remember enough to offer explanation. She will, however still be the true ruler of these lands, and as such she too will need to know all that you discovered."

Lilly turned to Kyrel, beckoning with a nod. Without question he approached as she said, "Do not forget who you are Fai Lek. Herrella is gone, and Lilliath will not always have me, but she does still have you."

"Yes Mai Mai." His arm went to his chest for the briefest of bows before he was reaching for her.

"Hey no. Wait!" Panic took over from the anger in Terrence's voice.

He'd recognised the finality of Lilly's words. Now hurrying toward them both he added. "I can't be your messenger!" He watched her slump forward into Kyrel's outstretched arms, "I mean, I wasn't even..." Again Terrence's words trailed off, the look on the Deebanaarie's face telling him all protest was now pointless. "She's gone?" he asked.

"The Kalaareem is ended." Kyrel nodded. "This body could not sustain so much power without it."

"But I... I could have been wrong about loads of things," said Terrence. "How could she just trust me like that? What if I had it all arse backwards? I never even got the chance to check on half of what-"

"Hey," feeling a hand on his shoulder, Terrence turned to see Harper at his side. "Don't worry," she shook her head, offering a smile. "Lilly knows how smart you are, OK. She knows she can trust you."

"That's right." Tobias joined them, his smile more of a mischievous smirk, yet every bit as comforting, as he added, "Besides Bro... We all know you're never wrong."

Epilogue

The sounds of conversation and broken laughter came out through the large wooden doorway at the end of the corridor. Poking his head inside, Arteth watched the three off-worlders: Harper and the twins; all joking over their meals as they discussed recent events.

At the back of the great hall, two female guards, one Da'ariel, one Deebanaarie stood either side of another set of double doors. Seeing him enter and head their way, they perked up, each with an arm across their chests, bowing their heads and stepping aside as he approached.

A hush had fallen over the table as the three classmates also watched him. Arteth glanced their way with a slight nod but otherwise, he paid them little mind, before speaking with the Da'ariel guard and opening one of the doors to go inside.

The second he opened the door Vereena was on her feet, the binding she'd been reading now cast aside and her hand at the hilt of her dagger. Then recognising her cousin she squealed, "Arteth!" and grinned as her hand left the dagger. The multitude of bindings she had open on the desk all but forgotten, she raced across the huge room and flung her arms around him. "When did you get in? I was not informed."

"We made better time than expected, so I chose to surprise you," he spoke in their native tongue; though he'd grown accustomed to speaking only the human language in an effort to teach their people, it felt only too natural to allow a lapse with her.

"Well, you should know better," she gently chided, also lapsing in her use of the human language. "Another second and my blade would have taken you at the jugular."

"Then I would have had two places from which to toast your Lady's triumph." He grinned, and receiving a disapproving smirk as she released him from her embrace his tone became all reassurance.

"Do not concern yourself too much with the abruptness of my appearance. All here do their duty. Had Kyrel not vouched for me I doubt I would have made it to the palace steps, let alone up them. You have done good work securing the city."

"A task less difficult than expected," she shrugged. "All the Deebanaarie here felt My Lady's touch when the Doloch Ty was proclaimed. They are loyal to her now and will all bow willingly when the time comes."

Taking in Vereena's robes and her hair piled high at the back of her head in dozens of fine shiny braids, Arteth said, "Still, it is good to see your warrior's heart has not dulled amid all this finery, Qin Am Ness."

"Yes, well, trusting Deebanaarie troops is not something which comes naturally to me cousin."

"As it should not, many outside these walls remain unaffected. Even among our own people there are those who doubt Mordrel's demise."

"Yes," she turned her back on him, returning to the desk covered in the ancient writings. "Our scouts bring word of many a rebellion. Most are small, easily quashed. Still, there may be cause for concern. Preliminary reports suggest the entire outer regions remain unaffected. And many of Mordrel's Du'Mirs remain heavily guarded in her name by those from her cohort who remain. Her general, Tarsem of House Val'dak is among those seeking to gather support from the other untouched houses. Should he succeed, it will surely threaten what peace the Doloch Ty achieved."

"And that is why you hide away in here. Studying these Deebanaarie bindings?"

"Partly," she picked up the one she'd been reading and sighed, "also in part to satisfy my own intrigue."

Taking a moment to gaze around the huge room: its walls lined to its high ceiling with shelves, and each of these laden with the bound writings, Arteth said, "Very different from our village room of writings."

"Yes," agreed Vereena. "The D'vey House certainly boasts a fine collection. So much of Azeron's history right here in this room. Arteth, there are writings here by the Nelaktanga! And some on Frik of the Velthrun! Why last eve I even found a recipe for roast Meelasknu stew." Seeing his brow rise, she shrugged, "hardly of much use to us now, especially since Meelasknu have been extinct for nearly two hundred cycles." Then, as he grinned, she sighed. "So much here, yet a way to bring peace in its entirety to our lands evades me."

Watching her give the binding in her hand a cursory glance before placing it back on the desk, Arteth, sensing her frustration asked, "Forgive my ignorance sister, I know there is much I could never hope to understand in these writings, and as a man I have never had your training; but isn't the knowledge entrusted to you as Qin Am Ness more than even this room could ever hold?"

"Even the Qin Am Ness have limits," Vereena turned back to him, "Generations of accumulated Da'ariel knowledge remains just that: Da'ariel knowledge. To truly bring the people of Azeron together again I fear so much more will be needed."

"And what of our new Mai Mai?" he shook his head. "Stories of her power are spreading across these lands as swiftly as the rebellions, if not swifter. Everyday more learn how the Lady Leyavanya herself returned to end Mordrel's reign."

"Just as every day more of them will learn how that ended when our cousin's Kalaareem did. As things are, we still have no way to know how much power she retained; if indeed she retained any at all."

"Then it is true?" His voice became glum, "She still does not wake-"

As if on cue the door burst open behind Arteth. He spun around, about to give a mouthful to whomever had interrupted them, but was caught off guard by Baxter's excited grin. Gasping for breath, one hand over his chest, he looked to Vereena. Struggling at first, with nothing but strained croaks before managing, "She's awake! Lilly's awake!"

***

Squinting, Lilly turned her face away from the sliver of light that shone in through a slight crack in the long drapes to the right of her. Ensconced in quilted bedding, it took her a moment to realise her surroundings were unfamiliar, and another to realise Kyrel was at her side on the edge of the bed.

With a groggy, fog-filled head and her throat feeling drier than she'd ever known, she was more than willing to sit up and accept the cup he was holding out to her.

Swigging back a huge gulp, she immediately gagged. Then coughing, she shoved the cup back into Kyrel's hand so she could grasp at her throat in a futile attempt to ease the intense burning the Gaawa juice had brought on.

"Perhaps a little at a time." He offered it again when she recovered enough to let her hand drop from her throat.

"God no," she waved it away. "I don't think I can."

"I am sorry," refusing to take the cup away he shook his head, "It really is the best thing for you right now."

Eyes watering, Lilly took the cup again, and forced down a reluctant sip. Again it seemed to sear her throat on its way down, but suppressing the urge to cough she felt the pain subside and managed to take a few more small sips.

"Good," Kyrel nodded, his voice as matter a fact as ever, "You will recover."

A couple more sips was all she could manage, partly because his intense stare was now adding to her discomfort.

"No more," she said, handing the cup back. "Not now."

Kyrel took it with a nod, cradling it in his hands as he asked, "How do you feel?"

"Like I've had hot coals shoved down my throat," she croaked. "What happened? Where..." she looked around at the room. It was all so unlike the village and everything else she'd come to know of Azeron. From the huge ornate wooden bed she was in, to the heavy dark red drapes covering the three huge windows on her right. The walls were a lighter shade of red, the floor was a polished stone and all about them were grandiose furnishings. "Where are we?" she turned back to him. "How did we get here?"

"We are in Crizoleth," said Kyrel. "D'vey Palace. This is the home of *my* ancestors."

"Oh God," devastation took over her face. "Then it's over! We lost! All those Da'ariel counting on me and I let them down-"

"Nydrel," Kyrel shook his head, his smile a stark contrast to the misery she felt. "You did not let anyone down," he assured her. "We are not here because you lost, we are here because Mordrel is no more. You were... Magnificent!"

Seeing her lip tremble he leaned forward, placing the cup carefully on the small cabinet near the bed's head and sliding closer, took her dubiously into his arms as she sobbed. "But I don't understand," Lilly said through the tears. "We were in that cage thing. I couldn't use my powers. How is this even possible?"

Kyrel let her cry a moment longer before pulling back to look down at her face.

"How much do you remember?"

"Errrm," Lilly swallowed, wincing at the pain it brought, before shrugging. "Enough to know Mairiel is dead. Oh God." She whimpered. "Mordrel killed her because of me."

"You must not think on it that way," his voice was firm. "Mairiel believed in you. She did what she could to give you the time you needed."

"You're telling me I should accept the fact that my own Grandmother just gave up her life for mine."

"Yes."

"I don't think I can do that Kyrel, don't you see, I was never anything but rude to her and now, now I-"

"Lilly," he lifted her chin, with a finger, forcing her to look him in the eye. "Had Mairiel seen what you became in the cho'odzi, had she seen the true strength of your powers; I know she would have been proud of you!"

"But I don't remember doing anything to make anyone proud. All I know right now is that so many of the Da'ariel died trying to protect me. I remember how they surrounded us. How you helped me with that chant thingy"

"Diun Sela Lekaa."

"Yeah," sniffed Lilly, her tears subsiding. "Like I said, the chant thingy." Rubbing her cheeks clean with the back of a hand she sighed. "I remember them fighting so hard to protect us... to..." Confusion filled her eyes. "What about Baxter? Oh God, he didn't make it did he?" Seeing Kyrel's mouth open she spoke before he could answer, adding, "Course he didn't, he was hurt so bad. Did any of my friends even make it? How many did we lose in that cage Kyrel?"

"A lot less than you believe!"

Baxter's voice had them both looking up, as Lilly's face split with a smile and she all but shrieked. "You're OK!"

In seconds her friends had piled into the room, with Vereena leading and Arteth waiting just inside the doorway.

Pushing past the others - Kyrel included - Harper threw her arms around Lilly.

"Girl, you gave us such a scare."

"Seriously..." Tobias agreed from Harper's side. "Do you think you could have dragged out the beauty sleep just a little while longer?"

"Yeah," added Baxter, "we were finally beginning to forget what a sorry sight you are."

Looking up, she grinned his way.

"It's real good to see you too... asshole."

"Hey," he stuffed his hands in his pockets. "Least I ain't still at your beck and call."

"Err... OK," Lilly raised an eyebrow, glancing from him to the others. "When were you ever-"

"Long story," Harper let her go and apparently noticing Kyrel for the first time, she offered him a smile before adding, "But hey, if it's any consolation, he's a little foggy on the details too."

"You are?" Lilly frowned up at Baxter.

"Meh," he shrugged, the slightest hint of embarrassment in his eyes. "Bits and pieces. Seems being healed by an all-powerful ancient being comes with a certain degree of... well.... haziness, but hey... sure beats a half a tree sticking out my ribcage."

"Yeah, I bet it does," Lilly was smiling again. "I'm glad you're OK," her gaze swept over the others; including Terence, who for reasons unknown to her seemed intent on hanging back, keeping a noticeable distance from Vereena. "I'm glad you're all OK..." she told them before settling on her younger cousin. "I'm really sorry about Mai Mai, I know how much she meant to you, to all the Da'ariel."

"Our people are strong," asserted Vereena, "And with the news of her passing comes the news of your triumph. That brings them swifter recovery than you would expect."

"Indeed," Arteth stepped forward from the shadows, "Word of Mordrel's defeat spreads fast and when they learn you are woken there will be rejoicing across all the lands in the name of the new Mai Mai."

"The new Mai Mai," Lilly gulped, her gaze flitting between Vereena and Kyrel. "I... I don't think-"

"There is much for you to think on," Kyrel offered an encouraging smile, before turning to Vereena. "Qin Am Ness, we overwhelm your Lady. She still has much strength to recover and I believe, much to discuss with her friends." Watching him, Lilly couldn't help noticing how he glanced Terrence's way and how, seeing this; Terrence, yet to speak, seemed to shrink more into the background. "Perhaps we should take our leave for now," added Kyrel.

"Yes," Vereena sighed, looking to Arteth. "The Fai Lek is correct; my lady does not yet remember her pledge. Time with her friends is what she needs most now."

"No, wait," pleaded Lilly as Kyrel stood to leave. "Please," she shook her head. "Won't you stay?"

He smiled. "I will never be far from you." Then nodding to the cup he added, "Finish your Gaawa, it will help."

As the door closed behind the three native Azeronians she looked to her friends. "I made a pledge?"

"Err... yeah..." Harper and Tobias stepped aside as Terence finally stepped forward. "About what happened in the cho'odzi, there's some things you wanted me to tell you."

"Things *I* wanted you to tell me?" Lilly's eyebrow rose, as taking Kyrel's place, Terrence sat on the bed beside her.

***

With her child strapped to her back Herrella hopped across the tree-tops, moving faster through Shadowwood than she had ever done before.

The extra weight on her back threw off her balance, but there was little time for caution. Thin branches whipped her arms and face, leaving welts and thin cuts. In her haste, she barely noticed their sting. Still her name carried to her over the whistle of the wind and she knew Kyrel continued his pursuit.

The clearing she sought was now visible, less than half a league from her position, and relying on her gaashmay, she took one last leap before spinning through the air and descending gracefully to the ground.

With bent knees, she landed on her feet and tearing the pouch from her belt pulled out the milky orb while gazing up to scan the tree line.

Again she made use of her gaashmay, tearing at the ground with one of its thin blades, before scooping out enough dirt with her hand to make a fist sized dent in the forest floor.

Another glance upward, still spying nothing, she placed the orb in the hole, pressing it down hard and pushing the dirt back on top of it. She patted that down with the heel of her hand before tugging at the straps of her papoose.

Laying the huge swathe of dirty brown fabric on the ground she retrieved her daughter from it, taking a moment to cradle the tiny child in her arms. Tears stung her eyes as she whispered words of comfort. The child, sensing her mother's distress, whimpered a little before letting loose a torrent of screams.

"Be safe my daughter," Herrella held her baby all the tighter; hoping in vein that with comfort she would cease her crying.

Yet over it all, she heard a slight but unmistakeable rustle above, and looking up, watched Kyrel somersault through the air and land standing only a few feet ahead of her.

With no more time to spare she placed the tiny child atop the buried orb muttering words to herself that she knew he could not hear.

"Do not do this," Kyrel approached them. "Herrella, please, if you take this path I cannot protect either of you."

"Protect us!" Herrella got to her feet, gaashmay in hand and disbelief on her face. "By betraying my people to your sister? By betraying me! Is that how you protect us Kyrel? That cannot truly be what you think you do?"

"It is not as you think, I did not reveal to my sister where your people are, Herrella. She is content for me to bring the child home. As long as I do that, I have her word she will leave your village alone."

"Then I should be content knowing it is only Lilliath that you give up for the sake of your own redemption?"

"What choice do I have?" He took another step forward. "I heard your mother Herrella," he shook his head. "Mordrel offers sanctuary."

"Sanctuary?" A bitter laugh escaped the Da'ariel princess. "What are the terms of that sanctuary Kyrel! My daughter would be raised Deebanaarie; never knowing anything of her Da'ariel blood, of her people!"

"Is it not better than never knowing anything at all?" he implored. "You would rather see her dead?" Kyrel spat the words at her. "I will not allow-"

"Allow?" her eyes grew wide. "By what do you claim the rights to allow anything? You speak as though I took you as a life mate Kyrel. What happened between us…" She shook her head. "It should never have happ-"

"Then you agree with Mairiel?" Kyrel's expression darkened. "You too would see her ended for the sake of your mother's fears."

"You left too swiftly," she assured him. "There is much you do not know."

"Like how her powers are a curse?" he scowled. "I heard plenty!"

"No," insisted Herrella. "Like how Niamma was able to convince my mother otherwise..." seeing him reach for his sword, disbelief filling his eyes, she added, "Think on it Kyrel. Lilliath would be dead already had my mother not changed her mind!"

Taking a moment to think as she suggested, he shook his head, "I know too well how the Da'ariel think of the magicks. How *you* feel about the Tuâoch. I know you can not believe your mother will truly let her live."

"You are right: of the Tuâoch my people have good reason to fear, but Lillliath is our daughter Kyrel. She has Da'ariel blood flowing through her veins. All magicks follow the side of the mother. My side Kyrel! She may be the first in generations to be born with active Laîoch essence. Mother sees this now. She knows how important that could be to our people. This child may be the hope my people have been waiting for. Mother would never harm her."

"You cannot know that!" he all but screamed the words at her. "You know as well as I there is no way to be certain. Mairiel knows it too. You cannot truly trust her in this. You know she would never risk it."

"Perhaps not," conceded Herrella. "That is why, if you *truly* are here to protect her, you will let me do what I must."

"What you must? What can you hope to achieve here? My sister's troops are at our back," He gestured behind them with a nod, "no matter what I believe they will be here before either of us can prevent it. Give her up willingly and there is a chance I can still protect both of you."

"Your sister's interest in Lilliath goes no farther than the essence in her blood. She will drain her thar the moment she deems it worth it and you know it." Herrella shook her head. "If you truly seek to protect her, you will not stop me from-"

"There is nothing you can do!" Kyrel growled, taking another step forward.

"Do not come any closer..." she waved her gaashmay at him.

"Herrella," he shook his head, pulling his sword from its sheath. "I beg of you, let me claim her as a true heir of the D'vey family. I know it is not what you want but she will be safe. I give you my word I would never let my sister harm her."

"Neither will I," Herrella raised her gasshmay high above her head.

"What are you doing?" his voice rang with confusion. "You cannot hope to hold off her troops alone."

"And I cannot again put my trust in the word of a D'vey."

"Herrella..." he took another step toward her.

"I said stay back!" she spat the command at him.

Ignoring her words, Kyrel kept moving forward.

"This is foolish; there is nothing you can do."

"You are wrong," insisted Herrella, bringing her gassmay back down as she added, "Even we Da'ariel have access to the essence," realising too late what she was doing Kyrel raced forward screaming, "Nydrel!" as she plunged the long thin blade deep into her own belly.

Seeing her drop to her knees beside baby Lilliath, he took a flying leap and was almost upon them when Herrella's body dropped forward concealing the child, and a huge wave of shimmering energy came hurtling from her body, knocking him clear off his feet.

For the next few seconds Kyrel was pinned by a force he could not see, unable to do anything but stare at the unmoving mound of mother and child.

The second he felt the pressure ease he was on his feet again, racing toward them. He also dropped to his knees, pulling Herrella backward and finding nothing but the ground and a slight indentation where the child had been. Staring down at this bare patch his voice became little more than a whisper.

"Ny Mech! What have you done?" Shaking his head he dragged Herrella's body closer, resting her head on his lap as she coughed up blood and whimpered through her tears.

"All that I could Kyrel; our daughter will be safe now."

"How can you know this?" he hissed, tears springing to his own eyes.

"Because now, she is far from both our families."

"You could have sent her anywhere! The blood magicks are unpredictable! How did you even learn this?"

"You are not the only one to make sense of the ancient writings Kyrel."

"Tell me..." he pleaded, "tell me what you've done. Tell me so I might bring her back."

"Ny," sniffed Herrella. "Even D'vey magicks cannot accomplish this."

"What have you done?" he asked again. "You must know my sister will not rest until the child is found. She will hunt your people to their end to find her."

"Not if you keep our secret Kyrel; if your word is truth."

"It is! I swear to you by the lady it is."

"Then without you she will never find my kin."

"Herrella, Please..."

"Keep our secret Kyrel. You say you do not betray us. All I ask is that does not change." Reading acceptance in his eyes, she pulled the Gaashmay from her belly with a mighty gasp, its blades retracting at her touch, and she shoved it into his hands. "My blood sent our daughter to her new home. With it you can watch over her."

"Herrella." Kyrel's entire face quivered as he spoke, but she was not about to allow him time to grieve. "I know you have access to quiesscence," she told him. "A Deebanaarie Prince... With my blood you can form a bond strong enough."

"Nydrel," Kyrel shook his head. "This was never what I wanted."

"It is all I could give her." Herrella choked, blood seeping from her mouth. "Be her Fai Lek, make the bond and see." She spluttered once more, blood escaping her mouth in thin tendrils, her lips red with it.

"Herrella."

"See!" She told him again. "See and *know* she is safe."

This last time Kyrel said her name it was a low moan that went unheard by her because all life had left her body.

"Herrella!"

***

"Kyrel?" Lilly looked in at him from the doorway of the huge meeting room.

Turning to her from his seat at the head of the table, where Deebananaarie and Da'ariel sat on opposite sides, he shook his head, pushing out his chair and hurrying toward her.

"You should be resting."

"I've been out cold for three days," she stepped over the door's threshold as he approached. "I'd say I'm rested enough."

"You drank the rest of your Gaawa?"

"Really?" Lilly's eyebrow went up. "That's what you want to talk about? Whether or not I'm getting my vitamins? I kinda figured we had more important things to discuss." Seeing her eyes go to the others at the table he sighed. "Then you have spoken with the human, Terrence Emerson."

Getting all the confirmation he needed from her eyes, he turned back to the others adding, "Cat Ya Vac!" and waved them toward the door.

There was no argument from any present, at least a dozen men and women all made a swift exit, each bowing their heads at Lilly as they passed her at the door.

Kyrel closed it behind them and turned his gaze back on her,

"Come... sit down, I will fetch you more Gaaw-"

"I didn't come here to sit down," snapped Lilly "And I sure as hell don't need any more damn juice!"

"Of course not," he shrugged. "Clearly stubbornness is something you get from your mother."

"And what do I get from you?"

"From me?" Kyrel raised an eyebrow.

"This isn't the time for playing dumb," insisted Lilly. "Tez told me what I called you... what... what Leyavanya called you." Seeing Kyrel suck in a deep breath, she added, "Fai Lek?" immediately his head snapped back and he fixed her with a knowing stare. "That's right," nodded Lilly. "He also told me it means: Honoured Father!"

A long and awkward silence followed as they stared at each other, until pursing her lips she raised both eyebrows, prompting him to sigh.

"I would have told you. I swear to you it was always my intention."

"Then why didn't you?"

"Because keeping you safe was of far greater importance and Mairiel was adamant about the terms of our deal."

"You're telling me she made you keep the truth from me?"

"Yes," shrugged Kyrel.

"Why would she do that? You both had to know what knowing would have meant to me..." Stalking away from him, Lilly paced the room. "You both watched me Kyrel. All of my life you watched me!"

"The Da'ariel have lived in fear of the magicks so long they've forgotten what it was like to embrace their own powers, let alone those of the Deebanaarie.

The stronger you became, the more evident it was that your powers were as much Tuâoch as they were the Laîoch. Mairiel did not feel it safe to nurture that part of you."

"Then that's the real reason I can use both so well," Lilly paused to shake her head at him. "And why you kept trying to stop me. This whole time you've been lying to me. Telling me those arguments with Mairiel were..." Lilly shook her head "She was the real reason you were holding me back, which must mean Mordrel was right... My own grandmother wanted me dead."

"Only at first," said Kyrel "When you were a baby-"

"Oh, well that's all right then, she just wanted to kill me as an infant when I was still too young to even consider fighting back."

"She feared that side of you which came from me," he shrugged. "If you knew more of our people's history you would understand."

"What I understand is while you both claimed to be protecting me, you were both lying to me. That the only person willing to tell me the truth was Mordrel."

"Perhaps, but she did so only to confuse you."

"Well, I guess it worked," Lilly stopped her pacing and turned to face him. "I'm definitely confused."

"About what?" asked Kyrel. "Whether or not you should remain in Azeron? Because that is not something I can answer for you. I know you had a life on the other side of the veil. People who matter to you-"

"Don't be such an idiot!" Lilly rolled her eyes and seeing him raise an eyebrow added, "We both know that's not even a choice anymore."

"We do?"

"The others have already made up their minds Kyrel. I might have been out since taking on Mordrel but they've had plenty of time to, shall we say... weigh up their options."

"Weigh up their?"

"They've made their choice!"

"Oh... And their choice... it is to be your choice?"

"Sure," she shrugged. "We all came here together. We've gone through... well... all kinds of bullshit here together, and ancient powers or not, you and I both know I never could have succeeded against your sister without them."

"We cannot know..." he shook his head. "They did only what was necessary to survive. This tells you nothing more than-"

"They're staying Kyrel!" Lilly glared at him, then seeing his mouth snap shut she nodded. "That's right. Definitely not the best decision for their survival, but hey... back home none of us was ever going to amount to much more than petty criminals. So... yeah... I guess you could say they've found their niche."

"Then you..." he looked dubious. "You also choose to stay?"

"You think I should leave?"

"What?" His hand went to his chest. "No! I... I thought..."

"Why Father," Lilly smirked. "I do believe that is the first time I have ever known you to stammer."

"Forgive me." He shook his head, "It is just... Given all that you came from... The way the human world reveres the role of the father-"

"You thought after all I've just learned: How you deceived me, I would want to be as far from you as physically possible?" Watching him drop his gaze she added, "You're right. In the human world we do revere the father." A feint snort escaped her as she added, "It's taken a lot of time and effort but, well... generally we try to respect both parents equally."

"Yes," nodded Kyrel. "This is something I have seen; but this is not the human world. Azeron is a world in which Herrella and I both disgraced our people."

"By falling for each other?" suggested Lilly.

"Falling?" he frowned "I recall no-"

"You loved her, Kyrel."

"Loved..." he shook his head with a smirk. "...A silly human concept. One which bears no significance here, Herrella and I respected each other and our thars were drawn to one another - nothing more."

"Nothing more?" Lilly's eyes rolled. "A Da'ariel princess getting it on with a Deebanaarie prince? She risked everything to be with you. You're not really going to stand there and act as though that meant nothing to her? To *you*!"

"You do not understand. How could you? There was so much we did not understand. Herrella needed to please Mairiel. There had been so much disagreement between them. To placate your grandmother and the village council she agreed to undergo her Taeleska."

"Aah, yes," Lilly nodded. "Some age old ritual said to increase the fertility of Azeronian women right?" Seeing the surprise in his eyes she sighed, "Tez has told me about that too; all chants and sacred herbs."

"I see." Kyrel nodded before asking. "And did he also tell you how the Taeleska heightens the senses? How it adds to a female's desire to mate?"

Before she could respond he was sighing. "They say it can be maddening. I was, as the humans say 'In the wrong place, at the wrong time' Herrella... she was upset..." Closing his eyes as if to reminisce Kyrel muttered, "What happened between us... it... never should have. Lilly, our peoples do not lie together. Such things have been forbidden since-"

"Does it heighten the man's senses too?"

"What?" he shook his head, eyes opening with obvious confusion.

"The ritual..." explained Lilly. "The Taeleska... Does it affect men as well?"

"Nydrel," he sighed, hands going up with obvious frustration. "Still you do not understand. Only females take the Taeleska. Azeronian men require no such ritual. We remain unaffected."

"You're the one who doesn't understand," she insisted. "You weren't affected by the ritual! Yet still you let it happen. Why?"

"Because... Because..." At a loss for words he shook his head.

"Because you *were* affected Kyrel; not by herbs, or chanting, but by that silly human concept: you loved my mother."

"Ny..." this time when he shook his head there was amusement on his face. "That isn't a possibility."

"Why, because there's no such thing here in Azeron?"

"Well, yes..." he told her. "We are people of duty, not affection. We do what we do because... well, because our people have been enemies so long, we know little else."

"Yeah, well I already know that isn't true," as he frowned, she added, "Vereena already opened my eyes to plenty of ways the people here show love. And now, more than ever, I know she was right: just because you guys don't have a word for it doesn't mean it doesn't exist."

"At least you are half right." Kyrel shook his head at her. "I should have left Herrella's tent as soon as I knew what was happening. Instead I doomed us both. The truth of that is obvious. I was a fool."

"Funny," she shrugged. "To the humans, that's just another word for being in love."

Seeing his jaw clench as he fought the urge to argue she smiled.

"It's OK if you can't get your head around it. I understand enough for the both of us. But I do need you to understand that I'm not choosing to stay here because I apparently pledged to ensure some lasting peace between the Da'ariel and the Deebanaarie OK. I'm not even staying for the chance to recover my powers, which by the way, Terrence seems pretty certain I will. Nor is it because as he tells it we actually all have pretty much no choice until my grandmother's youngest sprite Merly and hopefully that other orb she has are recovered. Oh and I'm also not staying because that lot all suddenly think, this place and you and heck me are like the coolest things since-"

"Then why are you staying?"

"See now I know you didn't watch over me my entire life, or come flying through the forest to rescue me because you believed the Da'ariel were your enemy."

"Perhaps not... but Lilly... that is not-"

"I'm staying because I have a father who is capable of love, and gives a crap about me, and because I deserve this chance to get to know him."

"Then I fear I am destined to disappoint you."

"Yeah, well," Lilly frowned, punching his arm lightly. "Welcome to the world of being a Dad."

***

Peeking in through the keyhole Vereena grinned at the sight of them; then almost toppled over with surprise at the sound of Terence's voice.

"You know, beyond the veil we call that eavesdropping," straightening up, she found herself face to face with him. Raising an eyebrow at her, then the door he added, "It's considered pretty rude, Lilly might well take offence."

"I... I listen only for what decision My Lady has come to," whispered Vereena. "As Qin Am Ness I should know. It is in the best interests of my people."

Noticing her uncharacteristic stammer he shrugged.

"Well, we're staying if that helps."

"Veyhi, yes it does," she nodded. "Thank you, I..." her face became contemplative as she asked, "All of you? Even if Merly is located? You have all chosen to stay?"

"Well, it turns out Baxter can't leave, something to do with being healed by Leyavanya's magicks. According to him, if he returns all bets are off. Course I'm guessing you already knew that, and me... well she pretty much asked me to stay when she gave me back those memories you took from me." Seeing her suck in her bottom lip, he sighed, "About that..."

"I am not sorry!" said Vereena. "I did my duty. That was all."

"Good thing I wasn't expecting an apology."

"That it is." She nodded before turning to leave.

"Wait!" he caught hold of her arm, only to receive a look from her that made him immediately drop it. "I was looking for you," said Terrence "I... I was hoping we could maybe clear the air."

"Clear the air?"

"Discuss the situation," he explained.

"I know of no situation we need discuss."

"Well, all the same," shrugged Terrence. "I've had quite a bit of time to think since we got here and I realise that maybe I reacted... badly."

"You did?" her eyebrow rose.

"Sure," he nodded "You had your duties. A responsibility to your people, friendship or not, I'm still just a stranger here. I knew that from day one. I was wrong to think you would put me first."

"You were trying to help."

"Yeah, well, I stumbled onto something I shouldn't have, not exactly the first time," he was shrugging again. "I'm pretty good at getting myself in trouble that way. But see the thing is..." He sucked in his lower lip, and misreading his frustration as he took a moment to consider the right words, she shook her head.

"There is no need for you to apologise either. You did only as Lilly requested. You cannot be blamed for your efforts. Your help meant a great deal."

Seizing the opportunity her words provided, Terrence added, "See that's just it. None of this was about Lilly for me. I would have helped anyway I could, whether she'd asked me to or not."

"Because you are a good person."

"No," he shook his head then seeing her frown added, "Well sure, I... I like to think I am, but Veer... I was only ever really helping because of you," with a slight shuffle of his feet he dropped his eyes muttering, "Because I like you."

"I like you too Terrence Emerson." Seeing him look slowly up at her she smiled. "And I am glad to know that we are still friends."

Closing his eyes a moment, he took a deep breath before opening them again and saying.

"That wasn't exactly what I meant."

"Oh?" her eyebrow rose again. "Then we cannot be friends again?"

"You know what," reaching out, he grasped her head gently between his hands adding, "Sod it!" before planting a somewhat drawn out kiss on her lips.

As he let her go, taking a dubious step back, Vereena's eyes grew wide - and dumbfounded she put a hand to her lips.

"The human kiss; that is how you..." then she was gulping. "Oh!" and nodding again Terrence sighed.

"Yeah..." then smirking added, "as I was saying: I like you."

The End

Additional Sketches From the World of Azeron

Toleth, Vereena and Arteth

Lilly, Early Concept Art

Baxter, Tobias, Terrence, Sandra Harper and Sandra Morris

"Warrior's Lament" – Early Flashback Scene Concept Art

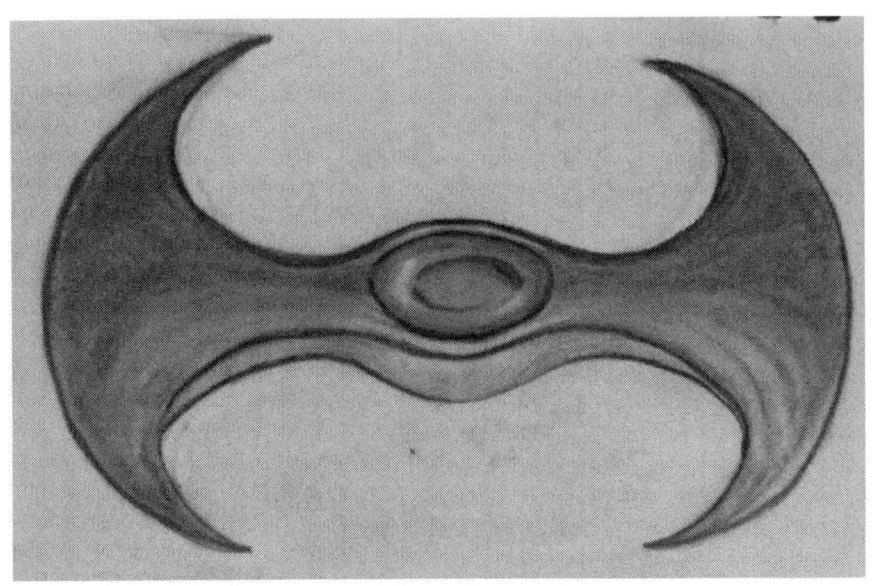

Early Gaashmay Concept Art

Printed in Great Britain
by Amazon